Key HOLES

ROSIE POLITZ

Book Three of the Key Series

Author photo © Debbie Medlock

Cover and interior design by Damonza

ISBN: 978-0-9998877-4-5 (Paperback)

ISBN: 978-0-9998877-5-2 (eBook)

Library of Congress Control Number: 2023910775

Published by Cypress Moon Publishing

8165 Rustic Rose Drive

Baton Rouge, LA 70818

First Edition

For Mom.

I miss you.

ACKNOWLEDGEMENTS

If you've been with me since the beginning, when my first book, *Key Moments*, came out in the summer of 2018, I want to apologize for making you wait so long for book three. I began writing this one in the fall of 2019 (soon after the release of my second book, *Key Elements*), but when Covid hit in March of 2020, my head just wasn't in the game. Life got crazy. I took a break. A long break, writing very little during that time. Then, last year, my life got even crazier. But that's when I jumped back in full force. I needed the distraction, and Clay and Lynn were there for me. I know it's taken me almost four years to finish this one, so I hope it's worth the wait.

Janna, Terri, and Billy — my editing team. The three of you gave me so much good advice while I wrote. Thank y'all for the corrections, pointing out small plot holes, helping me add depth to Clay and Lynn, as well as adding more banter between them. Janna, I love that you picked up on our inside jokes that I wrote into their story, and how you would sometimes leave comments for certain scenes with eye roll emojis (Clay's a horndog, what can I say?). When I was excited about a scene and called you to read it on the spot, I adored listening to you crack up laughing at what I wrote. Terri, whenever you would make a comment wanting more from a certain scene or extra background, I would add and add and send it back, which garnered comments of "YES! THIS!" and made me feel tons better. Billy, as always, your suggestions on ways to improve my writing and content help tremendously. Thank you for challenging me.

Chantelle, so much gratitude goes out to you for jumping in after my final draft was done, and doing a final proofread for me. And especially for telling me, "Lynn would never care about any of that." You were so right! And off I went to rewrite that scene from Clay's POV.

Josiah, thanks for the suggestion you gave me at Janna and Serkan's rehearsal dinner. I used it.

Erin and Chad, continuous thanks for your advice in all things Army related, especially the aspect of deployment, and letting me know what I wrote was indeed plausible.

Rick, thanks for the JROTC/ROTC information. Sometimes even Google makes me question, so I needed to know from a pro.

Katie, thank you for all your paramedic and EMT expertise. It was a big help.

Faith, thanks for your insight into everything related to (spoiler, so I'm not saying). But *you* know. (Wink) I hope I did that leg of Clay and Lynn's trip justice.

George, thanks so much for taking time out of your busy chef schedule to video Zombie Burger for me and telling me about the cool stuff you have there. I can't wait to come visit and eat there one day!

Heather and Cherie, thank you both for going to HSP and scoping it out for me, getting inside info and taking pictures and videos to send me. Same goes for Zombie Burger. Heather, thanks for putting me in touch with George and also for going *back* to HSP just to check something in person when I had one little question.

Tracy, thank you for picking up the phone without me even realizing what you were doing after you heard my frustrations, talking to myself wondering what the hell year that vehicle was in the (spoiler) museum. You immediately googled and called that place and freaking asked them. I may need more of that with book four. You better not go anywhere. The capitol and I need you!

Darrell, Murphy, Stan, Louis, Brad, Eddie, Keith, Marvin, and Joe — thank y'all so much for all the information dealing with state police, the academy, guns, ballistics, and situation protocol. It's nice having all my questions answered on the fly, being in a work environment with retired and current law enforcement officers. Thanks for being so accessible and making sure those portions of my plot were credible.

Tommy, thank you for your continued support and encouragement in this whole process from the start. I love and appreciate you. Thank you for believing in me.

PREVIOUSLY, IN THE LIVES
OF LYNN AND CLAY...

CLAY AND I exit Eureka Springs, Arkansas and head toward St. Louis, Missouri. I thumb through my playlist to find some good music. Pressing the random button on my phone, "Chandelier" by Sia starts.

"Cool song. I dig Sia," Clay says.

"Best wigs since Dolly."

Clay laughs. "Hey, can you book us a room in St. Louis? We should be there before lunch."

"Already ahead of you. I booked us a room before I fell asleep last night. You conked out as soon as your head hit the pillow. I don't blame you though. Driving takes a lot out of you. Are you sure you don't want me to drive at all?" I smile and bat my eyelashes.

Clay looks at me with a smirk. He knows I'm joking. He's pretty possessive of his truck. "Don't be silly. I got this."

"I know. I just like getting under your skin."

"Mmm. I like you under my skin. And on top of it. Sideways. And, speaking of swinging from chandeliers, that sounds fun."

I can't help but laugh. "I totally set myself up for that, didn't I?"

"That you did."

My phone rings. It's Annie. It's odd for her to be calling me so early on a weekday. I answer the call. "Hey girl, what's up? Everything okay?"

"I think Stone and I may have broken up last night." There's a crack in her voice.

"*What*? What happened?" Clay looks at me with concern. I cover the phone with my hand and whisper, "Stone and Annie got into a fight."

"He went a little crazy," Annie says.

"Crazy how? Start from the beginning."

"My car wouldn't start after I got off work yesterday. I tried calling Stone to come pick me up, but he didn't answer. Called again, no answer. Texted him. Nothing. So, I figured he must have left his cell at home or something. I was about to call his office phone, but Jim saw me standing next to my car. He asked me if I was okay and I told him my car wouldn't start. He offered me a ride home."

"Which Jim? Jim, the John Stamos look-alike? Or Jim, the rotund guy with the bad comb-over?"

"John Stamos."

I scrunch my face and suck in air through my teeth (that thing you do when you stub your toe) because I know this isn't going to be pretty. "Oh boy. Okay. Keep going. Where did it get crazy?"

"Jim pulled in my driveway and as I was getting out and thanking him, he asked if he could come inside to use the bathroom."

I didn't like where this was going. "I'm assuming you let him."

"Yes. I sat down at my kitchen table, rubbing my temples, trying to get rid of a headache. I didn't hear him come out. Before I knew it, he was behind me, massaging my shoulders, asking me if our boss was working me too hard. Said if he was, Jim would talk to him and get our team deadlines pushed back. I told him no, I just had a headache. At that second, Stone was inside. I gave him a key after we got back from Indianapolis and told him he was welcome to come in anytime, twenty-four-seven."

"That's a big step, Annie."

"Yeah. I thought it was the right one at the time. Anyway, he came in, saw Jim rubbing my shoulders. He asked what the hell was going on and proceeded to punch Jim in the face before I could even answer."

"Jesus. Over a massage?"

"Yeah, a little extreme, don't you think?"

"Slightly, especially without giving you a chance to explain first. So what happened?"

"Jim punched Stone back."

"Shit. What did you do?"

"I screamed at them to stop. I apologized profusely to Jim. Stone had given him a bloody nose, while Jim had given Stone a bloody lip. Jim left, telling me he'd see me tomorrow, which is today, in a few minutes actually, and I'm freaking out. I should have called in sick."

"What happened with Stone after Jim left?"

"He wanted to know who the fuck Jim was, why the fuck he was there, and what the fuck possessed him to think he could give me a fucking massage. His words."

"Sounds like Stone," I said.

"I mean, it's not like I was laying across the couch and he was giving me a foot rub with my legs across his lap, you know? It was just an innocent little shoulder massage."

"Exactly."

"But apparently, it's not so harmless in Stone's eyes. I couldn't understand why he was so pissed, and he couldn't understand how I didn't see that it was a big deal. He said it looks like Jim has a thing for me. Wanted to know if he flirts with me at work, does he ever take me to lunch, and so on."

"So how did you leave it with Stone?"

"We talked. I answered his questions, but he didn't seem to like any of my answers. I mean, yes, Jim flirts with me a little, but he flirts with everybody. That's just his personality. But I don't flirt back. And, of course we go to lunch sometimes. But it's all about business. We're both leading the same team project. I'm not sleeping with him, Lynn."

"What? I know that!"

"Stone left," she cries. "He threw my key back at me, walked out slamming the door behind him, and peeled out of my driveway. Didn't call at all last night," she sniffles. "If we don't spend the night together, we at least talk on the phone before we go to sleep. I don't know what to do. What this means. It feels like a break-up."

"Clearly you need to talk to him, Annie. Maybe he just needed to sleep on it and has cooled off this morning. He was a total ass for what he did and needs to apologize to you. And Jim."

"Yeah. I think so too. Shit, I need to get inside."

"How did you get to work this morning?"

"Called my brother and he said I could borrow my nephew's car since he's in a submarine somewhere in the ocean right now. Cody's car has been sitting in Brett's garage for a few months. He said it needed to be driven anyway. I can keep his until I get mine fixed. I'm going to call when I get inside and have mine towed to the shop today. Thanks for letting me vent."

"No problem. Call me later and let me know how things are going. You'll work it out. Love you."

"Love you too, Lynn. Thanks."

I hang up and let out a long breath. "Wow."

"What did my numbskull brother do to screw things up with Annie?" Clay asks.

"Stone can be such an idiot."

"Agreed."

"Annie thinks it might be over." I told him everything Annie said.

Clay scrubs his face and lets out a breath. "I don't know, Lynn. I probably would have reacted the same way Stone did."

"What? Why?"

"If I caught somebody else rubbing your shoulders, they'd get a beat-down from me too."

"I don't get it. I don't see anything wrong with a simple squeeze of the shoulders if it helps relieve a little tension. I get massages all the time. You know that."

"Yeah, in a professional atmosphere. At a spa. And Hope is the one you make appointments with, not any dudes. Sorry, Lynn. I'm with Stone on this. He didn't overreact."

"Annie's not cheating on him."

"That may be. But for my brother to do that, whatever he walked in on must have looked along those lines. Not that he might've thought Annie was cheating, but just the fact that another man had his hands on her. A massage is sensual, regardless of the part of the body it's performed on, especially if it's given by the opposite sex outside of a professional facility."

"I still think Stone owes Annie an apology. She didn't do anything wrong."

"She let her co-worker massage her, Lynn. Jeez. Haven't you been listening to a word I've said? You know the meaning of 'sexual harassment.' I know you do. You had to watch as many stupid videos for your job as I did for mine. Annie may have been innocent in her thoughts, but her actions showed Stone something different. It's about perception."

"He took it the wrong way. If Jim has a thing for Annie, then that's on Jim. It's not Annie's fault."

"No, I'll give her that, but I can tell you, as a man, Jim knew better. He took advantage of her." He pauses. "Do you remember that Christmas party we went to about ten years ago and some of your work people were there?"

"Yes. What's that got to do with anything?"

"Your old boss was there."

"Alex?"

"Whatever. I was on the other side of the room when he came in and saw you near the door. He hugged you."

"That's a normal reaction. I hugged a lot of people that night, Clay. Other men included. It was Christmas. A merry time of year. The air was bright and cheery. You hugged other women at that party, even kissed a couple on the cheek. I didn't get my panties in a wad."

"I didn't smell their hair."

"What?"

"Alex? Your boss? Smelled your hair when he hugged you. That's a blatant come on."

"My lord, Clay. When you hug someone, you can't help but smell their hair half the time. It's right by your nose."

"No, Lynn. That fucker closed his eyes and breathed you in. I watched him. I wanted to punch his lights out right then inside of that doorway. There are some things you just don't do to other women when they're taken. Like breathing them in and giving them massages."

"You're absurd."

"Really? How long after that party did you switch jobs?"

I start to think. I remember shortly after that Christmas party that Alex had given me the cold shoulder. I wasn't sure why, but I didn't feel like I should ask. I knew I hadn't done anything wrong on any of my assignments at work. I thought he was just keeping his distance because of the promotion I had applied for; he told me in confidence (a week before the Christmas party) he was going to make sure I would get it. But after the party, our conversations dwindled to strictly business and mundane niceties. He was curt with me and started giving me projects that he would have normally given to more junior people in the office. I did ask him about that part. He'd told me that he was just 'spreading the love' and 'giving others a chance to shine.' And then, I didn't get the promotion I was promised. The board 'decided to go in a different direction.' How freaking cliché, right? It wasn't long after that, I began to feel less challenged. Less needed. Less important. Figured it was time to move on to something else.

"Did you… did you say something to him?"

"You bet your sweet ass I did."

"What the hell, Clay!"

"You were in the bathroom. I cornered him and told him he better keep his hands, eyes, and *nose* off of you or he'd be sorry."

I shake my head. "You're the reason. The cause of his standoffishness. I felt so underappreciated at work after that. I was up for a promotion. I didn't get it. Because of you. I loved that job, Clay. I quit because of… I can't believe you did that. Alex never touched me, Clay!"

"Damn right he didn't."

"This is a lot to process. Pull over."

"Lynn, come on. That was so long ago. You moved on to a better job where you were challenged every single day. Your dream job. The one you retired from. You worked your way up all on your own. And you didn't have to deal with a hair-sniffing perv."

"Pull! Over!"

Clay exits the highway and drives to a gas station. He parks on the side of the building near the dumpster, away from the storefront where we can have a little privacy. I jump out and take a few deep breaths. He rounds the front of the truck to my side and tries to tug me into him. I wrench my hands away. The putrid smell of garbage invades my nostrils.

"You're being ridiculous, Lynn."

"Regardless of where I ended up, and how much I loved my last job at the museum, the fact that you interfered and who knows, could have sabotaged me from something great… that really pisses me off, Clay. You had no right to do that."

"The fuck I didn't!" he yells in a whisper. "You're *my* wife, and nobody breathes you in but me!"

"Are you listening to yourself?"

"I'm not apologizing for protecting you. That scumbag could've forced himself onto you at some point."

"God," I raise my hands in exasperation and look up at the sky. "I'm going in to get me something to drink." Clay starts to follow me. "Stay here. I just need a few minutes to breathe and wrap my head around this. I don't care how long ago this happened."

"Fine," he says calmly.

Before I round the corner of the building, I look back at Clay to glare at him. But his hands are on his hips and he's looking at the ground, shaking his head. Is he thinking about what he did? Or is he mad at me because I'm mad at him?

I go into the store and grab a bottle of water (although I feel like I could down a bottle of wine). I look for a snack, all the while thinking about what I'd just learned. I peruse the snack aisle and decide on a couple of trail mix varieties, peanut butter cheese crackers, and a Slim Jim.

What had Clay done by saying that to Alex? Where might our lives have ended up without the butterfly effect of Clay's actions? Of Alex's actions? If Clay hadn't seen him do that, would I have gotten the promotion? Would I have ever even left that job?

I get into the long line at the register. When I'm finally able to check out, I see Clay walking up and we make eye contact through the door. I look away as I grab my water and bag of munchies from the counter and head for the exit. Clay catches my arm after he enters the store and scoots us out of the way. I pull away from his grasp, this time with a little less abrasion. I don't want to cause a scene.

"I'll be in the truck," I tell him without looking at him.

"Yeah, okay," he says softly. Out of my peripheral vision, I see that he notices the lone bottle of water in my hands. "I'm gonna pick up some more drinks. And some peanut butter M&M's."

My favorite kind of chocolate candy. Clay gives me a small apologetic smile. He could buy me a truck load of peanut butter M&M's and it wouldn't make much of a difference in how I feel right now. I'm still pissed. My eyes finally meet his, but my expression remains vacant. He lifts his hand to touch my face, but I turn my cheek and walk out.

Back at the truck, I fumble with my keys and they fall on the pavement with a jingly crash. I bend over to grab them and as I stand back up, an arm wraps around my waist and pulls me backwards, forcing me to drop everything, including my purse. My water bottle rolls under the truck. Frantic, and noticing it's not Clay's arm, I start to scream. But a red bandanna comes over my mouth and nose, smothering my plea. It's a weird, strong smell, like rubbing alcohol and gasoline. Ether. As I'm panicking, I begin to get a little lightheaded. My limbs feel heavy and it becomes too hard to fight back.

A man's voice is at my ear. "Stop struggling or I'll kill you." I immediately steel myself. He lets go of my waist and points a gun at my side. "Go with me quietly or you're dead." I do as he says, as he leads me to a beat-up Mustang parked next to Clay's truck. "Get in and keep the rag over your face." I slowly open the passenger door of his car, hoping Clay will be rounding the corner any second. But I remember how long that damned line is.

The man, his face still hidden to me, slams the door and walks around the front of the car to get into the driver's seat. I'm still getting woozy from the ether. I see his profile through the windshield as he strolls around. He seems familiar, but the combination of ether and adrenaline is battling inside my body for a state of consciousness, and my mind is nothing but a thick cloud of fog. I can't think clearly.

The disheveled man gets inside the car, continues pointing the gun at my side, and smiles at me. I've seen that smile. Oh my god. This man, this loner, this kidnapper… is the handsome stranger from Hildene in Vermont.

CHAPTER 1

CLAY

I'M STANDING IN line to check out at the gas station, thinking about what I've done. Did I make the right decision all those years ago? Hell yes I did. I did it to protect my wife. And I would do it again. Taking care of Lynn is my job. My number one priority. Telling Alex to keep his fucking hands off her was for her own safety. And his too, frankly. He's lucky I didn't kick his ass in front of God and everybody at that Christmas party over a decade ago.

As I think about the look on Lynn's face when I tried to touch her cheek just moments ago, it breaks my heart to know I put that look there myself. Her eyes were rock hard and stone cold. She's livid. Hurt. Resentful. I know I need to apologize to her, but I also need to make her understand.

Alex was a snake. I know his kind. One thing I learned from all my years as a trooper is how to read people at a glance. All it took was a single look at him and I could tell he wanted Lynn under him, and not just on the organizational chart.

I'll explain everything to Lynn, even tell her about the background check I ran on Alex way back then, which revealed a misdemeanor assault charge from his squandered twenties. I hope that knowing what her old boss was like will make her feel better, see things my way, and realize I had her best interest at heart. I just need to get back to the truck.

Finally walking out the doors of the Circle K, I freeze when I round the corner of the building and see Lynn's keys and purse on the ground, along with her bag of snacks spilled out on the concrete. Her bottle of water is stuck under the right front tire, where it must have rolled after she dropped her bag. But no Lynn. My heart drops. Stomach flips. Veins run cold. I shout her name and swivel my head back and forth, searching the surrounding area looking for her.

I grab her purse and keys off the pavement and throw them into the truck. I start to back out of the parking space. But I don't have a plan. Where the hell do I go from here? I stop for a second and take a deep breath.

A knock to my left scares the shit out of me and I jump. I don't even bother asking the man what he wants. All I can think is that he might know something about what happened to Lynn. The man is older, scruffy, and a little dirty. He looks friendly enough, though not sure how reliable he'll be since he's holding a paper bag molded to what looks like a forty-ounce beer. But he's my only hope.

Rolling down the window, I get my phone out of my pocket and show the man standing there a picture of Lynn. "Have you seen this woman?"

"Oh. I think so." He scratches his beard. "That might be her."

"You saw her? Where is she?"

"I don't know, but I heard you calling a woman's name and I thought you might be looking for who I saw. That's why I came over here. I think I saw that lady leave with a guy in a red Mustang. Seemed kinda fishy. She was kind of slumped over in the passenger seat. Guy peeled out of the parking lot."

"Which way did they go?"

"That way." He points down the street to the right.

"How long ago?"

"Maybe five minutes or so."

"Did you happen to get a plate number?"

"Uh, no, sorry, I didn't think of that. But I think it was from out of state, 'cause it was bright yellow."

"Thanks, that'll help," I tell the man. He says something, but I don't hear because now I'm the one peeling out of the parking lot.

This is my fault. How could I have let this happen? Didn't I *just* tell myself that Lynn's safety was my number one priority? I should have never let her out of my sight. What the hell is wrong with me?

I'm trying to stay calm and react in detective mode. But I'm also in husband mode, freaking the fuck out.

"Goddammit!" I exclaim, as I pound the steering wheel, looking all around for a red Mustang. It could be anywhere by now. If I were still a trooper, I could easily call and have the traffic cameras checked, put in an inquiry to find out which states have yellow license plates, and use cell towers to ping her phone, assuming it's still on her person. But I can't do that now, especially since we're outside of Louisiana. I have nobody to call. "Shit! Lynn, I'm coming for you, babe. Hold on. It's going to be okay. I'm going to kill that motherfucker, whoever he is."

CHAPTER 2

I OPEN MY EYES. What happened? Where's Clay? Where am I? Not in the truck. Whose car is this? My head droops to the side and I squint to look out the window. A blur of wildflowers and utility poles rushes past on my right as we speed down the road, making me even dizzier. How long have I been out? Am I okay? I don't think I'm hurt. I don't feel any pain, except for a slight headache. And my vision is fuzzy, my head foggy.

The stench of stale cigarettes is strong. I also smell what reminds me of old, greasy cheeseburgers and leftover french fries as I notice a variety of fast-food bags balled up on the floorboard at my feet. The radio is on, set at a low volume. Thank goodness for that at least.

I loll my head to the other side to look at the driver. He's holding a gun on his lap. What happened is coming back to me now. This is the guy that flirted with me way back when we were at Hildene in Vermont. Has he been stalking me since then? What does he want with me? Is he going to kill me? Does Clay know I'm missing? Oh my god. Clay, please find me.

"Who are you?" I ask the man in a groggy voice.

He takes one hand off the steering wheel and puts it on the gun. Is the safety on? I hope so. He answers me without taking his eyes off the road. "Oh good, you're awake." Just before he turns the radio off, I realize that the song playing is Rick Springfield's "Don't Talk to Strangers." The irony is not lost on me.

"My head," I rub my temples.

"That's the ether. You'll be fine."

"Who are you?" I ask again. "What do you want with me? Where's my husband?"

"All in good time, sweetness," he says with condescension.

I huff out a breath in annoyance. I'm anything but sweet right now. I'm bitter. And sour. "Where's Clay? Did you hurt him?"

"I didn't hurt him, and I don't know where he is. But he's about to get a dose of his own medicine."

"What does that mean? What did he ever do to you? Where are you taking me?"

"No more questions." He readjusts the pistol on his lap.

"I remember you. At Hildene. You wanted to show me around. Have you been following us all this time?"

"Ah. You're catching on. Not just beautiful. Smart, too. Some trip you guys are on. I wasn't really in the mood for this long of a joyride, but then I figured, why not? I ain't got nuttin' better to do. This some sort of second honeymoon for you or something?"

"None of your business, asshole."

"Oh, you're a feisty one, aren't you? Don't forget, I'm the one with the gun, babe."

"Don't call me that. What do you want? Money?"

"I don't want your fuckin' money." He's eerily calm. "I want your husband to know what it's like to have the only thing in the world he cares about taken away from him."

"What are you talking about? There must be some kind of mix-up. We haven't done anything. Tell me who you are."

"You're not in the position to be making demands."

"How do you know Clay?"

He doesn't answer. He just looks at me. Then he says, "You know, at first I thought I'd never have a shot at getting the drop on you. The two of you never leave each other's goddamn sides. I mean, for fuck's sake, don't you ever get sick of each other?" He scoffs and takes a sip of something from a brown bottle that he was holding between his legs. It's a Bud Light. The bottle isn't sweating. Warm beer. Gross. He's drinking and driving, but doesn't seem drunk, or even tipsy. He sets the bottle on his thigh; it clinks on the gun. "I thought I'd gotten lucky at Lincoln's house. You were finally alone. If you had taken me up on my offer to escort you to the observatory, I could have snatched you then. I would've done it if there weren't so damn many people around. I couldn't even get you out of the house. Turned on my full charm and everything." Oh my god. My stomach is turning. "But I almost got you at that house with the waterfall. I was watching you in the woods while you took about a thousand pictures. He finally left you alone again and I was just about to make my move when I tripped on a fucking rock. Lost my balance and nearly fell flat on my face. You must have heard me because you looked around for a second and then took off."

I remember that. At Frank Lloyd Wright's Fallingwater in Pennsylvania. Clay was tired of waiting for me while I was trying to take pictures of that wonderful house from so many different angles. So he went to wait for me inside. I knew I heard rustling in the woods, but I figured it was a deer. And I distinctly remember getting an uneasy feeling. Now I know why.

"That was you. In the woods," I say. He smiles and nods. "Oh my god," I whisper to myself. "I think I'm gonna be sick."

"Don't fucking throw up in my car."

"Then pull over," I beg. I don't think I'm really going to hurl, although my stomach does feel queasy. But maybe if I can get him to stop the car, I can escape. But seriously, how can I do that when he has a gun trained on me? I have to try though. Right?

He whips into an abandoned strip mall parking lot and kills the motor. The man pops his trunk and gets out, tucking the gun in the front of his jeans like a TV gangster. Too bad my phone is in my purse. I can't sneak a call to Clay. I attempt to open the door and make a run for it, but my hands fumble all over the place. I can't even find the handle. When I finally get hold of it and pull it to get out, the door doesn't open. I try to flick the lock to open the door, but it's stuck. Of course it is.

The guy slams his trunk and strides to my side of the car. He's got a backpack on now. What's in there? He opens the door and pulls me out by my upper arm, rushing me to the back of the building. I stumble and would've fallen if he weren't gripping me so tightly.

"Please, let me go. You're hurting me."

"That's kind of the point."

"Wait," I say. And I can't help it. I do, in fact, lose the contents of my stomach right there. Half of it lands on his shoes.

"Oh shit, bitch! Dammit!" He jumps back, wiping his shoes off in the grass to clean them the best he can. "Fuck."

"I told you," I say weakly.

"Come on. Walk, goddammit," he says as he grabs me again and ushers me further.

He pulls on the gray metal doors in the back of the shopping center. The fourth one opens. He shoves me inside and tells me to sit on the deserted office chair. Still armed, he unzips his backpack and takes out a coil of rope along with some duct tape. My stomach drops again.

CHAPTER 3

CLAY

As I speed down the road, I notice a vacant strip mall up ahead. When I get closer, I see that the only car in the parking lot is a red Mustang with a yellow plate. Bingo. Hang on, Lynn. I'm coming. Please be okay.

Screeching to a halt, I slam the truck in park, and kill the engine. Reaching under my seat, I grab my gun case and arm myself with my Glock 22 as well as my Glock 19 for backup. I run around to the rear of the building.

I release the safety on my weapon, and the click sounds like thunder in the silent alley behind the shopping center. With my pistol at the ready, I take a deep breath and listen for a second. It's hard not to yell for Lynn, but I don't want to let whoever has her know that I'm here. I need to catch him off guard.

I hear some muffled yelling a few doors down from where I'm stalking. I can't understand what he's saying, but I can hear Lynn crying. She's alive. Thank fuck.

As I get even closer, I can finally hear him telling Lynn to shut up before he tapes her mouth

closed. When I get to the door, I see enough through the dirty, vertical glass window that this asshole has tied her to an office chair and has a Raven MP-25 pointed at her. One of the worst pistols on the market. The original Saturday Night Special. That could work in my favor though; they're not known for their reliability. I whip the door open and get him in the sights of my weapon.

"Put the gun down, *motherfucker*," I shout at the asshole, "and step away from her."

He has the audacity to laugh. "Well, look who found us. Welcome to the party, shithead. You're just in time to watch your future explode."

Lynn shuts her eyes tight and shakes her head. "Please," she whispers through tears.

"Lynn, are you okay?"

"Yes," she says with a sniffle.

"I'll blow a hole in your chest big enough to drive through, asshole, I swear to God," I say through clenched teeth. "Put… your fucking… gun down."

"No. You can't do this," the asshole squeals. "You don't get to win again."

"Win? This isn't a fucking game, you son of a bitch."

"You put *your* gun down! Or she gets it, right now." He walks up to the office chair and puts his gun at Lynn's head. She squeezes her eyes shut.

"Alright. Okay." I engage the safety and put my gun down on the ground.

"Kick it over here," he orders.

I do as he says, wincing as my pristine Glock slides across grimy linoleum. He picks it up and tucks it in the waistband of his dirty jeans. Thank God I brought my backup gun. My gut told me I would need it. I'll have to play it just right without spooking this nut job into shooting Lynn. He may be holding a piece-of-shit pistol, but that's not a guarantee that it will misfire.

"What do you want from us? Who are you?"

"Oh, you don't remember me? We met in Vermont at that big fancy house of President Lincoln's son."

"What?" I ask with disbelief. Then it hits me. He is the one who was checking Lynn out as we were leaving Hildene. His clothes are rumpled, hair wild, eyes red, with at least a week's growth of beard, but I know it's him. I knew he was up to no good the second I saw him two weeks ago. "*What?*" I repeat. "You've been following us since then?"

"No," he scoffs. "I've been following you since you left Baton Rouge."

"What the actual *fuck?*" I ask in horror as Lynn's eyes go wide. I start to lunge for him, and he places his hand on top of his gun, racking the slide back, loading a bullet into the chamber. For the first time in my life, that sound shrouds me in genuine fear, with Lynn's precious life in the hands of this lunatic. I immediately halt. "Tell me what the hell you want!" I demand in a rage.

"I want you to feel *pain*, you son of a bitch. I want you to know what it's like to have the one person you care about taken away from you forever!" He's screaming, and his hand starts to shake. He actually starts to cry. "I'm going to kill Lynn so you know how it feels."

Lynn whimpers.

"Please," I beg with anguish in my tone. "Please don't do that. Tell me what happened. Tell me what I did. How can I fix it?"

"You can't fix it."

"I'll do the best I can. What is it?"

"You killed my brother!"

"*What?*"

"Gus."

"Gus? I'm sorry, but I don't know a Gus. You've got the wrong guy."

"Augustus Chambers, asshole! He was in the truck that blew up in Afghanistan. Because of you! I read the report."

Oh, fuck. Shit. Goddammit. I don't know what to say. "I—I—I'm sorry," I stammer out. I close my eyes for a second, shaking my head at the loss I still feel for him and the others. "Chambers was a good man."

"Yes, he was. The best. I didn't even get to say good-bye."

"What's your name?" I ask, almost feeling sorry for him.

"Ross," he nearly whispers. He starts pacing back and forth. Good. At least his gun is away from Lynn's head now.

"Ross, I'm sorry about what happened. The way the truck blew…" I shake my head and take a deep breath, "It was a fluke. But I blame myself every single day for that accident."

"As you should. I didn't even get to say good-bye," he repeats. "I couldn't even go to his memorial service."

I look at Lynn and see that she's trying to undo the rope around her wrists behind the chair. I need to keep Ross talking.

"Do you want me to explain exactly what happened?"

"No need to. I read the report a hundred times to make sure my tracking you down was the right thing."

"This isn't right, Ross. What you're doing right here, right now… it's wrong."

"Not according to my calculations. If you hadn't been so impatient and just waited till you got back to base to see the drill route Mack drew up, none of it would've happened."

Fuck. He's killing me. I live with the guilt of that decision every day. "Look, I know how you feel."

"Not possible. You have a wife and a family who I'm sure all love the shit out of you. I ain't got nobody. Nobody!" He puts his gun back to Lynn's head and she stiffens.

"Ross, look at me." I need to keep him focused on me so Lynn can resume trying to untie herself. "Look at me." He finally does. "You said you didn't get to go to his service. Why is that?"

"None of your fucking business."

"Come on, Ross, I'm trying to understand."

He's breathing hard, rubbing his left temple while his right hand is still pointing a gun at my wife. But it's like he's wrestling with whether or not he wants to give me more information. "Fine," he finally says. "I was… in jail."

"I'm sorry," I tell him again.

"I want you to know… no, I *need* you to know, how you screwed up my life." He sighs. "My big brother was all I had after our parents died. We were a very close family. Damn near as perfect as the fucking Cleavers from *Leave It to Beaver*. I was so lost after they were gone, only eighteen when they died. I was depressed. Got mixed up in drugs. Gus was the only one who cared about me, believed in me, looked after me. Sent me to rehab and got me clean. He gave me a chance to make something of myself when nobody else would. Then he got deployed. He had to leave, and my life fell into shambles again. Ended up in prison for breaking and entering, drugs, whatever. And then you killed him. I vowed to myself that I would avenge his death, as soon as I was released. It took me a few months to track you down, but I found you. And then imagine my surprise when I found a 'SOLD' sign in your front yard."

"We moved," I said.

"No shit. So I had to do a bit more digging. Do you know how nice your old neighbors are? Told me everything I needed to know."

I picture sweet, little Mrs. Jenkins, in all her naïveté, doing just that. "Ross," I say calmly, "please put the gun down. Hurting Lynn will not bring your brother back."

"Maybe not, but you'll know how it feels."

I hope Lynn is still trying to work her way out of the rope. I can't look to check though. Don't want to clue Ross in. "Hey, I swear, I do know how it feels. I miss him too. It hurts like a motherfucker. And I didn't just lose one brother that day, I lost three. I miss all of them." I take a step closer as I see Ross start to crumble. "If you do this, you'll just go back to prison. For life."

"What the fuck do I care? I don't got nothin' or nobody left to live for anyway."

"You can change that. I'll let you walk away."

"No you won't. You're a cop."

"Ex-cop."

"We both know there's no such thing as an ex-cop. Once a cop, always a cop."

He's right about that. "Look. We can work something out. All I want is for Lynn to come out of this safely. Come on, Ross. Just give me the gun and you can walk out of here." I start to reach out for it.

"No!"

He fires the gun at where Lynn is sitting just as she lunges from the chair and falls to the ground with an oomph. I reach behind my back, pull my other pistol out, and shoot at the kidnapper, hitting him twice in the chest. He drops to the floor, blood oozing from his upper body and spurting from his mouth. I run over and retrieve his gun and mine before turning my attention to my wife on the floor.

"Lynn! Lynn! Are you okay?" I roll her over and there's blood on her right side, soaking through her shirt. She's pale, but conscious.

"I think I'm hit," she cries.

I take my t-shirt off over my head and ball it up, putting pressure on Lynn's wound with one hand. She yells out in pain, squeezing her eyes shut. "Fuck. I'm so sorry, love." Pulling my phone out of my pocket with my other hand, I dial 9-1-1 while keeping an eye on the dying man. After hanging up, I lift Lynn's shirt up and breathe a sigh of relief.

"Babe, you're okay. You're going to be fine. The bullet just grazed you. It's bleeding, but I don't think it's that deep. You probably won't even need stitches. Thank Christ you moved out of that chair when you did. Jesus." I cautiously pull her into my arms and hug her the best I can with one hand pressing her side with my shirt.

"Holy shit, Clay. Is he dead?"

"Oh, he's dead. God just hasn't told him yet." I look over at him lying on the filthy floor.

He meets my eyes. "Thank you," he gurgles, as he takes his last breath and expires.

"He's gone."

Lynn is trembling. "Why do you think he thanked you?" Her speech is shaky.

"Probably for putting him out of his misery."

I don't let go of my wife until I hear the sirens of the police units and ambulance arrive at the parking lot a few minutes later.

I tuck the guns in my jeans and carry Lynn over to the paramedics so she can get checked out. "She needs to go to the hospital."

"She's in good hands."

At this moment, the policemen walk towards me. Stepping in their direction, I introduce myself and turn over the weapons. "Clay Sinclair. That's my wife, Lynn," I say, pointing a thumb back at the ambulance.

"Lieutenant Les Michaels."

"Officer Dominic Lewis."

We shake hands as news crews start pulling up in the parking lot. Great.

"What happened here?" Lieutenant Michaels asks me.

"I did what I had to do. I'll talk to your investigators at the station.

But I'll need to contact my attorney. Look, I'm a retired state trooper from Louisiana. I know the drill. And I'm not saying shit in front of this circus." I nod to the media vans.

"Fair enough."

"He's in there." I cock my head towards the inside of the building where the gunman is, telling the officers where to find him. "Fourth door."

"We're going to have to detain you. Both of you."

"I understand that. But can I please check on my wife first?"

"Sure, I'll walk with you," Lieutenant Michaels says, as Lewis and a couple of other officers head to the back of the shopping center where the body is.

Michaels and I turn back in the direction of the ambulance. Upon assessing her injury, the first responders determined that Lynn doesn't need the hospital. "She can certainly go, but we can fix her up just fine right here."

"Are you sure?" I ask one of the medics.

"Positive. We'll take great care of her," the other one says as he starts bandaging her up.

"I'll be fine, Clay. Just let them do their job."

I reluctantly give in. "Alright," I sigh.

After the paramedics finish with Lynn, I break the news to her. "They're gonna have to take us in for questioning."

"I figured as much."

"Separately."

"I know. Protocol."

"Correct. Are you okay?"

"I guess I will be."

I give her a quick kiss and brush my thumb across her lips. "You'll be fine. Just tell them exactly what happened."

"Sinclair? We need to go," Officer Lewis says. Lynn and I are directed into separate units, and we head to the police station to give our statements.

I tell them everything I can remember, including the part about the guy who tipped me off in the parking lot at the gas station.

Hours later, when all is said and done, my killing of Ross Chambers is ruled a justifiable homicide.

Lieutenant Michaels hands my Glocks back to me. "We'll call you if we need any more information."

"Thank you." Michaels starts to turn away. I stop him. "Um… any chance you can take us back to our truck?"

"Lewis can do that, as a courtesy."

"Thanks. We'd appreciate that."

And with that, we exit the Hollister, Missouri police station.

CHAPTER 4

WHEN WE FINALLY have a moment to ourselves before leaving the empty parking lot of the strip mall, Clay wraps me in a strong embrace, careful not to squeeze my side too hard. He takes a deep breath and whispers something, but I can't understand him.

"What?" I ask.

"Nothing, just talking to myself." He pauses for a second and then lets out a long and tired sigh. "God, I could've lost you. I could've fucking lost you. Fuck. Fuck, fuck, *fuck*. Goddammit. This is my fault. This is all my fucking fault. Lynn, I'm so sorry, babe." I can tell he has more to say, but he's trying to work out in his head how to say it. "We... I think... shit."

"What, Clay? What is it?"

"We need to go home, Lynn."

"What? No, Clay. No. I don't want to."

"I can't do this anymore. Not right now. Let's take a break. My mind's a fucking mess. I just can't fucking—"

"Clay, please. No. I'm fine. I want to finish the trip."

"But—"

"No 'buts,' Clay. I mean it. I'm okay. I want to finish our trip." I have to. I need to keep my mind occupied and not think about what could've happened.

He sighs again. "Alright. Are you sure you're okay?"

"I'm fine. I'll be fine." Wait. Maybe *he's* not fine. He just killed somebody. "Unless… do you need a breather for yourself? You ended somebody's life. I know you, Clay, and I know you were feeling sorry for him before that happened."

"Fuck that. I stopped feeling sorry for him the second he pulled the trigger on you."

"Okay. You promise you're alright?"

"Yes. I just… I should've never fucking let you walk away from me at that gas station."

"Clay, I—"

"Let's just get the fuck out of here."

"Okay. Yeah."

He guides me to the truck and helps me get in. We drive in silence (for the most part) to the nearest hotel, somewhere on the outskirts of Branson, Missouri. I'm having flashbacks of the time after my encounter with the hitchhiker in Tallahassee. But this is worse. Way worse. Clay seems to have totally checked out since we left the police station. I know he generally curses more than I do, but he doesn't usually swear that much, that fiercely, all at one time. He's blaming himself. Nothing I say right now will be able to soothe him. I can't imagine the thoughts that are going through his mind, knowing this all stemmed from the accident he was involved in when he was in Afghanistan. He blames himself for that as well and suffers from PTSD because of it. I hope what happened today doesn't make his condition worse.

As the sun sets, we check into the hotel. Once we get inside our room, we crash on the bed without saying a word. Exhausted, I fall asleep in Clay's arms.

CLAY

I'm lying here wide awake while I'm wrapped around Lynn, who is sleeping soundly. My mind is racing. So much shit went down today. I can't believe I could've lost my wife. And it would've been all my fucking fault. But thank God it ended with her safe and alive. I killed a man. Just a few hours ago. I've never point-blank killed somebody before. I never even saw combat in either of my deployments overseas. I never even had to fire my weapon at anybody as a state trooper. My thoughts are all over the place. I killed a man. But I'm not sorry. I'd do it again to save my wife. I'd do it a hundred times to save my wife. I killed a man. A man who was the brother of my brother in arms. The brother of Augustus Chambers. Gus. Chambers. I know you welcomed your little brother with open arms. I'm sorry, Chambers. Wait, no, I'm not sorry. He was going to kill Lynn. I did what I had to do to save my wife. I did the right thing. I killed a man. This shit is undeniably therapy fodder. Fuck, I need to get out of here.

I gingerly untangle myself from Lynn. Rising from the bed, I'm as quiet as I can be while I search for the hotel notepad and pen. I scribble a message to Lynn, change clothes, and hightail it out of the room to clear my mind in the gym.

After my workout, I look at the time. It's after ten. I know it's late, but I need to call my doctor. He said I could call anytime I needed him, day or night. And I need him.

He picks up on the third ring. "Clay?"

"Dr. Hart. Hi. Sorry to call so late."

"No problem. What's up? Are you alright?"

"No." I explain everything that happened today. Lynn's kidnapping. Me killing her abductor. How I feel like I let Lynn down by not being there to prevent it all. How it will always feel like it's my fault. "This whole thing goes back to what happened in the past. In Afghanistan. Again, something terrible that happened because of something I did. I feel like all the progress I've made just came crashing back down, setting me back. I feel so worthless. So hollow. So… lost." My voice cracks.

"Clay, what happened back then was a result of circumstances that were outside of your control. Same as what happened today. Take that inner voice and turn it around. Beat the shit out of it. Don't give it power. Acknowledge the negative, but accept that it's based upon things bigger than you. You are not the blackness you feel inside of yourself. What happened doesn't define you. It doesn't make you who you are. You choose who you want to be. The paradox of misfortune is that it has the power to destroy you *and* gives you the power to transform and rebuild yourself. You choose which one you want. You have the courage and strength to overcome those burdens, Clay. Claim it. Choose it."

"I try. Every fucking day."

"Don't just try, Clay. Do it."

"Okay. Yeah."

"The more you fight it, the easier it will get. And it's okay to be vulnerable. I know you've got awesome support in Lynn for those times."

"Yeah, she's the best."

"So you've said."

I smile. "It's true. She saves me every day. Thanks, doc."

"Anytime. I'm here for you. Have a good night."

"You too."

LYNN

I wake up and see that it's dark in the room. Clay is not in the bed. The suite is eerily still. I check the clock on the bedside table for the time. The red digital numbers show 10:33. Wow, I've been asleep for a couple of hours. I flinch as I sit up, grasping my side where the bullet hit me. There's a note on Clay's pillow. *Went to the gym. Had to get out of here. Don't leave the room. I love you.* I wonder what time he got up and left, how long he's been gone. Should I go look for him? I know he said not to leave, but… I'm kind of freaking out. This is the first time I've been alone since everything happened. I know he probably just needs to decompress after all the shit that went down in the last fourteen hours. But how could he just leave me here? My anxiety is taking over. I should search for him. Right? No. Maybe. Ugh. I don't know what to do. What if I can't find him? What if we miss each other and he gets back to the room and I'm gone? He'd be that much more worried and probably undo any progress he made clearing his mind in the gym. I finally decide to just get out of bed and take a shower instead of going to look for him.

When I'm halfway finished with rinsing my hair, the bathroom door creaks open and I see Clay's form through the opaque glass of the shower stall. I watch as he strips his gym clothes off, opens the door, and steps in. He pulls me to his hard chest and wraps me in his strong arms. Hugging me with delicate tightness, he silently cries. Full on body-shaking sobbing. My husband, usually filled with strength and vigor, is breaking down. And it's tearing me apart inside.

I hug him back as hard as I can, letting my body reassure him that this is not his fault. I give him a soft kiss on his shoulder while rubbing my hands up and down his back, hoping my actions comfort him. My eyes begin to sting, and tears stream down my face, mixing with the water.

Clay breaks the silence. "Lynn." I look up at him. His eyes are red. He traces his fingertips across my cheeks. "I have no words," he sniffs. "I'll never be able to apologize enough. No matter what I say, it'll just... never be enough."

"You don't have to say anything, Clay. I don't blame you for what happened. It was beyond our control."

"I shouldn't have let you walk out of the store like that."

"Wrong. If anything, I shouldn't have walked out the way I did. I was just so angry. I'm the one who's sorry, Clay."

"*No.* Don't you dare try and blame yourself for this. It's on me. I'm your husband and I wasn't there. I didn't protect you."

"You *were* there. You *did* protect me. Clay, you *killed* for me."

He sighs. "But if I hadn't gotten a tip on what happened to you, if I hadn't gotten to that parking lot when I did, you could be..."

"Shh." I put my fingers over his lips. "No words, remember?"

"I love you," Clay whispers.

"Okay, I'll take those words." He smiles. "I love you too, Clay. Don't dwell on the 'what ifs' and the hypotheticals. I'm safe and here with you. That's a fact. We're done talking about this. We don't need to mention it ever again." But I know that's inevitable.

He covers my mouth with his and takes me up against the tiled wall of the shower with dominance. His possession of me is commanding but tender, which brings me to heights that I've never seen, never felt, never tasted. The intense love and passion between us right now is downright tangible. Palpable. Visceral. This is about power. Clay is trying to regain some sense of control. And I let him. Definitely no words needed.

The next morning, I wake up entangled in Clay's nakedness. I can barely move. His solid body is dead weight draped over my side. "Clay." I nudge him. "Get off."

He stirs. "Mmmm… that can be arranged," he says in that sexy, raspy, sleepy voice of his, as he presses his semi into my backside.

I playfully slap him on his thigh. "That's not what I meant, goofball. Didn't you get enough of me last night?"

"There's no such thing."

I snicker. "Come on, babe. I need you to move off me so I can get up. You're hurting my side."

"Oh shit. I'm so sorry." He bolts away from me. "Are you okay? Fuck. Last night in the shower. I wasn't thinking about your injury. I was being selfish and lost my mind in you. Did I hurt you? Did I make it worse? Let me see." He raises my shirt to check my bandage.

"No, it's okay. I mean, yeah it hurt a little in the shower when you held me against the wall, but it was worth it."

"Fuck." He jumps up in a rush and retrieves a new bandage and the antibiotic ointment along with some Aleve and a bottle of water. "Dammit, I'm sorry, babe." He sits back on the bed and tends to my wound.

"I'm fine, Clay. If it had been that bad, I would have said something. I'll be okay. It's not that deep. It'll heal in no time."

"Still. I'm a selfish asshole."

"No you're not. We both needed that last night. We needed to get out of our heads for a little bit." He finishes cleaning my wound and puts a new bandage on. I sit up and take the Aleve, then reach for my phone and look at the screen as Clay pulls the covers back up to his waist. "Shit. I've got five missed calls from Annie and six unread texts. I need to check on her. I wonder if she and Stone worked things out or decided to break up. Have you talked to your brother?"

"No. I had four missed calls from him, but I wasn't in the mood to chat last night. Had to get out of here and blow off some steam in the gym.

You're right though. We need to check on them. And," he sighs, "let them know what happened yesterday."

"Yeah. As much as I don't want to relive it. We should tell them." I get out of bed and walk to the bathroom. A thought hits me and I turn around to face Clay, still sitting in the bed. "Clay?"

"Yes, love?"

"We still need to talk about what you did. Regarding Alex. And my job."

"Shit, Lynn. Isn't that a moot point now? Fighting about that is what got us into this mess. Can you please just forget about it?"

"No. Not entirely. I just don't understand why you threatened him."

He sighs. "Come here." He pats the bed. I walk back over and sit down next to him. He sits up and wraps his arms around me, pressing the front of his torso to my back. Resting his chin on my shoulder, he says, "Because nobody touches you like that but me."

"But he just hugged me, that's it." I shrug.

"I'm not arguing with you about this again, Lynn. He didn't just hug you. He breathed you in. And before he came up to you and did that, he fucked you with his eyes from across the room. He wanted you, and I did something about it. And speaking of nobody else touching you like that… that includes personal massages."

I withdraw from his hold to turn around and face him. "We're back to this now? You still think what Stone did was justified and Annie is the villain in their situation?"

"He thinks the same way I do, Lynn. You don't give another man's woman a massage."

"That's ridiculous. It was innocent."

"Maybe for Annie. But not for the fucker who was rubbing her shoulders, I guarantee it. And besides, you know Daisy cheated on Stone, so he's very sensitive to that kind of shit to begin with. All I can say is, I better never catch anybody of the straight male variety giving you a backrub."

"Whatever."

"I mean it, Lynn. I'm fucking serious."

"You were there last year when Brett rubbed my shoulders and you didn't say anything."

"Okay. So maybe there's a very rare exception to the rule. But Annie's brother is like a brother to you. And you're like a sister to him. We both know that. Besides, he meant absolutely nothing by it except literally trying to help you feel better. You wanna know why? Because he's a *physical therapist*. A professional. Plus, that was when my wrist was broken. Otherwise, it would've been my hands on you instead of Brett's. His actions were harmless and completely clinical. He even looked at me before he touched you, non-verbally asking for permission, and I nodded at him while I raised my broken wrist. Bet you didn't know that. I gained even more respect for Brett that day.

"On the flip side, Alex wanted to nail you, and he wanted it badly. He had nothing but sex on the brain. Even if he would've never acted on it, I didn't want him *thinking* about you in that way. Do you see the difference?"

I sigh. "Okay. Fine. You're the only guy allowed to give me any kind of massage outside of a licensed facility."

"Damn skippy," he smiles, obviously putting an end to this argument. He pulls me down onto him and gives me open kisses along my neck to my shoulder.

"Stop it, Clay."

"Mm-Mm," he coos along my skin, saying 'no.'

"I need to call Annie now and check on her." I get up again.

"It can wait," Clay says as he pulls me back down to the bed by the tail of my sleep shirt. "There's something I want to massage you with first." He winks at me and throws the covers off his body, revealing his fully hard shaft.

CHAPTER 5

A FTER WE SHOWER and eat breakfast, I call my best friend and Clay calls his brother.

Annie and Stone were able to talk everything out, explain each other's point of view, and managed to make up. Thank goodness, because I'd hate to see them split over something as trivial as a misunderstanding over a massage. Maybe it wasn't that incidental to Stone, and I get that now, because of what Daisy did to him. But still, I don't think Annie did anything wholly wrong.

I give her the rundown on what happened with us yesterday, while Clay is on the phone in the other room telling Stone.

"Holy shit, Lynn. Are you alright? Is Clay?"

"Yes. We're fine. I mean, we're both a little shaken up of course, but really, we're okay. Clay saved me. It was a big mess, but we're good."

"Thank God. Jesus, what a cluster."

"I know. It was insane. Like something out of a freaking movie."

"Wow. So what are your plans now? Are you coming back home or what?"

"We're staying on the road. Clay wanted to come home, but I don't want to. I think we need the distraction. Plus, we're more than halfway through now. I just want to keep up our momentum. I'm having such a good time. Except for yesterday."

"Yeah, I can only imagine. I think it's good though, that y'all are continuing. Hold on a second, Lynn." I can hear Stone through Annie's phone asking her if she's ready to go and she tells him that she is, she'll just be another minute.

"Oooh, what do y'all have planned?" I ask, intrigued. Clay comes back and sits down at the table with me.

"Well, since we just had our first fight, and made up, well into the night I might add, we're taking a long weekend trip to Navarre Beach. We're leaving shortly and coming back Monday."

"Nice. I love Navarre. The water is so beautiful in that part of Florida. I'm glad the both of you were able to work things out."

"Yeah. Me too."

"Tell her how *we* worked it out *three times*," Clay says loud enough for Annie to hear. He grins and winks at me.

Annie laughs. "It must run in the family."

I chuckle as I playfully slap Clay and turn my attention back to my conversation. "I'm guessing you gave him back the key to your house?"

She snickers. "Yeah. He actually asked for it back, which surprised me a little. I thought he might have had second thoughts about me giving it to him in the first place, that it was too soon in our relationship. I figured he wouldn't mention it, but after our third round, he said he wanted it back."

"That's great, girl. Well, you better go. Don't keep that man waiting. Sinclair men are not known for their patience." I look at Clay and he winks.

"So I'm learning," she laughs as he calls her name again. "I'll talk to you later. Y'all be careful. Love you, Lynn."

"Love you too. You and Stone have a safe trip and have fun. Catch some rays for me."

"I'm sure I will. Bye."

"Later, girl." I disconnect and put down my phone.

"They made up," Clay says.

"That they did."

"I'm glad."

"Me too. What did Stone say about everything?"

"First he said, 'Holy fuck, dude.' Asked if we were okay. Then told me I did the right thing." He sighs. "You know, when I started looking for you, I told myself I was going to kill that motherfucker, but I didn't think I meant it literally." He shakes his head. "I still can't believe that happened. But I stand by it, and I'd do it again and again if it meant keeping you alive."

"Thank you for saving me."

"No 'thanks' necessary. I made a vow to you. I'll always do everything in my power to protect you, Lynn. You're my wife. You're my life." He kisses me softly. "Okay, now, back to this road trip deal. If my memory serves, we were on our way to St. Louis before we were interrupted. Is that right?"

"Yes."

"A blues museum?"

"Right. I'll need to look at the clue again though to refresh my memory on what exactly it is that we're looking for."

"Yes, please. Everything has been such a blur since I last heard the clue."

"Everything?"

"Well, not the parts where you were naked. Those are crystal clear," he says with a sly smile. "But the last twenty-four hours have completely thrown me off my puzzle-solving game."

"Understandably." I smile back at him and read the clue again. "Okay. 'The King of Beers was born in this city. A case for suits with the blues awaits without pity. In this gallery of artifacts, you'll find legends of names. Like King and Waters and Berry and James.' I remember now. We figured out that it was the National Blues Museum in St. Louis and that we're probably looking for a suitcase. Does that sound about right?"

"I think so. Refresh my memory on what the key and keychain look like."

I pull it out, showing Clay the Budweiser bowtie logo along with a tiny key. "It looks like it will open a suitcase."

"I still want it to be Elwood's briefcase."

"What?"

"Elwood Blues. Jake and Elwood. The Blues Brothers? Ring a bell? They had an album, *Briefcase Full of Blues*."

"We've been over this, Clay. Jake and Elwood weren't real blues men."

Clay looks shocked. "How can you say that?"

"Because they weren't Jake and Elwood. They were Dan Aykroyd and John Belushi. Actors. Comedians."

"But—"

"Okay, we won't rule it out. But let's just see what we find when we get there."

"Alright, babe." He starts singing "Soul Man" and doing some of the same dance moves as Jake and Elwood.

I laugh. "Having fun?"

He stops. "Yeah. Now that I got that out of my system, are you almost ready to get back on the road? It'll take us about four hours to get there."

"Yep, just lemme finish packing up a few things. That'll put us there at about three o'clock. We'll need a room."

"Already taken care of. I also checked the hours of the museum online and they stay open till eight thirty on Fridays. So we'll have plenty of time to rest for a minute and then head to the museum."

"Oh good. Okay. Give me five minutes and I'll be ready."

As we stand at the check-in desk of our hotel, I notice the clerk has the same kind of peanut butter cheese crackers on the counter that I bought at the gas station before I was taken. The sight of the bright-orange wafers takes me back and makes me shiver. I take a deep breath and grab Clay's shirt to ground myself.

When we get to our room, I see a fantastic view of the Gateway Arch, and for some reason, that calms me down some more. Seeing the arch marks another surreal moment for me. I've never been to St. Louis before, and I'm looking forward to taking the tram ride to the top tomorrow.

After we rest for about an hour, we get ready to go to the National Blues Museum to search for our suitcase.

We arrive and step into the breezeway. A large piece of glass with an emblazoned National Blues Museum logo is situated between two sets of wood-framed glass doors. We enter, learning that we're just in time for happy hour, which lasts from 5:00 until 7:00, at which point their weekly 'Howlin' Friday' concert starts. Tonight's performer is Jackson, Mississippi's own Zac Harmon and the clerk behind the counter asks us if we'd like to purchase combo tickets that will include the museum tour and the concert.

"That sounds great," Clay says as he purchases our tickets. "Looking forward to hearing some live music."

"Yes, thanks," I tell her. While blues isn't really a favorite genre of Clay's or mine, we both thoroughly enjoy live music. "So, we can just tour the museum on our own?"

"That's right. Just let me know if you have any questions."

The interior is beautiful. The museum is housed in a historical building that opened in 1906 as the Grand-Leader department store, a locally owned retail chain. The ceiling was designed using some original railroad ties from around the area, and some sections of the museum incorporated wood that was reclaimed from the Mississippi River.

There are several cases with memorabilia. One is presenting an outfit and guitar from Chuck Berry, and another showcases one of B.B. King's 'Lucille' guitars. Placards and photographs of many famous blues musicians are exhibited throughout the museum. There's even a small section on Robert Johnson, which reminds me of the second stop on our trip that landed us in Clarksdale, Mississippi where we learned about the infamous musician who allegedly made a deal with the devil for fortune and fame.

We finally get to the part of the gallery where I see a wall of additional black-and-white pictures with information on the blues performers, set in between suitcases and trunks of all shapes, sizes, and colors. Well, as far as colors go, they're mostly neutral. But I'm pretty sure this is what we've been looking for.

There aren't many people in this section, and what few there are don't seem to be interested in the suitcases. That's good for us.

"Clay, there it is. That wall full of suitcases."

"I see it. Any idea which one is ours?"

"No. There's nothing in the clue that points to a certain one. I can't imagine it's one of the

trunks though, since we had one of those already back in Philadelphia."

"Right. Plus, the key is too little to fit a trunk's lock. It's probably one of the smaller suitcases."

"Okay. I see a couple of medium-sized suitcases on the floor. I may start with those since it seems like they'll be easier to reach."

"And you'll be a little less conspicuous." Clay scans the room for security cameras. "Go for it."

"I'm not even that worried about getting caught."

"Me either. We have a story that gets us out of trouble. At least it's worked for us so far."

I squat down on the floor and put the small key into the first brown suitcase on the floor. It doesn't unlock. I try the tan one sitting next to it, and holy cow, the lock clicks.

"Yes," Clay whispers. "Don't raise the top up all the way. Just lift it slightly and stick your hand in to feel around."

I push my arm inside and feel not one, but two items. "There are a couple of things in here," I tell Clay. First, I come out with a greeting card in an envelope. I hand it to Clay.

"What else?" he asks.

"I'm working on it." The other article I come out with is a plastic tube with a strap, like one you store art, posters, or blueprints in.

"What the hell?" Clay wonders.

"Hmm. No idea. Let's get back to the truck and see what's in here before we come back for the concert."

"I'll trade you." He gives me the card and I hand him the tube.

"Hold on tight to it."

"I feel like Nicolas Cage in *National Treasure*, trying to keep the Declaration of Independence safe."

"Well, I know it's not that. But I can't wait to find out," I say as we walk out of the museum.

Chapter 6

"You want to read the card first or would you rather me open this baby and see what's in here?" Clay asks, holding the tube out in front of himself.

"Go ahead and open it. The card will probably have some sort of explanation, so I don't want any spoilers, if that makes sense."

"Alright, babe. Here goes."

Clay unscrews the end cap off the tube and pulls out a rolled-up piece of what appears to be some type of artwork paper. It's slightly aged, but seems to be in decent condition. As he unfurls the paper, we are stunned. There is no mistaking what we're looking at: an authentic Picasso print. The image is stamped onto the paper from the master etching, then signed and numbered in pencil by Picasso himself.

"Holy shit," I say, looking at the couple in the print.

"Are they fucking?" Clay asks with a laugh.

"It would appear so," I snicker back. "If not, they're about to be."

"Her tit's all askew," he continues laughing. "And, are her tits on her back or is her head on backwards?"

"That's Picasso for ya. Gosh, this can't be real."

"Are you talking about our life or the Picasso?"

"Both?" I chuckle.

"This is real life, Lynn. We're living it. And I'm willing to bet the Picasso is legit too." Clay views the artwork again. "Jesus, babe, look. There were only fifty of these prints created. And we freaking have one. Must have cost thousands," Clay says in awe.

"It's unbelievable."

The figures in the etching are lying down, with the man behind the woman. One of her arms is reaching up, grabbing the back of his neck, while one of his arms hugs her boobs, though only one is showing, skewed as it is. And their legs are all kinds of tangled up in each other. You can't tell whose legs belong to whom.

I open the card from Aunt Mitzi. "Let's see what she has to say about this." I read out loud to Clay.

"'My Dear Sweets,

'I hope you're not offended by this find. If I know you as well as I think I do though, you won't be. To answer the question that I'm sure is on your mind, yes, this Picasso is real. The title of this piece of work is Étreinte IV. Translation, 'Embrace,' in French. Picasso did a whole series of these with couples in various positions of embracing. This was the fourth one. Hence the IV.

'Flo helped me with this one. It was her idea to acquire this print for you. I thought it was a little suggestive for my taste, but she thought you would both like it and would display it with pride and joy.

'As I'm writing this, Flo and I are actually here in St. Louis. Remember when I told you we two old ladies were going to Branson? Well, we didn't. We came here for the grand opening of the museum and she helped me put the Picasso in the suitcase. We both donated money to help get the museum up and running, so we were allowed access to do this for you.

'I hope Flo was right in that you like this piece and you are continuing to enjoy your trip.

'Love Always,

'Aunt Mitzi.'"

"Well, isn't that something," Clay muses.

"I'd like to see the whole series of what these different stages of, ahem, 'embracing' are."

"Ha. Right? I guess Picasso was quite the lover." Clay rolls the artwork back up and slides it into its protective holder. "You ready to go back inside and listen to some blues?"

"Sounds good, babe. Lead the way."

While we drink a couple of beers and listen to a spectacular performance by Zac Harmon, Clay nudges me and shows me his phone. He has looked up all the Picasso prints with *Étreinte* in the title. He scrolls through them and points to one. Leaning over to me, he says in my ear, "We're doing that later." Then he kisses me on the cheek and I wink at him.

Walking back to the truck after the show, Clay raves about the music. "You know, I'm not much of a blues man — except when it comes to Jake and Elwood — but that was great. His rendition of 'Knockin' on Heaven's Door' was kick-ass."

"I agree. That was awesome. He was really good."

"Hey, you hungry?"

At the mention of food, I realize the answer is 'yes.' It dawns on me that we never ate dinner. "Uh, yeah, actually. I could eat. But I don't want anything too heavy. It's so late."

"Me either. I don't want to have to break out the Tums at three a.m."

As we settle in the truck, Clay searches on the GPS for nearby late-night eateries around town. My eyes perk at the one named Peacock Loop Diner.

"Ooh, that sounds interesting. Let's go there."

"Alrighty, ma'am. I've never had peacock. Bet it tastes like chicken." I snicker as he punches the button and we follow the route to the diner.

As we arrive, I see a magnificent neon sign in the shape of a peacock welcoming us. It's resplendent, with the bold, brilliant hues of the restaurant's eponymous fowl. The alternating neon lights emulate the bird fanning its feathers in a courtship display.

Clay grabs me by the hand and we enter. The interior atmosphere does not disappoint. It's freaking awesome. There are four white U-shaped counters with changing colors of light bordering the edges: purple, blue, green, turquoise. The same thing is happening on the ceiling as well, with vivid colors streaming out of huge fixtures. Diner-style barstools topped with turquoise cushions surround the counters. There's a wall of display cases with all things peacock and retro diner ephemera. Naturally, the song "Peacock" by Katie Perry starts streaming through my mind.

"Wow. This place is fabulous," I say.

"Yeah. It's like hipster meets fifties diner. You know how to pick 'em."

A hostess approaches us. "Good evening. I see we have a couple of lovebirds with us tonight," she says, eyeing our clasped hands. "How would you like to sit at our Peacock Carousel of Love?"

"That sounds pretty special," I say, with a questioning look on my face.

"It is." She smiles.

"Lead the way," Clay tells her.

She brings us to a circular booth with a marquee above, highlighting the title of said love carousel. The booth is set in its own little separate cubby, away from the rest of the patrons, with tan walls and a white curtain backdrop. Sconces with white lights are evenly spaced, three on each wall. A feather-like, white, glass chandelier hangs above the round, white diner table. The cushions in the booth are plush turquoise. As we slide in, the side walls of the booth practically cocoon us.

"Your waitress will be right with you."

"Thanks," I tell her. Clay gives her a smile.

"Well, I can see why they consider this a love nest," Clay says with a wink.

"It's definitely cozy."

Our waitress approaches, dressed in a cute blue and purple gingham shirt, jeans, turquoise Converse tennis shoes, and a peacock feather barrette in her braided hair. She must have heard what I said because the first thing she says to us is, "I can rotate the booth for you if you would prefer some privacy."

"It spins?" Clay asks.

"We don't call it a carousel for nothing. Here, I'll show you." She rotates the booth and we face the curtain. "There's a TV behind the curtain. You can play video games if you want."

"You serious?" Clay asks.

"Mmm hmm."

"That's bad-ass."

"That really is cool," I tell her, "but I think we'll be fine without the games. I'd much prefer to people-watch while I eat."

"So, no *GTA* then?" he asks.

I give Clay a look to indicate I truly do not want to sit and watch him play *Grand Theft Auto* during dinner.

"My wife has spoken. Spin us back around, please, uh, Miss Waitress."

"Oh, gosh, I'm so sorry," she says as she turns the booth back to where we are facing the restaurant. "Caroline. My name is Caroline. I'll take care of you guys tonight. What can I get you to drink? Soda? Or would you like one of our spiked milkshakes? We also have a full bar with some great specialty cocktails."

"Hmm," I think aloud as I peruse the menu. "I wasn't really planning on having a drinky-drink, but that Peacocktail sounds great. I mean, you kind of have to get it, right? Like a rite of passage when dining here?"

Caroline chuckles. "Sure, it's pretty popular." She writes it down then looks to Clay. "You?"

"I'll try the St. Louis Weather."

"Another good choice. That's our take on the Dark 'n Stormy. Be right back with your drinks." Caroline flits off to put our orders in at the bar.

"Look what I see over there," Clay nudges me and tilts his head towards the right.

"What is it? I can't tell what you're looking at."

"Check the reflection in the windows."

I adjust my eyes to focus on what he's talking about. "Holy crap. Is that Skee-Ball?"

"It is. From the looks of it, the lanes are right outside this little love dugout."

"It's so on when we finish eating."

"Challenge accepted."

Caroline brings our drinks and takes our order.

"Grilled cheese," I tell her.

"That sounds good. I'll have the same. And add an order of fried pickles to that please."

"You got it. Coming right up."

I take a sip of my drink. It's a pretty, blue-green color, like a peacock, of course. The combination of blue curaçao, vodka, and peach schnapps dances delightfully on my tongue.

"How's your drink?" I ask Clay.

"It's good. Kind of like a Moscow Mule, but with rum instead of vodka. Wanna taste?"

"No thanks, I don't think it will mix well with all this sweetness going on in this glass."

"Alright." He takes another sip. "We had a good day, I'd say. Wouldn't you?"

"Yeah. First a Picasso and live music, and now we're about to have super grilled cheese sandwiches. Then, I'm gonna kick your butt in Skee-Ball."

"Whoa, whoa, whoa, woman. Slow your roll. You know it's me that will outscore you."

"It's not pinball."

"Doesn't matter."

"I beat you at bocce."

"That wasn't fair. You grew up playing bocce."

Caroline comes back to the table with our grilled cheese sandwiches and fried pickles. "Here you are. Anything else I can get you? Another drink?"

"Not for me, thanks," I tell her.

"Me either. But I will take a glass of water."

"Oh, me too."

"Gotcha. Be right back. Enjoy your meal." She walks off to fetch our waters.

"Okay," Clay resumes our conversation. "Are you willing to bet something over Skee-Ball?"

"What do you have in mind?"

"You give me another strip tease if I win, like you did when I outplayed you in pinball back in our cabin in Tennessee." He takes a bite of his sandwich and I try the fried pickles.

"Um. No."

"Why not?"

"I already did that."

"So, was that a once in a lifetime thing then?"

"No. Not saying that. Just pick something different."

"I'll have to think a minute. What about you? What do you want? *If you win, that is.*"

Caroline comes back with our waters. "Need anything else?"

"No, thanks," we say in unison.

"Enjoy."

"If I win…" I pause as I take a bite of grilled cheese. "I want you to sing karaoke in the next week."

"No fucking way," he says as he shakes his head.

"Why not? You have a great voice, babe."

"It's just for you."

"Well, that's what I want if I win."

He sighs. "Fine. Then if I win, you're getting up with me three times a week for a month to work out in the gym."

"A month? No. Not happening. One week."

"Three."

"Two."

"Done."

"Shake on it?"

"Kiss on it." He leans over and gives me a peck on the lips.

"Only one game though. We don't have time for two out of three. It's getting late."

"Deal."

"And no sabotaging. I know you."

"Alright," he says with a sigh. Then he mumbles, "Buzzkill," and smiles at me.

We finish eating and head over to the Skee-Ball lanes. Clay inserts a couple of dollar bills and nine wood and resin balls come rolling down the chute, making that old familiar clacking sound as they stop at the end.

"I'm first," I say.

"Of course." He gestures for me to take my turn and moves to the side to watch.

Nearby customers of the diner observe me, as Clay explains our wager to a couple of them.

I grab the first ball, pull my arm back, and roll the ball up the alley with decent velocity, aiming high. It flies up the ramp and over the edge of the ball-hop at the end, landing in the center hole for thirty points. My next two balls hit the forty-point slot, good for eighty more points.

"Damn, Lynn. Not bad."

"Thanks. Now, please be quiet. I love you, but you're breaking my concentration."

"Yes, ma'am." He gives me a playful salute.

I rack up a total of 220 points before I pick up my last ball. I rub my hands on it and blow it for good luck. I release it up the alley, and seemingly in slow motion, the ball hikes up over the ball-hop and lands in the corner pocket for a whopping one hundred points. I almost scream. I hear a guy whistle at my ability to hit the highest mark. I look at Clay and his jaw goes slack. I'm in shock myself.

"Oh my gosh," I say. "I can't believe it. That was a complete fluke." Then I correct myself with mock arrogance. "That I only got a total of seventy points with my first two balls. That part was the fluke. I totally meant to do that with the last one."

Clay walks over to me with a smile. "Sure you did. Nicely done, babe. That was impressive." He gives me a kiss.

"Think you can beat three-twenty?" I ask, blowing on my nails and buffing them on my shirt.

"Please. Let the pro show you how it's really done."

He releases another set of balls and scores fifty points off the bat. By the time he grabs his last ball, his score totals 310. Great. I guess I'll be hitting the gym with him for two weeks. When he pulls back for his last shot, he aims for the corner slot worth a hundred points. Even if he misses, he will still get at least ten points and we'll be tied. Which we didn't plan for, but this way we will both win. Or both lose, however you look at it.

I think Clay was a little overconfident though, because when the ball nears his goal, it doesn't go in. It doesn't even fall into any other score slot. The ball bounces off the rim with a harsh thud and finds itself in the outermost section of the scoring area, falling into the beautiful gutter, leaving him with a total score of 310 to my 320.

I. Freaking. Win. Clay's face turns white as I jump up and down in my victory.

"Shit," he says. "Well done, love. You win."

Girls all around give me high-fives and congratulate me as the surrounding guys give Clay a consolation slap on the back, with a few of them saying things like, "Nice try," and "You were robbed, dude."

"Guess we'll be hitting up a karaoke bar somewhere in the next week," I tell him with a smile.

"I can't believe I agreed to that." He leans a little closer to me where only I can hear and says, "I was so sure I'd be watching your tits bounce on the treadmill for the next two weeks."

"Sorry not sorry."

"Come on," he smiles. "Let's pay the check and get out of here. I'm ready to practice some Picasso positions. One way or another, I'm watching your tits bounce."

I laugh as Clay puts a hundred-dollar bill into Caroline's hands with the check and tells her to keep the change.

CHAPTER 7

THE NEXT MORNING, I'm getting out of the shower as Clay comes into the bathroom, all sweaty from the hotel gym.

"Have a good workout?"

"Yeah. Missed you though," Clay says as he starts stripping off his clothes.

"If you weren't so cocky, you might have made that shot last night."

"I'll show you cocky," he says as he rids himself of his boxers. I laugh. "Seriously though, I love watching you work out, Lynn. You know that."

"But I need nature. I miss my runs on the trail at the park back home."

"You're still getting exercise though, of the horizontal variety. And sometimes vertical."

"I guess that's true," I smile as I dry myself with a fluffy towel.

"Can you order us some breakfast while I take a shower?"

"That was my plan. I've already put a pot of coffee on."

"Yeah. Smelled it when I walked in."

"We can figure out the next clue while we eat."

"Sounds good, love." He gives me a peck on the lips, steps into the shower, and turns the water on.

I adorn myself in one of the luxurious bathrobes that was hanging on the back of the bathroom door, and head back into the room to order us something to eat.

Our breakfast arrives just as Clay comes out. He answers the door, and we sit down for eggs, bacon, pancakes, and fruit.

"You ready?" I ask as I pour a ton of syrup over my blueberry pancakes.

"Hit me with it."

"Okay. 'Bulls, Cubs, and Bears… oh my! Stop by the Field Building and say, 'Hi!' In the heart of Lincoln Park, there are plenty of vessels to be seen. Harbor the one called Mt. Bel. It slipped in 216. What you'll find there is your legacy. Use it when you need some therapy.' Awesome. We're going to Chicago. I'm so excited, Clay!" I look up at the ceiling and cheer, raising my arms, but I forget that my fork is in my hand and a piece of pancake falls on my face and slides back down into my plate.

"Me too, babe," he laughs as he wipes syrup off my cheek. "What do you make of the rest?"

"I'm too thrilled to think. But let's see. A vessel is some sort of container, right?"

"Could be."

"Maybe a storage container."

"Or…" Clay pauses for dramatic effect. "A boat."

"Oh yeah. Okay, next up is 'Harbor the one called Mt. Bel.' If you harbor something, you hold it. Protect it and keep it safe. I think we need to find a place called Mount Bel and maybe that's what we need to unlock. 'Bel' is spelled weird though, just B-E-L. So I'm not sure if it's a person's name or maybe a monument. Probably not an actual bell since it's missing an 'L.' What do you think?"

"Maybe instead of Mount Bel, it's actually Bel Mountain."

"Okay. That's good. And what about the 'slipped in two-sixteen' part? Maybe there was a mudslide. Are there even mountains in Chicago, Clay? I think we might be on the wrong track."

"You're overthinking. We're just brainstorming. And I don't think there are any mountains in Chicago, but that doesn't mean there isn't something named Bel Mountain. Or Mount Bel. The 'slipped' part may be a ranking. Like if this Mount Bel is a tourist attraction of some sort, maybe their ratings slipped. And instead of two-sixteen, maybe she meant the year twenty-sixteen. Forgot a digit in the cipher."

"Oh my lord, maybe she did. That could really throw us off our game."

"The 'legacy' and 'therapy' parts though, I'm not sure what to think," Clay says.

"Me either. I mean, this trip isn't *our* legacy. Everything she and Uncle Sid have left us is part of *their* legacy. Why does she say we'll find *our* legacy? And therapy? Are we supposed to meet a therapist there?"

"Maybe she thought at this point in our trip, we'd need some therapy," he chuckles.

"She didn't leave a name. Maybe it's another kind of therapy. Like aroma therapy or physical therapy."

"I could definitely use some physical therapy," Clay winks.

"Seriously, dude? I just bent over all kinds of backwards for you last night, Picasso. Was that not enough?"

"It's never enough. But I can wait. If I must."

"Yes, please practice a little patience. Let's get back to the clue."

Clay laughs. "Fine. Maybe 'therapy' is Aunt Mitzi's way of just telling us to relax. Which brings me back to physical therapy."

I roll my eyes. But a smile breaks free, refusing to be kept behind my lips. "You'll get your physical therapy later, Sinclair. Way later. I want to figure this clue out before we leave this morning."

"Okay, okay. How 'bout this. Look up Lincoln Park," he says as he takes a bite of his scrambled eggs.

"Thank you. On it." I go to Google on my phone and get the results. "It's a neighborhood. Looks like a great area of the city."

"Anything specific stand out? Is the Mount Bel there? Maybe it's a statue."

"Let me add more criteria to my search." I add 'Mt. Bel' and come up with nothing. "No, that didn't help. Not even Bel Mountain helps. I get results for Taco Bells nearby."

"Search for 'heart of Lincoln Park,' since that's what the clue says."

I change the search again. And sigh. "Cardiologists, anyone? What are we missing?"

"Let me try something." Clay gets his own phone out and starts searching. He pulls up a map of Lincoln Park. He scrolls all over his screen, zooming in and out, moving left, right, up, and down, looking at all the pinpointed landmarks. "Boom!" he says, scaring the crap out of me.

"Shit, Clay." I put my hand to my chest. "What is it?"

He slides his phone over to me. "Belmont Harbor."

"You sure that's it?"

"It's a great place to start."

"But…"

"Lynn, please. Humor me. So far it makes the most sense. She used the word 'harbor' which could be a marina. And then she said, 'vessel.' We know that's another word for a boat. Moored in a harbor. 'Mont' is French for 'mountain.' That much I remember from high school French class. So, there's our Mount Bel. It's Belmont."

"Okay. That seems logical. And the 'slipped' part?"

He smiles. "I'm not getting my hopes up, but… I'm thinking it's a boat. In slip two-sixteen. Named *Legacy*."

"Holy shit. Now she's giving us a freaking boat? What's next?"

"We don't know it's a boat. It's just the most rational assumption."

"So, she didn't skip a digit in the code. It's not really supposed to be twenty-sixteen."

"Probably not. Because here's something else that I thought about: two-sixteen… February sixteenth."

"Oh my gosh. My birthday."

"Exactly."

"Wow."

"Yep. So, what does the keychain look like?"

I dig the keychain out with the label number 29 on it. "It's one of those foam ones that float."

Clay smiles wide. "So you don't lose your boat keys," he winks.

"Well. You might be right then. Especially since there are two keys on the fob."

"Still not getting my hopes up."

"How long will it take us to get to Chicago?"

"About five hours. You finished eating, pancake face?" he laughs.

"Yes, goofball."

"Okay. You get dressed. Then let's pack up, check out, and make our way to the Gateway Arch."

We arrive at the arch and buy our tickets for the tram to the top. There's a replica of the tram car so you can see how small it is and if you will be able to stand the four-minute ride to the top. It's quite small. Like a pod. There's only room for five people to sit. If you're claustrophobic, you might have to sit this monumental tourist attraction out.

The ride to the top is a strange one. A bit shifty, the capsule tilts here and there and then readjusts itself back to an even keel, but it's kind of fun at the same time. It feels kind of like riding a Ferris wheel. But unlike riding a Ferris wheel, my ears begin to pop as we ascend.

After exiting, we climb a few stairs and reach the pinnacle. Slim, horizontal windows are set throughout the hallway where you can see either side for miles.

Signs are posted throughout with facts about the arch. For instance, it's 630 feet tall. Construction began in 1963 and was completed in 1965. The Gateway Arch is made of stainless steel. It's the tallest arch in the world. Things like that.

On the west side is downtown St. Louis, with skyscrapers standing tall and mighty. We can see the old courthouse, which is a Federal-style building topped with a dome, the color a pretty greenish-blue, like the Statue of Liberty. That tells me it's probably copper, or at least has a copper exterior. The dome itself is probably made of iron or wood. Also in our sights is Busch Stadium, home of the St. Louis Cardinals.

On the east side, we're looking at Illinois. The Mighty Mississippi River feels like a lifeline back home to Baton Rouge. I guess in a way, it is.

After getting our fill of the fabulous view from the top, we head back to the ground. The ride down is shorter and faster, taking only three minutes, thanks to gravity and all that.

"That was great," Clay says. "Glad we did it."

"Me too. Always wanted to visit the 'Gateway to the West.' I love checking things off my bucket list. Another icon down, plenty more to go."

"We'll get there, love. I'll make sure you see them all."

"I love you."

"I know."

CHAPTER 8

"S o, who's turn is it for music?" Clay asks.

"I'm not sure. I'm so lost. You go ahead and take it today."

Yesterday, on our way to St. Louis, neither one of us was in much of a music mood, so I just put on my *Instrumental Pop* playlist and let it ride.

"Sweet, babe. Thanks." He hits a button and Pink Floyd's "Another Brick in the Wall, Part 2" starts.

We sing along to the next few songs that play from Clay's bank of music. If I don't know them or like them, he skips to the next one. In addition to the Pink Floyd number, we sing our hearts out to "Blister in the Sun" by Violent Femmes, "Once in a Lifetime" by Talking Heads, and "No Rain" by Blind Melon.

I take a swig from my water bottle as Clay lowers the volume of the radio when the traffic slows down on the interstate. All that singing made me thirsty.

"Hey," I say, "how would you like to hear more entries from Aunt Mitzi's diary?"

"Oh, that sounds intriguing. Read away."

"Okay, let me dig it out of my bag." Pulling it out of my purse, I open it to a random page. "August 9, 1950. '*Sid had an allergic reaction to straw-berries today after eating one of my pies. Guess I won't be making it anymore. That's too bad. It's a family favorite.*' Well, that explains why we never had her famous strawberry pie that we read about in her diary a couple of weeks ago."

"Wow. I didn't realize people could just develop allergies like that out of the blue."

"Yeah. It happened to my cousin Benny. I think it was a fruit for him too."

"Hmm. Okay, next?"

"Let's see. March 16, 1947. '*Sid and I took a Sunday road trip today. Drove to New Orleans, walked around the French Quarter. Shopped. Took a ride in the Desire streetcar. Ate at Antoine's. Had a wonderful time. Now to relax.*' Sounds like it was a fun day. They rode 'a streetcar named Desire.' How fabulous. That was before the movie even came out."

"Very cool."

"And I love Antoine's."

"Me too."

"Did you know that Antoine's is the oldest restaurant in New Orleans? It's been open since the 1840s I believe."

"I did know that. Here's some more trivia for you. Did you know that Oysters Rockefeller was invented there?" Clay asks.

"No. I didn't."

"Yep. Because the sauce was so rich, it was named after John D. Rockefeller, the richest man

in the country at the time."

"Wow. I love that."

"Yeah. Cool fact. So, what would you like to see when we get to Chicago? Besides the Field Building."

"Hmm, I'm not sure. Maybe the Sears Tower."

"It's the Willis Tower now."

"Whatever. I don't know why they feel the need to rename buildings."

"Money. It's always about money, babe."

"The almighty dollar. Well, anyway, I think I might like to go to Navy Pier too."

"It's 'Old Navy Pier' now."

I crack up laughing. "That would be funny. Not really though. They don't need to sell out. Anyway, I'd like to go, if we have time."

"We can make time. And instead, if you want, I heard there's a great bar called The Signature Lounge on the ninety-sixth floor of the John Hancock Building, if I recall correctly. We can see the city and have a drink while we're at it. They say the view is better from there, especially at night."

"Okay, that sounds good. Are you sure it's still called the John Hancock building?"

"As of today in 2017 it is. That could change at any minute though. Can you book us a room?"

"Sure." I get my phone out, look for centrally located hotels in Chicago, and reserve a suite at the Talbott Hotel near the Magnificent Mile. A big cow, painted like a ladybug, is climbing the building. Just by looking at the picture, I can't tell exactly what medium the cow is fabricated from, but my best guess would be fiberglass. And the fact that it's there, climbing the wall, is so random. Makes me like the hotel even more. I've always loved ladybugs. They remind me of Aunt Mitzi. She always said they were good luck charms. "All set for a room."

After settling into our room, we rest, and each take a shower before finally deciding to go down and eat at the hotel restaurant.

"I'm starving," Clay says, looking at the menu.

"Me too. I think I'm going to have the turkey bacon club."

"Turkey bacon? Gross."

"No, silly. Honey smoked turkey breast, with bacon. Real bacon."

"That's my girl."

"It's also dressed with a pickled green tomato, basil, lettuce, and avocado."

"That is a totally 'you' sandwich."

"Can't wait to try it. Never had a pickled green tomato before. What are you ordering?"

"I'm eyeing the overstuffed French dip."

"Oh, that looks good too. I'm gonna stick with my club sandwich though."

The waitress comes and takes our orders.

After she leaves, Clay asks, "Drinks at the Hancock building after?"

"Sounds like a plan. So, what do you think about the hotel?"

"It's great. You always book good hotels. This one is in a perfect location. But, what's with that ladybug cow climbing the building?"

The waitress brings our sandwiches, and we dig in.

"About the cow." I snicker, "I looked that up while you were in the shower earlier. It was from a public art exhibition in the city back in 1999 called *Cows on Parade*. They're made of fiberglass and there were over three hundred of them, all painted differently by talented artists. After the exhibit was over, they were auctioned off for charity. Only about half, maybe less, remain spread throughout Chicago."

"Really? That's cool." Clay dips his sandwich in the cup of au jus and takes another bite. "Mmm. Man, this is good. How's your club?"

"Delicious." I take a sip of my water. "So, the cow at our hotel is named 'Cowccinella Novemnotata,' a play on the scientific name of the nine-spotted ladybug."

"Which is?"

"*Coccinella novemnotata.*"

"Ah. Clever. And look at you, learning trivia about the city."

"I had to find out. It was bizarre for a ladybug cow to be climbing the façade of our hotel. I knew there had to be a story behind it."

After finishing our tasty sandwiches, we take a leisurely walk to the John Hancock building. It's a beautiful evening. The temperature is in the lower eighties and the humidity is low as well.

We stroll hand in hand for a few blocks and walk past a shiny Lamborghini. That's not something you see every day.

Clay notices the extravagant vehicle, of course, and he can't ignore it. "Looks like somebody drove my car here," he says with an envious smile and stars in his eyes.

"Riiiight," I laugh.

Clay chuckles, then points to our destination. "We're here."

I immediately recognize that the Hancock building is of the Structural Expressionist style of architecture, with a distinctive X-braced exterior. This indicates that the building's skin is part of its tubular system, which is an engineering technique designers use to achieve great heights in construction. This method keeps the building upright during high winds and other lateral loads.

We enter the Hancock building and take the elevator to the Signature Lounge on the ninety-sixth floor. We wait a few minutes for a table and are seated near the windows. The view of Chicago from up here is spectacular. The skyline is glittering with city lights almost as far as the eye can see. Several rooftop pools sparkle as overhead lighting reflects off their surfaces. The Ferris wheel of Navy Pier is a kaleidoscope of color in the distance.

I order the Godiva chocolate martini and Clay opts for a classic dirty martini with extra olives. He points with his head towards the panorama of windows. "Outstanding view."

"It is. I could have never imagined how beautiful it would be from up here. So, what's on the agenda for tomorrow? Harbor first?"

"I think that's probably wise. Once we're through with that, we can do Navy Pier since we'll be right there on the water. You up for the Ferris wheel?"

"Of course."

We finish our drinks and take a few pictures of the city view and one of us together. Then we head back to the hotel.

"Big day tomorrow," Clay says. "Let's get some sleep."

"Yeah," I say as I pull the comforter over me. "Goodnight. I love you."

"Love you too, babe. Night." He kisses me and I drift off.

I'm in the dark. I can't see a thing. I can't move. I can barely breathe. My mouth is gagged. My hands are tied. What's happening? Gunshots pierce my ears. Blood splatters everywhere. And I scream.

Something is shaking me. "Lynn, wake up!"

I sit up with a start. My chest is heaving. My body is sticky with sweat. "Oh God, Clay."

"Are you alright, love? You were screaming." He hugs me close.

"I had a bad dream. A nightmare, I guess," I say breathlessly. "I was trapped."

"You're okay. I've got you."

"It felt so real. Gunshots. Blood. Oh my god, Clay. Do you think it's because of what happened?"

Clay nods in solemn assent. "Yes. Probably so."

"Now I know how you feel when you dream about Afghanistan."

"And now I know how you feel when you have to wake me up."

My heart settles and I lay back down. "I'm sorry. It was just so scary."

"I know. It's okay. You don't need to apologize. I'm here. I'm right here. You need anything?"

"Um, yeah. Can you get me some water please?"

"Sure." Clay gets out of bed and walks into the bathroom. I hear the clink of the glass as it hits the faucet of the sink. It reminds me of the beer bottle clinking on the kidnapper's gun. There's a rush of water from the tap. It reminds me of the wind rushing by the car window as my abductor drove. I start to shake again. Clay returns with my glass, none too soon. I'm relieved to have him back in my presence.

"Thanks." Hands trembling, I gulp the liquid down, the glass vibrating against my teeth. After chugging the water, I wipe my mouth with the back of my hand. Clay takes the glass from me and sets it on the nightstand. I rearrange myself back under the covers and start to cry.

"Talk to me, love."

"I just… I was so…" I sob between words and breaths. "I was so afraid he was going to kill me. I thought I would never see you again and that I was going to die without you knowing what happened to me. And we just had that huge fight and I felt like the worst person. I just wanted to see your face again before he…" I can't finish my thought.

"Lynn. I know, babe. I know." Clay gets behind me and enfolds me into him, my back to his chest. "You can't imagine what was running through my head before I found you," he says with a crack in his voice. "I've got you now. You're safe. In my arms." He takes a deep breath, followed by a profound sigh of relief.

"Thank you for saving me."

"I wasn't going to stop until I found you. Are you sure you don't want to go back home?"

"I'm sure. I need this. It's a good distraction. What about you?"

"I'm okay with staying on the road if that's what you need, love."

"Okay," I sniffle. "I've been trying to stay so strong for you so you wouldn't have to worry about me."

"Lynn, that's what I'm here for. You know that I know how you're feeling. I live with those feelings every day. I'm still haunted by memories of what happened while I was deployed. It's not easy to stave them off."

"I just didn't want to trigger anything for you by bringing up the chaos that's been going on in my own mind."

"Forget about that. I've lived with it long enough that I can control it. For the most part. You know that. Don't bottle your feelings. If you need to get something out, you tell me. I'll help you through it." He pauses and then adds, "But to know that this guy got to you because of all the shit that went down over there. Because of me. It's all my fault. What happened to you." He sniffles.

"No, Clay. We're not doing this again. It was his fault. He was the crazy one."

"But—"

"Stop it. I don't blame you. So stop blaming yourself. Please, babe. Okay?"

"Okay, Lynn. Okay." He kisses my cheek. "I love you."

"I love you too." I bring his hand to my lips and give him a gentle kiss on his knuckles. "I'm afraid to go back to sleep."

"I know," he whispers. "It'll be okay. Just think good thoughts and close your eyes. I've got you. I'll slay your dragons, love."

CHAPTER 9

I WAKE UP WELL rested, despite the horrible dream I had in the middle of the night. I think spilling my guts out to Clay helped me. I'd been so restless the past few days and nights, trying not to think about what happened. I just didn't want to send Clay back to his dark place by taking him to mine. Thank God he understands and knows how to pull me out of it. I hope he knows how much I appreciate him.

I stretch my arms over my head and look over to Clay's side of the bed. Empty. Where is he? "Clay?" I call nervously, my anxiety rising. The aroma of fresh coffee hits me and I start to relax.

"In here, babe," he replies from the living area of our hotel room. "Ready for some coffee?"

"In a minute." I get up and head to the bathroom to wash my face and brush my teeth. When I get to the room where Clay is, he is sitting at the table reading the paper. My coffee cup is ready and waiting next to a bowl of fruit and yogurt with a side of granola. I grab my mug and lean over to give him a kiss.

"I wasn't sure how long you'd sleep and I didn't want to wake you, so I didn't order you a hot breakfast. I can still get something else for you though, if you want."

"No, this is perfect. Thanks." I mix the granola into the vanilla yogurt and blend in the plump berries as well. A blueberry leaks and the juice swirls into my breakfast as I stir, making my yogurt a pretty shade of pastel purple. "What time is it? I know we have a lot to do today. The harbor, the Field Building, Navy Pier. And whatever else." I take a bite and savor the perfect combination of tart mixed berries, smooth sweet yogurt, and crunchy granola toasted with honey and cinnamon.

"It's almost nine. I think we have plenty of time. It will be a full day though. You up for it?"

"Yeah. Looking forward to it."

"You good? After last night, I mean."

"Yes. Thank you for helping me fall asleep. I may need that again."

"No problem. Always here for you, love."

"You ate already?"

"Yeah, I had the same thing. Those berries taste like they were freshly picked this morning, don't they?"

"Mmm hmm," I hum with a mouth full of yogurt parfait goodness. "They're delicious," I say after I finish swallowing my bite.

Once I finish eating and we dress for the day, we take a cab to Belmont Harbor in Lincoln Park.

"Wow, it looks like there are more sailboats than any other kind of vessels in this marina," Clay says. "I wonder if one of them is ours."

"I guess we'll find out soon. I'd love a sailboat." I survey my surroundings. "It's very peaceful out here."

"Yeah. I love the sound of the water slapping at the pylons and hulls."

"Me too."

Various sizes and classes of boats are moored in the harbor, their hypodermic masts impaling the sky. Some are yachts that probably cost a million bucks. Gentle waves rock the docked watercrafts as the smell of the freshwater lake hits my nose. Several different species of gulls fly above our heads, searching for their next meal in the deep blue water below them. The jangling of metal blocks and rigging equipment against hollow aluminum masts of the sailboats is relaxing; windchimes of the marina. Flags snap as the wind picks up while simultaneously blowing my hair in my face, blocking my view of everything. I quickly put it up in a ponytail.

As we walk, the wooden planks clatter underneath our feet. Ahead of us, a family loads their boat for a day on the water, laughing and passing trays of food. The seagulls circle, hoping to be tossed a crust of bread or a sliver of sandwich meat.

"We're almost there," I say. "Here we are at the two-hundreds."

"Wanna race to two-sixteen?"

"No," I chuckle. "We'll be there soon enough."

We continue walking and when we reach the boat slip numbered 216, my mouth drops.

"Holy shit," Clay says in awe.

A beautiful yacht floats before us. I'm almost as in shock as I was when I saw the cabin she left us in Tennessee. The name of this vessel is *Legasea*. Clever, Aunt Mitzi. Real clever. The fact that this entire trip, including this boat, is her and Uncle Sid's legacy for us, and the name of the yacht is a pun… it's totally perfect.

"I love the name," Clay says.

"Me too."

"Told you what it was called. Just had the spelling wrong."

"Close enough. And she can definitely be used for therapy. You were right, it was the relaxing kind of therapy."

"Of the physical variety."

"That's a different kind of therapy and you know it. I'm picturing the wind in my hair, a drink in my hand, and music set to the good vibes."

"Exactly. Good vibrations with wetness all around," Clay laughs.

I playfully punch him in the arm. "You're incorrigible."

"Incorrigible, thy name is Clay." He then turns to the boat and gives it a quick once-over. "Man, this baby must be at least thirty-five or forty feet long."

"It's a lot bigger than I expected. Should we board?"

Clay dangles the keys. "Let's do it."

We climb aboard and Clay uses one of the keys on the yellow floatie fob to unlock the sliding glass door to the salon.

"Oh my god, it's gorgeous," I gush.

A tan leather sectional sofa is to my right with a glossy cherry-wood coffee table in front of it. Two matching chairs sit across from the couch, a table in between. There's an entertainment center with a nice-sized TV and stereo system facing the large seating area. The galley sports dark granite countertops, a decent-sized sink, and several cabinets, drawers, and cubby holes for plenty of storage. There's a two-burner stove, which is perfect. A convection microwave oven sits above the counter, and a small, side-by-side refrigerator/freezer combo is nestled under the counter. It's a little bigger than a dorm-sized fridge.

A curved dinette seat that's big enough for four people is set across from the galley, matching the couch. The dining table is oval and is the same glossed cherrywood as the coffee table.

"This is incredible," Clay says.

"Yeah," I breathe out.

"Look," Clay points. "Let's go down there. It's probably a stateroom."

We take a couple of steps down from the galley into a roomy cabin with a queen-size bed.

"Oh wow, Clay, this is… I just…"

"I know. I'm speechless too."

He opens a door to the right of the bed. "Whoa." I peek around to see what he revealed. It's a spacious bathroom, with the same granite counter-tops as the galley. "Here's the head. Generous amount of space in here."

"Impressive. I never would have thought a bathroom would be this big on a boat. We might even both be able to fit in that shower."

Clay winks at me. "We'll have to try it."

I step back into the stateroom to really check it out. The walk-around bed is covered with a lavish, silky comforter in shades of blue, with matching pillows. A TV is mounted on the side wall near the bed. We see two cedar closets and plenty of other storage areas surrounding the sleeping space.

Clay turns a small corner by the bathroom. "Sweet Jesus. There's another stateroom here with another bathroom."

"Are you serious?" I follow his voice and see that he's right. This cabin is a little smaller than the other one, but still has plenty of room to walk around the bed and includes all the amenities as the master stateroom. The bathroom is a bit smaller as well, but with ample space to do all your business.

"Lynn?"

"Yeah, babe?"

"Can we have this girl shipped home?"

"I'm sure that can be arranged."

"We haven't even seen the cockpit yet and I'm already in love."

"I hear ya. Let's go up to the bridge."

We exit the salon area and walk up the steps to the flybridge. There's an L-shaped sofa, a wet bar, and another small fridge. Clay sits at the helm in the captain's chair and takes in all the gauges, controls, and screens. Another sitting area is adjacent to his chair, large enough for at least two people.

I sit next to him and make myself comfortable as a brisk wind blows across my face. "Do you even know what all these buttons and joysticks do? Have you ever driven a boat like this?"

"Yes and no. I know what some of the gadgets are for, but I'll have to learn the rest. I've never commanded a yacht before, so I may need some lessons. I might even need a license."

"Does that mean we can't take her for a spin?"

"We could try, but I don't want to screw anything up. Maybe we can find somebody who knows what they're doing to take us out. But I'd have to make sure I trust them to drive this sweet girl."

"Well, you could at least crank her up. See how she sounds."

"I was just about to do that," he winks.

"Cool."

He puts the second key in the ignition and turns it. The yacht purrs to life and the monitors light up. I get chills.

"Beautiful sound," he says with a huge smile.

I give Clay a kiss and rub my hands through his hair. "I can't believe this is ours."

"How many times have you said that on this trip?"

"I know, but it's true. Just so much to take in, everywhere we go."

"I agree. It's all unbelievable."

"Hey, I think I saw an office near where we parked. I bet there's somebody there that can help us, or at least point us in the right direction if we want to get out on the water."

"That's a good idea. There are probably some yacht clubs around here too. Did you find a letter or anything from Aunt Mitzi? There's gotta be something, like at the cabin in Tennessee. You should go back down to the master stateroom and check the drawers."

"Aye aye, captain. You stay up here and look for a manual or something that might show you how some of these controls work."

"Aye aye, first mate," he smiles. And then smiles wider.

"What's that look for?"

"Ahem. Well, speaking of 'first mate.' Maybe we should do just that before you go looking for an envelope."

It takes me a second before I realize he's talking about having sex. Again. "Jeez, Clay." I turn to walk away, smiling a little.

He cracks up and yells as I make my departure, "You gotta admit, that was a good one! First, mate!"

His voice chases me as I shake my head and take the steps back down to the cabin to search the drawers for a letter or an envelope, hoping for something that appears to be from Aunt Mitzi. I rummage through the drawers in one of the bedside tables and come up empty. But in the top drawer of the other one is, of course, an envelope with our names on it in her handwriting. It makes me smile.

I pick it up and bring it back to the bridge to read it to Clay.

"Hey," I say. "I found it. Haven't opened it yet. Wanted us to hear it together."

"Awesome. I knew there would be something. Go ahead."

I open the letter and read.

"'Dear Sweet Loves,

'I hope you like this yacht. Uncle Sid and I bought it several years back. It's a 40-foot 2008 Meridian 391 Sedan Bridge. I know it's not brand new, but I'm sure it will still be in excellent condition when you find it. You know Uncle Sid takes care of everything to a T.

'We named it 'Legasea' thinking that would be the perfect name considering the intentions we hold for it. We've had some great times on this boat. I know you never knew about it, but that was the point. Sid has some wonderful friends up here that belong to the Belmont Yacht Club, which we're also members of. They have agreed

to maintain this vessel since we aren't able to be here year-round. And if anything has happened to them in the years that have passed, their kids have been instructed to maintain it.

'You may arrange to have it sent to Baton Rouge if you wish. Or you can leave it here and come when you want to have your own fun on Lake Michigan. It's really beautiful out here on the water. Whatever you decide, I hope you enjoy this little ship as much as we have.

'Please contact our friends to let them know you've found it. If you want to have it moved to another place, tell them that they will no longer need to be responsible for keeping it ship-shape.'"

I scan the end of the letter. "She left the names and numbers of their friends for us to call, then she just says that she loves us and hopes we're having fun."

"Okay. So do you want to leave it here or have it moved?"

"I think I'd like to have it shipped home so we can enjoy it there. I guess we'll have to find a boat storage place to keep it since there aren't any marinas in Baton Rouge. It's too big for us to keep at home."

"Plus, I'm not sure I could legally tow it with my truck and a trailer. Might be certain street regulations for its size."

"Yeah, so maybe we should just keep it here for now. Unless you think Stone can help get it home. Are his trailers big enough to haul a forty-foot yacht?"

"I don't want to bother him again with hauling something for us. I'll call and make arrangements after we get home. You go ahead and call the number in the letter and let them know we found it, but they'll still need to keep it up until we can have it moved, and we don't know when that will be."

"Okay."

"I think we should just not worry about getting out on the water with it now. Especially if you still want to go to Navy Pier and the Field Building. The pier isn't as close as I thought it would be from here. We'll have to cab it. Besides, I don't know what the requirements for needing a boat license in Illinois are. I don't have one, ya know?"

"Right. Well, you close stuff up here and I'll go downstairs and make the call to a Mr. Joseph Manchester."

"Why don't you just call him from here?"

"It's too windy. Might be hard for him to hear me."

"Mm'kay, babe. Meet you down there."

I make my way back down into the salon area of the boat and take my phone out. After the phone rings three times, a man answers.

"Hello?" he asks into my ear with a strong voice.

"Hi, is this Mr. Joseph Manchester?"

"This is his son, Anthony. Can I help you?"

"Hi, Anthony. Yes. My name is Lynn Sinclair. My husband Clay and I are here in Chicago. My Aunt Mitzi and Uncle Sid Santini were friends of your parents, and they left us their yacht. We wanted to let your mom and dad know that we found it, but we'll still need their help maintaining it for a while until we can have it moved to Baton Rouge."

"Ah. Lynn Sinclair. I'm familiar with your story. My parents are a little too up-in-age these days to take care of those sorts of things themselves, but my sister and I have stepped in to help. In fact, I just had your boat cleaned last month."

"Oh, that's great, thank you. So, your parents aren't doing well then?"

"Well, they've got the usual complaints… mostly arthritis, Dad has a bad knee, and Mom has trouble with her back sometimes, but all in all, they're in pretty good health for a couple of octogenarians."

"That's good to hear."

"I was sorry to hear about Mitzi's passing. I had met her and Sid several times over the years. Great people."

"Yes, they were. Thank you."

"Are you and Clay going to take your yacht out today?"

"Well, we wanted to, but Clay has never driven a boat this big and he's not sure how all the controls work or which screens display what. Plus, we're not aware of the laws here. He doesn't have a boating license or any kind of certification."

"He doesn't need one. I'll tell you what. We were just about to go grab some lunch to bring out on my mom and dad's boat. If it's alright with you and Clay, we can pick up some extra and meet you at yours. Take you out for a spin on the lake. Would love to meet you both. I can show your husband a few things about the *Legasea*."

Clay joins me in the salon and I smile wide at him.

"Anthony, that would be perfect," I tell him. "If you're sure your parents won't mind."

"They won't mind. They'd love to meet you too. You'll get to meet my wife, sister, and brother-in-law as well. Cheeseburgers okay?"

"Absolutely."

"Any allergies or aversions to certain condiments?"

"Nope. We're from Louisiana, so we'll eat almost anything."

"Ha. I'll grab my bottle of Tabasco for good measure."

I chuckle. "Thank you so much. We're looking forward to it."

Clay gives me a questioning glance.

"Sounds great," Anthony says. "We'll see you in about an hour."

"Wonderful. See you then."

I hang up the phone and Clay is shaking his head with a smirk.

"What are you up to, wife of mine? Who's Anthony?"

"I called to explain to Mr. Manchester what was going on, and his son answered. They were on their way to the harbor to take their boat out. They're going to meet us here instead and take us out on ours. Even bringing us some lunch."

"You serious?"

"I am."

"That's freaking fantastic."

"I know, right? I'm so excited. They'll all be here in about an hour."

"All?"

"Mr. and Mrs. Manchester, Anthony and his wife, and Anthony's sister and her husband."

"Sweet."

"I know we planned on doing Navy Pier and the Field Building this afternoon, but can we just stay another night and do the touristy stuff tomorrow?"

"You bet. I think we'd totally wear ourselves out if we still tried to fit all that into the rest of the day and night."

About an hour later, while Clay and I are lounging in the salon, I hear an elderly man ask, "Permission to come aboard?"

We stand up and open the sliding door.

"Of course," Clay says. "Please, watch your step. Come on in, y'all."

Clay helps the man, Mr. Joseph Manchester I presume, climb aboard. The rest of the family enters, and bags of food with the initials LBW printed on them are placed on the dinette table. It all smells divine.

"Mr. Manchester, it's so great to meet you," I tell him as I shake his hand.

"Please, call me Joseph. Mr. Manchester was my grandfather."

I laugh. "Okay, Joseph. I'm Lynn." I gesture to Clay. "My husband, Clay."

Introductions are made all around and we sit down to some of the best cheeseburgers I've ever eaten. The buns are buttery, the patties are well seasoned (I think I detect a hint of Worcestershire sauce, but I could be wrong), ample slices of American cheese that aren't lost between the meat and the bread, and onion-flavored mayonnaise.

"Have you ever had burgers from Little Bad Wolf?" Leah, Anthony's wife, asks.

"No, we haven't," I tell her. "Oh, is that what the 'LBW' on the bags stand for?"

"Yes," she chuckles. "We eat there all the time and order from them whenever we come down to take the boat out. It's a great place and they have wonderful crafty cocktails as well."

"Awesome. I love a good crafty cocktail. These burgers are delicious," I tell her.

"Yeah," Clay adds. "Thanks so much for bringing us lunch."

"No problem at all," Alexandra, Joseph's wife says. "Happy to do it."

Anthony's sister, Julie, lifts a container from the table. "Would anybody like some macaroni and cheese?" She spoons a small helping of the elbow noodles smothered in toppings onto her plate and looks around the table. She sees Clay salivating and passes the carton to him.

"Oh, God yes," Clay says. "Thank you. It's been too long."

Vince, Julie's husband, grins. "You're fond of mac and cheese, I take it,"

"Founder of the fan club," Clay laughs.

"It's his favorite food group," I tell Vince.

"A connoisseur then." Julie smiles. "Let me know how you like it, Clay. There's bacon, scallions, and toasted breadcrumbs in Little Bad Wolf's."

"Sounds delicious." I clear a space on my plate. "Pass it to me after."

Clay puts some on his plate and hands me the container. After he takes a bite, he closes his eyes and nods his head. "Very, very good," he says when he finishes.

After we eat, the guys head up to the bridge while we ladies clean up.

"I'm really surprised at how much room and storage the galley has," I muse.

"There are all kinds of tricks you'll learn about how to store things," Julie says. "One of my favorite hacks is putting a small tension rod in the pantry and using hangers with the clips on them, you know, the ones you get when you buy pants?"

"Yeah, I have tons of those taking up space in my closet at home."

"Good. So, use those as chip clips and hang them on the tension rod."

"That's a great idea. Thanks."

It's not long before we feel a vibration in the floor and hear a low *chug-chug-chug* as the yacht starts up. Julie continues showing me where all the hidden storage is around the galley and salon.

Alexandra tells me some stories of when Uncle Sid and Aunt Mitzi spent time here with them over the years. Her last anecdote is about her retirement party back in the early nineties, when they were all together celebrating the end of her nursing career. "If I recall correctly, Mitzi was a bit tipsy and dared Sid to jump in the lake in his underwear," she giggles.

"*What?*" I'm stunned and amused at the same time. "Did he do it?"

"Of course he did." We all laugh.

"I remember that," Julie says, still smiling. "I had just started working at the bank and Mom's party was the perfect ending to the stressful week. Sid and Mitzi were fun people."

"They were." I smile. "Are you still with the bank?"

"I am. Branch manager now."

"Awesome. Leah, what do you do?"

"I'm a veterinarian."

"How sweet. I love that. When I was little, I wanted to grow up to be a vet, but then I found out I was allergic to cats and rabbits, so that was the end of that."

"Aww, well, seems like you still ended up choosing a great career path. Something with history, right?"

"Yes, I was one of the head curators at a museum in Baton Rouge."

"Very cool," Leah says.

"Can you tell us more about the trip you and Clay are on right now?" Julie asks.

"Of course, I'd love to." I tell them how we found the box of keys, which states we've been to so far, and everything we have found. They were all familiar with our quest. I left the part out about my abduction though. No need to put a damper on this wonderful day.

When we're finished talking and cleaning up everything, we head to the flybridge to relax. Anthony is showing Clay what the screens display, how the controls work, and what all the gauges measure. Vince is busy unzipping and rolling up the panels surrounding the bridge so we can have the full breeze.

"Would you like a beer?" Joseph asks me. I notice all the guys have one, including Clay. Where did that come from? Was the boat stocked?

"We brought an ice chest," Leah says, noticing my confused look. "We also have wine if you'd prefer."

"You thought of everything," I tell her with a smile. "Actually, a beer sounds wonderful."

Joseph reaches down beside the sofa and grabs a beer for me out of the ice chest and twists off the cap. It opens with a hiss. "A girl after my own heart," he says with a wink as he hands me the cold bottle.

"Thanks." I take a big swig. "Ahhhh. That hits the spot." Its light, crisp taste is perfect.

Before I even realize it, we're moving. At some point, they must have untethered us from the dock.

Anthony is talking Clay through guiding the boat out of the slip. "Ease up on the throttle a bit. Good. Now, hit the horn to let everybody know we're coming out of the marina."

Clay presses the horn button and even though I was prepared, the loud sound still scares the shit out of me. I laugh as my body involuntarily jumps. It reminds me of the blast from a trucker's horn on an eighteen-wheeler. I get excited and move closer to Clay. Vince is in the seat next to him and Anthony is standing behind him. Once we clear out of the boat slip, I start to cheer.

"Great job, babe. You'll be a pro in no time." I give Clay a kiss on his cheek.

"Thanks, love."

When we make it out of the harbor and into open water, Clay picks up speed. The diesel fumes mix with the freshwater air and hit my nose. Lake Michigan is teeming with boats of all sizes. The steady *whump-whump* of a speedboat cuts across another boat's wake. Jet skis race in the distance, with plumes of water behind them that shoot skyward like the spouts from a pod of whales. I can hear Kenny Chesney's "Summertime" playing from a nearby boat. As we pass them, we all wave to each other, raising our glasses and beer bottles in a quick toast, as if to say, 'Cheers! Have fun!'

We stay out on the water for a few hours, getting to know each other, laughing and telling stories. Anthony continues to show Clay more about our new toy, showing him how to set the anchor and bringing him down to the engine room, explaining everything. This is a great bunch of people and I only wish we'd met sooner.

We head back to the harbor and Clay expresses how nervous he is to park the boat back in the slip. "I don't know, man. I've never docked a boat this big," he says to Anthony.

"You'll do fine," Vince says. "We'll talk you through it."

Once we're back in the harbor, Vince and Anthony verbally guide Clay with parking the boat. He masterfully slides the yacht back into the slip, like he's done it a hundred times. "Like a glove," he says as he buffs his nails on his shirt.

"See? Told you," Anthony says with a slap on Clay's back.

"Good job, bro," Vince tells him.

"Thanks, y'all."

We gather everything and throw out the food bags from lunch when we get back onto land. As we walk the Manchester family back to their vehicle, we exchange contact information, give hugs, and say good-bye. We promise them that after our road trip is over, we'll be back to visit. Possibly next summer.

"You should come back in the winter for some ice fishing," Vince says to Clay. "We usually take a guys' trip up to Green Bay. It's only about a three-hour drive from here."

"Oh, I don't know if I could handle the cold." Clay visibly shakes.

"It's not so bad. You get used to it," Anthony says, pantomiming drinking from a flask.

We all chuckle.

"I'll think about it," Clay says.

"Fair enough."

We give one more round of hugs and make our way out of the harbor parking lot.

It's late in the evening, and when we get back to the hotel, Clay and I crash on the bed.

"I'm worn out," I tell him.

"Me too. I had a blast today though."

"Same. I wish we'd known we were getting a boat so we could have checked out of the hotel and stayed the night on *Legasea* instead."

"That would've been fun. I can't wait to bring her out on the Gulf when we get back home. Stone and Annie will have to come."

"That sounds great. I'm sure they'd love that. You and Stone can do some deep-sea fishing."

"That's the plan. I wonder if there's a water route from Chicago to Baton Rouge using the Mississippi to get her back home."

"I'm sure there is. I bet that would be an interesting trip."

"I'm not so sure I'd be able to navigate that though."

"Maybe you can talk to Vince and Anthony and figure something out."

"Yeah. So, tomorrow we'll do Navy Pier and the Field Building. Then head to our next destination."

"We need to figure out where that is. In the morning though. I'm too tired to think right now. I don't even feel like getting up to take a shower."

"I hear ya. Let's take a quick cat nap, then we'll shower after."

"Deal." I close my eyes and drift off to sleep.

CHAPTER 10

CLAY AND I take a cab to Navy Pier. I take out the clue sheet on the way there. "Okay, ready for the next clue?"

"Sure thing, love. Hit me with it."

"Alright. It says, 'Head north to the Cream City and find the collection of all things H-D. In the Experience Gallery, find the steel horse with a side satchel and use the key.' Do you have any idea where the Cream City is?"

"No. But with the words 'steel horse' in the clue, I bet it has something to do with motorcycles."

"You think? It could be a statue of a horse."

"Maybe. Let me see the clue sheet." I hand Clay the paper.

"Look," he points. "There's a hyphen between H and D. So, now are you thinking what I'm thinking? It probably doesn't stand for High Definition."

"Probably not Howdy Doody either."

Clay laughs. "It's gotta be Harley-Davidson."

"Ah… yes. Probably a museum, since she says to look for a collection of all the things. And 'Experience Gallery' is capitalized, so that must be the title of an exhibit or something."

"Agreed. I'm still not sure where that is though, besides north. Look it up, babe. You could either search for Cream City or the Harley museum."

"I'll hunt for Cream City. I'd like to know why wherever we're going was given that nickname." I put my fingers to my phone and look it up. "It's Milwaukee. And the name Cream City has nothing to do with the fact that Wisconsin is known as America's Dairyland. It's because of all the cream-colored brick buildings that were built there throughout the nineteenth century. Interesting."

"Cool. Home Depot must have had quite the bargain on those bricks back then."

I laugh. "Says here they were made from glacial lake deposits along the lakeshore of Lake Michigan. The settled silts and clays were used to make the bricks."

"Nice. So, I'm guessing the part in the clue about side satchels is probably a saddlebag on the motorcycle. That's where we'll find our prize."

"Makes sense."

"Do you think we'll find the title to a brand-new Harley-Davidson there? Or a classic? Oh, maybe it'll be a voucher that allows me to have one custom built."

"No," I tell Clay. "Aunt Mitzi knows how I feel about motorcycles. And nothing has changed, you know that. She'd never do that to me."

"But—"

"But nothing. I'm not having this conversation with you again, Clay. So don't get your hopes up about coming into possession of a new, classic, or even a bike that's FUBAR. It's not happening."

He sighs. "Alright."

"It's because I love you, Clay."

"Yeah. Love you too," he says, without much feeling behind the words this time. He takes a breath. "Let's talk about something else."

"Okay," I say a little somberly. "Like what?"

"What does the keychain look like?"

"Crap. I forgot to dig it out of the box before we left. Shit."

"That's okay. We know where we're going. Maybe it's another beer keychain, since Milwaukee is another city full of breweries. Care to check one out while we're there?"

"Only if it's the Shotz Brewery."

"Are you making that up?"

"No."

"Shots? Like shot glass, or gunshot? I've never heard of that beer before. You must be joking."

"I'm not. But it's S-H-O-T-Z. The brewery where Laverne and Shirley worked."

"Oh jeez. I knew you were joking."

"It was real though. In the world of television. But seriously, we should find something different to do. I wonder if there is a *Laverne & Shirley* museum. Or a *Happy Days* museum, since that show was the parent of *Laverne & Shirley.*"

"Oh yeah, I forgot *Laverne & Shirley* was a spin-off of *Happy Days.*"

"Yeah. *Happy Days* spawned several shows. Anyway, I hope there's a museum for them. That's different. And would be fun."

"Sure," Clay says sarcastically. "Let's bet on how many schlemiels and schlimazels we'll come across."

"Don't forget the hasenpfeffer," I laugh.

"A Fonzie museum would be pretty cool though. Ayyyy," Clay quotes and gives me a thumbs up.

I snicker. "Maybe there's a cheese bar. We've gotta eat some authentic Wisconsin cheese. Be honorary cheeseheads."

"Hmm. What about fried cheese curds?"

"Mmm, yes. That sounds good."

We pull up to Navy Pier and exit the cab, heading towards the outdoor entrance.

The sweet aromas of funnel cakes, waffle cones, and kettle corn permeate the air. I can smell savory, grilled meats; french fries; and the freshwater from Lake Michigan. It's hot though, so there's also a hint of sweat in the atmosphere.

We ride the Centennial Wheel, a Ferris wheel nearly two hundred feet high with enclosed climate-controlled gondolas. The view from the top is awesome.

After the wheel makes a few revolutions around, we get off and make our way over to the area where carnival games are being played. I try my luck at throwing darts to pop balloons, which scores me a small fuzzy bear with crooked eyes. Clay plays the shooting gallery and hits every target. He doesn't win a prize, only gets the satisfaction of earning the highest score of all for his expert marksmanship.

Once we finish playing games, we shop until I find a Navy Pier Christmas ornament. On our way out, Clay and I snack on some of the best kettle corn. We've had a great time.

When we get to the Field Building, I almost start crying because of how close I feel to Aunt Mitzi here. The Art Deco building is massive, rising from a four-story base that takes up the whole site. Looking up at the sky-scraping center tower, the vertical lines of the building against the passing clouds give the illusion that it's falling over, and it almost makes me dizzy.

The entrance is framed in black granite. Five white marbled pilasters separate the bays that contain revolving doors which provide access to the lobby. I take some pictures of the imposing frontage of the building, trying my best to emulate the close-up shot of the entrance that hangs in the foyer of our home. I'm pleasantly surprised at how well I can recreate the image with the camera on my cell phone. The photo in our foyer is abstract, and I would have never known it was a zoomed-in photograph of the Field Building if it weren't for doing some research on the postcard Aunt Mitzi left for us as our treasure on the first stop of this quest at Houmas House. And as great as the shot in our foyer is, it doesn't do the building justice.

I take a deep breath as we enter. The amount of white and tan marble is astounding. Opulent. Reminds me a bit of the Empire Building in Birmingham. But this building, now more commonly known as the Bank of America Building, is larger than the Empire Building, therefore, there is a much greater expanse of marble. The linear pattern of the nickel silver and bronze metalwork is just as impressive. Such a shame they don't construct buildings like this anymore.

The lobby sports a multi-level corridor between Clark and LaSalle streets, allowing pedestrians to walk between the two roadways. A meeting of art, commerce, and convenience, it gives access to all the retail space without making people leave the building, which must be great during the Chicago winters. Part of the floor in the lobby is a terrazzo mosaic star pattern.

I take some more pictures of the inside as we walk around. Clay and I take a selfie in front of the big fancy mailbox that has an integrated design matching the building's exterior framework.

"I can't believe this is the place where Aunt Mitzi and Uncle Sid fell in love. Well, at least partly. This is where it all started."

"Um, didn't it actually start before they came to Chicago?"

"Maybe on Uncle Sid's part. I know he was interested first, but Aunt Mitzi didn't really fall for him until they came here to Chicago with all the Al Capone stuff. When he had to explain everything about what they were actually doing here."

"She was a pretty ballsy woman, confronting Uncle Sid with what she saw back then."

"I know. I didn't think I could admire her more, but as the days go on, my admiration grows."

Uncle Sid's father had been one of the whistle blowers on Al Capone and had to sign a bunch of paperwork regarding the case. He'd sent a young Uncle Sid as his proxy to Chicago to get it all done for him, as he was afraid for his life if he'd gotten caught on Chicago soil. Aunt Mitzi, just out of high school at the time, was sent along with Uncle Sid (under the guise of training for her new job at the bank that Mr. Santini owned) to throw off Capone's cronies. All the meetings with the men were conducted in Italian, so Aunt Mitzi hadn't understood a word. She had a sharp eye though, and caught sight of Al Capone's name on one of the documents. She knew something was up, and later demanded that Uncle Sid tell her what the hell was going on. He did, albeit reluctantly. But knowing what a good guy he truly was on the inside, and the fact that he trusted her with that big piece of information, she began her fall for him.

Clay brushes a fallen lock of hair behind my ear and sweeps his thumb over my cheek in the process. "You about ready to go, love? We've had a long day. I'm beat."

"Yeah, me too. Can we stay here another night though? I mean, since it's close to dinner time and all. I'm getting hungry. Plus, I really want to stay on the boat."

"Sure. I love that idea. What do you feel like eating?"

"I want something that's authentically Chi-Town. Like maybe a deep-dish pizza or one of their famous style hot dogs. What are you in the mood for?"

"Hmm... tough choice. But since we've had pizza a couple of times on this trip already, let's try some hot dogs. I'll find a good place. You get us an Uber."

"On it." We exit the building and I pull up Uber on my phone to reserve a car. "Our ride will be here in four minutes. What did you find for hot dogs?"

"Portillo's. Looks like a great place. Comes highly recommended through Tripadvisor."

"Sounds perfect."

"I wonder what it is exactly that makes Chicago dogs different from the rest of the country's hot dogs," Clay says. "And I wonder how they compare to the Lucky Dogs of New Orleans and the Sabrett hot dogs of New York."

"Guess we'll see when we get there. Here comes our car." I point to the white Camry pulling up to the curb. We hop in and head to Portillo's.

Once inside the restaurant, I look around at all there is to see. It's a very nostalgic vibe and the place is buzzing with customers. There's a long, walk-up counter where you place your order. Colorful neon lights in red, blue, green, pink, and yellow are above presenting various items on the menu. The upper part of Portillo's has life-size dioramas portraying traditions, customs, and the lifestyle of decades past. A family of mannequins is posed in a 1930 Chevy four-door sedan, complete with a realistic German Shepherd hanging its head out of the window. A clothesline with shirts, pants, even bras and underwear, hangs between the façade of two homes. A gentleman gets a haircut in the barber shop. The silhouette of a photographer and his glass plate camera is evident behind curtains.

As Clay and I get in line, we peruse the large chalkboard menu behind the counter.

"What are you getting?" he asks.

"I think I'm gonna get the regular hot dog. Dressed just like it's supposed to be, with everything." According to the menu, their definition of 'everything' includes mustard, relish, celery salt, freshly chopped onions, sliced red ripe tomatoes, a kosher pickle spear, and sport peppers. And of course, it's not complete without the steamed poppy seed bun. Chicagoans call this style 'dragging the dog through the garden.' It sounds delicious.

"I'm going for the jumbo dog."

"I would expect nothing less. You want to split an order of cheese fries?"

"Lynn, you know I would share just about anything with you, but, get your own cheese fries, woman." He gives me one of his sexy half smiles.

"Sir, yes, sir," I laugh as I playfully salute him.

We sit down with our food and thoroughly enjoy our Chicago dogs and cheese fries.

"Can't really compare these dogs with New Orleans or New York," Clay says. "They are a style all their own. I don't think I've ever had sport peppers before. Especially on a hot dog."

"Me either. I've never even seen them for sale in the store. Then again, I've never looked for them. I'm going to get some when we get back home. I don't know if I can eat another hot dog without them. They're not that spicy. Perfectly tangy and vinegary and pickle-y. Kind of reminds me of a pepperoncini. The sport peppers really make all the flavors piled on the hot dog come alive together."

"Agreed. I just wonder how many Peter Piper would pick."

"Pickled peppers?"

"Yeah."

"At least a peck."

"How many pickled peppers are in a peck?"

"However many Peter Piper picked."

"Touché."

"It's a mystery." I wink. "So how do you like the cheese fries, Sinclair?"

"I stand by my previous suggestion. Glad we didn't share."

"Well, you can have the rest of mine. I'm stuffed."

"Much obliged, ma'am," he says in a horrible Southern accent as he takes them from my tray. I laugh and shake my head at him.

After we finish eating, we talk for a few more minutes about our day, then head back to the hotel to gather our things and check out so we can spend the night on our yacht.

CHAPTER 11

I WAKE TO CLAY slowly shaking me from side to side and open my eyes. But he's not shaking me. He's not even in the bed. Then I remember, we're on the boat, and it was the bobbing of the vessel in the water that gently stirred me. After a big smile, wondering again how this is my life, I get up and start my morning.

Walking up the steps to the galley, I smell coffee. When Clay spots me, he pours me a cup.

"Mornin', love."

"Mornin'. Bless you for this," I raise my mug to him and take a sip. "Man, I slept like a baby. I think that's one of the best nights' sleep I've had on this trip. How 'bout you?"

"Same. The light sway of the boat lulled me to sleep. Wanna head up to the bridge to finish our coffee?"

"Sure, it looks like a beautiful day."

We head up to the next level, sit down on the sofa, and chit-chat about Chicago as a light breeze blows.

Out of nowhere, Clay bursts out laughing, startling me.

I put my hand on my chest. "Shit, Clay, you scared me. It's too early for that. You're lucky I'm almost done with my coffee or I probably would've spilled it. What's so funny?"

"Sorry, babe. Look at the name of the boat across from us."

I crane my neck a little to see our neighbor and start cracking up too. "Oh my gosh. That's hilarious."

The name of the boat is *Master Baiter*.

"That wasn't there yesterday, I would have definitely noticed it. It's the mother of all fishing puns. And sex puns are the best." Clay shakes his head, still laughing. He takes a picture of it. "I'm texting this to Stone."

"I figured," I chuckle.

After we finish our coffee, we go back down to the galley, clean up, and get everything ready to leave the *Legasea*.

By 9:30, we're all packed up and back in the truck.

"Okay, it'll take us a little less than two hours to get to Milwaukee," Clay says. "Can you book us a room?"

"Sure." I get my phone out, search, and book a suite at the Hilton Garden Inn, located in downtown Milwaukee, less than a mile from the Harley-Davidson Museum. "Done."

"Thanks, babe. Sorry, I should've done that before we left."

"No biggie. You don't need to apologize for that. We've pretty much been sharing the booking duties." I smile at him and he winks at me.

"I forgot what the clue says. I know we're going to the Harley museum, but what are we looking for when we get there?"

"The Experience Gallery, whatever that is. And something inside saddlebags."

"Oh that's right. And what about the keychain?"

"Ah, yes." I smile and dig out the number thirty keychain. "Oh my gosh," I laugh. "It's a little slice of Swiss cheese. It even feels like real Swiss cheese." The small piece of rubbery cheese on the keyring is about one-inch square. I dangle it in front of Clay. "Feel it," I snicker.

He rubs it between his fingers. "Eww," he chuckles. "Weird how close it feels to the real deal. So, whose turn is it for the radio?"

"It's mine."

"Again?"

"You know we alternate. You can have it tomorrow." I pick up my phone and hit shuffle on my *Night and Day* playlist. "Night Fever" by The Bee Gees starts, and I immediately begin to shimmy my shoulders.

"Good lord, woman, don't do that. You're embarrassing yourself."

"I can't help it. It's involuntary. Something about the Brothers Gibb just makes me wanna get my boogie on." I continue dancing in my seat, exaggerating my moves to get on Clay's nerves.

"Stop it," he laughs. "You should see yourself."

"So, it's you that I'm actually embarrassing then," I laugh back. "Because I'm not embarrassed at all."

"Whatever, just please, chill. All that jiggling is distracting me. You're killin' me, Smalls."

"Ohhhh, okay. I get it. No jiggling while driving." I wink at him and stop my wiggling. For now, anyway. "Let me get this straight. It's not so much that I'm embarrassing you with my skillful truck-dancing moves, it's just getting you riled up. Is that right?"

"Something like that," he says with one of his sexy half smiles.

"Okay. I'll save it for later."

"Good plan. Otherwise, I'm pulling over and I know you don't want me to do that."

"You are correct, sir."

"I love it when you call me 'sir.' It's hot."

"Slow your roll, Christian Grey."

"Is that you actually giving me fifty shades of permission to pull over?" he asks with a smile.

"What? No," I laugh while shaking my head.

"That's too bad." He reaches over, snakes his hand up my thigh, and squeezes my core. I give him a sexy look and carefully take hold of his hand. He slows the truck down. I remove his hand and slowly place it back on the steering wheel. His jaw drops. "You're so wrong for that."

"And you're out of your mind, Sinclair. Get it out of the gutter while you're driving."

"Fine. But you'll pay for that later."

"Promises, promises."

"Oh, that's a promise," he says with a wink.

I pick up my copy of *Entertainment Weekly* with Jon Snow from *Game of Thrones* on the cover just as "These Days" by Rascal Flatts comes on. Clay looks at me and makes a face. I know he's not a fan of country music, so I roll my eyes at him and pick another playlist. "Have You Ever Seen the Rain" by Credence Clearwater Revival begins to play from my *Cats and Dogs* list, which consists of songs about rain, or has the word 'rain' in the title.

"Better?" I ask.

"Much." He turns it up and starts to sing along. I love his voice. He really is a great singer. He may act like he doesn't want to sing karaoke since he lost the Skee-Ball bet, but I think deep down, he likes the idea.

After a minute or so, he turns the volume down and asks, "Are you sure you don't want to tour one of the most famous breweries of all time while we're in Milwaukee? We could go in search of The Beast."

"The Beast?"

"Yeah, you know, Milwaukee's Best. It's also known as The Beast. Is that not common knowledge among women?" Clay smirks.

"I vaguely remember guys at the college frat parties I went to chanting about 'going to get the beast,' but I thought they were talking about a rival school's mascot or something."

Clay shakes his head with a laugh. "Man, Tyler and I used to drink the shit outta that stuff. It was nasty, but cheap. The halls on the tenth floor of the Kirby Smith dorm would be littered with cans of The Beast the next morning after a party."

"I bet your RA loved y'all."

"Shit, he was the one that bought it."

I laugh. "Speaking of Tyler, have you heard from him lately?" Tyler is Clay's best friend from high school. They both joined the Army National Guard at the same time, but Tyler liked it so much, he transferred to active duty and eventually became a Special Forces Weapons Sergeant. He then went on to do some private military contracting when he aged out of the Green Berets, and now owns his own security company. He and other retired Special Forces soldiers train men who want to join the Special Forces. But early last year, he was offered an opportunity he couldn't pass up and temporarily returned to private military contracting that took him overseas.

"No, not in a few weeks. The last message I got from him said he was coming home sometime soon though, remember?"

"Oh, that's right. He may make it back to Louisiana before we do."

"Yeah," Clay chuckles. "He just might."

About an hour later, we've checked into our hotel and pull up to the Harley-Davidson Museum. We look around after entering. There are bikes everywhere, of course. I'm not much of a motorcycle enthusiast, but even I'm impressed with all the horsepower surrounding us. The smell of new tires, freshly waxed floors, along with the faint scent of exhaust fumes and motor grease hits my nose.

"Alright," I say. "Let's find the Experience Gallery."

"Wait, babe. Can we just look around for a bit? I'm sure we'll come across it."

"I don't want you getting any ideas. You're not buying a Harley."

"Don't worry. I won't. But you gotta admit, this is the mecca of motor-cycles. You know who would kill to be here right now?"

"Who?"

"Tyler," he laughs. "Come on." He grabs my arm. "I know you're antsy to find our prize, but let's just walk around a bit."

I sigh. "Fine."

CLAY

We amble around the showroom, and I scope out the evolution of Harley-Davidson motorcycles. Lynn lags behind, looking somewhat bored, but I stop and read the placards of all the ones I'm interested in. I learn some information about how these bikes came to be, as well as fascinating facts on some of the motorcycles. Lynn finally sidles up to me, wrapping her arm around mine, and putting her head on my shoulder while I read about each one. Some of the most notable bikes we come across are 'Serial Number One,' the oldest known Harley in existence; a World War II-era bike pro-duced for the Army to use for scouting, courier duties, police work, and transportation of radio equipment; a 1956 KH V-Twin once owned by Elvis; one of the original bikes created for the 2011 movie *Captain America: The First Avenger*. And speaking of Captain America, we also find a replica of the Captain America chopper on display that Peter Fonda rode in *Easy Rider*, as well as a replica of the Billy Bike ridden by Dennis Hopper in the movie.

One of the most prominent motorcycles we see is a 1973 FLH V-Twin known as the Rhinestone Harley, a bike blinged-out by a customer and was sold to the museum after he died. There are about three thousand dollars' worth of rhinestones on that bike. If Liberace had been a biker, this is what he would've ridden. I think it's the most bedazzled thing I've ever seen.

The next crazy Harley we come across is a one-of-a-kind customized bike called King Kong. It's a 1941 FL 74 model, combining two V-Twins and transmissions, making it over thirteen feet long. I'd call it a Harley-Davidson limo. I picture a biker guy in a sleeveless leather tux pulling up on this thing to pick up his biker chick for a biker ball. This motorcycle was built by a Harley enthusiast that was also a mechanic, and it took him over four years to customize. Completely astounding. The dual 1200 cc Knucklehead engines run through one electric start, which was unheard of at the time of production, making the creator of this monster bike a genius. Along with the two engines and transmissions are four pipes, two saddles, and two sets of handlebars. Some of the fun parts of King Kong include randomly placed doorknobs, vintage bullet-shaped Cadillac taillights, and scuba tanks used for airhorns. According to Lynn, the best part of the bike is an old-school boombox located in front of the passenger seat.

My favorite bike that we see in the museum is the 1991 Fat Boy model that Arnold Schwarzenegger rode in the movie *Terminator 2: Judgment Day*. That was a badass movie with a badass actor on a badass bike.

The most memorable Harley-Davidson motorcycle that we come across is a rusted, corroded, broken-down 2004 Night Train model. That may not sound like anything special, but this particular bike was found on an isolated beach in British Columbia after drifting for more than a year over four thousand miles across the Pacific Ocean in a storage container, thanks to the catastrophic tsunami that struck Japan in March of 2011. The owner was tracked down and per his request, the bike was to be displayed as is in the museum, thereby establishing it as a memorial to those who perished in the tsunami. Seeing the bike really puts things into perspective. You know about the tragedy, you saw the devastating news reports on television, you heard about the monumental loss of lives. But to see the effects of it up close and personal, it humbles you. Lynn and I say a prayer for the people that died, and for their families. Even now, many years after the destructive force of nature wreaked havoc on Miyagi Prefecture and other parts of the northeast coast, the country of Japan still feels the loss that the tsunami inflicted.

Lynn closes her eyes and takes a deep breath.

"Love? You okay?"

"Yeah, just releasing the tension and letting go of the somber mood that just enveloped me. It's just sad. You know?"

"I know. Mother Nature can be a real bitch sometimes. You ready to go find what we came here for?"

"Yes. I can use a pick-me-up after this." She smiles. "Let's go."

We find the Experience Gallery and realize that this is a place where we can actually sit on the bikes and get a feel for them. There's only one other guy in here. Bolted to the floor are many Harleys to choose from in various models, sizes, and colors. A huge screen with a video projection gives you the feeling of being on the open road while saddled up on a bike.

I pick an FLHR Road King, all sleek and black, and start singing Bon Jovi's "Wanted Dead or Alive," particularly the line about riding a steel horse.

The older guy sitting a couple of bikes away from me starts belting out Steppenwolf's "Born to Be Wild," as if to say that's a much better Harley anthem.

We all start laughing.

"I wonder how many times those songs have been sung in this room of road rovers," Lynn says.

"Probably at least a million times," I chuckle.

Lynn sits on the bike next to me, a Sportster Superlow with a deep-blue tank and fenders. We look up at the screen. It really does feel like we're riding. It's not exactly virtual reality, but it gives the illusion. Lynn runs her fingers through her hair, pretending that the wind is blowing it. I smile. At least it seems like she's having a better time now.

"This is pretty cool," she says. "And you look super-hot, babe."

"Oh yeah?" I smirk.

"Yeah. Let me take a picture of you." She gets her phone out.

"Do you want me to pose or—"

"Just act natural. Like you're really riding it."

I reposition myself and look at the projector, pretending to drive the bike. "Like this?"

"Yeah. Got it."

"Okay, now let me get one of you." I take my phone and Lynn poses and smiles instead of acting like she's steering the bike. "Beautiful, love. So, Lynn, let me ask you something. If you think I look super-hot riding this badass motorcycle, does that mean—"

"No. It doesn't mean you can buy a Harley. You can sit and look sexy all you want, but you know how I feel about you getting on the road with one. I know you think it's an irrational fear, but I just can't have you out there on a bike. I'm sorry, Clay."

I sigh. "Alright. Whatever." I turn my attention back to the screen in front of us, then fiddle with some of the controls on the dashboard of the bike. I don't want to begrudge Lynn her feelings or her fears. I'd never do that. But sometimes I wish she'd get over the ones she has when it comes to motorcycles.

LYNN

I know there are millions of people that ride motorcycles and never get so much as a scratch in their life, but ever since I was a little girl and witnessed an accident before my eyes, I just can't imagine how I would live if something like that happened to Clay. The fatal accident I saw when I was young led to recurring nightmares of my dad dying in a motorcycle accident, even though he never had a motorcycle. I still have a bad dream every now and then, with Clay lying in the street instead of my dad, covered in blood, limbs twisted in unnatural ways. I shake the memory off.

"Hey," I say. He looks at me. "I just can't."

He gets up off his bike and steps up to me while I remain seated on mine. "I know." He swipes his thumb across my cheek. "But for what it's worth," he leans into me and whispers in my ear, "you look sexy as fuck on that bike." He bites my earlobe. Christ almighty.

I take in a surprised breath. "You are so bad at doing shit like that to me in public, Sinclair," I say in an exhale.

"Don't you mean I'm so good at it?" He licks the shell of my ear.

"Jesus, Clay, stop it."

"Damn good thing nobody else is in here, huh?"

I glance at the bike occupied by the Steppenwolf fan, relieved to see it empty. "Damn good thing," I say as I push his hard chest away from me. He doesn't budge, but then backs away on his own, giving me that crooked sexy smirk of his.

"Then let's find the right bike and see what's in the saddlebags, because I'm ready to get you back to the hotel and finish what I just started."

"Saddlebags. Right. Quest. Keys." I nearly forgot why we were even here in the first place. My husband has that effect on me. I take a deep breath and continue. "Besides, there might not be any people in here right now, but there's a camera up there. You want to give the security team a show?"

He lets out a low, deep, throaty laugh. "Why not? It might be the highlight of their day."

"Clay." I give him a look that is one step away from an eyeroll.

"Okay fine."

I hop off the Sportster and give the room of bikes a quick scan. "Alright. We know we can narrow the search down by skipping the ones without lockable trunks or saddlebags."

"Correct. Let's start in the corner over there on the other side of the room and work our way back to the entrance of the gallery."

"Okay. This shouldn't take long."

We move to the row on the opposite side from where we are and start looking for the bikes with locked saddlebags. When we reach the middle, not far from where we both sat on our respective bikes to begin with, I find the one that unlocks.

According to the sign, it's a 1960 FLH Duo Glide with fiberglass saddlebags. Further reading tells us this bike includes a 74ci engine linked to a four-speed transmission, polished ports and high compression heads, and a twin fishtail exhaust (whatever all that mumbo jumbo means). All I know from looking at it is that it's red and white with chrome, white hand grips, and a large white seat.

"Holy shit," Clay says. "This is one retro bike. It looks like the badass big brother of Pee-Wee Herman's bicycle."

I laugh out loud and it carries enough to turn heads, if there were any heads to turn.

Clay positions himself along the lone camera's line of sight, blocking its view of the saddlebags. "Okay, you should be good."

When I finally get the saddlebag open, I lift the lid and we peer inside.

CHAPTER 12

"An envelope," Clay says.

"I could've guessed." I open it and read a short note from Aunt Mitzi telling us to find someone who can let the manager know we're here. That's it.

"Well, I assume the boss will give us something," Clay muses.

"Let's go see." I fold the note back into the envelope. "Should we ask for Mr. Harley? Or Mr. Davidson? Do their descendants even run the place now?"

"I have no idea."

We walk back to the area where we bought our tickets. Clay steps up to the counter in front of a cute girl with blue hair and a nose ring. She wasn't here earlier. He proceeds to lay his charm on thick. "Hi. Mandy?" He smiles while gesturing to her name tag.

"Yes. Hi," she says, returning his smile.

"Is it possible for us to speak with the manager?"

"Sure. Is there a problem with anything?"

"No." Clay winks. "We just have something to give him. Or her." He points his thumb over his shoulder at me. "We don't have an appointment or anything. Can you just tell your boss that Clay and Lynn Sinclair are here?"

"Okay, give me just a second and I'll call him."

"Thanks, doll."

'Doll'? I look at Clay and roll my eyes. He just smiles at me and winks as he joins me off to the side, away from the line forming in front of the counter.

"You're too much. A wink, a smile, and a term of endearment."

"Don't be jealous, babe. You know I only have eyes for you. And hands. And fingers." He leans into my neck and whispers, "And a tongue." Then he gives my neck a discreet light lick.

I slap him softly on his chest. "Stop that. We're still in public."

"Mr. Sinclair?"

Clay clears his throat. "Yes, Mandy?"

"Mr. Moretti can see you both now. Follow me."

"Great. Thanks."

Clay and I follow Mandy up a flight of stairs and turn down a hallway of opaque glass with several unopened doors. We are officially behind the scenes of the museum. She knocks on the door with the name Dante Moretti etched in the center.

"Come in," a strong male voice replies.

Mandy opens the door, revealing a guy who appears to be in his early fifties. "Hi, Mr. Moretti. Mr. and Mrs. Sinclair are here to see you."

The man stands as we enter. He has shoulder-length, jet-black hair; a goatee; wide shoulders; and tattoos up and down his thick, muscular arms. Holy wow, he's hot. He's wearing a black Harley t-shirt and ripped black jeans. I can't see his feet, but I imagine he's wearing black biker boots with a silver ring and straps at the ankles. There's a black leather jacket hung on the coat rack behind him, and his helmet sits on a side table next to his executive desk. I may not be much into motorcycle fashion, but this guy serves it well. This hulk of a man embodies every one of my stereotypes when I think of bikers. At least hot bikers. This dude looks like an older, dark-haired Jax from that TV show *Sons of Anarchy*. I've seen a few episodes at Annie's. Charlie Hunnam is one of her favorite actors, so she watched that show religiously.

"Thanks, Mandy." She exits and closes the door. "Hello. I'm Dante Moretti," he says, as he extends his hand out to Clay for a shake.

"Clay Sinclair. My wife, Lynn."

I shake his hand. "N-nice to meet you, Mr. Moretti." Holy shit, did I just stutter? Clay gives me a side-eye glance. Busted. Well, screw that. He flirted with Mandy at the front counter, even though I know it was just to smooth things over from the start. But damn, shouldn't I be allowed to have a moment of weakness when looking at this ultra-sexy piece of motorcycle man meat?

Dante grasps my hand a bit longer than necessary before he brings my knuckles to his lips and gives them a kiss. He looks directly into my eyes when he says, "Pleasure to meet you as well. Have a seat. And please, call me Dante."

Oh. My. God. My cheeks heat and I'm a little wobbly in the freaking knees. Clay clears his throat, which sounds more like a warning as he leers at Dante. I quickly recover and pull my hand back. "Okay, thank you, Dante." We sit across the desk from him in two black leather wingback chairs. I get down to business, trying to ignore the way Clay is giving Dante the once-over. "We retrieved this note from one of the saddlebags in a bike downstairs," I tell him, handing him the slip of paper.

"Yes, yes. Good." He takes it from me, brushing his fingers against mine. If he's not careful, Clay is going to kick his ass, or get hurt trying, given the size of Dante's massive arms. Clay's no weakling and can hold his own, but Dante probably has at least twenty pounds of muscle on Clay. "I know why you're here. We've been waiting." Dante smiles and winks. "I was sorry to hear of Mitzi's passing."

"Thanks."

"I've got a special treat for you from Sid and Mitzi." He gets up, walks over to a closet, and fetches a thick cardboard mailing tube about three feet long and four inches in diameter with white plastic end caps.

My eyes meet Clay's. I know we're both wondering if it's another painting. At least that's what I'm wondering. Clay might be wondering how he can pummel Dante six ways to Sunday. With his combined years in the police force and in the military, he probably learned some dirty fighting tricks. Plus, I'm sure Tyler has taught him some as well.

"A cardboard tube. You can never have too many of those," Clay says with heavy sarcasm.

Dante smiles. "Ah yes. There's nothing better than a cardboard tube to defend all pillow forts. They make the best swords. Am I right?"

"So right," I say with a giggle. Shit, I actually giggled. Clay rolls his eyes.

Dante walks back over and takes his seat in his worn leather desk chair. Setting the tube on the desk, he puts his hands on it and says, "This is a real treasure. I, for one, am jealous as hell that it's not mine," he laughs.

"Wow," I say. "Now I'm really anxious to see what it is. May I?" I reach for the tube.

"Of course." He hands it over with a smile. "Be careful though. It's delicate."

I pop off one of the end caps and put my fingers inside, mindful of his advisement. I grip the edge of a piece of paper and gently pull it out of the tube. Clay and I unroll it together.

"Holy shit," Clay says.

"I'll second that. Holy shit." I'm floored.

It's a signed movie poster of *Easy Rider*. The autographs of Peter Fonda, Dennis Hopper, and Jack Nicholson are scrawled across the yellow portion of the poster.

"This is outstanding," Clay says. "Wasn't this one of Uncle Sid's favorite movies?"

"It was. Part of it was filmed in Louisiana."

"Yeah. One of the best worst endings of a movie ever," he says. "If that makes sense."

"Totally get what you mean," Dante says.

I chime in. "I'm familiar with the movie, but ashamed to admit that I've never seen it. So, it's not a happy ending?"

"Depends on what your definition of 'happy' is," Dante says with a chuckle.

"Well, at any rate, I'm proud to have the movie poster." I turn to Clay. "We can frame it and hang it in the theater at our cabin in Tennessee next time we go back."

"That's a good idea, but I'd kinda like to have it at home so I could see it all the time. Maybe I'll hang it in my office."

"Oh, I like that even better. It would look great in your office."

"I'm not sure if you're aware," Dante says, "but this is actually the movie poster from the re-release of the film in 1972." He points to the line of text under the title. "See how it says '*Rides again!*'? Honestly, it's more sought after and rarer than the poster from the 1969 release."

"Are you serious?" I ask.

"Hand to God," Dante says, holding his right hand up.

"Whoa," I say. "That's extra special then."

"Sure is," he replies. "That's a pretty exclusive piece of Americana you've got there, especially with it being autographed."

I look over at Clay. He's being too quiet. Normally, he'd be all over the fact that we've got an incredible treasure of this magnitude. But he's just sitting there with his eyes on Dante, the muscles in his jaw ticking in irritation.

"Thanks for taking good care of it for us," I tell Dante. "How did you know my Aunt Mitzi and Uncle Sid?"

"I met them, but didn't really know them that well. My dad was great friends with Sid's younger brother Vince. Vince was really into the bike culture. We had a weekend-long party a little over ten years ago to celebrate the groundbreaking of the museum. Vince, his son Enzo, your aunt, and your uncle were present. Sid approached my dad with an idea. I was there when he did. He asked my dad if he would mind keeping something safe for him. Your Uncle Sid and Aunt Mitzi told us about the quest they were doing for you. It sounded like it would put you both on the American road trip of a lifetime."

"It really has," I say. I grab Clay's hand and he looks at me, softening a bit as he interlocks our fingers together.

"I bet." Dante smiles. "Sid asked if he could leave a special gift once the museum was opened. He didn't even have it yet, but he had an idea of what he wanted it to be. He promised it would be something Harley-Davidson related. Once he acquired it, he would bring it up here for safe-keeping, if we allowed it. Of course we said yes.

"When he called my father to tell him he had the poster and wanted to bring it, the museum still wasn't quite ready, so my dad invited both your Uncle Sid and Aunt Mitzi to come to the grand opening of the museum in July of 2008. We let Mitzi choose which Harley-Davidson she wanted to lock the note in. She picked the FLH because she said she liked the colors." He smiles. "Fast forward nine years, and here you are."

"I love hearing the stories of how aspects of this trip came to be," I say with watery eyes. I stand up, ready to go. "I don't want to take up any more of your time. Thanks so much for meeting with us today and relaying your story."

"Yeah, thanks," Clay says, feigning politeness as he stands and shakes Dante's hand. Clay rolls up the poster and places it back in the tube.

"It's been my pleasure. Anytime you're back up this way, feel free to drop in."

"Thanks. The museum is truly a great place. We really enjoyed it," I tell Dante.

"Thank you. I appreciate that."

"So, do we just go out the way we came in?" I ask.

"Yes. Just down the stairs to the left at the end of the hall. It was great meeting you both. Take care."

"Bye, Dante. Thanks again," I say as we exit his office and head down the hall.

"Fucking finally," Clay mutters under his breath.

"You know we're not leaving until we hit the gift shop to look for an ornament," I tell Clay when we get to the bottom of the stairs.

Clay sighs. "Christ," he says to himself. But I heard him and he knows it.

"What is wrong with you?" Like I don't know.

"Nothing. Let's go check out the shop." He walks ahead of me.

"Clay."

"*What?*" He whips around and stops for me to catch up.

We're still out of the public's view, so I put his cheeks in my hands and kiss him, softly and deeply. "I love you."

He rests his forehead on mine. "I know. I just… I wanted to kick his ass the way he was eyeing you and touching you and shit."

"Clay, come on. I'll admit he was a little out of line, but—"

"Out of line? And don't think I didn't notice how you reacted to him. Stumbling over your words, blushing, giggling and shit. I was standing right the fuck there!"

"Clay, I—"

"I wanted to fucking deck him, Lynn. Ever since the other day, I've been so much more protective over you. He just got my hackles up. Rubbed me the wrong way."

"Well, when we get back to the hotel, I'll rub you the right way. How does that sound?"

"I'm not joking, Lynn. I'm fucking serious. I almost lost you last week. I just… fuck. Can we just go now?" Clay's chest is rising and falling faster than normal, so I know I need to be careful of what I say next.

Putting my hands on his heart, I tell him, "Please, take a deep breath and listen to me. Dante was harmless." He scowls. "Harmless," I reassure him. "A little overly flirtatious, I know. But I'm fine, Clay. I'm fine. And no, we can't leave yet. I know you're ready to get out of here, but I want to find the gift shop first."

"Ugh… Come on, Lynn. Can't we just skip this one?"

"You know the drill. But I'll repay you later. Like I said I would. Deal?"

Clay sighs and then gives me one of his sexy smirks. "Deal."

We make our way to the Harley-Davidson gift shop and look around.

"I'm going to find me a t-shirt while you look for an ornament," Clay says.

"Okay. Get me one too. Different from yours though, we don't need to be twinsies."

Clay laughs. "Alright. What color and style do you want?"

"Surprise me. But I don't want black unless it's long sleeves."

"Gotcha."

Clay goes off in search of some t-shirts. I mosey over towards the Christmas ornaments and once again, I can't seem to make up my mind. I finally decide on one that is about two inches in diameter. It's metal, with 'Harley-Davidson Museum' arcing over the top and 'Milwaukee, WI' at the bottom. In the center of the ornament is a piece that swivels. The logo is on one side and there's a picture of Earth on the other, with people riding various styles of Harleys along the equator. I keep browsing and decide to pick up a shot glass as well. It's ceramic, shiny, and black on the outside with the museum logo in orange. The inside of the shot glass is solid orange.

Clay finds me in the checkout line and I can see he has more than two t-shirts draped over his arms. "Is that all you're getting?" he asks, pointing to what I hold in my hands.

"Yes. An ornament and a shot glass."

"Okay, cool. Give them to me. I'll check out and meet you near the exit."

"What? Why? I can stand in line with you."

"Alright, fine, but don't look at what I picked out for you. Turn around." He smiles.

"Okay, silly." I smile, give him the merch I selected, and turn around.

After Clay checks out and we make our way back to the truck, he places one bag in the back seat and hands me the bag with my shirt in it. "I hope you like them," he says.

"Them? As in, more than one?"

"Yeah. I couldn't decide."

I open the bag and pull one out. It's a hot pink tank top with a Harley on the front. "Oh, cool, I love it, Clay. Good choice." I reach back in the bag and grab the other one, but instead of just one more shirt, two come out in my hands. "Three shirts, Clay?" I laugh. "You're too much."

"I told you. I couldn't decide. And they all screamed your name."

I hold up the orange one. It's short sleeved with the H-D logo on the front, and the museum logo on the back. "Nice. I love this one too." Raising the other one up from my lap, I see it's a baseball tee with rust-colored sleeves. 'Harley-Davidson' is printed on the front over a shadow of the H-D logo. I look at Clay and smile. "I think this is my favorite. You made the best decision by getting each one for me."

"Good. I'm glad you like them all."

"I do. Thanks, babe." I put my t-shirts back in the bag.

He reaches over the center console and gives me a peck on the lips. "You're welcome, love."

"Show me what you picked out for yourself."

He reaches in the back to grab the other bag and pulls out a black t-shirt with the Harley-Davidson logo (different from the one Dante was wearing). Of course he got a black t-shirt. Typical Clay. Most of his wardrobe consists of black t-shirts. Next, he pulls out an army-green t-shirt, depicting a cream-colored star in the middle of the chest with the words 'Harley-Davidson' curved above.

"Oh, Clay, I love that one. Both are your style, but I love that they had a military one."

"Yeah, this one's my favorite," he says, holding up the army-green t-shirt. He smiles as he puts them back in the bag, reaches for mine, and returns both bags to the back seat.

"It's coming up on five o'clock. You hungry yet? Because I am."

"Yeah," Clay says. "Wanna find some place around here? Or order room service back at the hotel?"

"Room service sounds perfect. That gives me plenty of time for all the extracurricular activities I have in store for you."

"Good. You read my mind." He looks over and winks at me.

After we finish eating dessert, Clay takes a shower while I look up the touristy stuff to do

around town. I'm still hoping there's a *Happy Days* or *Laverne & Shirley* museum we can visit before we leave tomorrow, but I'm not holding my breath.

I scroll a little further down the list and can't believe what I see. I start laughing. It's ridiculously perfect.

Clay comes out of the bathroom and sits next to me on the bed. "What's so funny?"

"Well," I say, still semi-laughing. "I found something for us to go see tomorrow before we leave."

"And it's hilarious?"

"A bit."

"Spill it."

"Okay, you know how I was kinda joking about a *Happy Days* or *Laverne & Shirley* museum?"

"Yeah."

"I found something even better: the *Bronze Fonz*."

"What the fuck?" Clay asks, laughing.

"I know, right? It's a life-size statue of Fonzie on the Milwaukee Riverwalk downtown. Made of bronze. Hence, the *Bronze Fonz*. Isn't that hysterical?"

"Uh, yeah. We're totally going to see it tomorrow."

"And I think it's a lovely gesture for Milwaukee to celebrate one of the most famous TV characters of all time in such a way."

"Agreed."

"Smart too. I bet it brings die-hard Fonzie fans to the area, promoting tourism. I mean, Arthur Fonzarelli is an American pop culture icon."

"Italian American pop culture icon."

"Right," I laugh. "Okay, I'm going to take a shower."

"Good. Mine gave me a second wind, and I believe you made a promise to me earlier. So make sure you use the soap that energizes you. None of that sleepy-time relaxing shit." He winks at me.

I let the hot water sluice over my body as I wash my hair. After rinsing the shampoo out, I lather up with shower gel, rinse, and get out. After toweling off, I rub my arms and legs with lotion, followed by a spritz of body spray up and down my torso. Just as I'm finished blow drying my hair, Clay walks in and pulls me into his body.

"Clay," I laugh, "I need to get dressed."

"No. You don't." He walks backwards towards the bed, with me still clutched to him. "I've been waiting all day for this." He pulls the covers of the bed back and motions for me to get in. He strips and joins me. Lying by my side, he wraps a leg over me and nuzzles my neck. "You always smell so good. Like flowers." He runs his nose up my neck. "And peaches." He inhales me. "And coconuts." He gives me an open-mouthed kiss under my ear. "Pure Lynn."

Clay licks my ear and I shiver. "You do too. Not like flowers and peaches and coconuts though," we both laugh, "but like my clean, freshly-showered Clay, a splash of cologne mixing with your pheromones. So sexy. My man. That's my most favorite smell in the world."

He kisses me deeply as his hand finds my boobs. I run my fingertips up, then down his back, reaching and squeezing his perfect ass. Bringing my hand around to his front, I grab hold of his length. Damn he's hard. I pump my hand up and down and rub my thumb over the head, spreading the bead of his arousal around. He breaks the kiss and smiles against my lips. Then he moves my hand away.

"What do you think you're doing, Lynn?" he asks playfully.

"Um, I think that's pretty obvious, Sinclair. I'm rubbing you the right way. I told you I would."

He laughs, deep and throaty. "Well, stop. Right now is just for you. If you touch me again, I won't last five seconds, and I want to finish inside you."

"Fair enough," I say. "But why is this just for me? I'm the one who is supposed to be making this about you instead of the other way around. Remember?"

"Yeah, but, I'm the one who told you that I wanted to pick up where I left off earlier. Remember that scene in the Experience Gallery?"

"Oh."

"Yeah. Oh."

I smile. "But even before that, you said you were going to make me pay for teasing you in the truck. When I moved your hand from between my legs back to the steering wheel."

"Wow. I forgot about that. You're not really helping your case, woman. But I need this. Do you want me to pleasure you, or not?"

I can't argue. "Yessssss."

"I probably overreacted a little with the whole Dante thing. Even though I didn't appreciate how he was flirting with you while I was standing right there, I know you only have eyes for me. And that's all that matters. Now, just relax and let me continue loving my wife."

"Yes, sir."

"Mmmm… say that again."

"Yes, sir. Please, sir. Take me, sir. Pleasure me, sir." I'm kind of being a little silly, going a bit overboard with all the 'sir' talk. I'm smiling, and feeling a little ridiculous, but Clay looks serious. He's totally digging it.

"Yes," he whispers. "Again. Say it again."

What the hell. I'll keep playing along. "Sir. Kiss me, sir. Give me more, sir."

"Fuck yeah." Clay smiles and continues kissing me, then moves south, tracing my body with his tongue and kisses. After sending me over the edge with his glorious mouth at my center, he crawls back up and plunges into me.

"God, Lynn. Feels so good," he huffs.

"Yes," I whisper.

"Shit. I don't know how long I can hold off."

"I don't care. Just fuck me, Clay."

And with that, he picks up the pace. A few minutes later, he releases a gratified groan from deep within his chest as he spills into me.

CHAPTER 13

THE NEXT MORNING, Clay and I sit down for breakfast and go over the next clue before we head to the *Bronze Fonz* statue at the Riverwalk. I have my laptop next to me for any necessary visits to Google.

"What's it say?" Clay asks before taking a bite of his omelet.

I take a sip of coffee and then read it to him. "Okay. Listen carefully. It says, 'Travel to the Twin Cities, but not the apostle. A tower inspired by the U.S. obelisk was once considered colossal. In a room used to brief and confer, find a table where people concur.' Break it down for me, Clay. I'll see if I concur."

"Very cute." He smiles. "Okay. So, you really want me to break it down? Like, you want me to rap what I think it all means?" He starts beatboxing with his mouth and begins to rap freestyle. "*Well, listen to this, the Twin Cities on the list. Minneapolis, St. Paul cannot be missed. St. Paul was the apostle so we're not going there. Which leaves Minneapolis up in the air. The U.S. obelisk, now that's a bit trickier. I guess the D.C. Monument, not to be pickier. A place used for briefing and a table to agree at. We're looking for a conference room. Now, babe, do you believe 'dat?*"

I start cracking up laughing. "Holy shit, Clay. That was freaking impressive." I can't stop laughing as he continues to beatbox. "I've never heard you freestyle in my life. How have you never done that for me before?"

"I've never tried," he says laughing back. "Who knew I had it in me?"

"I just… I'm thunderstruck," I say, still smiling. "You're such a badass."

Clay rolls his eyes. "It wasn't *that* great. But I like when you call me a badass. I'll take that." He holds up his coffee cup and gives me a 'cheers' gesture before he takes a sip. "So, Lynn, do you concur?"

"Um, I was so distracted by you rapping that I actually have no idea what you said besides 'Minneapolis.' And yes, I agree with that much at least."

"That's the easy part. The rest is that I think we're looking for a conference room in a building that looks like the Washington Monument."

I reread the clue to myself. "Alright, yeah. That tracks. So we just need to find the obelisk in Minneapolis that resembles the Washington Monument. Shouldn't be too hard."

"What does the keychain look like? That might be a clue."

I dig out the one labeled with the number 31 and laugh. "It's Snoopy." I set it next to Clay's plate.

He shakes his head and snickers. "The fuck? Snoopy?"

"Don't laugh. I love Snoopy."

"I know you do."

"Maybe the Peanuts gang lived in Minneapolis. It snowed in the comic strip a lot during winter."

"Maybe. Or maybe Charles Schulz was from Minneapolis."

"Maybe it was both. Either way, we know we're going to Minneapolis. And now I have to look up where Charles Schulz was from." I google. "Sure enough. He was born in Minneapolis, but it says here he spent most of his life in St. Paul."

"Potato, po-tah-toh," Clay smiles.

"I wonder how Aunt Mitzi knew that."

"Maybe she actually knew Charles Schulz. Wouldn't put it past her and Uncle Sid to know the creator of one of the most beloved comic strips of all time."

"Nah. Surely I would have known if they did. She knows how much I love Snoopy. She wouldn't keep that from me. Not something that innocent."

"You're probably right. So, we need to find exactly where we need to go. If you still want to go see the *Bronze Fonz* and get some first-rate cheese curds, we need to get ready to leave. I'm not sure how long the drive to Minneapolis is, but I'd say at least four hours. Are you finished eating?"

"Yep. If you can make a sweep of the room to make sure we don't forget anything, I'll try and find the obelisk online. Don't forget the bathroom."

"On it." He gets up and leans over to give me a kiss on the cheek.

I search the internet using the keywords obelisk, Washington Monument, and Minneapolis. And, there it is. What pops up in the search results is a building called the Foshay Tower, though it is now a W hotel. Officially: W Minneapolis – The Foshay. It kind of reminds me of the Louisiana state capitol building. Guess we'll be staying there tonight. I book us a room online and then check us out of the hotel from the TV.

I straighten up the breakfast table, pile up our dishes on the tray, and pack up my computer. Clay comes back in the room with a pony-tail holder and one of his ankle socks, throwing the sock into his duffle bag and the scrunchie into our toiletry case. He gives me a raise of his eyebrows, non-verbally asking if I found anything.

"Yes. I know where we need to go. But first, Fonzie and cheese please."

We drive to the Milwaukee Riverwalk and find a parking place on the street near where the statue of Fonzie waits for us. With plenty of restaurants to choose from along the Riverwalk, the smell of glorious food permeates the air. An adequate number of benches are placed along the walk if you get tired and need to rest. Wrought-iron flower baskets containing pansies and daisies line the pathway. Boat traffic moves up and down the river, the sound of water breaking in their wake. Clay and I walk about a block towards the east side of the Milwaukee River before we notice the effigy of Arthur Fonzarelli. I get a little excited and start walking faster.

When we reach the statue, I'm surprised to see how short it is. The average height of American men is 5'10" and knowing that this is a life-size likeness, Henry Winkler must be vertically challenged. The statue stands on a slight pedestal of maybe one or two inches. I'm 5'7" and stand even with the *Bronze Fonz*, so that would make the actor about 5'6". Clay's got more than half a foot on him.

The representation of Fonzie is smiling wide, with both of his thumbs up, of course. His leather jacket is painted black over his white t-shirt. His jeans are painted as well, though they look a little more teal than the dark blue denim he wore on the show. We take a few pictures of each other with the Fonz, mimicking him with our thumbs up.

A lady dressed in a flourishing blouse and a pinstripe pencil skirt walks by and stops. "Would you like me to take a picture of you both with Fonzie?" she asks.

"Oh, yes, please. That would be great," I tell her. "Thank you."

"No problem. He's one of our city's favorite landmarks." She takes my phone and Clay and I pose next to the statue, each putting an arm around the metallic Fonzarelli between us. "I heard he's getting a new facelift in the next couple of weeks." She clicks my phone a few times as we smile with our thumbs up.

"Really?" Clay asks. "What kind of facelift?"

We walk back over as she extends my phone back to me. "See if those came out okay."

I check through the photos she took. "Perfect. Thanks so much."

"Sure. So," she turns to Clay, "to answer your question, every year the artist comes and touches Fonzie up. I believe he's going to fix his pants to more of an actual blue. It's my understanding that he's going to use a different paint formula or something like that. This Fonz has had blue-green pants for nearly ten years," she laughs.

"Good to know," Clay says. "I was wondering why his pants weren't exactly blue. Fonzie is too cool for teal jeans."

"Exactamundo," she says, and we all chuckle.

"It's nice to hear that the artist keeps up with his artwork and refreshes him every year," I say.

"Yes, he's very dedicated to his work. The *Bronze Fonz* is important to Milwaukee. A staple on the Riverwalk. And thank goodness *Happy Days* is still in syndication, keeping Fonzie alive for the next generation to appreciate."

Clay gives her a thumbs up and says, "Ayyyy."

"Thanks again for stopping and taking our picture," I tell her.

"No problem at all. Have a good day and enjoy your stay in Milwaukee." She starts to walk away.

"Wait," Clay says. "We're actually on our way out of town, but we'd really like to have some prime cheese curds before we leave. Any suggestions?"

"Of course," she beams. "You can get them almost anywhere, but my favorite place is AJ Bombers." She points down the road, then to the side. "Just around the corner and down the street from here. Take a left at North Water Street. It'll be on your left at East Knapp. If you're lucky, you'll find a parking spot on the street. If not, there's a pay lot behind the restaurant. Hope that helps."

"It does. Thanks again for all your help," Clay says.

"You're both welcome." The lady turns and heads the other direction after we wave goodbye to each other.

"Alright," I say. "Let's go get our cheese curds."

We walk back to the truck and head in the direction towards AJ Bombers. Fortune smiles upon us and we find a place on the street to park right near the entrance.

"Rock star," Clay says, talking about the spot we were lucky enough to find, like it had been reserved for us as if we were famous.

"The parking fairies are with us today."

Clay opens the door for me and ushers me in with his hand at the small of my back. The wonderful smell of deep-fried food and hamburger patties on the grill hits my nose. The hostess greets us and we are seated at a table for two in a corner. She tells us that our server will be right with us as she leaves us with menus.

The atmosphere is laid-back with World War II kitsch décor. Pictures of 1940s pin-up girls smile at us from the wall. Propaganda slogans are spray-painted on other surfaces of the restaurant. The floor is strewn with peanut shells that crunch under our feet. Hand-written graffiti covers the walls.

"Apparently, it's customary to leave your mark before you exit the establishment," I tell Clay.

"Or they have very lax security."

There is an aluminum chute fastened to the brick wall at our table with an empty metal bowl underneath it. That's interesting.

As we wait for our server, I notice several sets of tracks extended with airplanes dangling from them above the bar. I wonder what that's all about.

"You want anything besides cheese curds?" Clay asks.

"I don't think so. I mean, we just ate breakfast before we left the hotel. You?"

"Nah. I might get a beer though."

"It's not even noon," I laugh.

"You know what they say. It's five o'clock somewhere, right? Besides, how can I leave one of the most famous brewery cities in the country without having a beer?"

"Suit yourself, dear husband." I look over the menu at the drinks and I see something that surprises me. "Oh wow."

"What?" Clay asks.

The waiter comes to the table. "Hi. I'm Dawson. Can I start you off with something to drink?" He looks at me.

"I'll have a ginger ale. I've never seen that drink on a menu."

"Good choice. And for you, sir?"

"I'll have a Schlitz. It's not my favorite, but when in Rome."

Dawson chuckles. "I understand. We do have some pretty good craft brews though, and some great locals on tap, if you'd like to hear about them."

"Tempting. I do love a good craft beer, but I'll just take the Schlitz. Because I'll probably never drink it again."

"No problem." Dawson smiles as he writes it down.

"And we'd each like an order of the cheddar cheese curds," Clay adds.

"We're not that hungry, but we had to come get some authentic cheese curds before we leave Wisconsin," I tell Dawson.

He nods. "Good. We have the best. Would you like a complimentary peanut bomb?"

"Um, what's a peanut bomb?" I ask.

Dawson turns towards the bar, raises his arm up, and whistles loudly. Before we know it, one of the bombers hanging from the ceiling on the tracks is headed our way, slams into a bullseye attached to the wall above our table, and drops peanuts down the chute into the bowl at the bottom. Well, that explains the tracks above the bar. And the chute. And the bowl.

"Your peanut bomb," Dawson says.

I laugh. "That's fantastic."

Clay grins at Dawson. "Thanks."

"No problem. I'll be right back with your drinks." He smiles and walks away.

"I was wondering what these metal chutes were for," Clay muses.

"Me too." I pick up a peanut and crack it with my fingertips, throwing my shell on the floor with all the rest.

"Hey, what wowed you about the menu?"

"The ginger ale."

"Ah. Makes sense. They really should put that on menus everywhere. You love ginger ale."

"That I do. I also noticed that they have spiked shakes. I may not want a cocktail or beer right now, but I could definitely go for a Bourbon Salted Caramel shake."

"Holy shit, that sounds good. Yeah, let's get one of those to share."

"Share? You know there are certain things I don't do well with sharing."

"Well, make an exception today please. For me. At least let me have a few sips. Or bites. Whatever."

"Fine. You win."

Dawson comes back with our drinks. "The cheese curds should be out in a minute. Is there anything else I can get either of you right now?"

"Actually, yes," I say. "I would like—" Clay clears his throat and taps my leg with his foot. "I mean, *we* would like one of the Bourbon Salted Caramel spiked shakes. To share." Clay winks at me.

"Oh, that's my favorite. You won't be sorry. Two straws?"

"One straw. Two spoons," Clay tells him.

"You got it. I'll be right back with your cheese curds."

Clay grabs a peanut and peels the shell off. Following custom, he throws it on the floor. "Thanks, babe. I won't drink that much. I just want a good taste of it."

"I'm just giving you a hard time. You know I don't mind sharing with you. I can't believe you ordered a Schlitz," I chuckle.

"Like I said, 'When in Rome.' Here come the curds."

Dawson sets our cheese curds on the table along with my, I mean our, Bourbon Salted Caramel shake. "Anything else, guys?"

"No, I think that's it," I tell him as I reach for a cheese curd and dunk it in the chipotle ranch sauce, then take a bite. Wow, they taste divine.

Mild and slightly salty cheddar with a perfectly fried crust. The texture is a bit springy and they squeak against my teeth. That's how you know they're fresh. The chipotle ranch gives it a zing that makes the flavors come alive. These are so much better than the typical fried mozzarella cheese sticks at a regular bar and grill outside of Wisconsin.

"Okay, just so I'm clear, you're not ordering burgers or anything. Only came for the curds,

right?"

"Correct," Clay says. "And apparently this bomb-ass shake," he says as he lifts it off the table and sucks some out of the straw. "Shit that's good stuff."

"Agreed," Dawson laughs. "Enjoy. I'll be back to check on you in a bit."

"Thanks, man," Clay says.

I take a sip of my ginger ale while Clay tries the cheese curds. "They're so good," I tell him as he pops one into his mouth.

"Mmm. They are. Curd is the word." I laugh as he picks up one of the spoons and scoops up some more of the shake.

"Hey. Stop, dude. I haven't even tasted it yet."

Clay laughs. "Sorry. That's all I want." He slides it across the table to me and I pick up my spoon to dip some out.

"Oh my gosh. It really is delicious. Damn, that vanilla custard really makes it. So creamy. Just enough caramel with a hint of salt and the perfect amount of bourbon that you can definitely taste it, but it's not overpowering."

"I'll have to try to make one when we get back home. Too bad we don't have this kind of vanilla custard anywhere around Baton Rouge though. Guess we'll have to make do with Bluebell ice cream."

"It'll still be yummy," I say.

We sit in silence for a few minutes, eating our cheese curds and sipping our drinks. Something pops into my mind and I decide I'm going to mess with Clay for a bit. I smile.

"What are you smiling about?" he asks.

"Just thinking about later tonight."

"Oh really? What do you have in mind?" He winks at me.

"Well, I was thinking about you and your mouth."

"Mmm. I like the sound of that. Care to elaborate?"

"You're going to use it."

"That's obvious. How, exactly, would you like for me to use my mouth, Lynn? Do tell." He shifts in his chair.

I lower my voice just loud enough for him to hear. "I want your mouth, and your lips, to move up and down… to open and close… to hover…" I pause.

"Keep going, babe. Use your words."

"Over a microphone at a karaoke bar. Time for you to pay up."

"Shit."

CHAPTER 14

CLAY AND I leave AJ Bombers and start on our way to Minneapolis.

"Where are we going?"

"A building called the Foshay Tower. Here's the address." I relay the information to Clay and he puts it in the navigation system.

"Is that the place that looks like the Washington Monument?"

"Yes. We're spending the night there tonight."

"Wait. What?"

"It's a W hotel now."

"Oh," he chuckles. "Convenient."

"That it is."

"Okay. Only about five hours to go. Should be there in time for us to eat supper. Is it finally my turn for the radio?" Clay asks.

"Yes, babe, it's your turn," I snicker.

"Good." He hits shuffle on his phone and "More Than a Feeling" by Boston starts playing throughout the cab and Clay begins to sing.

"Is that going to be your choice for karaoke tonight?"

"Um… tonight?"

"Yes, I told you. The week is up. It's time for you to pay the piper, Sinclair."

"Babe, I'm going to be too tired to go out tonight after driving all day."

"Stop trying to make excuses, Clay."

"I'm not. I'm serious."

"Well, we'll take a nap when we get there before we go eat. You'll probably get a second wind."

"You have an answer for everything, don't you?"

I shrug. "So, is Boston your pick for tonight?"

"I don't know. Probably won't be this song. I'll have to think about it. Christ, though, Lynn, you know I hate singing in front of people."

"Then you shouldn't have been so cocky thinking you would beat me at Skee-Ball. You took the bet fair and square. And seriously Clay, you have a great voice. Don't be nervous. You'll be fine."

He lets out some sort of half sigh, half grunt noise. "Okay. But only because I love you."

"Jeez. You're such a sore loser. If I had lost, I'd be just as aggravated about having to work out with you in the hotel gyms. At least you only have to endure three to five minutes of agony. I was prepared for two weeks."

"I suppose that's true." He looks at me and smiles.

"See? It's a win for both of us."

"It's not a win for me."

Clay's phone rings, interrupting the song.

"Holy shit. It's Tyler." Clay punches the button on the dashboard to answer the call. "Tyler! How the hell are you, man?"

"Hey, bud. I'm doing well. How 'bout y'all?"

"We're great. Lynn and I were just talking about you yesterday. She's here with me. You're on speaker."

"Hey, darlin'."

"Hey, Ty. It's good to hear your voice. We've missed you."

"Same here."

"Are you back state side?" Clay asks.

"Yeah, that's why I'm calling. Got back yesterday. I'm going to rest up today but wanted to see if you and your lady wanted to get together tomorrow night and catch up."

"Oh, man. Can't. We're actually on a road trip right now. On our way to Minneapolis."

"Minneapolis? What the hell's up there?"

"Long story. I know you just got off a plane, but if you want to meet us at one of our stops that would be fucking awesome. Would love to see you."

"Hold up. One of your stops?"

Clay and I explain to Tyler all about the cross-country scavenger hunt we're on that Aunt Mitzi set up for us. "I don't know where our next destination is after Minneapolis, but once we figure it out, I'll let you know."

"Well, your next one might be too soon for me. Plus, Lena's fiftieth birthday is in two days and she'll kill me if I leave again so soon and miss her big five-oh celebration."

"Oh no," Clay laughs. "You can't do that because I don't want to be on the other end of your sister's wrath. She'll have my balls in a vice the next time I see her if you miss her party on my account."

Tyler laughs. "Yes she would. Tell you what. Give me a few days to reacclimate and then let me know where you'll be. I'm gonna take some time off for a bit so it won't be a problem. I know the boss."

"You *are* the boss," I laugh.

"Exactly." I can tell he's smiling. "Sounds like the two of you have had quite the adventure and scored some major kick-ass loot."

"It's been so much fun," I tell Tyler. "Seriously though, we'd love for you to fly out and meet us somewhere soon. There's no telling when we'll be home."

"You got it."

"Tell Lena happy birthday from us," I say.

"Yeah, man. Tell her she doesn't look a day over forty-nine."

"Fuck that. Then she'll have *my* balls in a vice. I'll just tell her you send your love. She's always had a soft spot for you, Clay. No idea why."

"Whatever," Clay laughs. "Talk soon, bro."

"Bye, Ty," I say.

"Later, y'all."

Clay shakes his head with a smile as he ends the call. "Man, it was good to hear from him. Glad he's home safe."

"Me too. I really hope he comes to meet us somewhere."

"He will."

"Good."

Clay turns up the volume on the radio and "Wait for Me" by Theory of a Deadman starts playing.

"You know," Clay says, "the first time I heard this song, it reminded me of the first time I had to tell you about being deployed."

"It did?"

"Yeah. I was scared to death of telling you," he says a little sheepishly.

"I remember. But you didn't need to be afraid."

"But we had just started dating and I didn't know how you'd react."

"I know." I grab his hand and kiss the top of it, keeping our fingers clasped together.

I remember the night he told me. We had only been dating about a month. He called me at work on a Friday afternoon.

My desk phone rang. "Lynn Boudreaux. How can I help you?"

"Lynn. It's Clay."

My heart did a little flip. "Hey, you. What's up?" He rarely called me at work so I knew there had to be a good reason.

"I need to change our plans for tonight."

"Okay. Did you think of a way to top our last date?" He had taken me to ride go-karts and play arcade games at Celebration Station. It was a really fun date. Plus, that was the night he told me he wanted us to be exclusive, and we became an official couple.

Clay chuckled. "Pizza and go-kart racing with a side of mini golf was definitely one of my top five favorite dates with you."

"We've only been on five dates, Clay."

"Exactly. Look, I know we're supposed to go out, but can you come over to my place instead? I'll cook dinner for you."

"You cook?"

"I have my moments." I could tell by the tone of his voice that he was smiling. "Is spaghetti okay with you? With a salad and garlic bread?"

"Sure, that sounds great. Why the change of plans?"

"I need to talk to you about something."

Oh shit. My heart sank. Nobody wants to hear that. Especially when a relationship was going so well. *He's going to break up with me. I thought we were off to a good start, but apparently, I misread him.*

"Um. Okay." My voice softened. I was on the verge of tears. Right there at my desk. "Is everything alright? Did I do something wrong?"

"What? No, no. It's nothing like that. I just need to tell you something and I'd rather us be alone." His voice was serious. Ominous. That definitely hadn't made me feel any better.

"Okay. Um, what time?"

"Seven. Or just whenever you want to come over after work is fine."

Jeez, he really wants to get this over with. I know he said he wasn't ending things, but a girl's mind wanders regardless. "Okay. Can I bring anything?"

"No. I've got it covered. I'll see you later, Lynn."

And with that, he hung up. He didn't even give me a chance to say good-bye.

After work, I went home, showered, and anxiously rummaged through my closet for something to wear. *How should I dress? If he's going to break up with me, I should look my best so I can walk away with my head held high and make him regret it. On the other hand, after being dumped, I don't want to be uncomfortable in a tight dress when I leave. It's too restrictive to cry in. And I know I'll cry all the way home.* At the last minute I finally decided on a jean skirt with a paisley top from The Gap.

I got to Clay's house at around 6:30 and knocked on the door. He answered it with a smile that didn't quite reach his eyes. "You look great. Come in," he said, and gave me a peck on the cheek. A peck. On the cheek. *He's definitely breaking my heart tonight.*

His dog, Shadow, met me in the living room and jumped up to my waist. He was a Catahoula Cur of only about eight months old. I reached down to pet him on the head. "Good boy," I told him. I put my purse down on the couch and followed Clay into the kitchen. "Smells great in here."

"Thanks. Do you want a glass of wine?" he asked as he began to uncork the bottle of Cabernet Sauvignon.

"Sure." I needed it more than I wanted it.

Clay poured the rich, burgundy liquid into a wine glass and handed it to me. "The garlic bread is almost ready." He took two dinner plates and two salad bowls out of the cabinet and set them on the counter. As he began to dish out the salad, he asked, "What kind of dressing would you like? Ranch? Italian? Blue chee—"

"Clay, stop," I cut him off and he swung around. "Please. I'm nervous as hell. What's going on? Are you breaking up with me?"

"What?" He dropped the salad tongs in the bowl with a *clang* and rushed over to my side. "No, Lynn." He hugged me and I relaxed with a sigh as I wrapped my arms around his waist.

I pulled back and looked up at him. "Then what is it? I can't deal with this small-talk right now. Please, tell me what it is you wanted to talk about."

"Let's fix our plates first, and I promise, I'll get right to it when we sit down," he said as the buzzer went off on the oven, indicating the bread was ready. He grabbed a potholder and took the garlic bread out, then proceeded to cut it into slices. "If you don't mind, would you get me the blue cheese dressing out of the fridge? And whichever one you want."

I just stood there for a second, speechless. *He's got to be kidding, right? He obviously can't sense the internal freak-out I'm experiencing, even though I practically begged him to tell me what the hell is going on right now. Just a couple more minutes. I can wait. Barely.*

Clay looked up from slicing the garlic bread and turned to me. "Lynn? The dressing?"

"Right." I walked over to the refrigerator, got the dressings out, and tried to relax. *Inhale. Exhale.* "How can you eat blue cheese? Gross." I wrinkled my nose.

He chuckled. "It's an acquired taste. What about you? What's your poison?"

"Ranch. All the way."

"I like ranch too. Sometimes I mix ranch with Italian. But I'm in a blue cheese mood tonight."

We dished our plates out and sat down at the table across from each other.

"Start talking," I said as I drowned my salad in ranch dressing.

"Okay." He took a deep breath. "You know I'm in the Army National Guard."

"Yes. That was one of the first things I learned about you, since you were dressed in your fatigues when we met." I took a bite of spaghetti. It was really good, with perfect tartness. Not sweet, thank goodness. I do not like a sweet spaghetti sauce. I wanted to tell Clay how good it was, but I didn't want to deflect from the conversation at hand. I wanted to know what the hell was going on.

"Right," he said with a smile. I assumed he was remembering that day just a month before. "Well…" His smile faded and he pressed his lips together into a line.

"Spit it out, Clay."

"You know things are crazy in the Middle East right now."

"Yes. I've heard."

"With everything going on over there… I've been activated for regular duty." He paused and looked at me.

"Um, okay. What does that mean, exactly?"

"I got my deployment orders today."

The blood drained from my face. I put my fork down. My voice was low and scratchy as I asked, "When do you leave?"

"Next month. Twenty-seven days to be exact. It's soon. I know. I'll be training to get ready for the mission for a couple of weeks and then I'm heading to the Middle East."

My eyes started to well and I sniffled. "So, you *are* breaking up with me."

"No, Lynn. No. Actually, I was afraid you would be the one to break up with me after I told you."

"Why would you think that?" A tear slid down my cheek and I swiped it away.

"Because. We just started dating. I don't know how long I'm going to be gone. Close to a year at least. Maybe longer. I can't expect you—"

I held my hand up in a 'stop' signal, cutting him off. "Let me tell you something, Clay Sinclair. You don't know me well enough yet to assume what I would do."

"You're right. I don't." Clay got up from the table and walked over to me. He grabbed my hand and gently pulled me up from my chair. Looking into my eyes, he said, "So… I'm just going to straight-up ask you then. Will you…" He cleared his throat. "Will you… wait for me? I know it's not fair of me to ask, but I don't want to lose you, Lynn. I don't want to lose this. Us." He gestured between our two hearts.

I smiled as the proverbial weight lifted from my shoulders. "Yes, Clay.

Yes. I will wait for you." I couldn't believe he thought I would really walk away from him because he was doing his job. I could not begin to imagine what in the world made him think that. It wasn't until after we were married that I found out his girlfriend before me broke up with him because of the high-risk nature of his job. Jobs, really. With Clay being a state trooper and a firefighter in the military, she couldn't handle the danger he put on himself, especially after losing an uncle and one of her good friends in the line of duty. I can respect that, but any job in the world can be a hazard. I mean, just walking out of your front door daily is risky, if you think about it. Bad things can happen to anyone, anywhere, anytime. Clay was worth taking a chance on, no matter how unpredictable his jobs might have been. Totally worth the gamble. I guess his ex did me a favor though. Score one for me.

Clay kissed me so wickedly sweet and hugged me as tight as he could without crushing me. "Thank God," he whispered into my ear. He pulled back and looked at me, shamefaced. "I didn't want to ask. I don't have the right. It's so selfish of me. We're so new. I'm sorry. I just…" He trailed off.

"I know," I said. My eyes teared up again. "You don't need to apologize. And it's not selfish, Clay. If anything, it's smart. You needed to know."

"It won't be easy."

"Nothing in life that's worth anything ever is."

He smiled so wide I thought his face was going to break in half. "Lynn, I… I…"

Oh my god. Is this it? Is he about to tell me he loves me? It's a little soon for that, but I've already fallen so hard for him, I'll definitely say it back. "You what, Clay?" I waited with bated breath. My pulse flashed and my heart hammered.

"I… can you stay here and keep an eye on things while I'm gone? And take care of Shadow? But don't feel obligated." His words were rushed. Like he changed his mind at the last second from what he was really going to say.

My heart fell to my stomach with a truckload of cinder blocks. *I guess he's not in love with me. Not yet at least.* "Um… yeah. Sure. I can do that."

"Thank you." He kissed me again. "God, I'm going to miss you so much."

"I'm going to miss you too. We'll just have to spend as much time together as we can before you leave. Jesus, that makes me sound clingy. I promise, I'm not clingy."

He laughed. "Cling away. I want to spend every second with you in the next twenty-seven days."

"That's not quite possible. We both have to go to work."

"Yeah, well… that part sucks."

"God, I was so scared you were going to dump me."

"Never."

I smiled. But I wondered something, so I asked. "Wait. If you never intended to break up with me tonight, why didn't you kiss me when I got here? Why did you just peck me on the cheek?"

"Shit, Lynn. I wanted to kiss you senseless the second I opened the door and saw you standing there. But, I didn't. I can be a dick. Not kissing you like I wanted to was a way to keep you at arm's length, I guess. I wasn't sure how this night would end. I'm sorry. I know that was a real asshole thing for me to do."

He grabbed my cheeks in his hands and looked into my eyes. I swear, I really thought I had seen love in his baby blues. But it's like he was scared to say those three little words. Wait, those are not three little words. Those are three big words.

He kissed me, softly at first. A few seconds later he deepened the kiss and I knew if I didn't stop him, we would probably go all the way and I wasn't ready for that yet. Yes, I was falling in love with him. But I was burned so badly by my last relationship, I swore to myself that I would wait much longer before sleeping with anybody else. I pulled away from Clay. "We need to stop."

"I know. I'm sorry."

"It's okay. I'm just… not ready yet. I know you're leaving next month and we don't have a lot of time, but I can't right now. Soon though. I promise."

He was so respectful of my decision for us to wait. I needed to be sure. One hundred percent sure. Though, I guess nobody can be that sure the person they're falling in love with would never hurt them.

Clay smiled. "Okay. Then, can we please get back to our dinner? I'm starving."

"Sure. It's delicious, by the way."

"Thanks. I appreciate that."

He gave me another peck, on the lips that time, and we finished our meal.

I look over at Clay and he's singing the song, word for word. Lyrics about a man not wanting to leave the woman he's always dreamed about having. Hating to be so far away from her. But just knowing that she's back home, waiting patiently for him, is everything he needs to get himself through his current situation, even though it's tough not being there for her. He's counting the days until he can return home.

Clay eyes me and says, "Hey. What's that wistful look on your face for? You okay?"

"Yeah," I smile. "Just remembering that night you told me about your first deployment. And you're right, this song hits that nerve pretty seriously."

"Doesn't it? I swear, I could have written it myself while I was away. The lyrics are spot-on for how I felt when I was overseas. Just knowing you were back home, waiting for me… it gave me strength. Hope. Something to look forward to. Someone to come home to."

"I would've waited even if you hadn't asked me to, Clay. I was falling so hard for you by then."

"I was falling for you too. It scared the shit out of me. I had never fallen so hard so fast for anyone in my life. And I wanted to tell you that night, I almost did, but I didn't want to drop two bombs on you at once. Wow, guess that's a poor choice of words. So, anyway, I waited until I went from falling in love with you to knowing without a doubt that I was totally and completely ass over tits for you."

"Ass over tits?" I laugh.

"Those were actually Tyler's words. He had gotten his orders before I did since he was already active duty, but when I called him to let him know I got my orders too, he could tell I was really upset. He asked me if it was because of you and when I confirmed it, he said, 'Fuck, dude. You're really ass over tits for this girl,'" he chuckles, shaking his head at the memory.

"And how did you respond?" I smiled.

"I told him I was getting there. And that I was scared shitless to tell you I had to leave. That I didn't want to lose you. Then he called me a…

that p-word you don't like, told me to find my balls, man up, and handle my shit. So I called him an asshole, but told him he was right. I hung up with him and called you at work to change our date plans."

I give Clay a sweet smile. "You know, I was scared too. I mean, I wasn't scared to love you. I was just afraid of being hurt again."

"I know, babe. I know." He takes my hand and kisses it. "Man, I really wanted you that night. I would've taken you on the kitchen table if you would've let me. Spaghetti be damned." We both laugh. "But I'm kind of glad we waited until the night before I left."

"Yeah, me too. That night was perfect."

"That it was. I love you, Lynn."

"I love you too, Clay."

CHAPTER 15

Clay parks the truck at the Foshay Tower. It's an Art Deco style building, faced with limestone. It's definitely similar in appearance to the Washington Monument, just with windows all around it. The sides of the tower have a slight inward slope, making each floor of the hotel a bit smaller than the one below it.

Clay looks the building up and down. "Damn. Are we back in Baton Rouge? I must have mistyped the address. Where's the Huey P. Long statue?" He laughs. "This building looks just like our state capitol."

"Almost."

We make our way through the lobby to check in. The interior is more extravagant Art Deco. Ornamental bronze entrances, mahogany, marble, and geometric terrazzo floors decorate the lobby. Waterfall chandeliers hang from an opulent ceiling plated in silver and gold. Gold-plated doorknobs, wrought iron, and more bronze embellishments complete the scene.

The reception desks glow with white lights while the ceiling over the area shines with a hot pink brilliance, creating a dazzling check-in experience. I feel like I've stepped into a more colorful version of the Emerald City of Oz.

Clay is talking to the lady while I'm taking in the beauty of the lobby.

"Here are the keys to your Marvelous suite," I hear her say as she hands Clay the small envelope with our key cards.

"Marvelous?" he asks.

"Yes, that's what you booked. Is that not correct?"

I step up. "No, that's right," I tell her. "I booked the Marvelous king suite. He's just clueless," I point to Clay and she smiles.

"You're all set then," she says.

"Yes, thank you." I loop my arm around Clay's and head towards the elevator.

"Marvelous?" he asks me, as we enter the intricate Art Deco elevator doors. He hits the button for the twenty-fifth floor.

"Yes," I laugh. "There was also a choice of Spectacular, Wow, Wonderful, and Fantastic. But I liked the Marvelous suite the best."

"That's a new one. I've heard of themed rooms, but never described as every synonym to the word 'great' before."

We exit the elevator and walk down the hall to our room. Clay opens the door and we enter.

"Wow," I say.

"Wow? But you said we had the Marvelous room."

I snicker. "Yeah. It's just nicer than I imagined from the pictures online."

The first thing I notice are the spectacular views of the city. A vibrant, royal blue, curved, Art Deco sectional sofa is to the right as we walk in. A matching chair with a table is off to the side of the couch and a round gold coffee table is set in the middle of the space. Hanging over the sofa, a funky, spiral light fixture looks as though someone blew a bunch of bubbles that all converged together. A large, flat-screen TV and the mini fridge station complete the living area.

We walk further into the room. There's a high-top, oval table with four chairs in what I guess would be considered the dining room. I'm loving the decorative lighting that hovers above it. It's stylish with cascading, spherical light bulbs arranged in an S-pattern.

City views continue as we round the corner into the bright bedroom where Clay drops our bags. The king bed is backlit with white lights in front of a wall patterned with geometrical shapes in various shades of blue. The lamps on the bedside table are classically chic, just a white globe sitting atop a golden inverted cone base. Love.

The bathroom is luxurious. There's a walk-in shower surrounded in slate gray tile with a rainfall showerhead. A huge soaking tub sits next to the shower. I can't wait to take a bath.

"That tub sure looks inviting," Clay says.

"That it does. Maybe we can take one together later, after we get back."

"Are you sure we have to go out tonight?"

"Yes, Clay. Why are you trying so hard to get out of this?"

"I'm not trying to get out of it. I know I lost the bet. I'm just tired. And by the way, that was a dirty little thing you did to me earlier at AJ Bombers. Getting me all riled up and then slamming that gauntlet down. You're gonna pay for that."

I smile and wink at him. "Okay, I promise I'll make it up to you later. But let's rest for a couple of hours. It's only five-thirty. Or do you want to eat first? Are you hungry?"

"Yeah. I'm hungry. But not for food."

Clay lunges for me and we crash together onto the bed. "Stop," I laugh.

He straddles my hips, hovering above me as he holds my arms down into the mattress over my head. "You just said you would make it up to me," he says as he interlocks our fingers. "Was that a lie?"

"No." I try to free myself from his hold, so he lowers his body, pinning me down. "But I said later."

"It is later. You said that like… thirty seconds ago. I'm cashing in. I want you, Lynn."

He slowly thrusts his hips into mine and the hard ridge beneath his shorts grazes my center. Sweet baby Jesus in a manger full of hay.

"You're not playing fair," I gasp as I wrap my legs around him and he rocks forward again.

"Oh, babe. This is as fair as fair gets. You wanna tease me and then remind me I have to sing in front of a bunch of strangers? You owe me."

"Fine then. But the only way I can pay you back is if you flip over so I can blow your mind."

"Now we're talkin'." He rolls off me and settles on top of the comforter with his hands clasped behind his head on the pillow, kicking off his shoes. "I was all in for a quickie, but if you'd rather blow me, far be it from me to stop you," he laughs.

"I didn't say anything about blowing you."

"Yes you did. You said—"

"I said I was going to blow your mind." I say this as I scoot down his body and start unbuckling his belt. I didn't say that I *wasn't* going to blow him.

"What are you doing, then, if not that?"

"Shh." I undo the button on his shorts and lower his zipper achingly slow, one notch at a time.

Clay raises up on his elbows and watches me. "Jesus, Lynn. You're killing me."

I look up at him and smile wide. He shakes his head and lowers himself back down to the pillow, exhaling a quick puff of air. When I finally get his shorts completely unzipped, I tug on them and Clay raises up an inch so I can drag them down his legs and throw them on the floor. He's wearing black boxer briefs. I slip my hands under the hem of each leg to rub his upper thighs. Clay lifts up again so I can remove his underwear. I lightly scrape my nails on his ass as I pull them off. He inhales through his teeth.

"You saucy little minx," he whispers with a smile. "You *are* going down on me."

I wink at him. "You ready?"

"Fuck yeah."

I kiss the tip of him and swirl my tongue around his head. Working him with my mouth, I take him deep, making a swallowing motion when he hits the back of my throat.

"God, Lynn. Fuck, that's good."

I move one of my hands up his stomach and rub around his muscular abs. He shoves a palm into my hair. I moan around his length which sends vibrations through him, and he lets out another curse. In a good way though. I take my other hand to the base of his shaft and twist around it in a pumping motion as I continue to twirl my tongue around the top and on the underside of his head, working him over as he squirms beneath my actions.

"Shit, babe. I'm close," he rasps out.

I know he is. I can tell by the way his breathing intensifies, the increased writhing of his hips, and the tightening of his hand in my hair.

I take him deep once more and that's all he needs before he lets out a groan and my mouth fills with his release.

Clay relaxes, exhaling contentedly. "Holy shit," he breathes. "That was…"

"Marvelous?"

Clay laughs out loud. "Marvelous doesn't even begin to describe what that was. You far exceeded marvelous. I mean, damn woman, you really know how to suck my dick."

I crack up laughing.

"What's so funny about that? I'm giving you a compliment."

"I just didn't expect you to say that, exactly. You make it sound like that was the first time I did that for you."

He chuckles. "I meant what I said though. So, thanks, love. I really needed that."

"Don't mention it," I say with a sly smile.

"Same time tomorrow?" Clay asks with a wink.

"Ha. You wish. Gotta give my jaw time to recover. Maybe next week."

"You know I would return the favor right now if I had the energy. But you've wiped me out. My limbs feel like Jell-O."

"It's okay, Clay. You don't need to. I owed you, remember?"

"Yeah, but I wish I could anyway. Jesus, that sounds lame. I can do it. Let me do it for you. I want to. I know I can muster up some strength."

"Oh, can you?" I smirk at him.

"Just. Need. Water." He comically pants and holds his hand out to me like he wants me to fetch him a glass. Then he laughs. "Seriously though. I feel like such a tool for leaving you unsatisfied."

"You think that was unsatisfying for me? I love knowing how much pleasure you get from that. It's a little exhilarating watching and listening to you unravel under my hands and mouth. How little I have to do to make you splinter."

He smiles. "So, it's like a power trip for you."

"Something like that. But it's the same when you go down on me. You make me lose control. I'm putty in your hands."

"Mouth." He gives me one of his sexy half smiles.

"Right." I chuckle.

"I get it. I love doing that for you too. I have to admit, my ego inflates when I drive you over the edge that way. My testosterone skyrockets. It makes me want to beat my chest and howl at the moon."

I laugh. "You're such a caveman."

"Hell yeah I am. And proud of it. So take your clothes off, woman. Let me taste you."

"No, Clay. It's fine. I'm fine."

"That means you're *not* fine."

I chuckle. "Most of the time that would be true. But I promise, I am fine. We don't always have to flip-flop favors for each other. You know that."

"Alright. I won't argue."

"Good. Now, Sir Alpha McSavage, let's get cleaned up. We have a karaoke bar to find."

A couple of hours later, we walk into a bar called the Vegas Lounge. Karaoke doesn't start until 9:00 so we decided to take a nap first and eat something before we left the hotel.

This place is a total dive bar. Very hole-in-the-wall. I love it. And they have karaoke every night. I know we'll have a great time.

The walls and ceiling are all made with wide, wooden planks. Plenty of neon beer and liquor signs light up the joint in a rainbow of colors. Pictures with various funny sayings are hung all around the walls. There's even a sign saying that they have meat raffles on Wednesdays and Saturdays. Unfortunately, we're too late for that. Not that we'd have anywhere to keep raw meat if we won something anyway. But that's a cool draw for the locals. I also see signs for Bingo and a pull-tab casino. We may have to partake in the latter as well while we're here.

Clay finds us a table and we settle in.

"What do you want to drink?" he asks.

"Well, since they advertise as having the coldest beer in town, I guess I'll take a Blue Moon if they have it."

"Yes ma'am."

While Clay is at the bar getting our drinks, I wonder to myself what song he's going to sing. Will it be something by Boston? Or, since we're in Minneapolis, will he honor Prince while we're here?

Clay comes back to the table with our beers and a couple of pull-tab casino games for us to play. He must have read my mind.

"Thanks, babe. I'm glad you thought of getting us a couple of games. I love these things." He sets my Blue Moon in front of me and I take the orange slice and squeeze the juice down the bottleneck while he does the same thing with the lime in his Corona.

Sliding one of the casino cards to me, Clay says, "Let's see if we're winners." He begins to pull the tabs on his game. I wait for him to finish before I start mine.

"Well?"

"Womp, womp, womp…" He shows me his card. "Loser over here. What about you?"

I pull the tabs on my game and, you guessed it. Same. "Loser," I show him and make a sad face. "Oh well, I'm still a winner because I get to watch you sing tonight in front of all these people."

Clay rolls his eyes as he takes a sip of his beer. "I still can't believe I agreed to that bet. I thought for sure I'd kick your ass at Skee-Ball."

"Well, you didn't. So here we are. What's it going to be?"

"I don't know. I'll have to go look at their list."

"Let me pick."

"Fuck that," he snickers. "If I'm doing this, I'm choosing the song."

"Fine." I take a draw from my beer and then lick the sweetness of the orange from my lips. "As long as it's not 'Tequila' or 'Rock 'n' Roll Part Two,' since those are ninety-nine point nine percent instrumental."

"Damn." He snaps his fingers. "Foiled again." He chuckles.

A couple gets up from their table when the DJ calls their names. The girl is a cute, young thing in her early twenties and is wearing a red and white polka dot dress with spaghetti straps. The guy looks a little older, wearing a polo shirt and khaki shorts. Frat boy gear.

"Ladies and gentlemen, may I have your attention," the DJ announces. "Please welcome back to the stage, your favorite karaoke couple, the newlyweds, the dynamic duo of ditties… Saaaandy and Deeeean." He drags their names out like they're about to get ready to rumble in a wrestling ring.

"They'll be singing their signature song, 'My Humps' by the Black Eyed Peas. Take it away, you two!"

We sit and watch Sandy and Dean sing their hearts out. Sandy shakes her rump as Dean sings the question about what she's going to do with all the junk inside her trunk. The crowd cheers as they sing with them. Sandy then jiggles her 'lovely lady lumps' as she and Dean go back and forth singing their parts of the silly lyrics. You can't help but love this song though. It's so catchy. We cheer along with the rest of the audience when they finish. They were very entertaining.

"Okay, Clay. Your turn."

"Not yet, Lynn."

"Well at least go pick out a song and put your name on the list. There are already people in front of you. I'm sure it will be a while before you're called. You're doing this, Sinclair."

He sighs and gets up, heading to the DJ booth. The DJ hands Clay a sticky note for him to put his name and song on. I watch Clay search the pages of the thick binder containing the many songs to choose from. He looks at me and shakes his head with a resigning smirk. He then asks the DJ a question and the DJ nods, flipping to a section in the middle of the binder and pointing at a page. Clay smiles. He writes something on his piece of paper and hands it to the DJ.

I bet he's going to sing something totally from his punk wheelhouse, like The Clash's "Rock the Casbah." Or something suggestive like "Feel Like Makin' Love" by Bad Company. Or maybe even an audience participation song like Queen's "We Will Rock You."

I smile when Clay walks back to the table as I take another sip of my beer.

"I found a good song," he says.

"Awesome. I knew you would. What is it?"

"Clay Sinclair ain't tellin'. You'll just have to wait and see."

"How far down the list are you?"

"I think there are three more people ahead of me."

When I finish my beer, I shake my bottle at him and he looks down at his, noticing he's almost done as well. He winks at me as he gets up to fetch us a couple more.

"You want another Blue Moon?"

"Yes please."

We sit and listen to a girl sing "Kiss" by Prince. She isn't half bad, but she doesn't quite hit the high notes nearly as well as His Royal Badness could. Then a guy gets the crowd going with "Don't Stop Believing" by Journey. A karaoke staple. Next is a couple that appears to be closer to our age. They sing "Close My Eyes Forever" by Ozzy Osbourne and Lita Ford. If I actually close my eyes, I'd think it was really Ozzy singing. That guy is pretty good. And the woman has long blonde hair just like Lita Ford did in the eighties.

"Shit, I'm next," Clay says. He takes a long swig from his beer.

"You'll be great, babe. I know it." I grab his hand and give it a squeeze.

The DJ then announces his name. "Clay, please step up to the mic. Your turn, man."

Clay takes a deep breath and heads in the direction of the stage. When he gets there, he says into the microphone, "Hey, y'all. I don't usually do this sort of thing. It's way out of my comfort zone, but I lost a bet to my wife. So, here I am." The crowd cheers. Clay looks at me. "This is for you, Lynn."

When the music begins, I almost start crying. I gasp as my hands go to my mouth and my eyes water. It's our wedding song. The first song we danced to as a married couple. "I Love You" by Climax Blues Band.

I've never heard Clay sing this song before. Not even once, in all our years together. We consider Styx's "Babe" our song, but we couldn't exactly use that for our wedding dance. The lyrics weren't fit for a typical wedding song. However, this tune will always hold a special place in my heart. Clay is the one who picked it for our first dance as husband and wife. A couple of days after he asked me to marry him, he told me that while he was deployed during Operation Desert Storm, one of his buddies was listening to some music and this song came on. Clay said as he listened to the lyrics, he knew he was going to propose to me as soon as he landed back on American soil. And he did. Right on the tarmac as I was hugging him so tightly after being away from him for eight months. He also told me he knew he wanted this to be our first dance song. And it was.

The crowd in the bar cheers as Clay sings about how I came along and stole his heart when I entered his life. That I've got what it takes, so he made me his wife. And ever since we've met, he's never looked back, and that it's almost like living a dream. A tear falls down my cheek and I wipe it away. He sounds just like the lead singer of the band. I knew he would be great. But never in a million years would I have thought he'd pick this song.

When Clay finishes singing, he looks at me and rubs his heart. Then he nods to the crowd in thanks. Everybody cheers and whoops and hollers. Clay looks surprised as he makes his way back to our table. Guys are slapping him on the back. Girls smile at him, giving thumbs up. He finally reaches me, and without saying a word, Clay takes my face in his hands, planting a long, sweet kiss on my lips as the crowd continues to whistle with enthusiasm.

"You were—"

"Let's get out of here."

He grabs my hand and leads me towards the door as everybody keeps cheering. I hide my face with my hands, a little shy for some reason at everyone having witnessed that seductive kiss. I'm sure they know why we're leaving.

As we exit, I hear the DJ get on the mic and say, "And that's how it's done, folks!"

"Clay, that was… I have no words," I say as he starts the truck.

"You don't have to say anything."

"Yes I do. Really though. You were incredible. I knew you would be good, but shit. That made me melt. Your song choice was a complete surprise."

"Good surprise?" He smiles.

"The best."

"I'm glad you liked it."

"I loved it. I love you."

"Love you too, babe. Now, I hope you got your fill because I'm never doing that again."

I laugh. "Fair enough. You can always sing just for me though."

"I will," he takes my hand and kisses my fingers.

We pull in at the hotel and when we get into the elevator, Clay picks up where he left off at the bar, crashing his lips onto mine. As we ascend to the twenty-fifth floor, his kiss deepens. It's predacious. Voracious. Rapacious.

Once we're inside our room, clothes fly in a frenzied fury and we scramble into bed in with an urgent need.

"I'm taking you, Lynn," he breathes in between kissing me. "Hard. Fast. Slow. Soft. All the ways."

Panting, I tell him, "Good. Do it."

His teeth wrap around the flesh between my neck and shoulder. I inhale sharply at the unexpected sensation. But it was good. So good. Clay juts his tongue out to soothe the sting of his bite and reaches between my legs, checking to see if I'm ready. I know I am.

"Fuck. You're so wet. So primed."

"About as wet as you are hard," I say as I grab hold of his length.

He positions himself over me and places my legs over his shoulders. Clay moans as he sinks into my body. A similar sound escapes from me as I involuntarily echo him.

He keeps his word, alternating between slow and fast, hard and soft, all the while holding on to my legs. Then he lowers them from his shoulders and bends over to take my breast into his mouth, circling the tip with his tongue, maintaining a wild drive inside of me.

Slowing down, he kisses me softly. Smoothly. Sweetly.

"I love the way you feel," he breathes. "The way you tighten around me. The way your body reacts to my touch. The way your soul intertwines with mine."

God, this man.

"I love you, Clay," I whisper in a puff of air.

"I know, love. I know," he smiles.

He kisses me again and picks up his pace, shuddering when he comes undone.

CHAPTER 16

A SERIES OF MELODIC chimes carries across the room to my ears. What the hell is that? Oh, it's Clay's phone.

"Clay." I nudge his leg with my foot. "Your alarm's going off."

"What the hell. I didn't set my alarm," he says groggily. He reaches to the bedside table and picks up his cell. "Shit. I must have accidentally turned it on. Sorry, babe."

"It's okay." I stretch. "We probably need to get up anyway and come up with a game plan for getting into the conference room to see what's hidden in the table."

"That's true."

"What time is it?" I ask.

"It's eight thirty."

"Yeah, good time to get up."

"Want me to call for breakfast?"

"Yes please. I'll go shower. Will you make some coffee?"

"Yep."

I start to get out of bed, but Clay stops me, pulling me by my tank top.

"What are you doing? You're going to rip my shirt, Sinclair."

"I just need my morning sugar. Come here."

He nuzzles my neck and follows that up with a smack on the lips.

"Good morning," I say.

"Yes it is. Go shower, and breakfast will be here when you get out."

I get up and head to the bathroom. I take a long, hot shower, enjoying the steam as it enters my pores.

When I'm dressed and out of the bathroom, Clay has my coffee ready, but I don't see breakfast anywhere.

"Thanks for the coffee, babe, but where are my pancakes?"

"Well, I thought you might actually like to have breakfast in the restaurant on site instead of having room service delivered."

"Why?"

"Because. The name of the hotel restaurant is Keys Café."

"Oh, cool. Good call. Yes, I'd love to check it out in person then."

"That's what I figured. Let me take a quick shower and we'll head down."

When we get to the restaurant, the hostess greets us. "Welcome to Keys Café. Table for two?"

"Yes. Thanks," Clay says.

I look around and take in the atmosphere. The Art Deco motif continues. Speakeasy vibe included. Mirrored signs border the restaurant with slogans like 'Prohibition Ends Here,' 'Don't Take Any Wooden Nickels,' 'Know Your Onions,' and 'I'm All Alone But in Good Spirits.'

Framed artwork on the wall reflects the 1920s as well: women adorned in flapper dresses with fringe and feathers, draped with long strands of pearls; dapper men dressed in three-piece, pinstripe suits accompanied by fedoras and black patent leather shoes.

Colorful, custom tap-handles in the well-stocked bar advertise several local brews. A dozen chairs tucked under the counter patiently await the upcoming happy hour, or at least for somebody who lives by 'It's five o'clock somewhere.'

In front of me is a counter atop a curved glass display case of indulgent cakes and pies. I see one that I'd really like to order a slice from: a cake with white icing, dripping with chocolate ganache all around and down the side. I resolve to leave room in my belly. I can't see what it looks like on the inside since it's not cut. Hopefully it's a cookies and cream cake. One of my favorites.

We're seated at a table and the hostess hands us menus. "Your waitress will be right with you."

"You want another cup of coffee, love?"

"No. I think I might just have some juice."

The waitress comes over to our table. She has big poofy hair and her eyelids sport great, smeared arches of blue eye shadow. "Good morning. I'm Gladys, and I'll be taking care of you this morning. What can I get you two to drink?" She whips out a pencil hidden in her bouffant and sets it ready on a green and white striped order pad.

"Apple juice please," I tell her.

"And I'll have coffee. Black."

"Got it," she says. "Are you ready to order breakfast or do you need a few more minutes?"

I know what I want, but I look at Clay.

"Give us a few," he says. "When you come back with our drinks, we'll be ready."

"No problem." She returns the pencil to her swirls of hair and strides towards the kitchen.

I already know I want pancakes to eat, but as I scan the menu, I see that you can add bananas and chocolate chips. Yes please.

"What are you getting to eat?" I ask.

Clay is looking over the menu. "Thinking about the Loon Omelet."

"Loon Omelet?" I look for it on the menu and read what's included in it. It has Minnesota wild rice, mushrooms, onions, turkey, tomatoes, provolone cheese, and a special mushroom cream sauce. "Hmm… sounds good. I don't think I've ever had an omelet with rice in it before."

"Me either. That's what kind of drew me to it. And not just any rice… Minnesota wild rice. I need to see what that's all about."

"I'm sure it will be delicious."

"Yeah, I hope so. Although I am disappointed by the lack of loon in the ingredients. Never had loon before," he chuckles.

I smile and shrug. "I'm sure it tastes just like turkey."

Gladys comes back with my juice and Clay's coffee. She takes our order. "Good choices." She smiles as she heads to the kitchen, scratching her permed head of hair with her pencil before it disappears back into her do. Her coiffed curls don't even move. I bet she still uses Aqua Net.

As I pick up my juice glass, I notice that it has the Keys Café logo on it. I want it.

"What's wrong?" Clay asks, noticing me eyeing the glass. "Is it dirty? Got lipstick stains?"

"No," I smile. "It's nothing really. I just want one of these glasses." I turn it around so he can see.

"Ah. Well, maybe they sell them."

"Maybe. I'll ask Gladys when she comes back."

"So, do you have a game plan for this conference room or what?" Clay asks as he takes a sip of his coffee.

"Not really. I was hoping you would be the one that had something in mind. I mean, of course, we could just go and look for it and start unlocking drawers in the table. That's about the extent of my plan. I'm not as stealthy as you are."

"That's as good a plan as any. But we could also see about reserving the room."

"Oh, I like that idea even better. Let's check after we eat."

Gladys comes back with our breakfast.

"That was fast. Can't wait to dig in," Clay says, rubbing his hands together.

"Glad you're looking forward to it. Enjoy. Anything else I can get you?"

"No, but I do have a question," I say. "Do y'all sell these juice glasses?"

"No, we sure don't. Not yet anyway. We're planning to open a small gift shop, but we haven't ordered all our inventory yet. It'll probably be a couple of months before we're ready."

"Aww, that's too bad. I really like this glass."

"She has a thing for keys. Weird, I know." Clay winks at me and then smiles at Gladys.

She looks between the two of us and smiles back. "I'm sorry, dear."

"That's okay."

She walks away and then turns back around. "Tell you what, I'll ask my manager and see what she says about selling one to you now."

"Thank you so much. I would really appreciate that."

"No problem."

I turn my attention to the plate in front of me. "Oh man, these pan-cakes look so good," I say as I drown them in maple syrup.

"They sure do. Almost makes me wish I'd gotten the same," Clay says as cuts into his omelet and takes a bite.

I wait for him to chew for a few seconds before I ask, "How's your loon omelet?"

"Not too shabby. Very savory. Wanna try it?"

"No thanks. I don't think it will mesh too well with all this sweetness I have going on over here." I make a circular motion over my plate with my fork.

"Suit yourself. I want a bite of your pancakes though."

I cut him off a few triangular pieces and put them on his plate next to his hash browns. "Is that enough?"

"Yeah. Just wanted a taste. Thanks, babe."

Gladys comes back to our table to check on us.

"I could use some more apple juice," I tell her.

"You got it."

"Did you find out about the glass?" Clay asks.

"I did. And I'm sorry, my manager said I couldn't sell one to you. Until our new stock comes in, we're running low on logo juice glasses."

"Oh well. Thanks for checking," I tell her.

After we finish eating, I head to the bathroom to wash the sticky syrup off my hands. It doesn't matter how careful I am when I eat pancakes, I always manage to come away with sticky fingers. Sometimes I even wind up with a sticky elbow. I have no idea how that happens.

When I get back to the table, I realize I'm too full for that piece of cake. Too bad, because it looks so freaking good. Clay pays the tab and we head back up to our room to let our food settle for a while before we try and take on our mission.

"I got something for you," Clay says with a twinkle in his eye.

"You got me something? When?" I chuckle.

"When you were in the bathroom at Keys."

"What is it?"

He reaches into the pocket of his cargo shorts and pulls out a glass with the Keys Café logo on it. But it's not a juice glass. It's a pint glass.

And it's even better than the juice glass because it not only has their logo, but a silhouette of the hotel. Since the glass is taller, there's room for the Foshay Tower.

"Surprise," he smiles.

"Oh my gosh, how did you manage that?"

"When you went to the bathroom, I called Gladys over to our table and asked her if they had any glasses of a different size that I could buy instead of the juice glass. I gave her the short and sweet of our story, then she checked in the back. Returned to the table with this one. She didn't even charge me for it. She loved our travel saga and understood why you wanted it because of the name and all the keys we've used to unfold and unlock our story."

"Aww, Clay. I love that. I'm glad you thought about that, because I sure didn't. Obviously. Thank you." I give him a kiss and wrap the glass up in a couple of pages from the complimentary newspaper.

"You're welcome. I called the front desk about reserving the conference room, but it's occupied. Though the girl did say they were going to break for brunch, which should be," Clay looks at the time, "right about now if you want to go try our luck."

"She said we could use it while they're gone?"

"Um, no. She inadvertently mentioned they were leaving for brunch. I don't think she meant for us to have at it in their stead."

"Gotcha. Well…" I dig in the box of keys and find the Snoopy keychain. "I'm ready."

We leave our hotel room and head down to the level where the business center is located to find the conference room.

As we approach the door with the words 'Conference Room' on the plate to the right, Clay points. "This is it."

"Oh gosh, I hope the door isn't locked," I whisper. "We only have the one key and I assume it's for a drawer in the table."

"Let's see." Clay tries the doorknob and it opens. We eye each other and smile. "I can't believe they left it unlocked. Guess their meeting isn't top secret."

After we step inside, Clay shuts the door quietly. The conference table is about twenty feet long and six feet wide, black lacquered, with sweet, little vases of purple flowers decorating the table along the center line. Half-full water glasses are set on lavender napkins at every chair. Papers and manila folders are stacked neatly on the table.

I count the seats and there are twenty. Eight on each side and two at each end. A landscape painting of majestic mountains hangs on one side-wall and another of a sunset over a beach hangs on the other wall between two large windows. A TV is mounted on the wall at one end of the room opposite a projector screen.

There are small, narrow drawers under the table at each chair. But I notice something. There are no locks on the drawers.

"Shit, Clay. Do you see what I see?"

"You mean, what you don't see. Locks. Yes, I noticed that."

"What the hell do we do now? There aren't any other pieces of furniture in here that the key might open."

Clay walks all the way around the table, inspecting each drawer underneath. When he gets to the head of the table, he stops and smiles. "Come here."

I amble over to where he stands and look down at the drawer. It's different from the rest. It's longer, taking up the whole end of the table. And there's a lock on it.

"Oh, thank God." I stand there, staring at it, counting my blessings that we didn't just hit another roadblock.

"Well, what are you waiting for? Go ahead, babe. Get the key."

"Right," I say as I pull the Snoopy keychain out of my pocket.

Inserting the small key into the lock, I twist my wrist and it opens. I inhale deeply. The breath escapes from me as I open the drawer. Pens, note pads, paper clips, and various other office supplies take up space. Surely that's not what is meant for us. There must be more than one key to this drawer. I move a few things around, picking up a notebook to look through it. This must be it. I check for another clue written inside, but there's nothing that indicates it's for us.

"Anything inside the notebook?"

"No. I'm getting frustrated, Clay, and I'm scared we're going to run out of time."

"Hey, I have an idea. Remember the Empire Building in Birmingham?"

"Yeah. What about it?"

"We found a folder taped underneath the top of the filing cabinet. You smell what I'm cookin'?"

I smile and reach my hand up under the tabletop, feeling around for an envelope. My face falls. "Nothing there."

"Hold on." Clay squints. "Is it just me, or is the bottom of the drawer a different wood than the sides?"

I look to see what he's talking about. "It *is* different. The grain, the color... maybe it's—"

"A false bottom."

"Yes!"

Clay pulls his pocketknife from his shorts and slides one of the blades into the sliver of space between the bottom and the side. He shimmies it back and forth, until it starts to lift. I smile. "It's getting there," he says. Finally, it raises enough to where I can stick my pinky finger under it and bring it all the way up, removing the fake bottom, being careful not to let everything spill over the edges. "Good job, babe."

"Thanks. You too." I see a manila envelope with the name 'Sinclair' scrawled on top. "There it is. Grab it. My hands are a little full." Clay takes the envelope out of the real bottom of the drawer. I replace the fake one. "Let's go. They could be back any minute."

Clay hands me the envelope and drops the key as he tries to secure the drawer. "Shit."

I open the door. The hall is quiet, but won't be for long. "Clay, hurry. The elevator is on its way back."

"It might not stop on this floor, Lynn. But it's all good. I got it locked."

As we get to the elevator, the door opens and about six people come out, heading to the conference room. I give Clay wide eyes as we step into the elevator. "That was cutting it close," I say as the doors shut.

When we get back into our room, I unclasp the envelope and break the seal, unsheathing a small stack of 8x10 black-and-white, glossy photographs. Flipping through the dozen or so photos, my jaw drops.

"No. Fucking. Way," Clay says, sounding more surprised than I'm sure I look. "Plot twist."

CHAPTER 17

CLAY AND I sit and study the photos. One picture shows Aunt Mitzi and Uncle Sid sitting at a table in a restaurant laughing with Marilyn Monroe and Joe DiMaggio. Another of them posing with Audrey Hepburn at a black-tie gala. Seated at a formal dinner table next to Humphrey Bogart at what appears to be a banquet of some kind. Standing in front of the Sands Hotel with The Rat Pack in Las Vegas. The 'A List' of celebrities from the 1950s goes on for a total of fourteen photographs. Even the negatives are included (protected in sleeves), proving the authenticity of the pictures.

"How?" I ask, stunned. "How did I not know about this?"

"How did *nobody* in your family know about this? Or at least never mention it. Do you think your mom and dad know?"

"No. I'm sure they would have said something. Mom would have for sure, had she known."

"Well, if there's one thing we've learned about Aunt Mitzi and Uncle Sid along this trip, it's that they were private people. To an extent anyway. They didn't toot their own horns."

"But it's like they lived two separate lives. One where they were just down-to-earth and the other where they rubbed elbows with rich and famous celebrities. All this seems like it was such a key part of their lives. There are holes. So many holes."

"Key holes."

"Exactly!" I huff. "I feel like I never even knew them."

"Lynn. They *were* down-to-earth. And apparently still rubbed elbows with the rich and famous. But that doesn't mean you didn't know them. You did. If they had bragged about hanging around all those celebrities, that wouldn't exactly make them down-to-earth, would it?"

"I guess you're right. I just wish I knew the story. Or stories. How they knew them. What they did together. Why they never said anything. If anybody else knew."

"Well, love, I bet we'll find out. Remember how we came across all the Al Capone articles and then got the explanation in a letter after that?"

"Yeah. I'm sure there's a letter from Aunt Mitzi in our near future explaining everything about these pictures. Filling in the holes."

"I'm floored though," Clay says. "They were friends with The Duke, Lynn. John fucking Wayne. Or they met him, at the very least. Unreal."

"I know, right? I wonder if there's a secret photo album somewhere hidden in our house of all their celebrity get-togethers."

"We'll have to check around when we get back. Didn't you clean out her bedroom closet though?"

"Yeah, and I didn't see anything. But I haven't gotten to the others yet. There's no telling what we might find in them."

"Well, you ready to check out our next clue?" Clay gathers up the pictures and slips them back into the manila envelope.

"Yes. Let's see where we're off to next."

Clay gets our things together as I get the clue sheet out of my purse.

"Hey, babe?" Clay calls from the bathroom. "You still want to keep the little shampoos and shit? Our toiletry bag is overflowing with all of them."

I chuckle to myself. I don't know why I keep throwing them all in our bag. It's not like we're going to run out of shampoo or conditioner. I packed brand-new, full-sized bottles before we left home. "No, I guess not. But wait, let me smell the lotion. I might want to keep that." I walk into the bathroom and Clay has the lotion open, waiting for me to sniff it. When I put my nose over the top of the small bottle, he squeezes it, and it shoots out onto my face. He throws his head back in laughter as I let out a playful scream along with a snicker. "You ass." I smack him.

Wiping the lotion off my nose and forehead, I rub it into my hands and give them a whiff. I don't like it. "Ew. No. Chunk that shit. Smells like a funeral home. Blech."

"A funeral home? That's awful," he laughs. "Why would anybody make a lotion that smells like a funeral home?"

"I don't know, but smell." I hold my hands up to his nose and he inhales a bit. Then he scrunches his face up. "Ugh, gross, you're right. Definitely Eau de Mortuary. Jeez, that's bad."

"Told you," I smile. "It smells like carnations, but carnations remind me of funeral homes," I say as I wash my hands in the sink to get the smell off.

"Why do carnations remind you of funeral homes?"

"I guess because it's one of the cheapest flowers on the market, and funeral sprays are pretty costly to begin with, so florists use carnations as fillers to make them more affordable. At least that's my take on it. There could be a totally different reason why all funeral homes smell the same. Just like nursing homes and hospitals all smell the same."

"Ahh, yes… the unmistakable scent of antiseptic covering up death."

"Wow," I blanch. "When you put it like that… just… ew, again."

Clay chuckles. "Your reasoning makes sense though, why all funeral homes smell alike. It's not exactly illogical, though it could be that all funeral homes have a universal policy to use carnation scented air freshener."

"You're hilarious," I say facetiously, but then I snicker.

Clay circles back to the origin of this conversation. "You should have seen your face though, when I squirted you with that death flower lotion," he says, smiling.

"Hmph. Whatever. Stop clowning around and finish packing. I'll meet you at the living room couch after I make another pass around the bed for any of our stuff."

"Yes, ma'am." I hear the bottle of lotion hit the bottom of the trash can with a loud *kerplunk*.

I walk around the bed to make sure everything has been picked up from the bedside tables and make another sweep along the floor with my eyes. All good.

When Clay sits down next to me on the sofa, he puts his arm around me as I unfold the cipher and read clue number thirty-two.

"Okay. 'In the capital of Iowa, find the Place that was the first hospital in the state used by the Sisters of Mercy. Home of a man who was worthy of a curtsy. The Place has expanded, and now has a stage. Look under the space where performers make wage.' Hmm... that's a little vague."

"Well, at least we know we're going to Des Moines. I see that the word 'place' is capitalized. So that must mean something. Let's check out of the hotel and then we can try to figure out the exact destination while we head in that direction."

"Good plan. I think we're ready. All packed up. Let's look at the key first though."

"Oh yeah. Almost forgot," Clay says.

I dig in the box and look for keychain number thirty-two. It's flexible and rubbery, oval, with a black background and a weird stencil design in yellow. I'm stumped. The key itself is small, like for a padlock maybe. "What's this?" I ask Clay, referring to the crazy outline inside the keychain. "Another symbol to figure out?"

Clay takes it from me and holds it horizontally. "This, my dear wife, is the logo for the University of Iowa. The Hawkeyes. You should really brush up on your college football mascots."

"Whatever. But now knowing that's what it is, I can see the bird head in the stencil."

"Good. Okay, ready to go?"

"Let's hit the road."

We get into the truck and Clay plugs Des Moines into the navigation system.

"Only about three and a half hours. We should be able to knock this all out in a day. We can move on after that unless you want to stay in Iowa," Clay says.

"What about Tyler? Do you want to call him to come meet us there? You said you'd let him know where we'd be next."

"Not yet. Lena's party is this weekend so he can't leave till after that."

"Oh yeah. We should send her flowers or something."

"That would be nice. You're such a sweetheart, babe. So thoughtful."

I smile and turn to my phone, looking up florists to send her a bouquet for tomorrow. There's a beautiful summer arrangement with colorful pastel roses, gerbera daisies, and lilies. "What about this one?" I show Clay the picture of the flowers on my phone.

"Perfect. As long as there aren't any carnations in it."

"Nope. Not a single one," I laugh, and order the bouquet to be delivered to Lena tomorrow, with a sweet note wishing her the happiest of birthdays.

"Maybe wherever we go after Iowa would be a better place for Tyler to meet us," Clay says.

"Sounds good. And we'll just play it by ear today and see how things go, then decide if we want to stay there tonight or not. That okay with you?"

"Yup," Clay says, popping the 'p' at the end.

"Minneapolis was fun," I say as we pull onto the interstate.

"That it was."

"I really loved hearing and seeing you sing karaoke. That was a real treat."

"A once-in-a-lifetime event."

"It was so sweet though. You made my heart pound with joy and love. I think every woman in that bar swooned over you."

Clay smiles at me. "Stop it." His cheeks color.

"You're adorable when you blush."

"I'm not blushing. And don't call me adorable," he says as his face turns an even deeper shade of pink. "That's the last thing men like to be called. Try hot or sexy. Fuckable works too." He gives me a side-eye glance.

"But you *are* adorable, Clay. You can be adorable and sexy at the same time you know. And I love making you blush. Those moments are so few and far between."

He grabs my hand and kisses it, then interlocks our fingers. "Well, it takes a lot to catch me off guard. You're the only one that has ever had that effect on me. The blushing one."

"So, now you're acknowledging that I made you blush?"

"Yes, Lynn. You made me blush. Happy? I felt my face go warm, so I know it. It's just so out of character for me."

"No it's not. It might be out of character for Clay Sinclair, former first sergeant Army firefighter and badass Louisiana State Police lieutenant, but it's in no way out of character for my sweet, sexy, and insatiable husband."

"Fine. I'll take that." He winks at me as he squeezes my hand, then lets it go. "I don't know whose turn it is for music, but I'm claiming it."

"I don't remember either, so I'll let you."

He smiles as he punches the shuffle button on his Spotify list in his phone. ZZ Top's "La

Grange" starts playing and Clay sings along, overemphasizing when it gets to the repeating 'haw, haw, haw, haw' part. I look at him like he's crazy.

"What? That's my favorite line of that song. Fucking brilliant," he laughs. I shake my head. "Aw, come on, Lynn. At least admit their songs are fun."

"I have nothing against ZZ Top. I like them."

"I thought so. I was wondering why you were looking at me like I'm demented."

"I just don't know that I would call that part of the song 'fucking brilliant' per se."

"Don't you know when I'm kidding?" He looks at me and I snicker. "It is my favorite part of the song though."

"Mine too."

"Good. Glad we got that settled."

I get my phone out and text CeCe to see how things are going back home and to check on the house. Then I text Annie and make sure things are still going smoothly with her and Stone.

Fall Out Boy's "My Songs Know What You Did in the Dark (Light Em Up)" comes on. Clay increases the volume and drums his fingers on the steering wheel.

"Like this song much?" I ask, smiling.

"Yeah. First off, it's just a really kick-ass jam. And I like the title. It's kind of sexy and ambiguously voyeuristic, if that makes sense."

"Sure. Like all songs and lyrics, it's open to interpretation. I guess that goes for titles as well."

Clay smiles and starts belting out the chorus. I join him. This really is a great song.

After a minute or so, my phone buzzes. It's CeCe returning my text. Clay notices and turns the volume down.

"Who's that?" he asks.

"My sister."

"Everything okay?"

"Yeah. Things are all good back home."

"Good."

"Okay, we need to figure out exactly where we're going." I read the clue again. "I don't even know what to start with for my search online. There aren't even any real key words. All we know for sure is that we're going to Des Moines."

"It's okay, love. We've been in worse situations when it comes to the clues. Let's try to break it apart. She said something about the Sisters of Mercy, right? Aren't they nuns that run hospitals all over the world or something?"

"I think they do more than just run hospitals. But yeah, that's part of the clue."

"Alright. And the word 'place' is capitalized, so that's probably part of the name of where we're going. Or street name or something. As per Aunt Mitzi's usual M.O. It was somebody's house, correct?"

"Yes. And apparently whoever he was, he was a pretty distinguished gentleman, deserving a curtsy and all that."

Clay chuckles. "Okay. And what about a stage or something?"

"She said that the place has expanded and has a stage. To look under it."

"Look under the stage?"

"Well, she doesn't say that exactly, but she said to look under the space where performers make wage. So I assume she's talking about performers on the stage. That's how they make their money right? By performing. On the stage."

"Okay, let's roll with that. It might be some sort of performing arts theater."

"A performing arts theater that was formerly a hospital?" I ask, my face a little scrunched up in confusion.

"Um, well, it was also a house. Sooo…" Clay drags out the last word and trails off.

"Fair point."

"Try looking up Des Moines, Sisters of Mercy, and theater. See what you come up with."

I input those words into the search bar on my phone's internet browser and wait for the results. "Oh. I think this might be it," I say, reading the first heading.

"What've you got?" Clay asks.

"Hoyt Sherman Place."

"Well, it's got a man's name and 'place' in the title. I bet you're right."

"Let me just read a little about it and make sure that's it."

"Is it a theater?"

"Shh."

"Was it a Sisters of Mercy hospital?"

"Clay, hush."

"Who was Hoyt Sherman?"

I look up at him with what I'm sure is an annoyed expression. "Dude. I'm trying to freaking find out. Shut your cake hole."

Clay laughs. "Sorry, babe," he says, still smiling. I know he was bombarding me with questions on purpose just to irritate me.

I read some of the history about Hoyt Sherman Place. For a short time after Hoyt Sherman's death, it was in fact a Sisters of Mercy hospital. Then, after the hospital closed, it became the Des Moines Women's Club. They added an art gallery, which was the first public art gallery in the city. In 1923, the Women's Club had an auditorium built with 1,400 seats to use for their club activities and programs.

"Can I trust you'll listen?" I ask Clay.

"Of course. So? Is that it?"

"Yeah. For sure." I tell him what I learned.

"Okay, I'm going to pull off at the next exit and put in the address." Clay does so, and then we're back on I-35 heading south. "Now, tell me, who exactly was this Hoyt Sherman?"

"Hmm, let me see." I click on his name to find out more.

"Just hit me with the high points."

"Alright." I skim the information looking for something notable. "He was a lawyer. A banker. Postmaster. Brother to General Sherman. And at the beginning of the Civil War, he was appointed Army Paymaster by President Lincoln in the Union army with the rank of major."

"Wow. Okay. Mr. Sherman had quite the résumé."

"He certainly did."

"I mean, that's like four careers. Could he just not make up his mind or something?"

I snicker. "Who knows?" I scan more of Sherman's bio. "He was also the general manager of the Equitable Life Insurance Company of Iowa."

"Make that five careers."

"Shh," I smile and continue. "He built Hoyt Sherman Place in 1877. He died in 1904. The mansion has a collection of nineteenth and twentieth century paintings on display along with

intricately carved furniture from the seventeenth century. Cool."

"Sounds like we'll get a pretty good history lesson when we get there."

"I think I just gave it to you."

"Smart ass."

I smile and turn the radio back up. "Whiskey in the Jar" by Metallica is playing.

When we pull up to Hoyt Sherman Place a couple of hours later and park, I take in the impressive size of the former home turned hospital turned art gallery and theater. The exterior is not particularly fancy, but it's not exactly dull either. It's a late Victorian style of architecture. It kind of reminds me of a cross between an old brick high school and a church, although none of the windows that I can see are stained glass. The bricks are dark red, and you can tell from the building's details that the architect and builders took pride in their work. Most of the windows on the second level are tall and arched. There are even a couple of Palladian windows sprinkled along the sides.

We get out of the truck and Clay opens the back door to get his backpack.

"What do you need that for?" I ask.

"We're looking for something under a stage, right? Might be dark. If that's the case, we'll need the flashlights, and you never know what else I have in my trusty bag that may come in handy."

"Good thinking."

Walking up to the entrance, I notice how kempt the hedges are. An array of deep purple and hot pink petunias, orange and yellow marigolds, along with white and goldenrod daisies adorn the flower beds near a wrought iron bench.

Clay opens the door and we enter. There's a small reception station a few feet in front of us. A lady with gray hair wearing a red and white gingham shirt sits in a leather desk chair. I smile at her as she greets us.

"Hello," she says. "Welcome to Hoyt Sherman Place. How can I help you today?"

"Hi," I say to her. "We were wondering if we could get a tour of this beautiful place."

"Sure thing. Is it just the two of you or do you have a group? It's a five-dollar charge for each person in your group. A docent will give you a detailed tour, if that's the case."

"No, ma'am," I say to her. "It's just the two of us. What's the charge for that?"

"There's no charge. You're more than welcome to do a self-guided tour at your leisure. Here are a few pamphlets with information about Hoyt Sherman Place. If you don't mind though, would you please sign our guest log?"

I take the pamphlets from her with a smile. "Of course. We'd be happy to sign your register." I jot our names and address in the book.

Clay takes a twenty-dollar bill out of his wallet and slides it into the slot of an acrylic donation box where it stands out among the singles. The lady beams. "Oh, thank you so much. That's very generous of you."

"Not a problem," Clay says. "Thanks for the information. We're looking forward to our tour."

I sidle up alongside Clay, scanning the brochures for a floorplan. "According to the layout of the building, the theater is over here," I say, pointing to its location on the map. "We've got several areas to explore before we get there."

"Let's go then."

As we make our way through the house, I appreciate all the antique furniture. A large dining room table covered with a pale pink tablecloth is set with china and crystal. There's a dark wood buffet that's nearly the length of one wall. A silver tea service is centered on its surface and flanked by elaborate candelabras.

Penetrating further into Hoyt Sherman Place, we pass through the art gallery and check out some of the beauty hanging on the walls. It's quite an eclectic and intriguing collection: paintings of blurry, hazy mountains are juxtaposed with refined, sharp details; the Rocky Mountains and the Grand Canyon painted in intense, bold colors; random objects painted together on canvas, heavy with symbolism, open to interpretation; pale, nude women dappled in sunlight. The variety goes on.

The well-lit room is expansive, with shiny wood floors. Light smells of paint, lavender air freshener, and wood polish permeate around the room. Classical music flows softly from the overhead speakers. I bet if I were wearing heels I could hear them clacking across the floor. We learn from the brochure that the two areas of the gallery, separated by French doors and arched windows, can be rented out for events like wedding receptions or graduation parties.

As we look at all the art, I think I find my favorite piece. Titled *Summer Afternoon*, by Charles A. Cumming, it's a woman in a long-sleeved, pastel pink dress. She's carrying a parasol on a paved path, slightly bending, to touch a stalk of lavender. You can see she's stopping to appreciate the small things in life. A colorful field of grass surrounds the light purple blooms, and I imagine that the next thing she would do is to bend down further and smell the fragrant bunch of lavender, treasuring the simplicity of it. Literally stopping to smell the flowers, admiring how the sun can bring such beautiful things to life.

However, from her expression, she might be worried about something. Anxious. Distressed. This walk of hers could be her way of letting go of her pain, her troubles, just for now. And in this lovely bunch of lavender, she finds peace in the present moment.

"Lynn?" Clay breaks me out of my internal observation. "You ready to move on?"

"Yeah. I just really love this painting. It's beautiful." I snap a picture of it with my phone.

"Check out his last name. Cumming. I'd love to have that as mine instead," he smirks.

"Isn't that already your last name?" I ask with a raised eyebrow.

"Touché." He smiles and grabs my arm, leading us towards the direction of the theater.

When we make our way through the doors of the auditorium, I'm in awe. The space is completely lavish. Almost indescribable in all its rococo elegance. There's a red velvet curtain with a scalloped valance closed on the stage. Matching red velvet seats make up many curved rows, raked all the way to the back and up in the balcony. But it's the ceiling that gets me. Oh, the ceiling. It's so exquisite. A huge semi-circular medallion occupies the center (which looks more like a Victorian fan) with ten beams jutting out from it, some going all the way down to the floor. Each beam is carved with detailed rounded flowers, roses maybe. It kind of looks like a Victorian kraken is taking over the theater.

"Wow," Clay says, looking up at the ceiling.

"I know. This place is gorgeous."

"Where do you want to start?"

"At the stage I guess. Probably some trap doors we can get into and look for something underneath. Since the key is maybe for a padlock, we'll just have to go trial by error. Get ready to enter Hell, babe."

"Hell?"

"That's what they call the area under the stage."

"Hmm. Okay."

Clay and I begin to walk towards the side and climb the steps to get on the stage, but then he stops. "Look," he says, pointing. "There's a black drape curtain hanging off the front of the stage. Maybe it's covering some prop cabinets the key might fit. Let's check there first."

"Good idea."

As Clay pulls the shroud back, we indeed see some locked storage cabinets. We smile at each other. I take the key out and try to unlock the first door. Nothing doing. The key doesn't even fit into the lock.

"I don't think this is going to be it," I say, a little defeated. "If the key won't fit in this lock, it won't fit in any of the rest down the line. Shit."

"Hey, don't get upset yet, Lynn. This is just the first set of cabinets. Maybe all the locks are different. Move down to the next set."

"Okay. You're right."

"I know," he smiles. "Don't get so ahead of yourself. You always do that."

I scoot to the next set of storage doors and they do indeed have a different lock. Clay raises his eyebrows at me in an 'I told you so' look. "Don't even think about saying it," I warn him.

"Wasn't gonna say a thing." He crosses his heart.

I put the key in the other lock, but still nothing happens. We continue down the line to the next two sets of cabinet doors with the same result. "Can I sulk now?" I ask.

"No. We've still got plenty to search around the stage."

"That's true. Let's keep moving and go up the stairs to the right, here," I say pointing to the set of steps leading up to the stage.

We walk up to the side, climb the stairs, and start looking for something all around the stage floor. But everything looks flush. No evident separations in the wood where a door would lift up. Clay walks to the back corner off to stage right.

"Hey. Over here. I found something."

He bends down as I walk over and lifts a small flap of wood about three inches square. Lo and behold, there lies a lock underneath.

"This has to be it."

"You do the honors," he says.

I squat next to the lock and insert the key. It clicks when I turn it and we laugh. "Whew. I was getting nervous."

Clay lifts the storage door and there is a ladder that goes down inside. He opens his backpack, takes out one of the flashlights, and turns it on. "Let me go first and see what we're up against down there. It might be too cluttered for both of us."

"Okay. Be careful."

"Don't worry. I'm up to date on my tetanus shot." He snickers as he makes his descent into Hell.

I give him a few minutes to assess the situation down there before calling out to him. "What do you see?"

"Uh…" his voice echoes up to me. "Not much. Just a bunch of chairs, audio-visual equipment, and shelves with props and boxes. There's also a closet with a bunch of costumes."

"Can I come down?"

"Yeah, babe. It's fine."

I take the ladder to the belly of the stage. Looking around, I see exactly what Clay described. Various sizes of speakers, projection screens, a bunch of folding chairs, and shelves full of boxes fill the room. The air smells musty. Dust particles swirl in the beam of Clay's light.

"Wow, it's bigger down here than I expected."

"Yeah. So, what do you think we're looking for? We don't have another key. Do we?"

"No. There was just one on the keychain."

"Well, let's look around. There's got to be something here. Another clue at the very least."

"Check the boxes on the shelves to your left. I'll go right," I tell him.

"On it. Here, take my light. I'll get the other one out." He hands me his flashlight.

"Thanks."

We scurry to our respective shelving units and I start opening boxes, rummaging through stage props, looking for whatever it is that I know will stand out. Plastic fruit, crocheted doilies, dishes, blankets, artificial flowers, wooden swords, Christmas decorations, and a plethora of other garage sale items that must be used for plays are stored here.

I move to the closet, thinking maybe our prize is in there. I find a bunch of vintage clothing along with a box of wigs and get an idea. This should be fun. I take a colorful, tie-dyed mini dress off the hanger and slip it on over my clothes. It's a little big, but it'll do. Removing a long, black-haired wig out of its box, I tug it on. It reminds me of Cher when she was still married to Sonny. "I Got You Babe" suddenly pops into my head and I start singing it to myself. Stepping back to one of the boxes from the shelf I was looking around in, I dig out a silk daisy and a pair of John Lennon sunglasses to complete my ensemble.

"Heeey, maaan," I say to Clay in my best stoner voice. "Check me out." I hold up my hand in a peace sign.

Clay starts cracking up. "What the hell are you doing?" He's still laughing. "You're supposed to be looking for our treasure from Aunt Mitzi," he says, shaking his head at me.

"Who says this isn't what we're meant to find? Maybe she just wanted us to play dress-up. I used to do that all the time at her house with the old clothes from the closet under the stairs. Come here, I've got something for you."

"I'm not playing your reindeer games."

"Come on, Clay. Don't be a buzzkill. Get your ass over here."

He sighs and walks over to me, taking the pinstripe suit jacket and fedora I'm holding. Putting them on he says, "If I'm doing this, I'm doing it right. Hold on." He walks back over to his set of shelves, hunts around, and comes back with a fake Tommy gun. "Now we're talkin'."

"Nice touch. You make a hot gangster, babe."

"Do I?"

"Mmm hmm."

"Should I make you an offer you can't refuse?" he asks in the voice of Marlon Brando's Vito Corleone from *The Godfather*.

I laugh. "Um, not here and not now. But yeah. Later for sure."

He puts the gun down and wraps his arms around me. Squeezing my butt he says, "You make for one sexy hippie."

"Really?"

"Yep. Even in these baggy clothes."

"How is that sexy then?"

"Because I know what's underneath all those layers." He kisses me and I start to turn warm.

"Okay, we need to stop," I say, lightly pushing him away. "We can't do this here, Clay."

"Why not? Maybe *this* is what Aunt Mitzi had in mind for us." His hand travels up my layers of clothes.

"I doubt that," I say laughing. "Come on, let's keep looking."

"Who's the buzzkill now?" he asks, raising an eyebrow at me with a smirk.

"I should have known you'd turn this into a sex thing," I laugh.

"Well, I'm a guy. What do you expect? Besides, we've never tried role play."

"Never needed to." I give him a wink.

He gives me another quick kiss and turns back to the closet. "What else is in here?"

"Just more costumes I think."

Clay directs his light onto the top rack of the closet and squints his eyes. "Hmmm..."

"What is it?" I ask.

He reaches all the way to the back of the shelf and comes out with a lock box. The letter 'S' is engraved into the top.

"Well, well, well. What do we have here?" he asks with amusement.

"Oh my god. Do you think that's it?"

"Probably. I mean, it has our initial on it, plus it's a combination lock. No key required."

I look at the lock. It needs four numbers to open it.

"We could be here forever trying to figure out the combo."

"Is there maybe something in the clue that might give us an idea? Like a hint inside the clue that alludes to a set of numbers?"

I pull the clue sheet out of my purse and read it again. "No. I don't think so."

"Let's think then. It's four digits. Maybe her birthday?"

"July seventeenth. Zero, seven, one, seven."

Clay tries the numbers, but it doesn't unlock.

"What about the year she was born?"

"Maybe. That would be 1924."

Clay attempts the new set of numbers. "One, nine, two, four." He jiggles the opening. "Nope. Not it."

"Okay, try the year she and Uncle Sid got married. That's 1943."

"One, nine, four, three." Nothing. "Your birthday?" Clay tries zero, two, one, six. Still nothing.

"Try five, one, five, one."

"Why?"

"Fifty-one keychains."

"Oh, good thinking." He tries the numbers and the lock still doesn't open. "Shit. What other four number combos are significant that she knew we'd be able to guess?"

"Hmm…" I think to myself. "Oh! Try the year *we* got married."

"One, nine, nine, one."

It pops open and I let out a little squeal.

"What's in it?" I ask as Clay lifts the lid.

CHAPTER 18

"WHAT IN THE ever-loving…" Clay trails off.

I peer into the box and see two masquerade masks. They're black with silver filigree. The more feminine one is lacy with rhinestones. Small bottles of massage oil and bubble bath are also included in the box. And a cassette tape. That's right… a cassette tape.

I start laughing out loud. "What kind of kinky shit was Aunt Mitzi into?"

"I don't want to know," Clay deadpans.

"Do you see a note or envelope anywhere in there?"

Clay hands me the masks and says, "Nope."

"Shit," I huff. "And just what the hell are we going to do with a cassette tape?"

"That's probably where we'll find our message."

This does not placate me. "Thanks, Captain Obvious."

"You're welcome, babe." He smiles.

"What I don't know is how we'll be able to play it since we don't have one in the truck. They quit putting cassette players in cars back in the late nineties. Or early two-thousands."

"That's not true," Clay says. "The last car with a factory installed tape deck was the 2010 Lexus SC 430."

"Of course you would know that." I roll my eyes.

"Of course I would," Clay beams.

"Maybe we'll find a tape player down here," I say. "Keep looking around."

We search the shelves and come up short. I'm surprised there's not one in all this thrift store merchandise. Not even an oversized jambox. They must have never put on a play that required a cassette deck as a prop.

"Let's head back up," Clay says. "It's kind of dank down here. I feel like I need to — *achoo!* — sneeze," he chuckles.

"God bless you," I say with a sympathetic smile. "Okay, let's go."

"Thank you." He sniffles and sneezes again.

We climb the ladder back up to the stage. As he is locking up the trap door, I realize we are still in costume.

"Um, Clay, do you notice anything wrong with this picture?" He looks up at me and smiles.

"Shit. Well, let's make the most of the stage while we're still dressed in costumes, shall we?"

I laugh. "Our characters don't really go together. A roaring twenties gangster and a summer of love hippie chick?"

He stands up and walks to center stage, stretching his arms out. "Maybe one of us came here on a time machine."

"Oooh, I like where you're going with that."

He turns around in a full circle with a smile, dips his head down, then looks up at me with a serious face. He appears to be in character now.

Clay tips his hat at me and says in his best New York gangster accent, "Excuse me, miss. I seem to be a little jingle-brained."

"Jingle-brained?"

"Confused. I'm lost. What kind of get-up is that? You work in a candy factory or somethin'?" He points to my kaleidoscopic outfit.

I laugh. "No. It's called tie-dye. It's hip. Why? Do you dig it?"

"Do I *dig* it?" He laughs.

"Yeah, man."

"I don't know what that means. What's your name, doll?"

"My given name is Jane, but I go by Moon Sparkle now. What's your name?"

"John. But I'm better known as Johnny Salami."

I can't help it; I lose it. A loud laugh escapes me, and I shake my head. "Well, Mr. Salami. That's quite a moniker you've got there. How did you get that nickname?"

"How do you think?" He winks. "Ya know how dey call bald guys 'Curly'?"

"Yeah."

"It ain't like dat."

"Hmm. Maybe you can show me sometime."

"Okay, toots, but only if you help me hide it afterward."

I crack up again. "Deal." We both smile.

He looks around the stage with a scowl on his face. "Say, doll, what is dis place?"

"This is Woodstock."

"What's a Woodstock?"

"A music festival. I'm here with about four hundred thousand of my closest friends, celebrating peace, love, and music." I raise my two fingers in the peace sign. "Where did you say you were going?"

"I didn't."

"Oh. Right. Well, where are you headed?"

"I need to get to the city."

"New York City?"

"Yeah."

"It's about two hours south of here."

"What? How da hell I get upstate?"

"Maybe you're having a bad trip. Dropped too much acid and hitched a ride up here with some of my fellow music lovers. Or maybe I'm the one having a bad trip."

"A bad trip? Dropped acid? Dollface, I don't get your lingo."

"What do you mean you don't get it? Have you had a lobotomy or something?"

"Nobody's put the icepick up my eye. Okay, dish, this is going to sound crazy, but what year is it?"

I laugh. "What *year*? It's 1969."

Clay makes an overly dramatic surprised face and reaches into his jacket. When his hand comes out, it's shaped into a gun, and he points it at me. "Tell it to Sweeny, toots. Stop with the chewing gum. Just wait until I call for my chopper squad. You might be a looker with great gams, but I don't like how you're giving me the applesauce. No broad is worth this."

"Whoa, dude. Chill out, man." I put my hands in the air. "First of all, I don't get your lingo either. No idea what you just said. But we can figure this situation out. I can help you. Please put your gun down."

"No way, doll. Without my piece, you've got me behind the eight ball."

"What does that mean?" I ask.

"In a tight spot," he says with a smile. "But if you'd be willing to accompany me to the city, I'll forget about all this craziness. Put everything back to copacetic." He puts his 'gun' back in his jacket and walks towards me. Brushing my cheek with the back of his fingers he says, "I think you're the cat's pajamas."

I burst out laughing. "The cat's pajamas? Really, Clay?"

"Who's Clay? And yeah, the cat's pajamas. The bee's knees."

I snicker. "Well, I think you're very groovy. Why don't we get out of here and you can show me why they call you Johnny Salami."

"Now that's an offer I can't refuse," he says with a smile as his hand snakes down to my thigh, lifting the hem of my dress.

"Aaaand scene." I dip my head down and swipe my hand in front of my face as I remove Clay's wandering arm with my other hand.

Clay laughs and kisses me. "That was fun, Miss Moon Sparkle. Let's get back down there and put these costumes back in the closet where they belong."

"Good idea."

As Clay reopens the trap door, an older lady comes into the theater.

"What's going on here?" she asks. "Can I help you with something? Was that storage unlocked? What are you doing?"

"Uh… hi… we, uh…." I stammer.

"We were just looking for something, but we found it," Clay says, rescuing me.

"Something you lost here?" she asks.

"Not exactly. My aunt, well, she sent us here to retrieve something."

"Your aunt?" She crinkles her face up in confusion, then her expression changes to recognition. "Wait a minute. Her name wouldn't happen to be Mitzi Santini, would it?"

"Yes," I say smiling. "Well, it was. She died a couple of months back."

"Right. I'd heard about that. I'm so sorry for your loss. She was a fantastic lady."

"She was."

"I was unable to make her funeral." She looks sad for a second, but then smiles at me. "You know, you could've just told the front desk who you were. Somebody would've come gotten me and I could have taken you straight here."

"We like to see what we can get away with," Clay says a little pompously.

"Ah. Rebels. I love it."

"It makes the trip that much more exciting," I say. "So, you knew Aunt Mitzi?"

"I did. We met decades ago when my husband and I were on our honeymoon and she and Sid were vacationing in Italy. We were staying in the same hotel and struck up a conversation in the hotel bar one night. The four of us became fast friends. They would come up here a couple times a year to visit. You're Lynn, right? And Clay?"

"Yes, ma'am," Clay says.

"I'm Barbara. Pleasure to meet you both."

"Same here," I say. "So, you know about the box then? I assume you had something to do with hiding it on the shelf in the closet down there," I point to the opened door on the stage.

"Yes, dear. I did," she smiles. "I'm glad you found it. It's been on that shelf a few years. On one of Mitzi and Sid's visits, they were just starting to put the treasure hunt together for you and I offered to store one of your clues here. They didn't even ask but were so delighted I had volunteered. I knew it would be safe down there, no matter what they decided to save for you, or when they decided to leave it. Sadly, Sid died before they got a chance to come drop it off. She made a trip not long after his death. The box remained safe. As you seem to have figured out," she gestures to our costumes, "nothing gets thrown out of Hell."

I chuckle. "That's so sweet. Thank you for that. Do you happen to have a cassette player we could borrow? She left us a tape in the box that I assume has an explanation of the other contents we found inside."

"No, I'm sorry, we don't have one here. Maybe you can try Goodwill or a thrift store or something. Surely they would have one you could buy for pretty cheap."

"That's a good idea. Thank you so much for all your help in keeping the box safe for us." I take off the costume, wig, and accessories, stripping back down to my shorts and t-shirt. I hand the garb to Clay. "Would you bring these back down for me? I'll wait here with Mrs. Barbara."

"Sure thing, love."

I turn back to Barbara. "I'm sorry if we were making a lot of noise. We didn't mean to disturb anybody. We were just having fun with the props we found downstairs."

"Oh, nonsense. It's fine." She waves a hand in dismissal. "I'm just pleased to finally meet you. Wasn't sure I'd be around for this. I suppose if I hadn't walked by the security room and saw you on one of the screens, I would have missed out on this all together."

"Oh my goodness," I smile sheepishly. I can feel my face turning red as she points to the surveillance cameras in the corners of the theater.

"You would've probably been caught sooner if the guard hadn't gone to lunch yet." She smiles.

Clay pops back up onto the stage and locks the door, making sure it's secured. "Everything is as we found it. All back in order."

"Thank you, son. I appreciate that."

"No problem. We wouldn't have left a mess even if you hadn't caught us," he smiles.

"Well," I say, "Thanks for all your help and information. I'm glad we ran into you. Or, got caught by you, rather."

Barbara chuckles. "No worries. What do you kids say these days? 'It's all good.'? So, yeah. It's all good. Happy to help."

"Well, Lynn, are you ready to go?"

"Sure." I walk over to Barbara and give her a hug. "So nice to meet you. Thanks again for everything."

"Sure thing," she says, as I let go of her.

Clay gives her a hug as well. "Are you going to walk back with us?"

"No. I think while I'm here I'll grab a few light bulbs from the backstage storage cabinets to bring to the front. There are a couple around the lobby that need changing out."

"Alright. Thanks for not arresting us," he smiles, and then we exit the theater.

Clay puts his backpack in the backseat, shuts the door and climbs into the front.

"We need to find out where we're going next. I'm hungry though. My pancakes from breakfast went down a long time ago. Let's find somewhere to eat a late lunch and figure out the next clue," I tell him.

"Good plan." Clay picks up his phone and searches for somewhere to eat. "Oh my god, babe. I found the perfect place for us."

"Do tell."

"Zombie Burger."

"I'm sorry, I must have misunderstood you. Did you say something about zombies? You know I hate horror stuff. And you know what zombies eat."

"C'mon, Lynn. It's a restaurant. I'm sure it's family friendly. I can't find a place called Zombie Burger and not go there. It would be like you finding a restaurant that specializes in a disco theme and me holding you back from that."

I sigh. "Okay. You're right. I'm sure it will be fun."

"That's the spirit. Pun intended."

"Your puns are always intended. Do you think there are any vegetarian zombies?"

He chuckles and punches the address into the navigation system. "Oh cool, it's only seven minutes away."

"Good, because I'm starving."

When we arrive at the restaurant, I notice several planters with zombie heads and arms sticking out, giving them the appearance of crawling out of the plant boxes. There's also a garden gnome that's a little creepy, with red eyes, bad teeth, and blood streaking down his ceramic white beard. I shake my head, but Clay is in heaven, or wherever zombies go.

When we get inside and sit down at a table, a waiter comes over and welcomes us with a smile and a glass of water for each of us. "Hi, guys. Welcome to Zombie Burger. I'm Kirk." He gives us menus. "I'll be back shortly to take your orders."

"Thanks, man," Clay says.

I look up and down the columns at the many choices of burgers, snickering at some of the names. For instance, there's the East Village of the Damned, Juan of the Dead, and Helldorado just to name a few. Most of the burger names are a play on some sort of horror movie or television title, character, or scary stuff in general.

"What are you thinking about ordering?" I ask Clay.

"Definitely The Walking Ched."

"I knew it." I smile. The Walking Ched burger has a breaded, deep-fried macaroni and cheese bun. The burger itself is loaded with bacon, cheddar cheese, caramelized onions, plus macaroni and cheese. And we all know how much Clay loves his mac and cheese.

"What about you?" he asks.

"I'm going with The Poultrygeist." You guessed it. I'm having a chicken sandwich.

"These names are killing me," Clay smiles.

I roll my eyes. "Like a zombie?"

"Of course," he chuckles. "My love of puns and all things horror combined in one place. How much better can it get?" He takes a sip of his water and flips to the back of the menu. "Hmm… no ladyfingers in the dessert section. Seems like a missed opportunity. Have you looked at the drink menu?"

"I'm looking now. What are you getting?"

"Just based on the name, I'm going with the Red Death. It'll probably be a little too sweet for my taste with the peach schnapps, sloe gin, triple-sec, and orange juice. But I'm a fan of vodka and Southern Comfort, so we'll see. You?"

"I'm going to get The Socket. I don't think I've ever had blueberry vodka before, but it sounds good. Combined with strawberry purée, lime, and soda water, it sounds like something I would enjoy."

"I think that's a good choice for you. Definitely a 'Lynn' drink."

Kirk comes back and we give him our orders. "All great choices," he says. "You're gonna love The Walking Ched."

"I'm sure I will," Clay says as Kirk takes our menus.

"You know I'm going to have to try a bite of that when it gets here," I tell my husband.

"Sure, love."

Clay and I scan the décor of the restaurant. I would call it macabre chic. There are life-size zombie figures dressed in tattered clothes; a long, framed mural of a cityscape with the undead roaming around; a sign that says, 'Keep Calm and Eat Brains;' a baseball bat wrapped with barbed wire like *The Walking Dead* character Negan's 'Lucille;' framed movie posters that have been zombified and their names changed to *Toy Gory, Breakfast is Tiffany, Indiana Bones, Deadward Scissorhands*, and more.

"What's your favorite decoration?" I ask Clay.

"It has to be the wicker casket."

"What? Where?"

He points over my shoulder and above my head. "Looks like the real deal."

"No wonder I missed it," I say as I turn my head around and look up. "Holy crap. Did they really use those to bury people in?"

"No. I mean maybe some people did, but traditionally, they were used in the nineteenth century for viewings, before the bodies were transferred to wooden coffins and buried. They were also commonly used during the Civil War because they were easy to move and didn't cost as much to produce as the wooden ones."

"Wow. Very interesting. How do you know all that?"

"You do know who you're married to, right? I research shit like that for fun."

"Right. I should have known."

Kirk brings our food and drinks to the table. Clay's burger is massive and looks freaking delicious. My chicken sandwich looks good too, but I almost want to trade mine for Clay's.

"Enjoy your meal, guys. Can I get you anything else? Do you have any questions about anything?"

"Yeah," Clay says, "I have a question."

"Okay."

"Is that an authentic wicker casket?" Clay points to the object in question.

"It sure is. The owner is very proud of it. It's one of his favorite acquisitions."

"It's great. A perfect addition to this awesome place." Clay says. "And now I'm going to take down this feast of mac and cheese before me."

"Alright," Kirk laughs, "I'll leave you to it then."

Clay takes a bite of his gargantuan burger and moans. "Sweet Jesus," he says after he swallows it down. "That is one fantastic fucking cheeseburger."

"Okay, give me a bite."

"You haven't even tried yours yet," he snickers.

"Just gimme a bite, Clay."

"Alright, babe. Jeez. Impatient much?"

He holds it in front of my face, but I can only stare at it. "Whoa. It's really big. I don't know if I can get my mouth around it."

Clay bursts out laughing. "Well, you never had problems with putting your mouth around big things before." He winks at me.

"Oh my god. You're such a guy."

"That I am, babe. That I am. And by the way, that's what she said. Now, do you want a bite or not?"

"Can you cut me a piece?"

He stares at me blankly. "Um… sure. That's not how you do it, but okay."

I take a bite of my chicken sandwich as Clay cuts me a little slice of his heavenly burger and puts it on my plate. "Mmmm, my chicken is really good. The simplicity of the pickle, lettuce, and mayo on this delicious bread is perfection."

"Sounds boring," Clay says as he takes another bite of his burger, eyes closed, nearly looking like he's making love to it.

He opens his eyes and I shake my head at him. He winks at me playfully as I take a sip of my water. I need to cleanse my palate so I can taste The Walking Ched. "Oh wow. That is scrumptious."

"Told ya. How's your drink?"

I try it and it's tasty. "Love it. It's refreshing. And yours?"

"Not bad. A little too sweet for me, as I suspected it would be, but it's alright. You may have to finish it for me."

"That won't be a problem."

"Okay," Clay says after swallowing another bite, "You ready to figure out the next clue? Did you bring the sheet in?"

"Yep. It stays in my purse." I take it out and read clue number thirty-three. "It says, 'You're off to the state that brought us Kool-Aid, Fred Astaire, and Arbor Day. Here's to hoping you enjoy what's coming your way. There's a place in the capital that is state of the art. Present the key to gain access to something that's close to my heart.' Well that sounds sweet."

"Yeah. And a little vague. Any idea where we're going?"

"Not based on the clue. But I'm guessing Nebraska just by our proximity. Since north of us is Minnesota, east is Illinois, and south is Missouri. All of which we've been to already. That leaves Nebraska to the west."

"Makes sense," Clay says. "It's interesting that Aunt Mitzi threw Kool-Aid into the mix," he smirks. I roll my eyes and he laughs.

"Do you think you could go one day without making a pun?"

"Maybe if I tried. Seriously though, did you know Kool-Aid was invented in Nebraska? I didn't."

"No, I didn't know that either. Apparently, Fred Astaire was born in Nebraska and Arbor Day was established there as well. She's very cryptic on the rest of the clue though. Except for saying something about the capital city. That's Lincoln, right?"

"Right."

"But that's it. Just that there's some place in Lincoln that's close to her heart. Nothing else. How are we going to figure out where to go exactly?"

"We might not be able to decipher that part until we get the key once we get back into the truck."

"That's true. Some of the keychains have been more of a clue than the actual clue itself. So I guess we're at a standstill till we finish eating."

"I suppose we are."

"I don't want to rush with my food, but I'm anxious now."

"Babe, the key isn't going anywhere. It'll be fine. Take your time. Enjoy your chicken sandwich. I'm not gonna scarf my lunch down just to get back to the truck a little sooner. I'm going to savor this monster cheeseburger."

"Okay, fair enough."

Clay looks around the restaurant a bit more and spots a section of t-shirts hanging on the wall. "Oh, I have to check those out and get one before we leave." He points at the selection.

"Have at it."

After we're done eating, I finish off Clay's drink while he picks out a shirt. He decides on a black and white baseball tee that says 'Cell Block Z' on the front. He also picks out a pint glass with the restaurant's logo on it.

"Now we'll each have a pint glass that we like," he says. "Yours from the Keys Café and mine from here." He smiles.

"Love that for us."

Clay pays the bill and we head back to the truck to figure out our exact next destination.

CHAPTER 19

CLAY STARTS THE truck to cool it off while I search through the key box and look for the one labeled with the number 33 on it. The key itself is strange. I remember seeing this one when we first found the box of keys in the stairs. It looks like a wind-up toy key. There are no protrusions or notches on the blade. The shaft is rounded and hollow, but nearly flat at the tip. The bow of the key is odd, almost heart-shaped, with an open hexagon in one of the wings of the head. Like a small wrench.

"What is this?" I ask Clay. "It looks like some kind of tool or something."

He removes the key from my hand. "It's a roller skate key. The wrench part was used to tighten the axle nuts on the wheels of old-fashioned skates. The kind you had to fit onto your shoes and adjust to fit your feet."

"Oh yeah. The skate keys I've seen before looked a little different than this. So what do you think the key means for us? We can't open a pair of roller skates."

"Well, the place we're headed has to have something to do with skates, seeing as how the key fob is a three-dimensional bejeweled roller skate."

I take the key from Clay and examine the keychain ornament. It's quite beautiful. Rose gold with pink rhinestones all over the skate. It reminds me of my childhood. "I used to love to go roller skating at Leo's Rollerland back in the day. Did you ever go?"

"Yeah. It was the place to pick up chicks in junior high."

"You were 'picking up chicks' in seventh grade, Clay?"

"You know what I mean. Flirting and all that. It's not like I brought them back to my parents' house and banged them at that age. Jeez." He rolls his eyes and laughs.

"I know, it's just the way you said it. Like you were some kind of pre-teen playboy."

"I was." He smiles proudly.

"Whatever." I shake my head and chuckle. "I wonder if we ever saw each other."

"If we did, I doubt I looked twice at you," Clay smirks.

I smack him. "You're such an ass."

"I'm being serious." He rubs his bicep where I struck him. "Sheesh, you sure pack a punch for a small thing."

"Don't you forget it." I point at him, but then smile and wink.

"Anyway, like I was saying… we're three years apart. Which means nothing now, but I doubt I was twelve checking out a nine-year-old."

"Touché. Okay, you got me there. I wasn't even thinking about boys at that age, so I doubt I would have looked twice at you either. By the time Annie and I discovered boys, you had probably gotten your license and moved on from the roller rink."

"Yep. By that time, I was trying to pick up chicks at Cortana Mall."

I snicker. "I loved the mall. Annie and I would spend hours there on the weekends during high school. Times were so much simpler back then. My main concern while we were at the mall was what I was going to order from Taco Bell and trying not to get caught looking at the naughty stuff in Spencer's."

Clay cracks up laughing. "Oh my god, that's hilarious. I can picture you as a modest teenager, trying to hide the fact that you were looking at scantily clad men on greeting cards and shit." He continues chuckling.

I start laughing too. "It was the first time I ever saw a vibrator."

Clay guffaws. "You mean 'personal relaxation device.' Isn't that how they marketed them?"

"Yeah, I believe so. Something like that. I was so naïve and innocent. Everything always made me blush, but there was something so daring about looking at all that salacious stuff. It gave me a strange air of confidence. Like, in a way, I knew it was wrong, but it couldn't be wrong, because it was there for sale. Legally. It had to be okay. But it was taboo."

"The angel and devil on your shoulders."

"Exactly."

"Oh, to be that young again. I'd never go back though. I'm perfectly happy where I am in life."

"Me too, babe."

"Okay, that was a fun trip down memory lane. But let's get back to the task at hand and try to figure this clue out now," Clay says.

"Yeah, let's do that."

"Try searching for skating in Lincoln, Nebraska and see what comes up."

"Good idea." I look online and smile at what I see. "Well, besides several places to actually go roller skating and ice skating, there's also the National Museum of Roller Skating."

"I'd say that's our destination considering we have ourselves an antique skate key."

"Well, let's roll."

"No pun intended?"

"Oh my gosh, I didn't even realize," I laugh.

"Those are the best kinds." Clay puts the museum into the navigation system. We head out of the Zombie Burger parking lot and put Des Moines behind us.

"Cool, only three hours. Less than I thought. We might be kind of tired when we get there though. Why don't we get a room tonight and head to the skate museum first thing tomorrow?"

"Sounds good, love."

I book us a room online and then something dawns on me. "I've got the perfect song for us right now."

"Hit me with it."

I search my phone and find it. "Brand New Key" by Melanie starts.

"Oh, I remember this song," Clay says. "It's a little too sweet and sugary for my taste, but I definitely remember it. My mom sang it a lot."

"Yeah, mine too. I think she had the LP."

"After this song is over, I'm picking something. That's enough bubble-gum pop music for me today."

"Alright. Fair enough. You know, a lot of people thought this song was a sexual innuendo. Because of the key and lock. Never made sense to me though because she never sang anything about inserting any keys into locks or keyholes."

"Huh… interesting. Maybe *she* was the pair of roller skates, the keyhole, if you will."

"Hmm. Now *that's* interesting. But, it turns out she wrote it because, well, she was a vegetarian."

"Say what now?"

I chuckle. "One time when she drove by a McDonald's, the smell of the frying burgers in the air made her nostalgic for her childhood. And roller skating."

"Cool. How do you know that?"

"You look up zombies for fun, I look up meanings to songs."

We drive for a few more minutes and as soon the song is finished, Clay gives me his phone to switch the connection from mine to his so his music can now play through the speakers. He hits a button on his playlist and "Walk This Way" by Aerosmith begins.

As Clay sings the part before the chorus, I think I hear him singing the wrong words and I crack up.

"What's so funny?" he asks.

"What were you just singing? Say the words you just sang."

"What? Why?"

"Just do it."

"Okay, fine. Hey diddle diddle with your titty in the middle of—"

Yep, I crack up again. "Oh my god, Clay. How have you gone all this time getting away with singing those words?" I can't stop laughing.

"Those are the words. What am I singing wrong?" He gives me a smile like he knows he's right.

"It's not 'with your *titty* in the middle.' They wouldn't have played that on the radio. It's 'kitty.' Like a cat. Like the p-word. How many women have you seen with middle titties?"

Clay's face is blank. He shakes his head and scrubs his face with his hand. "Holy shit," he's laughing now too. "That makes so much more fucking sense. I just… I've just sung it that way since I was a kid and never thought about it. My mind is officially blown. Cyclops tit woman."

"That sounds like a sci-fi hero name."

Clay laughs again and shakes his head. "Man, I feel like such an idiot."

"Nah. Don't. I get it. There's a bunch of songs that I got wrong when I was younger, but as I got older, I realized what the actual lyrics were. Sometimes I still sing the wrong lyrics out of habit though. But it's still funny as hell, hearing you sing about a cyclops tit."

"You know, there was that chick in *Total Recall* that had a titty in the middle."

"Yeah, but she had three boobs. Not one. She wasn't a cyclops tit woman. She was a triclops tit woman."

"True. There's plenty of misheard lyrics."

"Yeah. There's even a word for it: mondegreen."

"What?"

I nod. "Mmm hmm. Mondegreen. Something about this writer whose mother used to read poetry to her as a child. One of the lines in the poem was 'Laid him on the green,' but she thought her mom was saying 'Lady Mondegreen.' So, as an adult, she came up with the term 'mondegreen' for misheard lyrics and phrases."

"You are just a fountain of knowledge today."

"I'd be a good 'phone a friend' for *Who Wants to Be a Millionaire?*"

"That you would. So, tell me some of your mondegreens, or at least some you've heard about. Help me feel better."

"Well, let's see." I take his phone and search for "Every Breath You Take" by The Police and start playing it. "Okay. You know the part where he sings about how his poor heart aches?"

"Yeah."

"Annie's brother used to sing it, 'I'm a pool hall ace.'"

Clay cracks up. "That's classic. Give me some more."

I pull up "Beast of Burden" by The Rolling Stones and as soon as the lyrics start, I sing, "I'll never leave your pizza burnin'."

Clay laughs so hard. "Shit, that's better than the pool hall ace. Who thought that's what it said?"

"Cecilia."

Laughing, he says, "Man, I can't wait to tease her about that."

"If you do, I'll tell her about your titty in the middle."

"That's fair," he laughs. "Because I'm totally going to give her shit about leaving pizza burning. I mean, the lyrics are in the freaking title of the song. How could she get that wrong?"

"I know, right?" I laugh. "But I guess you don't really make that connection when you're a kid."

"Okay, so now tell me some of yours. I know you must have some that you've gotten wrong yourself."

"Let me think." I run through song lyrics in my head that I know I've gotten wrong before. "Alright, I've got one." I play "Jet Airliner" by The Steve Miller Band. "Don't laugh."

"Oh, I already know I am, just by you saying that."

"I used to think he was singing, 'Big ol' Jed had a light on.'"

Clay throws his head back in laughter. "That's fucking hilarious. But again, it's the title of the song."

"Yeah, but in my defense, Steve Miller adds an extra syllable to the word 'airliner.' It totally threw me off."

He chuckles and shakes his head. "Okay, I can see that. I suppose I'll let that one slide. But still, that's a good one. What else?"

I pull up "Keep It Comin' Love" by KC and The Sunshine Band. "Remember this song?"

"Yeah."

"I used to think it was 'Keep It Common Law' when I was little."

Clay cracks up yet again. "Did you have commitment issues as a child? Proponent of de facto relationships?"

"I didn't even know what 'common law' was," I snicker. "I just thought that's what they were singing. Clearly I'm not opposed to legal marriage. But I don't think Louisiana even recognizes common law marriage."

"No, it doesn't."

We drive for a little while longer before Clay needs to pull off and fill up with gas.

"You want to go in and get us some snacks while I fill up?" he asks.

"By myself?" I feel a flash of anxiety wash over me.

"Shit. Sorry. I'll go with you."

"No, no. You know what? It's okay. I'll be fine."

"Are you sure?"

"Yeah, Clay. Yeah. I need to do this. I can do this." I take a deep breath. "Anything in particular you want?"

"Lynn, wait. I'll just—"

"No, Clay. I'm doing this. Tell me what you want to snack on."

"Okay. Um, something chocolatey, with nuts, caramel, and nougat."

"You literally just described a Snickers bar."

"Perfect. King size. Three of them. Please. And a large fountain Dr. Pepper with lots of ice."

"Three king size Snickers bars? You must be feeling pretty grumpy."

"No," he laughs. "Just stock up on them for me. I'll eat one now, one later, and one later than that."

"Alrighty then."

I walk towards the door of the station, a bit apprehensive. I need to push the flashbacks of being abducted from a gas station parking lot out of my mind. That was a fluke circumstance, and it won't happen again. I know Clay would've come with me, but I need to do this on my own. I look over my shoulder at my husband and see that he's watching me closely. That reassures me.

CLAY

I keep a sharp eye on Lynn as she heads towards the entrance. I almost went inside with her anyway, but I know that there's nobody else after her and the situation with her kidnapping was an isolated incident. Besides, lightning doesn't strike the same place twice, right? She'll be okay. She's got this. Lynn needs to rebuild her confidence. She won't be long. I scan the parking lot for anything peculiar just to be on the safe side. Nothing seems amiss. Just an old Pontiac Sunbird at the pump across from the one I'm using. When the gas tank of the truck is finally full, Lynn still isn't back. What the hell is taking her so long? I'm going in. No, I need to let her do this so she won't associate gas stations with bad memories. I wait another minute and still no Lynn. Fuck this shit, I'm going in.

LYNN

I enter the store and see that there isn't anybody in line, so I won't be long. I gather Clay's Snickers bars along with a few varieties of trail mix, Pringles, and beef jerky. I then head to the drink station to get his Dr. Pepper and a Diet Coke for me.

There's a little girl about six years old in the aisle with her mom near the bread and I hear her ask her mother if she can have an Icee. The mom tells her no, because she can't afford anything extra. She only has enough money for a quarter tank of gas, a pack of lunchmeat, and a loaf of bread. I look out of the window and see an old beat-up car that looks like it's on its last legs, with a missing hubcap and peeling paint. The battered Pontiac is parked near the pump next to our truck. I feel the need to say something, hoping I'm not overstepping.

"Excuse me, miss." She looks up at me with tired eyes, but doesn't say anything. "I couldn't help but overhear you. I would love to buy you and your daughter a few things, if you would let me. And fill your car up with gas."

She's speechless as her eyes begin to fill. "Um…" She smiles. "I… I… really?"

"Yes, really. Please. Let me help you."

"Wow. Okay. Thank you. Thank you so much." She sniffles and wipes at her tears. "This has never happened to me before. And you have no idea how much I could use the help right now. I appreciate it so much. Before we left our house, I prayed that God would let me get here without running out of gas, and somehow send me a reprieve, and here you are. An angel in the flesh."

"Oh, I don't know about the angel part," I chuckle.

"Can I get a cherry Icee?" the little girl asks me.

"Sure," I say with a smile, at the same time her mom tells her 'No.' "Please, I'd love to, if it's okay with you of course," I tell the lady. She nods as another tear falls down her face. I look at her daughter. "Cherry is my favorite flavor too." She beams at me with a gap-toothed grin.

"We like the same stuff," she says. "What's your name? My mommy is Janelle and I'm Amelia. I'm seven. I just lost my two front teeth."

"Hi, Amelia. I'm Lynn. It's nice to meet you." I put out my hand for her to shake, and she does so enthusiastically. "I'll be right back," I tell her.

I walk to the front counter and ask the clerk if it's okay for me to leave my items with him for a minute. He says it's fine. I grab two of those hand-held grocery baskets and give one to Janelle. "Fill this up with whatever you want. My treat."

"Oh no, that's too much. I just need…"

"Fill it," I say with lightheartedness. "Come on, Janelle. Please. I've got a few things I need to get as well. I'll meet you at the counter."

"Thank you," she says, as she reluctantly takes the basket from me and heads to the back where the refrigerated section is. She puts in a half gallon of milk and some other perishables.

I take the other basket and begin filling it for her with things like a jug of laundry detergent, toiletries, coffee, and snacks. Then I proceed to get Amelia her cherry Icee.

About that time, I hear the bell chime at the door as Clay comes frantically rushing in. I look over at him and when he sees me, his face calms and his body relaxes. He walks over to me and rubs my shoulders. "Jesus, Lynn, what's taking so long? I was getting worried."

"Sorry. I just wanted to help this lady and her little girl. We're filling their car up too."

"Oh. Okay. You're getting an Icee? You haven't had one of those in years."

"It's not for me. It's for Amelia." I nod towards the back of the store where Amelia and Janelle are still putting food items in the basket.

"Gotcha." He leans into my ear and whispers, "Are they in trouble? Stranded or something?"

"No, just having a run of bad luck. I offered to buy her some groceries and fill her car up."

"That's so sweet of you, love." Clay takes his wallet out and sifts through it, seeing how much money he has on him. He only has about eighty-five dollars in cash so he gets his bank card out, winks at me, and walks over to the ATM. I turn back to the Icee machine and finish my task of fixing Amelia her cherry-flavored treat.

A few seconds later, the seven-year-old runs over to me. "We're finished! Mommy let me get some of my favorite kind of cheese."

"Excellent," I smile down at her. "Here's your Icee."

She takes it from me with a sparkle in her eye as she gushes with glee and slurps some up the straw. "Mmmm. Thank you. This is my favorite drink in the whole wide world."

"You're so welcome. I love them too. Come on, let's get back to your mom." I walk her over to the counter where we meet her mother. Clay meets us there as well.

"Hello," he says to her.

"Hi," she says sheepishly.

"This is my husband, Clay."

"Nice to meet you. I'm Janelle."

"And I'm Amelia. I'm seven and I just lost my two front teeth." She smiles her toothless smile at Clay.

Clay laughs. "Well, it's a pleasure to meet you both, Amelia and Janelle."

"Did you thank Mrs. Lynn for the Icee?"

"She sure did," I say, and Amelia nods her head as she takes another sip through the straw.

We put the baskets on the counter and the clerk starts ringing everything up.

"I can't tell you how much I appreciate this," Janelle says, looking between Clay and me.

"No sweat," he tells her. "It's our pleasure."

"So, Amelia and I have two angels today. Not just one. It's refreshing to know that there are still good people in the world." She smiles.

I blush a little. "We're just doing what anybody else would do if they could."

"I'd nearly lost faith in humanity. My life, our lives," she looks down at Amelia, "have been in a shambles the past few weeks. Not to throw a sob story at you, but our place got broken into and everything we had that was worth anything, little as it was, got stolen. They even took…" her voice cracks, "most of our food."

"I'm so sorry to hear that," I tell her, putting my hand to my heart.

"Wow," Clay says. "That's really awful."

She sniffles. "I just wanted you to know how much I really, *really* appreciate your kindness."

"That'll be sixty-two thirty-five," the clerk says. Clay inserts his card in the keypad at the register.

We all walk back out towards our vehicles and Janelle puts her bags into the back of her car. "Climb in your booster seat, honey," she tells Amelia. As she finishes buckling her up, I stand there holding the other bags full of items that I bought for them, unbeknownst to her.

"What is… I didn't…" she stammers.

"These are also for you."

"No, I can't possibly… you've done enough…"

"I figured you wouldn't put any snacks in your basket. Plus, we can all use some coffee and the few extras I threw in there. Please." I hand her the bags.

"Gosh, I just… thank you. Thank you both." She accepts the few bags and adds them with the rest of the groceries in the back seat.

"You're welcome," Clay says smiling. "Can you pop your gas tank so I can fill 'er up?"

"Oh. Yes. Thanks so much for the gas too."

Clay puts his card into the gas pump while Janelle opens her gas tank.

I walk over to the side of the car where Amelia is sitting and stoop down to her level while Clay and Janelle make small talk. "Are you enjoying your Icee?" I ask.

"Yes. It's yummy. You want a sip?" She holds her cup out to me.

I smile. "No, thanks, darlin'. You get to enjoy every bit of it."

"Okay. Sometimes my mommy tries to make Icees out of my juice boxes. She puts them in the freezer and chops the juice up in a bowl for me when it gets frozen, but they just aren't the same."

"I understand. But your mom is smart for thinking of that and sweet for trying to make you a good substitute."

"Yeah. Sometimes we make cookies too. She's the bestest mom."

"She sure is." I hear Clay hanging up the gas pump so I know it's time to say goodbye to this sweet little girl. "It was really nice to meet you, Amelia. I hope you and your mom have a good weekend."

"I will because I got an Icee and some string cheese."

"I'm so glad. You enjoy that Icee and string cheese, sweetie."

"Okay." She smiles.

"Can I have a hug?" Amelia thrusts her arms around my neck, nearly knocking me over and I laugh. "Wow, you give great hugs," I tell her. "Thank you for that."

"My granny used to tell me I have good hugs, but she went to heaven."

"Oh, I'm sorry to hear that. It's hard to lose a grandparent, but I know she's smiling down on you. I bet she's very proud of the girl you are."

"That's what my mommy says too. Granny is always with us. In our hearts."

"That's right. Okay, I'm going to get back in my truck now."

"Okay. Bye!" She waves at me and I shut the door, waving back.

I walk over to Janelle and Clay as he is handing her a small stack of money. She's shaking her head and shoving his hands away.

"No, no. I can't take it. It's too much. Too much. You've both done more than enough already."

"Janelle," he says, "Please. Take it. It's fine. We want to. I've been where you are and know life throws curve balls. It's only three hundred dollars. Not that much in the grand scheme of things. But I know it will take a little weight off your shoulders, if even for a couple of days."

"Are you sure?"

"We're sure," I tell her.

"I've never been one to take charity," she says with a shaky voice. "I've always worked hard for what I have. But we were living with my mom, and she just died a few months ago. Without her income, things have just gotten a little out of hand. Then the break-in, and I'm worried about the effect all this will have on Amelia, and…"

I give Janelle a hug. She sobs into my shoulder. "I'm so sorry about your mom. It's alright. It'll be okay. You'll be okay. You're raising a sweetheart of a girl and doing the best you can. That's all anybody can do. And we're doing what we can. So please let us." I let her go and she looks at me, face crinkled as she wipes her eyes with the back of her hand.

"Okay. Okay," she nods. "I mean, 'thank you' doesn't even seem like it's enough to say. Doesn't even begin to express how I'm feeling. How grateful I am." Clay hands her the money again and she finally accepts it. "Now I can pay my water and electricity bill. And put more than a quarter under Amelia's pillow from the Tooth Fairy," she chuckles.

"Good deal," Clay says. "It was nice to meet you, Janelle."

"You too." She hugs him. "Thanks again."

"Take care, Janelle," I tell her as I give her a hug goodbye. Clay and I both wave to Amelia through the car window and she waves back.

We get in our respective vehicles and go our separate ways.

"Wow," Clay lets out a long breath. "That's some tough luck. I hope things pick up for her."

"Me too. Thank you for giving her some money."

"Not a problem. I knew she'd need it. Glad she can keep her lights and water on now."

"Yeah. I feel really good about what we did for her, but I almost feel like it wasn't enough. I feel like we should keep in touch and sort of adopt her and Amelia."

"Lynn, she's way too proud. It's one thing to accept help when you're in dire straits, but I can tell she's the type of person that doesn't do that often, if ever. I think she'll be okay. It's too late now anyway. They're long gone in the opposite direction."

"Yeah. You're right. But I should have given her my number and told her to call me if she needs anything."

"Babe. Your heart is so big, but you can't save the world. I love that about you though."

"Okay." I sigh. "How about some tunes to get us back in the groove?"

"Sure. Hit me with something upbeat. No disco. Or country."

I scroll through my *What's Your Number?* playlist and pick one I think Clay will approve of right now. "Edge of Seventeen" by Stevie Nicks begins playing, with that unmistakable guitar riff.

"Good choice." He starts bobbing his head. "Hand me one of my Snickers please," he says before belting out the first line of the song.

CHAPTER 20

Before we get back onto the interstate, I see a garage sale sign and tell Clay to slow down so I can see the address.

"Why?" he asks.

"Because we should go see if they have a tape player for sale."

"Can't we just order one through Amazon for next-day delivery to our hotel?"

"Probably. But I don't want to wait that long."

"Gotcha."

I write the address down as we pass the sign. "Pull into that neighborhood up ahead so we can put the address into the GPS."

As we turn into the subdivision, there's another sign for the garage sale with pointing arrows.

"Well, that's lucky, it's in here," Clay says.

We follow the arrows and signs to the house where the sale is. As Clay parks in the driveway, I see a good-looking guy in his mid to late thirties sitting at a table with a cash box, notebook, and a glass of wine. He looks up from his phone as we approach.

"Hi," he says in a smooth deep voice.

"Hello." I look over a table of knick-knacks and old kitchen gadgets. "Do you by chance have a tape player for sale?"

"Um, like a VCR or…"

"No. A cassette tape player. For music."

"I don't have one out here, but let me ask my husband. He might have one in the back of his closet he wants to get rid of. He keeps bringing stuff out," he chuckles.

"Thanks," I tell him.

He phones his husband. "Dex. You got a tape player you don't want anymore? Got a couple out here looking for one. … No, like a jambox or something. … Right. … Yeah, figured you might. … Okay." He hangs up. "He thinks he has one, but he's checking to be sure."

A few minutes later, another handsome guy, Dex I presume, comes out with a slim-line pastel purple boombox from the eighties. What a blast from the past.

"Hey, guys. Is this what you're looking for?" he asks us.

"Hi, yes, thanks. This will work. I used to have one just like this, but mine was pink."

Dex smiles and says, "This was my older sister's, but I always coveted it. Wore out Madonna's *Material Girl* tape on this thing. I hid this beautiful baby so she couldn't pack it when she left for college. My parents had to end up buying her a new one, and suddenly I 'found' the old one." He smiles cunningly. "It was all mine then."

I laugh. "Sounds sentimental. Are you sure you want to part with it?"

"Oh, it's fine. I'll always have the precious memory of stealing it from my sister. Everything is digital these days anyway, plus we're trying to get rid of stuff. Brody and I are moving into our dream home soon." He looks at his husband and they smile at each other.

"How much do you want for it?" Clay asks.

"Um, I don't know…" Dex thinks for a second. "How's ten bucks?"

Clay squints at the ancient tape player. "Does it work?"

"I think." Dex shrugs. "Five bucks."

"Sold," Clay says, and hands him a five-dollar bill from his wallet.

"Awesome," I say to them. "Thanks. We acquired a tape from my great aunt who died a couple of months ago. I can't wait till we get to our hotel so we can plug it in and listen to it."

"Sorry for your loss," Brody says.

"Thanks."

"If you want to, we can plug it in right now if you don't want to wait till then." Brody points to an outlet near the table where he's sitting.

"Really? You don't mind?"

"Not at all."

Dex looks a little anxious though. "I'll feel like a fool if it doesn't work."

"If that's the case, we'll figure something else out. Either way, thank you so much for even offering," I say.

"Let's also pray that it doesn't chew the tape up," Clay says.

Brody holds up a pencil. "We're prepared if that happens."

"Well, let's hear what Great Aunt…" Dex looks at me inquisitively.

"Mitzi."

"Oh, Great Aunt Mitzi, how sweet. Let's hear what ol' Mitzi has to say."

I smile. "This will be fabulous. I don't know what's on the tape, but I'd at least like to see what we're in for. It could be a message from her, some of her favorite songs, or another clue."

"Clue?" Brody asks with interest.

"Yeah. We're on a cross-country scavenger hunt."

"Oh, wow, that sounds intriguing," Dex says. "Can you tell us about it? We love stuff like this."

"Sure. I love talking about it." I smile.

"This calls for a sit down and more wine. Would you two care for any?" Brody asks.

I look at Clay. He shrugs and says, "Fine with me."

"Okay, hold on just a bit." Brody stands. "I'll go get a couple more chairs and glasses. But first, I need to know a few things. Do you prefer red or white? Dry or sweet? And what are your names? I'm Brody and this is Dex."

Clay laughs. "Clay Sinclair." He sticks out his hand to shake Brody's. "My wife, Lynn." He gestures to me and I give a small wave. "Nice to meet you both."

"Same," Dex says while Brody nods.

"Dry red would be great for the both of us."

"Excellent. I've got a smooth merlot and a smoky cab," Brody frowns thoughtfully, "but we opened that last night, so it might be a bit oxidized."

"The cabernet is perfect, especially since it's already opened."

"Yes," I say. "We love a good cab."

"You got it, Lynn. And Clay." He turns to his man. "Dex, you gonna sit down and have a drink with us or are you going back to fumbling around the closet?"

"Are you kidding me? I haven't fumbled around the closet since I was a teenager. No way I'm going back there." He pulls a pair of rainbow-framed sunglasses from his pocket and dons them with delight.

We all laugh.

"I'm definitely taking a break for this. I gotta hear what's on this tape. Besides, I'm the one who asked if they could tell us more, remember?"

"Right. Okay, babe," Brody says.

"Aww, you call him 'babe.' That's what we call each other," I say.

Dex blushes with a sweet smile and looks at Brody. "Bring me a glass of whatever you're having. Babe." He looks at me and winks.

"Well," Brody says, "I was going to ask if you could help me."

"Oh, sure. Duh. Sorry. I'll get the chairs while you get the wine."

"My plan exactly."

"Can we help?" I ask.

"Don't be silly," Dex says. "You're our guests. But thanks. We'll be back in a jiffy. If anybody comes up, ask for five bucks for anything on the tables, but take anything over a dollar. I trust you won't go running off with our cash box?"

"Your vault is in good hands," Clay says.

"That's what he said." Dex winks and steps inside without another word.

Clay and I look at each other, speechless at Dex's comment, and then silently burst out laughing.

A few minutes later, Brody and Dex exit their house. Dex is hauling two more chairs and Brody is carrying a tray with four glasses of wine, along with a bamboo charcuterie board bearing various cheeses, crackers, olives, and grapes. They are going all out for us.

"Wow, what's all this?" I ask.

"Oh, honey, please," Dex answers. "We love to entertain. We don't even need an occasion. Sometimes we just celebrate the sunshine."

"That's awesome. Thanks. Both of you."

"Yeah, thanks, guys," Clay says. "This looks great."

"No sweat," Brody nods.

"I love olives," I tell them.

"Oh good. I know I should have asked," Brody says, "but I took a chance. You either love them or hate them. These are garlic stuffed." He settles the tray down on the table in front of us and we all sit and gather around, taking our wine glasses.

"Let's make a toast to…" Dex thinks, tapping his finger on his chin. "Serendipitous friends and messages on tapes."

"And cross-country scavenger hunt stories," Brody adds.

"And being called 'babe' by your love," I say, then look at Clay for him to add something.

"Yeah, all of that. And garlic stuffed olives."

We all laugh, clink our glasses together, and take a sip.

"Ahh, so refreshing," Dex says. "I love a good glass of rosé on a crisp summer day. Now, let's get down to business."

"Yes," Brody claps his hands once and rubs them together. "Where is this tape?"

"Oh, it's in the truck. I forgot all about it since we decided to listen to it here with y'all," I say. "Clay, can you get it please?"

"Sure, love." He gets up and walks over to the truck.

"I thought it was 'babe.' What was *that*?" Dex asks.

I smile. "He calls me 'babe' and 'love,' but I usually just call him 'babe.' It started when we first began dating and the song 'Babe' by Styx came on the radio and he sang it to me."

Dex puts his hand to his chest. "Oh my god, that's the sweetest thing."

Clay gets back to the table with the whole lock box including the tape, masquerade masks, massage oil, and bubble bath. "What's sweet?" he asks, putting the box on the table.

"She was telling us about your song. 'Babe.' I love it. Cute story," Brody says. "And we love Styx too. We're suckers for old school eighties music. But we have a certain soft spot for the one-hit wonders. We once had a party where that's all we played."

"That's greatness," Clay says.

"So, what's with the box?" Brody asks, pointing to it.

"The tape is in here." Clay opens the box after entering the combination again, shuffles around a bit, removes the cassette, and closes the lid.

You couldn't help but see the other items in there while Clay was getting the tape, and Dex's eyes go wide, darting back and forth between Clay and me, and his mouth drops a little bit.

"Whoa, hold on. You can't just let us see all that kinky shit and shut the box. I know we just met, but spill it. What's the deal with those blindfolds and lube?"

"Babe," Brody says to Dex, with a deadpan 'seriously' expression on his face. "I hardly think you need an explanation."

I laugh. "Wait." I put my hands up in front of me. "First of all, they aren't blindfolds. They're masquerade masks. And that's not lube. It's massage oil."

"Okaaaay. You call it an avocado. I call it an alligator pear. My question still stands."

Clay smiles. "The answer is, we don't know."

"Well," Dex's eyebrows arch, "I can offer some suggestions." He winks.

Clay chuckles. "We're hoping to find out by listening to the tape."

"Hold up," Brody says. "Was this box one of your clues?"

"It was actually one of our finds. But we think the masks and stuff might be more clues and hopefully there's an explanation on the tape."

"From your aunt?" Dex asks.

"Yes. At least we hope so," I say.

"Great Aunt Mitzi. You go, girl." Dex snaps his fingers in the air.

Clay inserts the tape into the small jambox. "And so, without further ado…" He presses the play button.

"Hello, my lovelies."

I gasp and start to tear up at the sound of Aunt Mitzi's voice. I take a deep trembling breath, bringing my hands to my open mouth, and Clay pauses the tape.

"Are you okay, Lynn? Do you need a minute?" He puts a soothing hand on my leg.

I nod.

"Oh, sweetie, is that her?" Dex asks.

I nod again, fanning my face with my hands, trying not to let the tears fall.

Brody rubs my back and grabs my glass. "Here. Take a sip, hon." I do. "This is good though, right? It's what you wanted to hear."

"Yeah, but, wow. I guess I wasn't really prepared to hear her voice again. It just makes me miss her that much more. That sweet," my voice cracks, "cadence of her speech. Her accent." My words break to avoid a meltdown. "The way her… face lights up… when she talks." I take a deep breath, trying to hold my emotion in. "And her nose crinkles when she smiles. I can see her plain as day." But I can't help it. The tears fall and my chest bursts into quick, involuntary huffs. Clay consoles me by folding me into his upper body, wrapping his arms around me and hugging me tightly.

"It's okay, Lynn. Let it out," he says. I can feel him turn towards Dex and Brody. "Sorry, guys. It's been a while since she's had a good cry over Aunt Mitzi."

"Oh, no apologies necessary," Dex says. "I just lost my Lolli last year. That's what we called my grandmother. She didn't want to be called 'Grand' anything or 'Maw Maw.' She said it made her sound old," he chuckles. "My grandfather wanted to be called 'Pop,' so my mom gave my grandmother the name 'Lolli' and 'Lollipop' was born." I can hear the smile in his voice. "I'm sorry, I'm rambling."

"I loved Lolli. I miss her too," Brody says sincerely.

I lift from Clay's chest and smile over at Dex. "That's the cutest origin of a grandmother's name I've ever heard," I say as I sniffle and wipe my cheeks. "She sounds wonderful."

"She was."

"You feeling better, babe?" Clay asks me.

"Yeah. Sorry, y'all. Those emotions hit me like a ton of bricks."

"That's totally normal," Brody says. "It's all good."

"I think I'm okay." I look at Clay and smile.

"You sure?"

"Yeah. Go ahead. I should be alright for you to play the tape now."

"Okay. Here we go. Just let me know if you need me to pause it again." Clay presses the button to continue playing the message.

"*Once again,*" Aunt Mitzi continues, "*I'm sure you have so many questions. I will start with the rest of the contents in the lock box you found at Hoyt Sherman Place.*"

"Thank you, Jesus," Dex says. I can't help but snicker.

"*The masquerade masks will help you get into a destination in the future on your trip. Consider them your admission fee. The massage oil and bubble bath are just because I figure, at this point on your quest, you both could probably use a massage and a nice bubble bath. Order some champagne and have a long, hot bubble bath, followed by a massage you give each other. And whatever comes naturally after that.*"

"Ooh… you tell 'em, auntie," Dex says with a knowing look. "Get it, girl." He winks at me and I blush. Clay shakes his head with a snicker.

Aunt Mitzi continues. "*You are over halfway done with this road trip scavenger hunt and I thought you could use a little time to decompress and unwind.*"

"That's adorable," Brody says. "Sounds like she was amazing."

"She was," I smile as I let a tear fall and grab Clay's hand.

"*Now, let me back up a bit. I know you'll want to know how we were able to hobnob with all those famous people.*"

"Pause it," I tell Clay. He does. "Can you get the envelope to show Dex and Brody?"

"Sure, babe." He goes back to the truck and comes back holding the manila envelope with the photographs of Aunt Mitzi and Uncle Sid pictured with all the celebrities from decades ago.

Clay hands it to Brody and he opens it, revealing the photos. Dex and Brody sift through them with open mouths.

"Are you kidding me?" Dex asks. "Just chillin' with Marilyn Monroe. No big deal," he says facetiously.

"Holy shit," Brody says, his eyes wide. "How could your aunt and uncle have known all these celebs and we've never heard of them? This is amazing."

"I know, right?" I smile. "Okay, Clay. Keep going."

"*You know Uncle Sid and I were very comfortable. The Santini family donated money to a lot of charities and with that came certain privileges. We would attend banquets, fundraisers, and galas associated with each charity from time to time. Sometimes, celebrities happened to be there, as they would have*" *donated to the charity themselves. We'd be assigned to a table, sitting next to the occasional famous person, or people, and we'd talk. Exchange pleasantries and get to know each other a little. When at one dinner, we were seated next to J.P. Morgan's grandson, Henry. He and Sid got to talking about banking, finance, investment opportunities, et cetera. They even had a common interest in boating. They became fast friends and later that year, we were invited to their home for a dinner party. From there, we were introduced to other well-known wealthy individuals, and it just kind of snowballed. We've never been the kind to boast about our assets, so we always kept that part of our lives separate. Lynn, your grandmother was the only one I ever told about those times. She loved hearing my stories. And I loved telling them. Here's one secret little anecdote I'll let you both in on. I had a huge crush on Frank Sinatra. He was so handsome and very charming. Charisma to the nines. And you probably know, he had a reputation of being quite the ladies' man." She giggles. "Sid always held me a little closer whenever Frank was around.*

"Anyway, my sweets, I hope you are both having fun. Don't forget to take some time to relax. The following are some songs that might help get you in the mood. I love you both so much and I'm watching over you. Hugs and kisses. Love, your old Aunt Mitzi."

What follows her voice is Louie Armstrong's "A Kiss to Build a Dream On." It makes me smile.

I lean into Clay and he hugs me, rubbing my back up and down.

"You alright, love?"

"Yeah. I really needed to hear her voice."

"That was incredible," Dex says.

I sit up and take another sip of wine. "Yeah. It was. Thanks again for the opportunity. Inviting us to sit and listen."

"Don't mention it. Brody and I will be talking about this for years to come."

"Well, are you ready to get back on the road, Lynn?"

"I guess." But I'm a little bummed. Dex and Brody have been great company. For some reason, I feel like I've known them for years.

"Oh, do you have to go?" Brody asks. "Stay for dinner. Please. We'd love to have you."

"Yes. I'm a great cook," Dex says. "Chicken Pasta Primavera is my specialty. I was seriously just thinking about going to pick up the garage sale signs and start cooking. Brody read my mind by asking you both to stay. I can have it ready in about an hour or so. Whatcha say?"

I look at Clay and he winks. "Sounds good to us. If you're sure. We don't want to put you out."

"Please," Brody stands, "this is the most excitement we've had in a month. Come on, let's take this party inside. Just excuse the boxes."

"Brody, I'll go ahead and pick up the signs around. Can you take the chicken out for me and start the water on the stove?"

"Sure. We did pretty well here today." He looks around at what's left of their sale. "Sold a lot of stuff and made some decent money we can put towards decorating our new house."

"I know. And I'm glad nobody came and interrupted us while we were listening to the tape."

"Yeah, that was lucky," I say.

"Things started to wind down a bit before you both got here. We hadn't seen anybody in a while. We were busy early this morning though," Dex says.

"Glad everything worked out," Clay says.

"Yeah, me too. Let's head in." Brody finishes off his wine.

"I'll be back shortly," Dex says, walking to his vehicle.

I grab the tray with the nearly empty board and add our wine glasses to it. Brody picks up two chairs. Clay does the same and follows Brody into their house. I tag along behind them with the tray as Dex starts his car and backs out the driveway.

CHAPTER 21

Clay and I enjoy the delicious dinner and wonderful company. We have a great, long conversation, trading particulars of our families, jobs, and hobbies. Dex and Brody tell us all about their new house, and we tell them all about our trip and the things we've found along the way. I almost leave out the part about me getting kidnapped and Clay killing the guy in my defense, but it's such a vital part of our tale that I include it after looking at Clay for the go-ahead. He nods, giving me his blessing to tell the story. I even give them the background of what took place with the tragic accident when Clay was deployed and he lost his brothers in arms when the truck blew up. I know how strongly he feels about everything being his fault, but I think the more we talk about it, the more therapeutic it will be. Plus, I think Clay could really use an objective perspective. Besides, in just a few hours, I've come to trust Brody and Dex. As unconventional a way as this new friendship formed, I do now consider them friends.

After Clay and I finish telling them about the worst part of our trip, we sit in silence for a minute. Dex and Brody are stone-faced, shaking their heads.

"Clay," Brody says, "you have to know that wasn't your fault."

"Don't," Clay says.

"No, man. Brody's right. I can't imagine what you're actually feeling, but none of it was because of something you did or didn't do. And look, you did save her. She's here. Safe. With you." Dex puts a hand on Clay's shoulder and squeezes.

"I've told him the same thing," I say.

"Look, I appreciate y'all being supportive. Really, I do. It's just always been hard for me to cut myself some slack. Especially when it comes to this whole entire situation, starting from the accident when I was overseas to killing the fucker that took my wife. I've been dealing with this for years — though, the fact that I killed a guy is new, and that brings a fresh type of hell to the table — and I've been trying to tell myself everything that y'all, and Lynn, and my doctor have been saying. But they're just words. It's hard for me to forgive myself. Always has been. I find it difficult to truly feel the words and apply them. I know I need to work on allowing the dark corners of my being some more latitude in absolving myself of everything that's happened. Fuck, I don't know why I'm spewing all this shit to y'all. Maybe it's the alcohol flowing freely. Maybe it's the fact that y'all seem like old friends. Or the fact that it's easier to get shit off your chest when you're talking to people you'll probably never see again, like sending out a message in a bottle." Clay sighs heavily. "Look, I know deep down that it's not my fault. But I don't feel it in my bones and in my heart. Not yet anyway. That will take some more time."

"Of course," Brody says. "I'm sorry."

"Me too, man," Dex adds. "I can't imagine."

That's the most I've ever heard Clay talk about everything. I don't even mind that I wasn't the only one in the room when he got that deep. I'm just happy he did. I put my hand on his leg and he wraps his fingers around mine. We sit in silence in the heavy air of Clay's memories.

"How about some dessert?" Dex asks, appropriately changing the vibe of the room.

"Yes," I say, giving Dex a gracious look. He responds with a subtle nod.

"I've got homemade key lime pie."

"Oh, perfect. I love key lime pie."

"One of my favorites," Clay says. And he seems to be in a better mood already.

"Glad to hear it," Dex says. "It'll just be a second."

Dex gets up and grabs the pie from the refrigerator while Brody clears the table of our dinnerware. Back at the table, Dex serves the pie onto matching dessert plates.

"You really are a great cook," I tell Dex.

"Thank you," he says. "I appreciate that. Lolli taught me everything I know when it comes to the kitchen." He smiles.

"Yeah, it was so good," Clay says. "We haven't had many home-cooked meals during our time on the road, so this has been a real treat. Thanks, guys."

"You're welcome," Brody says. "Glad to have you both."

"Yes," Dex chimes in. "It's been our pleasure. When was your last home-cooked meal?"

"A couple of weeks ago," I tell them, taking my first bite of key lime pie. "Oh my god, this is delicious."

"Mmm hmm," Clay agrees.

"Thanks, you guys."

I swallow my bite and continue. "We spent the week in Indianapolis at my grandparents' house and of course she cooked up a storm for us while we were there."

"Yeah, everything else has been at restaurants, fast food drive-thrus, hotels, and gas station snacks," Clay chuckles.

"Well, I'm glad we could give you guys a bit of a change. Nothing wrong with fine dining or even fast food occasionally, but I can imagine it gets old. Dex really is a wonderful cook. I'm a lucky guy," Brody smiles.

"Clay's not a bad cook either, but his specialty is grilling. He also makes an incredible gumbo."

"Ooh, I've never had gumbo before," Dex says.

"Me either."

"Well," Clay says, "if you ever find yourself in Louisiana, let us know."

"Yes!" I say with enthusiasm. "That's an awesome idea. We'd love to return the favor."

"That sounds fabulous," Brody says. "I've never been to Louisiana."

"Y'all will love it," I tell him and Dex. "It's a bit of a culture shock, but it's a fun place to be."

"We should plan a trip for the fall. I've always wanted to go to New Orleans," Dex says. I cringe at how he pronounced 'Orleans,' but I let it slide.

"That's the perfect time to come," I say. "The weather finally cools down a little bit. Sometimes," I chuckle. "And there are tons of great festivals in the fall. Plus, Clay always makes a big pot of gumbo with the first cool snap of the year. You can't really rely on our weather when planning a trip, but October is a good time regardless."

"Yeah, and even if it's eighty degrees, I'll still make gumbo for y'all," Clay smiles.

"That sounds great," Dex says. "Guess that means you'll be seeing us again. Hope you don't regret spilling your guts to us now." Dex winks at Clay.

"Shit," Clay chuckles. "Nah, man. It's cool. Just don't ever bring it up again."

"Deal. So, Brody and I will talk about going down to New Orleeens—"

"Please don't call it that," I say.

"Nawlins?"

"Good god, no," Clay says. "It's 'New Or-lins.' Like my wife's name, but plural. Or even 'New Or-luns. Like 'lungs' without the 'g.'"

"Got it. Okay, so Brody and I will talk about going down to New *Or-lynns*," he winks at me, "and come up with a game plan."

"Yep," Brody says. "I'm looking forward to it. Let's exchange numbers."

Brody tells me his phone number. I save it and text him so he has mine. "Here's Clay's number too." I text it to him and he responds by texting Dex's number back to me.

"Great. We're all set now," he says.

Clay turns to me. "Okay, babe. I guess we should get back on the road. Still got about an hour to go till we get to our hotel."

"Yeah, alright. Are you okay to drive?"

"Yes. I only had a few glasses, and frankly, that conversation earlier totally sobered me up. I'm fine."

"Good." We get up from the table and I pick up our plates.

"Girl, put those down," Dex says. "We'll get them."

"I don't mind."

"Alright. Knock yourself out then," Dex gestures to the sink.

I laugh, grab the forks, stack the plates, and wait for Brody and Dex to add theirs on top of ours. I grab their forks as well and bring everything to the sink, turning the tap on to rinse the dishes.

"I'm gonna stop here, because if you're anything like me, you have a particular way you load your dishwasher."

"You are correct, my dear," Dex says. "Though Brody's way is different from mine, and we argue all the time about how the silverware should be loaded."

"Same with me and Lynn," Clay says chuckling.

"The silverware goes in handles up, not down," I declare.

"Exactly," Dex says. He puts his hand up for a high-five. "Put it there, sister." I meet Dex's raised hand.

Clay shakes his head, smiling. "Thank you both so much for your hospitality," he says to Dex and Brody, extending his hand for a shake.

"Oh, we're past handshakes now. I'm going in for a hug," Dex says, wrapping his arms around Clay with a laugh.

"Same," Brody says, making a Clay sandwich. I don't blame them.

They give me big hugs too. "It was so nice to meet y'all," I tell them. "Thanks again for everything."

"You're so welcome," Dex says. "It was wonderful to meet you both too and to hear your story. We can't wait to come visit."

"Yes indeed. I'm really looking forward to that gumbo," Brody says. "Okay. One more hug," he says as he engulfs me in his strong arms, and then Dex is behind me doing the same. These guys sure love to give sandwich hugs.

"Be safe on the road," Dex says.

"Always," Clay tells him. "Guess we'll see y'all in a few months."

"Yes, can't wait," Brody says. "I'm going to search for hotels on Bourbon Street as soon as we get inside."

Clay and I pile back into the truck and wave at Dex and Brody as we back out of their driveway.

"Well," Clay says, "that was an interesting and unexpected detour."

"It was. And a fun one too. I can't believe how fast I became so comfortable around them. They were great."

"Yeah. Good couple of guys. I enjoyed their company."

"Same. How about some music?"

"Sure. Not in the mood for anything too hard or fast right now though."

"Okay. I'll find something." I pull up my *Mellow Out* playlist, but before I hit the shuffle button, I turn to my husband and touch his arm. "Are you okay, Clay?"

"Yeah. I'm just in my head a little bit. I'm fine. I'll be fine."

"Okay. If you want to talk—"

"I don't. Not right now. I'm all talked out for tonight. Sorry, love. I promise, I'll be alright. Just play the music. Please."

"Alright." I finally press the play button on my phone and "Horse" by Live starts.

"That's perfect," Clay says. "Thanks, babe."

"Sure." I know he's probably thinking about the whole kidnapping, shooting, and killing again since we just brought it all back up with Dex and Brody. He just seems a little too on edge right now, so I put a comforting hand on his thigh and he grabs it, interlocking our fingers. He raises our joined hands to his lips and kisses the back of my hand.

We drive for a while, continuing towards Lincoln, Nebraska as "Fade Into You" by Mazzy Star, "Brighter Than Sunshine" by Aqualung, and The Jeff Healey Band's "Angel Eyes" play throughout the truck.

I turn to Clay and turn the music down. "I have a question."

"Hit me."

"Not that I'm complaining, but I just have to ask. What made you give three hundred dollars to Janelle earlier today? I mean, I'm all on board for it, but that just seemed a little over-the-top. Even for you."

He sighs. "It's because of Tyler."

"Tyler? What does Ty have to do with it?"

"You know we've been best friends since high school."

"Yeah, you met in ROTC, right?"

"Yeah. Well, technically, JROTC, since it was in high school. Anyway, he didn't always have it so easy growing up. At least for a while, times were hard for his family. His dad had been laid off from the paper mill and his mom was a teacher's aide, so she didn't make that much. And they had four kids."

"Tyler is the oldest, right?"

"Yes. Then Lena, Kurt, and Ellie. Ellie was only a toddler when we were freshmen. So, anyway, Tyler would sometimes bring Ziploc bags to school and put food from lunch in them for his siblings. Stuff like rolls, fish sticks, french fries, cookies, and things like that. He would eat all the items like the vegetables, meatloaf, and mashed potatoes. You know, stuff that would make a huge mess if you put it in baggies."

"Wow. I had no idea."

"Nobody really did. I don't think the younger kids realized, and Tyler never let on. I think I was the only one he told. The really hard times only lasted about a year, but that's long enough. They almost lost their house, but just before that happened, his dad got hired on at the Exxon plant and began making good money again."

"Thank God."

"Yeah. But still, during the worst of it, I wanted to help. I couldn't though, not really, since I didn't have much money. I mean, shit, I was a kid myself. My parents were separated then so things were tight on each side there. I told Ty I wanted to help but he wouldn't let me because his parents would be embarrassed if they knew I knew. I would still sneak him packages of Pop-Tarts though and canned goods here and there. He hated to take it, but I made him. I knew he'd never take my money, even if I had any, but I did the best I could with what he would let me. When I noticed his tennis shoes were wearing out, I gave him a pair of Nikes that didn't fit me comfortably."

"Awww."

"Well, I wasn't using them. They were practically brand new. Anyway, all that to say that I vowed to myself that if I could ever make a real difference for somebody, I would. That's part of the reason why I went into the kind of work I did. And when my parents got back together, and renewed their wedding vows, things were better for us again. Tyler and his family didn't really need as much help by then, but still. That stuck with me. I wished I would have been able to do more for him when he and his wonderful family needed it."

"That's so sweet, Clay. You always say that I have a big heart, but I think yours might just be a little bit bigger."

"Nobody's heart is as big as yours, babe."
"I love you."
"I know."
After driving a few minutes in silence, we pull into the parking lot of the Graduate Lincoln, our hotel in Nebraska. After we check in and make it up to our room, we shower and get into bed. It doesn't take long before sleep finds us.

CHAPTER 22

I AWAKE TO A loud crash and bolt upright. Clay is not in the bed. I get up to go look for him. "Clay? Are you alright?" I open the bathroom door.

"Hey, sorry. I dropped the toiletries bag and when I went to catch it to keep it from hitting the floor, I knocked the hairdryer off the wall and it smashed on the tile. I'm sorry I woke you up, especially in such a *Three Stooges* way."

I chuckle. "That's okay. I'm just glad you're alright. I thought you slipped and fell or something."

"No, I'm okay. Remind me when we get down to the lobby to let them know I broke the hairdryer."

"Will do. Have you been up long?"

"No, only a few minutes. I had to piss and then figured I might as well just stay up and smash the blow dryer." He smiles.

Standing in the doorway of the bathroom, I look over at the clock on the bedside table. "I can't believe I slept so late. It's after nine. I guess I really needed that sleep."

"Me too. I didn't even make coffee yet. Are you ready for today?"

"Yeah, I'm excited to find out what the National Museum of Roller Skating is going to tell us about Aunt Mitzi."

"I feel like we haven't heard the clue in ages. I need a refresher. Let me finish brushing my teeth and we'll go over it again."

"Okay. I need to brush mine too, but I'll go make coffee first."

"Good plan. We're not going to solve any riddles decaffeinated." He puts his deodorant back in the bag. Catching my eye in the mirror, he gives me a wink, his toothbrush sticking out of his mouth.

I make the coffee and head back to the bathroom to begin my morning routine. After I finish, I meet Clay in the living area of the hotel room and get the clue sheet out of my purse. He's ordered room service for us, a light breakfast of fruit and yogurt parfaits.

"Thanks for ordering food," I say as I pop the top off the cup and take a bite of the vanilla yogurt mixed with bananas, berries, and granola. "Mmm. So good."

"You're welcome. I didn't feel like a heavy breakfast this morning. I'm kind of anxious."

"Me too. This is perfect." I take another bite. The word Clay just used makes me wonder exactly what he's anxious about. Is it more of an excitement kind of feeling for today, or is it actual anxiety over revisiting everything last night? I clear my throat. "Clay, I know this probably isn't the right time for this, but I need you to tell me what's really on your mind."

"What do you mean?"

"You know what I mean. Start talking."

He sighs. "Babe, I'm okay. I swear. I mean, yeah, I'm a little tense about reliving everything last night, but that's not new for me. I deal with this shit every day in my head. I'm used to it. Maybe I just need to call Dr. Hart. Get some things off my chest."

"I think that's a great idea. It's been a while since you've seen him. I'm sure a phone call will do you some good. Your sessions with him have been the best outlet for you since you started therapy all those years ago."

"Yeah. I've actually called him a couple of times while we've been on the road. I'd sneak a quick call in when you were asleep or when I was going to get ice or something. And I called him right after everything went down last week."

"You did? Why didn't you tell me?"

"I didn't want to put my burden on you. Plus, I didn't want to make you think I was drowning in guilt. Even though I am."

"God, Clay. I would never think any less of you for calling your doctor. You know that, right?"

"Yeah. I know."

"And how many times do I have to tell you that you don't have anything to feel guilty for?"

"You can't dictate my feelings, Lynn."

"I know, but—"

"It's just… I feel how I feel and I can't help it. I just need to work through it. I'll give Dr. Hart a call later today. Promise."

"Good."

"Thank you, Lynn."

"For what?"

"Allowing me to process in my own way. Not forcing anything on me."

"You're welcome." I peck him on the cheek and get back to the task at hand. "Okay, I'm going to read the clue again. 'You're off to the state that brought us Kool-Aid, Fred Astaire, and Arbor Day. There's a place in the capital that is state of the art. Present the key to gain access to something that's close to my heart.' So basically, we just need to go to the skating museum and give them the roller skate key we have."

"And then I guess they will give us something that Aunt Mitzi loved."

"Or at least let us see it. It just says 'gain access to something' so we may not be able to take it with us if it's part of the museum."

"But didn't the letter at the beginning of the cipher say to take what we find with us? Plus, remember when we went to the Victrola Museum in Delaware? We were able to have the piece they had on display delivered to our house. So maybe it's kind of the same thing," Clay says.

"Maybe. I guess we'll see when we get there. But remember in the beginning of the cipher where she wrote us the letter, she said that there may not be anything tangible for us to take in every place."

"Oh yeah. But I would imagine that a museum would have something tangible."

"She also said for us to use our own judgment."

"Well then, I guess we'll see when we get there."

"Just like I said." I smile.

"Just like you said." He smiles back at me.

"Look up the museum and check to see how far it is from the hotel," I tell Clay.

He searches on his phone. "Shit."

"What?"

"You're not gonna like this."

"Do *not* tell me they're closed."

"Umm…"

"Are you freaking kidding me?" He shakes his head. "What kind of tourist attraction isn't open on the weekends? It's Saturday for crying out loud. That's when people go and tour things like that," I say with a huff.

"It gets worse. The museum doesn't open again until Tuesday."

"*What?*"

"I'm sorry, Lynn."

"I don't want to spend the next three days here. Not that there's anything wrong with Lincoln. It's a beautiful city. I just want to keep moving."

"We could simply chill and relax for a little bit. You know we're going to miss the road and this adventure when we get back home."

"Is that your subtle way of telling me you need to chill and relax, Clay? Because—"

"No, no, no. Not necessarily. I'm fine. I just thought maybe we could make use of the bubble bath and massage oil Aunt Mitzi left us." He winks at me.

"That does sound nice."

"But, if you want to keep going, we will."

"Hmm… tough decision." I mull it over and decide I really want to keep moving forward. "I think I want to continue. We can do the bubble bath and massage at the next place we stay. Are you sure you're okay with leaving though?"

"Yes. Let's go down to the concierge and see if some of the locals have any connections to the National Museum of Roller Skating. Maybe somebody can let us in for a special circumstance."

"That's a good idea."

"Come on." He stands up and reaches for my hand. I grab his and he pulls me up off the couch. "We're going to get into that museum before Tuesday, Lynn. I'll make sure of it." He ushers me out the door and down the corridor to the elevators.

"Are you going to break in if we can't find anybody to help us?"

"Don't be silly. I will scour the entire city until I find someone who can let us in."

"You're the best."

"I know."

The elevator doors open to the lobby and we walk towards the concierge desk. The hotel's logo is affixed over colorful panels of curtains that serve as the backdrop.

A young woman who barely looks old enough to be out of high school greets me. "Good morning. May I help you find something to do today?" She smiles.

"Hi, Carissa," Clay says, reading her name tag. "We really need to get into the National Museum of Roller Skating. But we saw that it's closed until Tuesday."

"That's right. It's only open Tuesday through Friday."

"Why aren't they open on Saturdays?"

She shrugs. "I guess they like their weekends," she smiles. "Wait, what do you mean you 'need to get in' there?"

Clay gives her our names and the usual abbreviated spiel of our trip. "Is there any chance you might know somebody that can help us and let us in? We won't take long and we'd be happy to make a donation."

"A nice donation," I add with a smile.

"What an unusual story. Let me see what I can do." She winks at us as she picks up the desk telephone and makes a call.

"I sure hope this works," I say to where only Clay can hear.

"Me too," he mutters.

"Hey, Aunt Betsy," Carissa says into the phone. "I have a couple of people here at the hotel with a request that's out of the ordinary and I hope you can help. Well, what I really need is to see if you can get your friend, Mrs. LuAnn, to help." She gives her aunt our story and our wish to enter the museum today. "Okay. ... Sure, that will be fine. ... Great. ... Thanks. Talk to you soon." Carissa hangs up the phone and gives us a smile. "Good news. My aunt is going to call her friend that works at the museum and see if she can let you in for a little bit. She's going to call me back as soon as she can. No promises, but she'll try."

"Oh, that's awesome," I say. "Thank you so much."

"No problem. I hope it works out. If you'd like to wait in the lobby, I can call you over when I hear from her or I can ring you in your room."

"We can wait here for a bit," Clay says. "Thanks, Carissa."

The fun atmosphere of the lobby eases my nerves. We approach a set of bamboo couches with green velvet cushions and take a seat. A white brick wall in front of us reads 'We Are All Students' painted in a whimsical font. Three old-school arcade games are just a few feet away from us in the corner: *Defender*, *Frogger*, and *Donkey Kong*.

"Fingers crossed LuAnn comes through for us," I say, actually crossing my fingers. I knock on the arm of the couch. "Does this count as wood?"

"No, love. Bamboo is actually a type of grass. Better to try your luck on the hardwood floor."

"Right." I rap my knuckles on the herringbone-patterned, chestnut floor for good measure.

"What do you think it is that we'll find?"

"I don't know. I mean, I know Aunt Mitzi loved roller skating, but I have no idea what could be so significant that she has something museum worthy."

Clay shrugs. "If there's anything we've learned the past couple of months, it's not to be surprised about anything when it comes to Aunt Mitzi."

"You're so right about that."

"Maybe it's a pair of twenty-four-karat gold roller skates with diamond encrusted laces."

I burst out laughing. "I wouldn't put it past her to have had such skates."

"Mr. and Mrs. Sinclair," Carissa calls, waving us over.

We walk back up to the counter. "Please, it's Clay and Lynn," I tell her.

She smiles and nods. "I heard back from my aunt. Her friend can meet you at the museum in about thirty minutes."

"Oh, yay!" I cheer. "Thank you, thank you, thank you!"

"You're so welcome. Mrs. LuAnn is very excited to meet you."

"Thanks, Carissa," Clay says. "We really appreciate your help." Clay tips her twenty dollars and she beams.

"Wow, thank you. It was my pleasure. I can't wait to hear the rest of the story when you get back."

"Well, since we know we're going to be able to get in today," I tell her, "we'll be checking out now. Since the museum is only about ten minutes away, we should have time to pack up and still get there within thirty minutes."

"Oh. Okay." She sounds a little bummed. "I guess I'll just ask my aunt how it all played out."

Clay smiles warmly at her. "Thanks again for all your help."

"It was no trouble. I hope you both enjoyed your stay here at the Graduate Lincoln."

"We certainly did," I tell her.

"Oh, one more thing," Clay says. "I accidentally broke the hairdryer in the room this morning, so it'll need to be replaced."

"Okay, no problem. Thanks for letting me know."

"Do we need to pay for a new one?"

"No, not at all. Stuff like that happens all the time. We're prepared," she smiles.

"Cool, thanks."

We wave good-bye to her and head back up to our room to gather our things and check out.

After we load our bags into the truck, we have fifteen minutes to get to the museum. We arrive with four minutes to spare. Built with schoolhouse-red bricks, I might think this was somebody's home if it weren't for the sign out front.

A brand-new, black Dodge Challenger is in the parking lot. I assume that's LuAnn's car. I hope she hasn't been waiting long.

We walk to the entrance. She looks up, sees us approaching, and comes to unlock the door for us. She's about our age, with brown hair in a bob cut.

"Hi, are you Clay and Lynn?" she asks, before opening the door all the way.

"We are," I say.

"Okay good. I'm LuAnn. Come on in. So nice to meet you both."

"You too," I tell her. Clay nods. "Thanks for opening for us."

"No problem."

"Nice car," Clay says, pointing his thumb behind him towards the parking lot. "I'm a Dodge guy myself."

"Thanks. It's my husband's. He took my Durango to get an oil change today."

"Ah. Lucky you then. I have a '67 Charger I'm restoring back home that I drove in high school."

"Oh, my man would be so jealous."

Clay smiles with pride.

As we enter the museum and see all the display cases, my mouth drops. I had no idea what to expect in general, but there is a ton of roller skating memorabilia exhibited throughout the museum.

The evolution of roller skates is displayed around the room. In addition to the various shapes, styles, and colors of roller skates, I see trophies, classic skate cases, pictures, costumes, uniforms, vintage ads, and so much more.

"So, what exactly do we do, now that we're here?" Clay asks.

"Umm… well," I turn to LuAnn. "Can we look around for a minute? There's so much more to see here than I expected."

"Sure. I'll be at the front desk if you have any questions."

"Thanks," Clay tells her.

We walk around the place and check everything out. I love the wall of wheels. It showcases the progression of the different types of skate wheels used over the years, from wood to metal to polyurethane. They're all mounted, and you can even spin them. I think my favorite part of the museum is the area displaying the various types of odd and unusual skates. Featured here are a pair of stilt skates; motorized skates; and skates for a horse, parakeet, and bear. There is even a roller skate that dates all the way back to 1819. In addition to roller skating memorabilia, the museum also includes sections with history and keepsakes of figure skating, speed skating, roller hockey, and more.

Clay and I explore for a few more minutes before I decide to ask LuAnn about the skate key we have. Just as I was about to go find her, she comes back to check on us.

"Hey, guys," she says.

"Hi. I was about to come get you."

"Well, here I am," she smiles. "So, did you find what you're looking for?" She gives me a bit of a suspicious smile, like she knows something.

"Um, not yet. I have this old skate key that my aunt gave me." I hold up the key and dangle it. "She left us instructions to present the key and we would gain access to something that meant a lot to her."

"Ah, yes. I was wondering how long it would take you to show me the key."

"So, you already know what Aunt Mitzi wants us to have?"

"Yes. Follow me. And I love the fact that you still speak of her in present tense."

I give her a warm smile and place my hand on my heart. "She's always here with me. In spirit at least."

We follow LuAnn to a door with an 'Employees Only' sign on it. As she unlocks it, she tells us, "This is our archive room. We have so much memorabilia that we often rotate things in and out of our exhibits. We store the rest in here. Mitzi's items have been displayed off and on throughout the years." LuAnn flips the light switch on and we enter.

"Oh wow," I say as I look around the room. Glass display cases, shelves with acid-free storage boxes, and cabinets with long shallow drawers occupy the space.

"Now, I have a few things to show you. You can decide if you want to take them or leave them here for us to keep on display. Mitzi left it up to you."

"Okay. I can't wait to see what you've got."

"Me either," Clay says. "I'm intrigued."

LuAnn unlocks a long thin drawer and pulls out what looks like some sort of program booklet, an old uniform shirt, a spiral notebook, and a lapel pin. The shirt is a long-sleeved jersey with red and navy-blue horizontal stripes, and a big number 13 on the back.

"I assume you're going to explain what all of this is?" I ask.

"Of course," she smiles.

"That looks like a roller derby jersey," Clay remarks, pointing to the shirt.

"It is. Your Aunt Mitzi was a trailblazer for roller derby in the Baton Rouge area back in the late forties and early fifties."

"What?" I'm stunned.

"Holy shit," Clay says. He looks at me. "You didn't know?"

"No. I mean, I knew she loved to skate, but had no idea that she was into roller derby."

"She kept it a secret. Sid knew of course, and I think a couple of her siblings may have known, but her parents didn't know. There was a bit of a stigma about roller derby when it first started."

"A stigma? Why?" I ask.

"Well, back then, women involved in roller derby gave off a negative impression of themselves, with the sport having an image of violence and impropriety. It wasn't considered lady-like, because it wasn't. Roller derby was rough. Anyway, because of that, many of the participants concealed the fact that they played to avoid unfavorable reactions and backlash from their friends, family, and coworkers."

"Wow," Clay says.

"She wasn't ashamed of being involved, but she didn't want her family to worry about her and didn't want the town gossiping about her, as if she were doing something wrong," LuAnn explains.

"I can kind of understand her wanting to keep this part of her life secret," I say, "but it doesn't really seem like it would be something so bad that her family wouldn't approve of it."

"Babe, from what we've learned about Aunt Mitzi this whole trip, we know that her parents were pretty protective over her."

I turn to Clay. "Yeah, but at that point in her life, she was married to Uncle Sid and her parents wouldn't exactly have been able to tell her what or what not to do."

"Regardless, she wouldn't have wanted to disappoint them if she knew they would disapprove of her being involved in roller derby."

"I guess that's true." I turn back to LuAnn. "So, is this one of her uniform shirts?"

"It is. Her team was the Louisiana Vivacious Belles Roller Derby. L-V-B-R-D. Better known as the Lovebirds."

"Oh my gosh, that's so cute," I say. "Did she have a special roller derby name for herself?"

"She did. Her name was Stork Raven Mad."

I laugh out loud. "That's perfect."

"Everybody on the team had a bird pun name. I think if you check out that program, you'll see the roster with a list of their names. And just as a little side note, that program is in near-mint condition. One of the best-preserved we have here."

I pick up the program. It's slightly tattered around the edges, but otherwise pristine. I thumb through the book and find the list of names.

"Read the best ones out loud," Clay says.

"Okay. Let's see. There's Lovey Dovey... Wren Too Deep... Robin Lanes... The Unpleasant Pheasant... and Lark My Words. There are a bunch more, but those stood out the most to me."

Clay chuckles. "I like 'Robin Lanes.' That's clever. But Aunt Mitzi's is the best."

"I agree," I laugh. "What's the notebook for?" I point to the spiral-bound tablet LuAnn is holding.

"Oh, this is definitely for you to take with you. It's filled with notes from the Lovebirds' bouts with stats, rosters, and even minutes from meetings the members had. But at the end, there's a special note for you."

"Wow. That's awesome." I smile. "So, wait a minute. We have a skate key to present to you, but Aunt Mitzi didn't have any skates displayed here?"

"We do have a pair of her skates. I was waiting for the right time to show you. You may have overlooked them in the case."

"That could've easily happened. We didn't exactly study the cases very hard, excited to get to the Aunt Mitzi part. Please, lead the way."

LuAnn shuts the drawer and locks it, then exits the room. We follow her as she meanders through the display cases, finally arriving at one in the corner. Several different styles of skates are featured from the forties and fifties. There's a pair of black leather skates with red and white laces and clay wheels, a pair of white leather skates with blue and white checkered laces and metal wheels, a black and brown leather pair of Reidell classic roller hockey skates with black laces and what appear to be rubber wheels, along with several other pairs of skates. But the skates that stand out to me the most are sitting in the corner of the case. It's a pair of cream-colored suede skates, well-worn with white laces and wooden wheels. They are nearly boots. I bet they come up to mid-calf. A row of five metal shoelace hooks is above the eyelets for the laces to continue up the skates for further tightening and support.

LuAnn points and says, "Those—"

"The ones in the corner?" I interrupt her. "I'm sorry." I give her a sheepish smile. "The suede ones?"

"Yes. Those were hers."

A broad grin spreads across my face. I knew in my heart those belonged to Aunt Mitzi. "I love them. I can see her wearing them."

"You certainly can." LuAnn smiles. "See the pictures surrounding them?"

I take notice of the several black-and-white photos in frames around the skates on the back panel of the display case. "Oh my gosh. It's her." My eyes burn with the want of tears.

"Holy shit," Clay says. "Look at her go." He chuckles, pointing at one of the pictures.

In the photo he's referring to, she and a few of her teammates are racing around the rink. Aunt Mitzi is wearing the jersey I'm holding in the crook of my arm. All the players have matching sets of striped shorts tightly fitted over a pair of snug racing pants. Large, leather patches are affixed to the knees and upper-outer thighs of their pants, protecting them against bruising when they fall. None of them are wearing helmets though.

Another picture shows Aunt Mitzi and a couple of the other girls on the team in mid-fall as a player from their rival team, whose position is apparently called the Jammer, must've gotten ahead of them, causing the Lovebirds to lose their balance and tumble down. Aunt Mitzi's mouth is wide open, eyes bulged, arms out, her right leg extended, and left leg bent at the knee. I can't tell if her expression is one of enjoyment or alarm. Probably a little of both.

In this picture, the members of the Lovebirds are wearing helmets, but the Jammer on the opposing team is not. This tells me that it was probably taken sometime after the previous photo we were looking at. Maybe team LVBRD finally decided it was smart to wear helmets. Since the other player isn't wearing one, it must not have been part of the regulations. Maybe it was left up to each skater's discretion. I don't know why anybody wouldn't want to wear a helmet when participating in this sport though. Perhaps to project more of a badass image, but I can only imagine how much damage and pain a velocious roller skate wheel to the temple could inflict. Not worth it in my opinion.

A few more pictures surround Aunt Mitzi's skates: one of the whole team, a photo showing one of the team members putting makeup on Aunt Mitzi (presumably backstage getting ready for a bout), and one more action shot with Aunt Mitzi hip checking another player.

"All of these are great." I take pictures of the photos the best I can with my phone through the glass of the display case, trying to avoid a glare.

"Agreed," Clay says. "She left some excellent stuff with this museum."

"That she did. And I'm kind of surprised we get another letter after hearing her voice from the cassette tape on our last stop."

"It's probably not a very long letter," Clay says.

"Sorry, it's not. There wasn't much room left in the notebook so it's just a note," LuAnn says. "But no doubt, it's still something you'll appreciate having."

"Of course," I smile.

"Okay, Lynn," Clay says. "Are you ready?"

"For what?"

He clears his throat. When he speaks again, it's in a horribly exaggerated game show host voice. "Welcome back to *Take It or Leave It*. Our contestant, Lynn, is trying to decide what course of action to take from here. We're all waiting for your decision. Will you take all the items, spin the wheel, leave some of the memorabilia, bid on the blue box, or go for what's behind curtain number three?" He starts humming the *Jeopardy* theme song and holds a fake microphone out to me.

I start laughing. "You just combined about four different game shows in one."

"I'm sorry, that's incorrect," he says, staying in character. "If you don't give us your answer in the next one hundred milliseconds, you'll be sent to the dungeon with the trolls, where you'll be forced to gargle peanut butter."

"Wha—"

"Sorry, time's up."

I keep laughing and shake my head. "This reminds me of that episode of *Friends* when Joey was rehearsing his audition for that crazy game show *Bamboozled*."

"Oh, I remember that one," LuAnn says, chuckling. "So funny."

I nod, agreeing with her and then look back at my husband. "Just give me a second, Clay. Jeez."

"I gave you a decisecond," he smiles, changing back to his normal voice.

"What is that, like half a second?"

"One-tenth of a second, actually."

"You expect me to make that big of a decision in point-one seconds?" I ask with a laugh.

"Seriously though," he says, grabbing my hand and bringing it to his lips to kiss my fingers. "What do you want to do?"

I tap my index finger on my upper lip, thinking for a minute. "Well, I think I would really love to have her jersey and the program. And her skates. Gosh, I love those skates. I will leave the lapel pin and the pictures." But then I think better of that decision. I'd hate to take everything and leave this museum with only a small commemorative pin and a couple of photos from The Lovebirds. They should have more recognition. "Wait. I'll tell you what. I'll leave the program too, but can you scan it and email it to me?" I ask LuAnn. "That way I can still kind of have it."

"Definitely. It's the least I can do for you if you're willing to leave it with us. I'll even get the photos out of their frames and email scans of those to you too, so you'll have a much better copy of them."

"Oh, perfect. That would be great. Clay, take a few pictures of me holding the program."

"Here," LuAnn says. "Let me. Clay, you stand next to Lynn."

"Yeah, that's a good idea. Come on, Clay. Get with the program."

He rolls his eyes but then smiles. "Cute."

LuAnn snaps a few pictures of us with Clay's phone. I then use my phone to take a few close-up shots of the pin.

"Thank you so much," I say to LuAnn as I hand her the pin and the program.

"No. Thank *you*. I'm so glad you're leaving the program since it's really one of the best we've ever had in circulation."

"It's no problem."

"Let me get the skates out for you. I'm sure I can find another pair to put in their place."

"You know what? Don't do that. I…" I can't believe I'm about to do this. "I absolutely love the thought of having her skates. But frankly, we don't have room for them in the truck, and—"

"We can have them shipped," Clay says for my benefit.

"No, it's okay." I look at him. "Thanks, babe, but really," I turn back to LuAnn. "I think they need to stay here. As much as I would love them, those skates belong here."

"If you're sure, love."

"Yes. I would like a picture with them too, though."

"Of course," LuAnn says, practically beaming that I've decided to leave them here. She unlocks the display case and removes the skates. "I can't believe you're going to let us keep these babies. Thanks so much for that. I'll put a special placard out saying all her items are on loan from you and Clay."

"Aww, that's sweet of you. Thanks."

I hand the other things I'm holding to Clay and accept the skates from LuAnn. They are heavier, but softer, than I imagined.

LuAnn snaps a few pictures and tells me to try them on. Why hadn't I thought of that?

Upon closer inspection, I notice an interesting fact about the skates. "They were made in Chicago." I smile up at Clay.

He smiles back. "Of course they were."

I tell LuAnn about how Chicago seems to be a running theme with us on this trip, popping up in places here and there. I give her a few examples of how Aunt Mitzi (and Uncle Sid) were connected to Chicago, including the Al Capone story.

"Wow," she says. "Well, I'm not sure if it's a coincidence or not, but the main manufacturer of roller skates in the United States was the Chicago Roller Skate Company. Since 1905."

"I'm sure it's not a coincidence," Clay says.

"Are they still in business?" I ask.

"Yes and no. The founding family, the Ware brothers, stayed in business until they sold it to the National Sporting Goods Company in the nineties. So now, NSG makes Chicago brand skates. But the Ware family had a run of it for nearly a hundred years."

"Not too shabby," Clay muses.

"I think I'll try the skates on, but not skate in them. Afraid the wheels won't be strong enough. Don't want to break them."

"I'll piggyback on that and ask, if you don't mind, that you sit down to put them on and not stand up in them at all," she smiles.

"Good call," I tell her. I sit down in a nearby chair and put the skates on. They are a little snug, but I manage to lace them all the way up. They go almost to my mid-calf, as I suspected they would. "I can't believe I'm wearing her skates. Skates that I never even knew she had."

"I'm sure you'll always remember this." LuAnn takes some pictures of me with Clay and then some of just me by myself in the skates, even asking me to strike some silly poses.

Then Clay chimes in. "Do one like Jennifer Beales on the chair in *Flashdance.*"

I laugh. "Just don't throw any water on me." I mimic the famous *Flashdance* scene the best I can in a pair of fifty-year-old roller derby skates.

"Ooh, that's hot," Clay says. He starts singing the theme song to the movie, "Flashdance… What a Feeling" by Irene Cara.

LuAnn laughs, but something tells me my husband isn't joking, even though I'm sure I look ridiculous. I certainly feel ridiculous.

"Okay. That's enough of that," I say, smirking at Clay.

I remove the skates and put my shoes back on. LuAnn replaces Aunt Mitzi's skates and takes the pictures off the back of the display case panel. "For me to scan this week," she says holding them up.

"Ah, thanks again for that. And thanks a million for meeting us here today and agreeing to open just for us in this crazy venture of ours."

"Oh, sure. I was happy to do it. I only met Mitzi the one time she came here to donate her stuff, share her story, and leave the notebook for you, but in that short of a time, I could tell she was a very special lady. We share such a love for roller skating and derby."

"Aww, look at you, talking about her in present tense too."

"Stork Raven Mad and I are kindred spirits," she smiles.

"I'm sure she would agree."

"Well, babe," Clay says as he claps his hands together. "Are you ready to go? We've taken up enough of LuAnn's time."

"Oh, it's been my pleasure," she says. "You two are a hoot. Clay, that game show schtick was hilarious."

"It's just a regular Saturday afternoon with the Sinclairs," he says.

"See what I put up with?" I laugh. "Thanks again, LuAnn. But yes, we should be on our way. Give you your day back." I drape the jersey over my arm and put the notebook into my purse.

As we walk towards the exit, LuAnn stops at her desk to pick up a pad of sticky notes. "Here," she says, handing it to me with a pen. "Write down your email address so I can send you the scans."

"Oh goodness, I can't believe I forgot." I jot down my email and hand the pen and pad back to her. "Thanks for remembering."

"No sweat."

Clay opens his wallet and takes out two twenty-dollar bills. "Here," he says. "Take this donation for your museum. We really appreciate your trouble."

"Oh wow, thanks for this." She takes the bills from Clay's hand and tucks them into a drawer in her desk. "I'll put this in the register when we open back up."

We exit the museum and head back to the truck. Clay and I wave good-bye to LuAnn while she gets into her vehicle as we pull away.

CHAPTER 23

As Clay and I get back on the road and situated, I thumb through the notebook skimming the details Aunt Mitzi wrote for the meetings she had with The Lovebirds. The stats. The rosters. The problems. The solutions. Game strategy.

Clay turns to me and says, "Wait. Where are we going?"

"I don't know."

"Maybe we should figure that out."

"Ya think?" I smile at him. "Pull over into that church parking lot and let's look at the next clue. Then I'll read the note from Aunt Mitzi."

Clay makes his way into the lot and parks the truck, leaving it running.

"I'm kinda hungry," he says. "It's after lunch time."

"Same. Okay, let's find a place to grab a bite and look at the clue there."

He pulls up the nearby restaurants on the GPS and starts calling out names of places to eat.

"Pizza Hut?"

"Nah," I say. "Not in the mood for pizza today."

"How about El Toro?" he asks, rolling his R. "Feel like eating some Mexican bull?"

"Ooh, yes. I could go for some tacos. Or fajitas. Or a chimichanga."

"Yeah, me too."

As we enter the restaurant, the aroma of grilled meat and fried tortilla chips hits my nose. Mariachi music is playing through the speakers in the ceiling. My mouth waters at the sound of sizzling fajitas on a cast iron skillet platter. I'm so hungry.

The interior of the restaurant is what you'd expect from a typical Mexican eatery. The walls are painted in a tan color with murals of Mexico. There's one with a lady in a colorful dress with a matching sombrero. Another with a man wearing chaps riding a bucking bull, the bull's hind legs nearly straight up in the air. On the opposite wall, a matador waves his red cape in front of a bull in an arena. Neon signs over the bar advertise Dos Equis, Modelo, and Corona beer. A few posters adorn the walls as well, promoting their weekly specials like Margarita Mondays and Taco Tuesdays.

The hostess seats us and hands us menus which, in our hunger, we study as if they were holy writ. Seconds later, our waitress appears with a bowl of tortilla chips along with a cup of salsa that looks homemade. Thank God, because again, I'm starving. I notice a sign in a plastic frame on the table that says, 'We will, we will, guac you!' that offers their tableside guacamole. I'm all over that. Clay and I give the waitress our orders and before I can even tell her that I want the tableside guac, Clay orders some. There he goes, reading my mind again.

"Great," she says. "I'll be right back with your drinks."

I pull out the clue sheet, scanning it till I get to number thirty-four on the list. I clear my throat. "Okay, are you ready?" Clay nods, shoving a salsa-dipped tortilla chip into his mouth. "Here goes. 'Enter the Sunflower State and look for a shrine. The one that belongs to the World's Largest Ball of Twine.' That's it?" I ask, a little stupefied.

"Where is the world's largest ball of twine?"

"I'm not sure. There could be more than one, you know? Multiple small towns could all be making the same claim to fame."

"True," Clay says. "The notoriety of being home to the world's largest twine ball would be hard to pass up." He chuckles and dips another chip.

The waitress brings our drinks and sets them on the table. "Our tableside guac specialist is on his way to make it live in front of your eyes," she smiles.

"Do we need a referral to see the specialist?" Clay deadpans, not even reacting when I kick him under the table.

"Ignore him," I tell her with a smile. "He thinks he's funny. And thank you. I can't wait." I freaking love guacamole. The stuff you get in tubs from the grocery is okay, but nothing beats fresh guac.

Clay takes a sip of his Corona and then says, "Back to the quest. Maybe it would be a good idea to first look up what state is known as the Sunflower State."

"Yes." I pick up my phone to search for the answer, but then see a handsome Latino guy pushing a cart full of fresh ingredients, kitchen tools, and bowls in our direction. He must be coming to make our guacamole, so I set my phone down.

"Hola," he says. "My name is Rogelio and I'll be creating your guacamole experience this afternoon." We watch him prepare a beautiful bowl of guacamole with avocados, onions, freshly squeezed lemon juice, a little salt, garlic, and a fresh jalapeno pepper sans seeds. He makes a spectacle of it all by quickly chopping everything with precision, singing to us in Spanish as he mashes the avocados, squeezing the lemon juice without letting one seed drop into the bowl, and folding the rest of the ingredients into the mix with expertise. The whole production is a piece of performance art.

Clay and I clap as he serves us and we each take a tortilla chip and scoop up some of the guac with it to taste.

"Holy crap. This is delicious, Rogelio," I say to our culinary maestro.

Clay nods to him. "I agree, mi amigo. Job well done. Rogelio? You're my bro-gelio."

"Gracias," he says with a chuckle. "Please enjoy the rest of your lunch." He gathers his tools and rolls the cart back to the kitchen.

I take a sip from my strawberry margarita and eat a few more chips with dip. I alternate between the salsa and guacamole, then dip one tortilla chip into both concoctions. The mix of the combined flavors of dip is so good.

"I think you can look up the Sunflower State now," Clay tells me.

"Ah, yes. I was a little distracted by some of the best guacamole and salsa ever." I pull up Google on my phone and search. "It's Kansas. We're going to Kansas to see a big ball of string and yet there's no mention of *The Wizard of Oz*?"

"There wasn't a big ball of twine in *The Wizard of Oz*. Well, maybe in the book, I don't know. Never read it. I know there wasn't one in the movie."

I shake my head. "I'm being serious, Clay. I can't believe it. I thought for sure when we got to Kansas that Aunt Mitzi would have us go somewhere that was significant to that movie."

"Come on, Lynn. That's too cliché for Aunt Mitzi. She's classier than that."

"How is a hoard of cord less cliché?" I screech.

Clay cracks up. "Shit. 'A hoard of cord.' That's hilarious, Lynn."

"Do you see me laughing?" Clay's face stills. "Asshole," I mutter.

"Hey, you might wanna check your attitude before somebody drops a house on you, missy."

If looks could kill, Clay would be deader than the Wicked Witch of the West. He smiles at me regardless. I roll my eyes and continue my diatribe. "This is so dumb. I can't believe she just… dismissed Dorothy and the whole thing. How could she do that?" I'm flustered. Flabbergasted. Flummoxed. "No Tin Man, no Toto, no—"

"Cowardly twine?" Clay's atrocious pun fails to calm me.

The waitress brings our food but I'm almost too agitated to eat now.

"Is there anything else I can get you right now?" she asks.

"No, thanks." I fake a smile.

"I'll take another Corona with lime please," Clay tells her.

"Sure thing. Be right back with that." She flits off towards the bar.

Clay turns his attention back to me. "Okay. What's the big deal, Lynn? So we're not off to see the wizard. Why are you so mad?" He starts piling fajita meat along with some grilled green peppers and onions, grated cheddar cheese, sour cream, and pico de gallo onto a tortilla.

I let out an exaggerated sigh. "I'm not *mad*, I guess. Not really."

"You sure as hell sound mad."

"Whatever. It's just that we always made a big to-do while CeCe and I were growing up to go and watch *The Wizard of Oz* at Aunt Mitzi's. She would make us big bowls of popcorn and bought us red slippers to wear. She even glued red sequins on them, and I just have really fond memories of those times. I mean… she loved Judy Garland. Hell, for all I know, she probably knew her. I just thought she would have incorporated those memories of us together for our stop in Kansas. I'm just really disappointed. That's all."

"I'm sorry, babe," he says sympathetically. "You know though, we're not even there yet. Stop speculating. Maybe there will be another clue when we get there."

"Maybe. But, you're right. As usual." I smile at him and finally cut into my chimichanga.

"I know." He gives me a wink. "And not that this will thrill you any, but if I remember correctly, the twine ball was mentioned in one of the novellas Stephen King wrote with his son Joe Hill."

"Really? What's it called? Not that I've read it. Wait, why does his son have a different last name?"

"It's his pen name. He wanted to see if he could succeed on the sole basis of his own merit and not because of who his father is. But after he achieved a bit of success, he came forward and confirmed that he was the son of Stephen King. I think some magazine article outed him first though."

"Gotcha. King of the Hill."

"Ha. That's cute."

"Does he write scary books too?"

"I'd say mostly yes. But he also writes graphic novels and has written some dark fantasy and post-apocalyptic stuff."

"Cool. I know Stephen King is your favorite, but I just can't read his work. I'm too chicken."

Clay chuckles. "It's okay, babe. He's not for everyone."

"So what's the name of the book?"

"It's called *In the Tall Grass* and it's about this brother and sister that go on a road trip. They get lost in a field in the middle of Kansas, looking for a little boy that they believe is in trouble because they hear him screaming for help."

"That sounds ominous. Say no more. That's all the synopsis I need."

"Yes, ma'am. Anyway, it's a short read, so I've read it several times. It mentions that the sister wanted to go see the World's Largest Ball of Twine, which they do. I'm a little eager to see it myself now because of the reference to it in their book."

"Very cool that you'll have another Stephen King connection with this trip."

"Yep. Nothing beats us seeing his house in Bangor, Maine though. That was truly a bucket list moment for me."

"I know, you were like a little kid, fanboying in front of his house."

"Can't blame me for that. It was freaking surreal. Cheers to Stephen King." He holds up his beer bottle and takes another sip, then changes the subject. "Hey, did we ever look at the key for this one?"

"Nope. Sure didn't. I forgot."

"And you still have the note from Aunt Mitzi to read from the roller skate museum."

"Now *that*, I remember. I wanted something to look forward to when we finished eating."

"When you get a second, see if you can find what city the ball of twine is in so we know exactly where we're going."

I point at him with my fork. "Good call. I almost forgot. I got stuck on the whole lack of Emerald City-ness that I neglected to keep searching."

"Okay," Clay furrows his brow at me, "you know all that stuff from the movie is in Oz, right? Not Kansas."

"Yes, Clay. I'm aware. Jeez. You're really on a mission to piss me off this afternoon, aren't you?"

"Just trying to shake things up. I like seeing your feathers ruffled. It's kinda hot."

I glare at him. "Keep it up, Sinclair. See what happens."

"Ooohh… I'm so scared," he says facetiously.

"You should be."

He laughs. "Anyway, I'm pretty sure they mention the town in the book I was talking about, but I can't think of it off the top of my head."

After I take a bite of refried beans, I continue looking on my phone and find the town immediately. "Here it is. Cawker City, Kansas."

"Yes. Rings a bell. That's it."

I click on the map tab and zoom in. "Dang. I wouldn't exactly call it a 'city.' It's in the middle of nowhere."

"Hey, ya gotta have a reason to pull people to your town. What better way to do it than with a huge-ass ball of twine? It got Aunt Mitzi there, right?"

"That it did." I check to see how long it will take us to get there. "It's about three hours southwest of here. We may need to stay there tonight."

"Where's the nearest big city?"

"Um…" I drag my fingers around the map. "Looks like Wichita. Another two and a half hours southeast of Cawker City."

"Surely there's some place in between where we can stay."

"Oh, I'm sure there is. But you asked for the nearest big city." I do another time and distance check. "Wichita is a hundred and seventy miles from Cawker City. If we go to the twine, do our thing there, then drive to Wichita, we'll be there around…" I look at the time and do the math, "nine or ten o'clock tonight."

"I'm okay with that. I can probably get us there in about two hours. And south is probably the best direction for us to head anyway. With Colorado to the west of us, I doubt Aunt Mitzi would send us that way before sending us down to Oklahoma. So, I would bet that's our next state. Go ahead and book us a room in Wichita, love."

"Okie dokie."

CHAPTER 24

Clay and I get back on the road with full bellies after a delicious lunch and head down towards Cawker City, Kansas and the World's Largest Ball of Twine.

"My turn for music," I tell Clay. I pull up my *Night and Day* playlist and hit the random button. "Sunglasses at Night" by Corey Hart begins playing.

"Whoa, that's a blast from the past," Clays says. "Reminds me of when I first joined the police academy."

I snicker. "I can picture you thinking you were such a badass that you actually wore your sunglasses at night."

"I didn't think I was a badass." He pauses. "I knew I was." He blows a hot breath on his nails and buffs them on his shirt.

"Oh, how I love it when your humility shines through," I say with heavy sarcasm. I shake my head at him. "I bet you gave your superiors fits."

"Who me?" He feigns incredulousness. "Seriously though, I wasn't really a badass. At least not in the beginning," he smiles. "But that song was all over the radio back then. Me and a few guys from the academy would go out to dinner sometimes after class was over. We'd all wear our sunglasses at night, inside, *looking* like badasses. We certainly *felt* like badasses. At least I did."

"I can totally see it."

"Glad you can, because we couldn't see shit." He laughs. "We looked cool though."

"And on that note, I'm finally going to dig for the Kansas keychain and then read Aunt Mitzi's note from the book she left us."

"Okay."

I dig in the box for the keychain labeled with the number 34 on it. "Aww, it's a sunflower." I show it to Clay. The fob dangling from the keyring is about one inch in diameter and has a picture of a beautiful sunflower under glass that is slightly convex. "So, this represents the Sunflower State of Kansas."

"How charming."

"Now for the little letter." I pull the notebook from my bag and turn to her message on the last page. "No wonder why it isn't very long. There's not much room on the page. She says, *'Hi, you two. Hope you're still having fun and had a bit of a surprise at the roller skating museum finding out about the Lovebirds. More info on that later. Much love to you both. XOXO, Aunt Mitzi.'* Well, that's definitely short and sweet."

"Guess we're in for another explanation at some point in the future on this trip."

"Sounds like it."

As we cross the state line into Kansas, I snap a picture of the sign welcoming us. It's not long before we're driving by fields of sunflowers. I make Clay stop and pull over so I can get out and take some photos of them. The sun is shining just right, with rays casting down, creating a spotlight effect across the flowers. It's so beautiful, like something out of a Van Gogh. I've never seen this many sunflowers in one place before. I wonder if I can go further into the field to get better pictures. A modest breeze blows across the field and the cheery sunflowers nod to me in waves, as if beckoning me to come closer. I turn back around and tell Clay to get out of the truck and come with me. He turns the hazard lights on and heads my way. Hand in hand, we walk into the warm and inviting field. We take a couple of selfies in the middle of the bright, welcoming flowers. They're pretty tall, taller than Clay, and he's six two. At my height of five seven, we have to put the camera at an odd angle to get both of us in the frame with the sunflowers. Then Clay has a suggestion.

"Get on my back."

"What?"

"C'mon. Like I'm giving you a piggy-back ride." He stoops down a bit. I grab onto his shoulders and jump onto his back. He grabs my legs under my knees and I wrap them around his waist. He hops once to get me better situated. "You good?"

"Yeah. You?"

"Yep. I much prefer you in this position in front of me though."

I laugh and kiss his neck. "Stop it. We can't do it in the sunflower field."

"Says who? Nobody's around, Lynn."

"Maybe not, but our truck is like a beacon on the side of the road. I don't want to get in trouble if a state trooper happens to drive by."

"Did you forget who you're married to? Helloooo… retired state trooper here." He chuckles. "I'm sure if we got caught it wouldn't be the first time for a trooper to catch somebody in the fields. Besides, we're all brothers in blue. He'd give us a pass. If I caught a Kansas trooper and his honey getting it on back home in a rice paddy, I'd look the other way."

I picture a couple thrashing about in the shallow water and mud amidst the crawfish traps. "I think everybody would."

Clay laughs. "Okay, sugar cane field."

"That makes more sense."

Clay squeezes my calf as he holds me on his back. "C'mon, babe. How 'bout a quickie?"

"No, Clay," I laugh. "Take the picture already. I'm about to fall."

"Alright, fine. But do you realize it's been like two whole days since I've been inside you?"

"Wow. 'Two whole days.' How awful of me to let you go *two whole days* without it," I say sarcastically. "You're such a sex fiend, Clay. Are you having withdrawals?" I laugh.

"Maybe I am. I miss you. You're irresistible."

"Am I?"

"Hells yeah."

I chuckle. "Clay, you know the last couple of days have been exhausting. Tonight, though. Okay?"

"I hope you mean that."

"I do. I've missed you too, babe." I bend my head down and give him a loud smack on his cheek.

He pops me up again and holds my phone out to snap a picture. We get a great view of the sunflowers in the background this time with me at this height. He snaps a few and then turns his head back for a kiss.

After about ten seconds of us kissing, I start to lose my grip and begin to fall sideways. Clay doesn't catch me in time and we tumble to the ground, laughing.

"Shit, Lynn. You okay?" he asks with a chuckle.

"Yeah."

"Sorry I couldn't save you from falling."

"It's okay. I'm alright. Just a little dirty now."

"Fine by me." He smiles, rolls on top of me, and goes in for another kiss, taking it deeper than the one from a minute ago.

I lightly push his shoulders. "You seriously need to stop."

"Ugh. Tease," he winks.

"C'mon, Captain Caveman. Lemme up."

After we get up and brush ourselves off, I scroll through the pictures. They all came out so good, but the best ones are of me on his back. Then I see that he took some photos of us kissing. They're so sweet. Like something out of a movie, the sun hitting us perfectly. It's dreamy, the way it's reflecting off my hair, creating a halo.

I show Clay my favorite one. "I think I want to frame this when we get home. I love it. You little sneak. Thank you for that little surprise." I love it so much that I make it the new background to the home screen on my phone.

"You're welcome, love. They did come out pretty good for me not looking at what I was doing." He takes a closer look at it. "It's damn sexy. Look at us."

"I know. We make a hot couple, don't we?"

"Mmm hmm." He slaps my butt. "Now, let's get back on the road. The World's Largest Ball of Twine is waiting for us."

We arrive in Cawker City, Kansas about an hour later. As we're driving into the town, we notice how desolate it looks. The streets are empty. Hardly any cars are parked out in front of the stores that line the road. Several of the buildings look abandoned, with rusted-out doors, peeling paint, and dirty storefronts. Some of the structures have broken windows on the second levels.

"It's eerie, isn't it? I feel like we're the only people within miles. Maybe they roll up the carpet early on Saturdays," I say.

"Maybe they roll up the carpet early every day. A lot of small towns are like that. Cawker City at five in the evening has quite the *House of Wax* vibe."

"I don't know what that means."

Clay snickers. "The movie?"

"Never seen it."

"Doesn't surprise me. The original movie with Vincent Price is better. The remake with Paris Hilton about ten years ago was a lot different, but it wasn't the worst film I've seen. The town in the movie has a bit of a ghost town feel. That's all I meant. Speaking of all that, this would be a great place to film a horror movie. It's got the perfect atmosphere."

"It is kinda creepy. Oh, look at the sidewalk. It's painted with a huge path of yellow twine that snakes all the way down. I bet it leads right to the," I throw my voice into an announcer's deep pitch, "World's Largest Ball of Twine... Twine... Twine..."

Clay laughs. "So instead of following the yellow brick road in Kansas, we're going to follow the yellow twine sidewalk."

"Works for me," I laugh.

"We should be getting close."

Sure enough, it's not long before we approach the gazebo with the giant coil of rope.

"There it is! The Earth's biggest globe of thread!" Admittedly, I was a little perturbed about this stop on our trip at first, but now that we're here, I'm excited. I put the keychain in my pocket.

Clay parks the truck and we get out, scanning our surroundings a little closer. "This place isn't so bad," he says.

The storefronts contain various works of art. In one, there's a model of a red and white barn taking up the whole front display window with a ball of twine sitting outside of the doors. The ball is relatively large in proportion to the barn, so maybe that's paying homage to the ball's origin. Other storefronts showcase paintings that poke fun at famous works like Van Gogh's *Starry Night*, where the moon is a ball of twine. Grant Wood's *American Gothic* has the farmer's wife holding a ball of twine close to her chest. In Andy Warhol's *Campbell's Soup Cans*, the golden center seal of the label is a ball of twine. In one of the most recognized pieces of art, da Vinci's *Mona Lisa*, a ball of twine sits in her lap.

Clay rubs his chin thoughtfully, looking at a foot-tall effigy of Michaelangelo's statue of *David* dangling a ball of twine from his hand instead of a sling. "I'm sensing a theme here."

"Okay, let's go take a look at the planet's jumbo sphere of string."

"How many ways are you going to try to say 'World's Largest Ball of Twine?'" he asks with a laugh.

"I dunno." I shrug with a smile.

"I still think the best one you've come up with is 'hoard of cord.' That's my favorite."

"Glad I amuse you."

We walk over to the gazebo. There's a wooden sign flanked in front with brick pillars marking the world icon's claim to fame. It touts that the ball is over eight million feet long, over twenty thousand pounds, and has a circumference of forty-three feet. The sign also mentions that it was started in 1953 by Frank Stoeber.

Clay and I come to a large, metal mailbox labeled 'Visitor Registration.' I guess that means it's okay to open it and we won't be breaking any federal laws. I open the box and pull out a guestbook. Scanning the entries, I'm amazed by how many people just from this year have been here and from how many different states and countries. The last record is from yesterday, written in by a family of six from Denton, Texas. I jot down our info into the next blank and before replacing the log book, I check to see if there is anything else in there that might have a lock on it. It's empty, except for a few more pens.

As we walk closer to the ball, the pungent odor of sixty-year-old twine makes itself known. It reminds me of what a century-old hardware store might smell like. There are benches at each corner of the gazebo surrounding the ten-ton orb of sisal.

"This thing is colossal," Clay says.

"That's what she said."

Clay laughs. "She did."

"It is massive though."

"Gargantuan."

"Enormous."

"We could play the 'big' thesaurus game all day long."

"That we could. But instead, let's see if we can find what we're here to unlock."

Clay walks around to the other side of the twine ball. "Lynn, over here."

I follow his voice and see him standing next to a locked donation box that's mounted onto one of the corner columns. "Voilà," he says, holding his hands out towards the box like a game show assistant.

"Oh, good deal." I pull the key out of my pocket and stick it in the padlock. And guess what… it doesn't budge. "Ugh. Of course this isn't it."

"Chill out, Lynn."

"Don't tell me to chill out, Clay."

He sighs. "Haven't you realized by now that not everything is always going to go our way? But we manage to find solutions and clear the hurdles. All I'm saying is, stop being so pessimistic. It's getting annoying." I huff. "Just give it a chance. Besides, most of everything we've come to hasn't been very hard for us to obtain. You need to appreciate that."

He's right. How is he always so right? What's wrong with me? Maybe I'm finally about to start my period. If my cycle were regular, I would know for sure. But it's so sporadic that I only have a few a year. "You're right. I'm sorry."

"It's okay, babe. Now, scoot over a little. Let me try. Maybe you're not holding your mouth right. Watch and learn."

I roll my eyes and let go of the lock. He sucks in his cheeks and lips, making a fish face. I can't help but laugh at that. He turns the key and doesn't have any luck either, even with his mouth twisted.

"See? I told you."

"Well, look at the lock. It's not that old. They might have had to change it. We don't know when Aunt Mitzi set this one up. It could have been years ago."

"Shit. So what do we do? Everything is closed. There's nobody around to help us."

Clay removes the key and hands it back to me. "I could break it open with a tool from my truck."

"No, Clay. You can't. This is a donation box with money inside. We can't just leave that open."

"Well, we could—"

Just then a car honks in two short, friendly bursts, interrupting him. The car parks and an older lady gets out. "Hi, can I help you?" she asks, making her way up to us.

"Um, I hope so. Are you in charge of the donations?"

"I'm in charge of all of this," she waves her hands around the gazebo with a proud smile.

"Oh, thank God," I say, relieved. "We didn't think anybody was around."

"I was just closing up shop and saw you from across the way." The twine mistress points to a store across the street. "Did you want to leave a donation?" Her pointing shifts from the store to the donation box. "You can just slip it in the slot there."

"No. Well, yes, actually, we'll leave a donation. But, um, I have this key…" I pull the keychain back out of my pocket.

"Oh, say no more," her hands go to her heart. "Your Mitzi's family, yes?" She gives me a wide smile.

"Yes, ma'am. We are." I smile back at her. "I'm Lynn, and this is my husband, Clay."

"I'm Shirley. So nice to meet you both."

"Nice to meet you too."

"Pleasure," Clay says, shaking her hand. "So, is this a new lock? Our key doesn't work."

"It is a new lock. Well, relatively new. We replaced it a couple of years back. I knew the day would come when you would get here and the box wouldn't open for you. I prayed to God and all the reverent beings, as well as just put it out there in the universe that somehow you would find me to get the right key, but I found you instead!"

I return the sunflower keychain to my pocket. "I'm so glad you did. So grateful that the cosmic beings led you to us. Right place, right time. We've been traveling for weeks and it's hard to remain hopeful and positive all the time that things will just work out the way I want them to. Like nothing is going to get in our way."

"Well, life happens, darling," she says. "If we didn't run into roadblocks every now and then, we wouldn't appreciate the times when everything runs smoothly and in our favor."

Damn. Is this woman related to Clay? "Yeah. That's so true."

"I was just telling her the same thing," Clay smirks. "Do you happen to have the key on you?"

"I certainly do. It's in my car though. I'll be right back."

While Shirley goes back to get the key, Clay and I pose in front of the World's Largest Ball of Twine and take a few selfies. When she gets back, she offers to take a photo of us that shows the whole ball fitting into the frame.

"Thank you, Shirley," Clay tells her.

"No problem. Now, here's the key," she hands it to me, "and I also brought a spool of twine for you to add to the ball, if you'd like." She holds up the reel with the twine wrapped around it. "It's only a few feet long."

"Oh, wow. We'd love to add to it. That'll be special."

"Wonderful. But I'm sure you'd rather open the lock first."

"Well, I could go either way. What's better for you?" I ask her.

"Oh, please open the box. I've been dying to know what's in there," she smiles.

"I'm guessing money for the upkeep of the World's Largest Ball of Twine," Clay offers as I cringe.

Fortunately, Shirley giggles. "Besides that, silly." She smiles and gestures to the box. "Go ahead."

"You got it." I unlock the donation box and look inside. I see a small pile of dollar bills reaching about halfway deep. Moving the bills out of the way, I see an envelope with our names on it taped to the back. I reach in, get it out, and show it to Clay.

He chuckles. "Another letter?"

"Looks that way." I start to lock the box back but Shirley stops me.

"Wait," she says. "I believe there's more in there for you. Dig around a little."

I swirl my hand around in the bottom of the coffer and hit something hard. It feels like a box so I grab it and pull it out, careful not to let any of the money spill over the lip of the donation box.

Clay sidles up next to me. "What've we got?"

"Not sure yet."

Our latest treasure is a small rectangular box, wrapped in red paper like a present. It's about three inches by four inches by two inches.

"What are you waiting for? Open it, babe."

I smile and hand the letter to Clay, then unwrap the gift. What I see brings a smile to my face and tears to my eyes.

CHAPTER 25

"SEE? I TOLD you," Clay says with an expression on his face that's somewhere between a smile and a smirk. But when he sees my eyes watering, he soothes me by rubbing my back.

Our prize is a Christmas ornament. But not just any Christmas ornament… Dorothy's ruby red slippers from *The Wizard of Oz*.

A laugh bubbles up and escapes me. "I shouldn't have doubted her." I sniffle.

"No, you shouldn't have."

I look at him sheepishly then turn my attention back to the ruby shoes ornament. "They're beautiful."

"They really are," he agrees.

"This one is a perfect addition to the other ornaments I've collected on this trip. We're going to have the best Christmas tree this year."

"That we will."

The box is stamped with the Lenox corporation brand logo and when I turn it over, I read on the back that the title of the ornament is *There's No Place Like Home*. I also see that this ornament was manufactured to celebrate the 75th anniversary of the movie.

I open the box and take the ruby slippers out to get a closer look. They are porcelain, about three inches in height, two inches wide, and one inch deep. There's a small gold rope with a tassel for hanging it on a Christmas tree. The shoes are glittery, sparkling, and shimmering in the Kansas sunlight.

"I love them so much. They're perfect."

"What have you got there?" Shirley asks. "Dorothy's shoes?"

"Yes." I tell her the backstory of how my sister and I had a tradition of watching the movie with Aunt Mitzi every year. I tell her how unnecessarily upset I was that Aunt Mitzi didn't have any *Wizard of Oz* plans for us here in Kansas. And I tell her how I've been collecting ornaments to commemorate our experience since the beginning of our road trip.

"That's so sweet. I love it. So do you feel better now, having a piece of our beloved movie included in your journey?"

"I do. I know it sounds silly."

"Not at all. Many of us, especially in Kansas, have big love for all things *Wizard of Oz*. It's near and dear to our hearts." She pats her chest.

"Would you mind taking a picture of us with the ornament in front of the twine?" I ask.

Shirley beams. "I'd be happy to."

I hand her my phone, and Clay and I pose in front of the ball again, but this time Dorothy's ruby slippers dangle between us. After she snaps a few pics, I pack the ornament back in its box and put it into my purse.

"Thanks," Clay says to her.

"No problem. Now, how about adding a few feet to Cawker City's pride and joy?" She grabs the spool of twine and hands it to Clay.

"This will be fun," I tell her.

"I love adding the new total to the ledger. Just make a lap around the ball," she tells us.

We each grab one of the handles and Shirley tucks the end of the twine into the threads of the ball to secure it. Clay and I drag the spindle around the circumference of the large ball until we get back to Shirley.

"I thought you said we were only going to add a few feet," Clay muses.

"Well, I mean, relatively speaking," she gestures to the ball, "forty-three feet really isn't that much." Shirley cuts the twine off the spool and ties it onto the ball. "I'll make note of it tomorrow when I get back to my shop. Are you guys staying in town tonight?"

"No," Clay says, "we have a room booked in Wichita for the night."

"Oh, that's a nice city. You'll enjoy it. Is that where your next clue is?"

"We believe we're headed to Oklahoma," I tell her. "But we'll figure it out when we get back in the truck for sure. Or at least when we get to Wichita. I can't leave without asking though, did you know my Aunt Mitzi? Or did you just meet her when she came looking for a place to hide our treasure?"

"I met her when she came a few years ago, with a friend of hers. Flo, I believe."

"Ah, Flo. Yes. I think after Uncle Sid died, Flo helped her with placing some of our prizes at our destinations."

"Love that woman," Clay says.

"They were both so sweet. Flo found me online and called. She gave me a brief synopsis of what Mitzi was planning and then put her on the phone. Mitzi made arrangements with me to leave your present here. I loved her story and what she was doing for the two of you. I was so sorry to hear that she had passed."

"Thank you."

"She was such an honest-to-goodness beautiful lady," Shirley says with a heartfelt smile.

"She certainly was."

"I could tell with just the little time I spent with her what a genuine person she was. She must have lived an astounding life."

"We're finding that part out," Clay says. "We learn something new about her every day."

"Not just new, but surprising."

"That's beautiful."

Clay nods. "She was into roller derby."

Shirley's eyes widen. "Cool!" She pantomimes skating and elbowing an imaginary opponent.

"Well, Lynn, are you ready to get back on the road?"

"I suppose so." I turn to Shirley. "But first, let's get a picture of the three of us in front of the twine, if you don't mind."

"Oh, I'd love to. Do you have a self-timer on your phone?"

"I do, but I never use it. Clay is good at selfies, with his long arms. He can get the perfect angle."

We pose in front of the ball and Clay holds his arm out in front of us with my phone and snaps a couple of pictures.

"Thanks so much for helping us with the lock," I tell Shirley. "I'm so glad you happened to see us here. I guess if you hadn't, we would have figured out what to do."

"Or we would've canceled our reservations in Wichita. Tomorrow we would've used our detective skills and eventually been led to you," Clay says with a chuckle.

I almost remind Clay how he wanted to break into the box, but decide that's not a good idea in front of Shirley. "Yeah. Probably that," I laugh.

"Well, it's been a pleasure to meet you both. I'm happy I could help. You two be careful and enjoy Wichita. I'll lock up here." She points to the donation box.

"Yes, ma'am. Thanks again for everything."

"Oh," Clay says, "speaking of locking up, here's the donation we promised." He reaches into his wallet, takes out a twenty, walks over to the box and drops it in.

"Thank you for that. I really appreciate it."

"No sweat."

Clay and I both give Shirley a hug. We take a few more pictures with the sun setting over the town, then get back onto the road and head towards Wichita, as we wave goodbye to Shirley and the World's Largest Ball of Twine.

Settling into the ride, I take out the letter that was in the donation box with the ornament. "Okay, let's see what Aunt Mitzi has to say now."

"Hit me with it, love."

I open the envelope and take out a couple of sheets of paper. "It's way longer than her note from the roller derby book. Here goes.

"'My dear loves, as promised, I'm going to give you a little bit of background with the Louisiana Vivacious Belles Roller Derby team. I always loved roller skating, but I became more interested in the roller derby aspect when Sid and I went to Chicago during the whole Al Capone situation. Chicago was the birthplace of roller derby and was huge there at that time. I read a lot about it while I was there. I asked

questions of the locals. I was intrigued, so I brought it up to Sid. He pulled a few strings and we were able to attend one of the bouts while we had some free time during our trip there. I fell in love with the zeitgeist of it all. The spirit, the noise, the colors, the camaraderie. I'd never experienced anything like it before. It was electric. I wanted to be a part of it. Roller derby hadn't really caught on in the rest of the country yet, and I wanted to be the one to bring it to our town.

'I mentioned to my parents, in simple conversation, what roller derby was, and before I could tell them that I wanted to be involved in it, they immediately expressed their distaste for such a pastime. They didn't understand how any respectable lady would subject herself to such mayhem and harm. So I had to hide the fact that I was creating a team for the Baton Rouge area. It took years for me to recruit other players and get the movement up and running while I learned more about it. New teams started forming. We were sort of underground. Like that movie from a few years ago, The Fighting Club, or something like that? The community didn't really talk about it outside of our sacred zone. It was a crazy time. But I loved it. Your grandmother knew about it, of course. But I knew Rita would never tell Mama and Papa about it. She kept my secret safe. So that's how the Lovebirds came to be.

'Now, about Kansas. I know you were probably expecting a whole Wizard of Oz experience, and I really wanted to give it to you. But there aren't very many choices when it comes to it, believe it or not. There are a couple of museums, but one of them wouldn't let me leave anything for you, and another one didn't have a good place for me to put something that couldn't be disturbed. We had already used a display case at the Museum of American Finance in New York, and we've tried not to repeat the type of item for you to unlock. So, Flo helped me and found the World's Largest Ball of Twine. I knew I still wanted to have something Dorothy-related for you though, hence the ruby slippers ornament. I hope I didn't disappoint you.

'I love you both very much and I hope you are enjoying your trip.

'Love always, Aunt Mitzi.'

"Oh my gosh, Clay. I feel so terrible for acting like such a baby about it all. At least I understand now why she didn't send us to a *Wizard of Oz* museum. She knows me so well and she knew I would be looking forward to something in the land of Oz. I feel like I'm the one who disappointed her for even feeling slightly bummed earlier."

Clay laughs humorlessly. "Oh, that's rich, Lynn. 'Slightly bummed'? Um, babe, do you remember how upset you were at first? You were *very* disappointed," Clay chuckles and shakes his head. "Downright mad if I recall."

"Touché," I say sheepishly. "I was never mad though."

"The hell you weren't. Which was silly. I mean, not that I'm trying to tell you how to feel, you know I would never do that. It's totally fine to feel what you feel. To be mad and upset and disappointed. You're only human and entitled to let your emotions get the best of you. But with that, you just need to remember and recognize that Aunt Mitzi put her blood, sweat, and tears into creating this quest for us. As did Uncle Sid. And even Flo. Aunt Mitzi did everything she could to make our road trip special. Trust in that. Trust in her. Okay? Eventually it's going to take us over the rainbow. I think today proved that."

My eyes start to water and my silence speaks for me. Once again, I know he's right. I nod my head, feeling ashamed. From my periphery, I see him look my way and when he notices the look of sadness on my face, he brings his hand to my cheek and swipes it with his thumb.

"Lynn. C'mon, babe. I'm not trying to hurt you. I'm sorry, love. I just don't want you to get in your head too much about things that may or may not happen the way you want them to on our trip. It's supposed to be fun. Aunt Mitzi wouldn't want you to get upset over any of the places she's sending us to or any of the things she's leaving us." He takes my hand and kisses my fingers.

"I know," I say quietly. "But what about how we learned they tried to adopt two babies that didn't work out?"

"Well, I think that's something she just wanted us to know. I'm sure she figured you would be a little upset about that, but she wouldn't want you to dwell on it."

"Yeah. Okay. And I'm sorry too, for getting so worked up about the whole thing earlier."

"It's okay. You're just passionate. And sensitive. Two things I love about you."

I squeeze his leg. "But you're totally right. And I hate that you keep having to remind me. You're always the voice of reason. You're so good at putting things into perspective for me."

"I try."

"I can't promise you won't have to do it again though. I'm just temperamental like that I guess."

"Not a problem. You keep things interesting." He smiles at me. "So, are you happy with the way things turned out in Kansas?"

"Of course. I think we ultimately had a great experience at the most bountiful intercontinental orb of jute."

Clay laughs. "Now, that's my favorite." He gives me a pat on the leg as if to say 'Good job' for coming up with yet another way to verbalize 'World's Largest Ball of Twine.' "And kudos to Aunt Mitzi for giving *Fight Club* a shout out."

"Yeah," I snicker. "I guess what happened at roller derby, stayed at roller derby."

When we pull into the Ambassador Hotel in Wichita, it's 9:15. Clay gets our suitcases out of the back and I grab the duffle bag with our toiletries.

The lobby is beautiful, with velvet furniture, royal purple carpets, and natural slate tile. Double-stacked round chandeliers hang from the ceiling and create a sparkle throughout. Silver sconces resembling torches with tapered ends and metal lampshades adorn the dark, wood-grained columns. This place is pretty posh.

We check in and head to our room. The same luxe style of furniture and plush carpeting has carried up here. Even the bed scarf is royal purple.

I'm so tired that I drop the bag at the foot of the bed, crash onto the mattress, and kick off my sandals.

"No, ma'am. Get up."

"I know I promised you, but I'm exhausted, Clay."

"That's too bad."

He lies down next to me and starts rubbing my back, kissing my neck, licking my ear. That wakes me up.

I turn over. "What are you doing?" I whisper.

"I think you know." He gives me a devilish smile. "I'm giving you a second wind."

"I need to shower first. I feel so dirty."

"No. You're not showering. The dirtier you are, the better."

"But, the fields today, Clay. I'm filthy."

"I don't care. So am I. We can shower after."

I give up. I mean, I do want him too. Right now. "Okay."

"Mmm. Good. I've missed you. I've missed this." He moves his hand to my center and rubs me through my shorts, but only for a second before he stops.

"God, Clay. Who's the tease now?"

"Oh, I'm not teasing. I'm totally serious."

He unfastens my shorts and slides them down, taking my underwear with them. Then he lifts my shirt up and I take it off. My bra follows. I'm totally bare.

"Your turn, Sinclair. Get naked."

"Yes, ma'am."

He sits up and undresses in seconds. I scoot up the bed to put my head on the pillows. He practically pounces on me and I laugh.

"Eager much?"

"I don't think 'eager' is the right word. I'm way past eager." He takes my breast into his mouth and swirls his tongue over and around the tip. "I'm ravenous," he growls between licking and sucking and grabbing. "Do you feel what you do to me?" He pushes himself into my hip.

"God, you're so hard." I reach down to grasp around his length. "What are you waiting for?"

He kisses me passionately, then looks into my eyes and says, "I want you so much that I can't decide if I should take things slow and make love to you or go hard and fast and fuck you."

"Do both at the same time, Clay. Make fuck to me."

And so he does.

CHAPTER 26

CLAY

My eyes open, but it's still dark. Reaching over, I check my phone and see the time is 5:37. I look over at Lynn, sleeping peacefully. I can make out the silhouette of her face in the ambient light coming from my phone. She's so beautiful, even while she lightly snores. I smile to myself. I guess I really wore her out last night. We both needed that.

I should hit the gym. It's been a few days since I worked up a good sweat, not counting last night.

I get up and make my way to the bathroom for a piss. I wash my hands, brush my teeth, and throw on some workout gear.

I jot down a note on the pad by the bed to let Lynn know I'm going to the hotel gym. I bend down and give her a light kiss on the cheek. She stirs.

"Shit," I say softly. "Sorry, babe. Didn't mean to wake you. I left you a note. Stay in bed, I'm just going to the gym to work out for a bit."

"Okay," she rasps. "Have fun with that."

"I will."

"I know." Her eyes are still closed.

"Love you." I give her another kiss on the cheek.

"Mmm. I know that too."

I chuckle. "Okay, I'll be back in about an hour."

The temperature of the gym is cool and comfortable. And it's clean. I'm the only one in here. Good. I kinda figured I would be at this hour.

It's time for an upper body workout, but I start with a ten-minute warm-up on the treadmill. I replay the last week in my head. I really should call Dr. Hart again. I know everything that happened with Lynn being abducted wasn't my fault. But it still feels like it was. I can't quit blaming myself.

When my ten minutes on the treadmill are up, I move to the chest press for a fifteen-minute set to work my biceps, triceps, and pecs. Being in the gym really helps clean the cobwebs out of my brain. It's as much mental therapy as it is a physical workout.

I move to the lat pulldown to work my back and shoulders for fifteen minutes. A guy walks in and raises his chin at me in greeting as he heads for the treadmill. He's built like a WWE wrestler, looks to be in his thirties, with a totally bald head, tattoo sleeves, and a full goatee that hangs a few inches off his chin. After I finish my set on the lat, I move to the hanging leg raise to work on my abs.

Another bodybuilder walks in, this one with a bleach-blond crew cut and a clean-shaven baby face. He's tatted up as well, but definitely younger than the other one. Buzz Cut gives Baldy a fist-bump and hops on a stationary bike next to the treadmill. Maybe there really is a WWE match in town. Sweat drips down my back as I hear them talking about 'the concert last night' and after about three minutes of their conversation, finally deduce that they've been in town for something called Riverfest. Apparently it's a big deal in Kansas with carnival rides, concerts, water sports, and all sorts of events that last about a week. From what I gather, they were part of the strongman show. That tracks.

They haven't moved from their equipment. It must be cardio day for them. I don't want to invade their personal space, even though I was here first. I don't really want my personal space invaded either, so I decide I'll just make a few laps up and down our hall to cool down instead of taking up the last treadmill next to the bald-headed beefcake. I nod at the guys when I leave and head back up to our floor.

LYNN

I'm awakened from deep slumber by the sound of the heavy hotel door shutting when Clay comes back from his workout. I don't move though, still too sleepy and tired. I hear Clay ruffling through his suitcase, probably picking out some clothes. Then, the bathroom door closes.

I don't know how much time has passed when he exits the bathroom. He leans down to move my hair out of my face and kisses me on the cheek.

"I'm back, love."

I open my eyes and stretch, catching him by the bottom edge of his t-shirt before he fully walks away. "Come snuggle me."

"Mmm. Is that your way of telling me you want morning sex?"

"No. It's my way of telling you that I want you to snuggle me."

He snickers and slips back into bed under the covers, wraps me in his arms, and tucks me against himself with my back to his chest.

"You smell good," I tell him. "Fresh and clean."

"Thanks to my shower," he chuckles. "I definitely needed one."

"What time is it?"

"A little after seven."

"How was your workout?"

"Fine. You should've joined me."

"No thanks."

"You might've liked it. There were a couple of hulks in there."

"Really? Were they green and wearing shredded clothes?"

"Ha. No. In town for some festival. They're in the strongman show."

"Wow. Yeah, sorry I missed out on that. Not really though. You're the only strongman I want."

He pulls me closer and whispers in my ear, "Is that your way of telling me you want morning sex?" he asks as he pushes himself into me.

I laugh. "Jesus, Clay. No, that's not what I'm saying." But now that I think about it, I wouldn't mind a little morning nookie. But I play hard-to-get.

"No? You just said you wanted me. Are you sure you didn't mean you wanted some a.m. lovin'? A roll in the hay? A little rumpy-pumpy?" He says that last one in a British accent.

I crack up laughing and put on my best British accent possible, which is still terrible. "A 'rumpy-pumpy' did you say? Now you're just being cheeky." Clay laughs, so I continue in my awful impression. "Do you fancy a cuppa? Bloody hell, mate. It's a brilliant day, innit? Cheerio." I switch back to my normal voice. "But speaking of cheeks…" I reach around, grab his ass, and squeeze.

"Is that your way of telling me you want morning sex?" he asks, for the third time in five minutes.

"Yes."

"You ready for breakfast?" Clay asks as he gets redressed.

"Coffee first, please. But yes, I'm getting hungry. I don't want anything too heavy though."

"Fruit and yogurt parfait with granola?"

"Perfect."

It's after eight now and I definitely need my caffeine. I get out of bed and walk to the bathroom, grab the plush robe off the back of the door and put it on. Then I proceed to brush my teeth and wash my face.

"I ordered breakfast for you, love. Should be here in a few." Clay brings me a cup of coffee.

"Ahh," I say after my first sip. "Thanks." I sit back on the bed and get comfortable while I have my coffee and wait for breakfast.

"Anything you want to do in Wichita while we're here? Shirley seemed to think we'd enjoy the city."

"Sure, we can look online and see if there is anything that sounds like fun."

Clay grabs his phone to start looking stuff up. There's a knock on the door so I get up to answer it, knowing it's breakfast.

"Sit your butt down, woman. You're not answering the door naked."

"I'm not naked, I'm wearing a robe."

"With nothing underneath. I'll get the door."

"Sir, yes, sir." I salute him with a smirk and go sit down at the table with my coffee.

The steward enters the room, wheels the cart to the table, and deposits our plates of food. Clay tips him and the attendant leaves.

"Oh wow, your bowl of fruit and yogurt actually looks really good."

"Sure does. It's quite fancy. They even added whipped cream."

"Can I have a blackberry?"

"Of course." I stake one with my fork and drag it through the creamy goodness on the side. Clay opens his mouth and I feed it to him.

"Mmm. Man," he says as he chews, then swallows it down. "So good. I forgot how much I like blackberries. Thanks, babe."

"Sure. What did you get?" I look at his plate. "Oh my gosh, is that Eggs Benedict?"

"The menu called it Tuscan Eggs Benedict, with smoked capicola instead of Canadian bacon."

"What is capicola?"

"It's kind of like prosciutto, but it's from the neck and shoulder of the pig, whereas prosciutto comes from the leg. And capicola has a lower fat content, so it's more tender."

I look at him, stunned by his knowledge of Italian deli meats. "Okay, Chef Boyardee."

"I googled it before I ordered it to make sure it wasn't some kind of kale."

I laugh. "I knew there had to be a reason for your expert explanation."

Clay smiles. "So, you wanna bite?"

"Um, yes please. That sounds so good."

"Here." He cuts a piece and loads his fork. There's something so selfless about him giving me the first bite of his meal. He signals for me to open my mouth as his utensil draws closer.

As I chew, I moan. I savor the taste and finally finish the bite. "Holy crap. That was delicious. I think I've had that meat at Aunt Mitzi's before, but didn't know what it was. That hollandaise sauce is some of the best I've ever had. And do I taste basil?"

"Yes. Do you want to trade?"

I can tell he hopes I'll say 'no,' but would swap with me in a heartbeat if I said 'yes.' "No, babe. I'm fine with my fruit and yogurt. Really. But thanks for the offer."

"Anytime." He winks at me and cuts himself a piece. "Shit. You're right. That's good," he says when he finishes his first bite.

"So, what is there to do in Wichita?"

"Not sure." He pulls his phone back towards him and resumes his search. "Looks like they have quite the nightlife scene, but we won't be here for that. Several cool museums too, but not in the mood for a museum right now, is that okay with you?"

"Sure. What else?"

"Shopping. No. Breweries. Nah. Bowling. No thanks. Oh, this looks interesting. Wanna go throw some axes?"

"Throw axes? I don't know about that."

"It looks fun. We could make another wager."

"One that you would probably, I mean, most definitely win, so no."

"C'mon, Lynn."

"I have an idea. Let's save the axe throwing for when Tyler gets to meet up with us. Then y'all can go to town with wagering bets and heaving hatchets."

"You know, that's a fantastic idea. We can just get back on the road after we figure out the next clue. Maybe drive around a bit first and see Wichita's downtown area or something."

"That sounds good."

"Okay. It's settled then. So what's the next clue?"

I get up and retrieve the clue sheet from my purse. "Let's see. Number thirty-five. Wow, I can't believe we're on thirty-five already."

"I know. We've accomplished a lot in the last month and a half."

"Seems like we've been on the road a lot longer than that. This has been the best trip, Clay. I'm really glad we're spending this time together, making these memories."

"Me too, babe. Me too. I'm treasuring these days with you. But I treasure all my days with you." He reaches over and squeezes my hand. I don't react and instead keep my face neutral. "What's wrong?" he asks, his eyebrows furrowed.

"Nothing. I'm just waiting for the joke to follow."

"A joke?"

"Yeah. Surely there's a 'treasure full of booty' joke coming from you with that previous remark."

Clay guffaws. "Babe," he's still laughing. "I was being serious." Chuckle.

"But yeah, I treasure all my days with your booty too." Snicker. "That was a good one. Now, tell me…" He shakes his head, smiling, "What does the clue say?"

"Right. The clue. But just so you know, I treasure all my days with you as well. Okay. Now, on to number thirty-five. 'Head south to the Mother Road and get your kicks. There's a place in Clinton with lots of old pics. Find the booth where you can drop a dime. Inside you'll find something made with time.' Hmm… wonder what all that means."

"Well, let's pick it apart. Obviously, we're heading south to Oklahoma, just like we thought. To a town called Clinton, on Route 66."

"Yeah, that part's easy. I've heard of Route 66 being called the 'Mother Road,' plus the whole song about getting your kicks on Route 66. So if we're headed to a town named Clinton that has lots of old pictures, I'm assuming it might be an art gallery or maybe another museum."

"Or a photography studio."

"Could be."

"The part about finding the booth where you drop a dime might be a phone booth. Maybe there's a lone phone booth on the highway that's still there for posterity's sake."

"Oh, that would be cool. But what would that have to do with old pictures?"

"Maybe the booth is decorated in old pictures from landmarks along Route 66," Clay says.

"Okay. That's a stretch, but a decent idea nonetheless. Oh! Maybe it's a toll booth."

"Hmm, that's a good guess. Though, I'm not sure if Route 66 had any tolls. It certainly could have. I just don't know. It could also be like a booth in a diner. There were plenty of diners along the Main Street of America, and you could drop a dime on the table for a tip."

"Oh, that's another good guess. Let's see what else. Well, speaking of photography studios, it could be a photo booth. Like the old ones where you would pay to have a strip of four pictures come out."

"Excellent guess, babe. I bet we still have several strips of those with us around the house from when we first got together."

"We do. They're in my scrapbook. And I know I have tons of them with me and Annie through the years. We used to fight over which ones we wanted to keep for ourselves. We both always wanted the best one. Which is why we have so many. We took them every time we went to the movies, Fun Fair Park, the mall… any place we came across those old photo booths."

"Funny how those booths faded out over time, but now they're all the rage at weddings and corporate events."

"Oh wow, I hadn't thought about that. So true. Except now they're semi free. Whoever is hosting the event pays for them."

"Yep. Plus, fun props. So, do you have any other kinds of booth guesses? I'm at a loss now," Clay says.

"Hmm… what about a kissing booth? You could drop a dime for a kiss."

"That's a really cute guess, love, but I doubt there were any kissing booths that had anything to do with Route 66."

"You're probably right. But look at us, coming up with all kinds of possibilities."

"We're smart like that."

"That we are. We make a good team, babe," I say to him. "Alright. Moving on. So the other part of the clue is about finding something made with time. Like maybe a watch?"

"Possibly. Could be anything really. Maybe it's the Hope Diamond. That took time. It's like a billion years old."

"Isn't the Hope Diamond in the Smithsonian?"

"Not if it's in some type of booth in Clinton, Oklahoma."

"Ha. Yeah, that's pretty doubtful. Although that would be cool as shit. The Hope Diamond is gorgeous."

"Do a search for Route 66 and Clinton, Oklahoma. See what we've got."

"On it." I pull up Google on my phone and investigate. "The Oklahoma Route 66 Museum. This has to be it."

"I'm sure it is. And what does the keychain look like?"

Digging in the box, I immediately see which one I believe it is and pull it out, double checking the number on its label. Yep, this is number thirty-five. "It's the classic highway sign for Route 66."

"Cool."

"Look at the key though. It's very odd. There are all kinds of crazy teeth cut into the shaft." I show it to Clay and he takes it from my hand.

"Babe, please don't talk about teeth cutting into shafts," he chuckles. "You're making my junk hurt."

I snicker, bare my teeth, and make a loud chomp.

"Augh!" Clay's hand darts to cover his crotch.

I grin. "Sorry. Let me rephrase. There are weird notches cut onto the blade."

"Better," he smiles, lifting his hand from his guarded manhood to inspect the key. "Kinda small too, only about an inch long."

"Let's hope that's not what she said."

Clay laughs. "That's not what you would say." I wink at him. He smiles and clears his throat. "The key is clearly not for a door. Maybe some sort of desk or lockbox. Could even be for a piece of machinery like a cash register or something. Okay," he hands the key back to me and I put it in my pocket. "So how far is the museum from here?"

I do a distance check. "About three and a half hours southwest of Wichita."

"Alright, perfect. We can be there by lunch. You about done with breakfast?"

"Yep. I'll pack up our stuff if you fix me another coffee for the road."

"I gotcha, babe."

"Thanks."

We check out and load up into the truck. I settle in and pick up my phone, scanning my playlists. I know just the song to play.

"Isn't it my turn for music yet, Lynn? I feel like you've been hogging it," he chuckles.

"Yeah, yeah, yeah. I know it's your turn. But lemme just play this one song first. Then it's all you. Deal?"

"Deal."

"There are lots of versions of this song, but this one is in your wheelhouse."

"Let's hear it then."

"Okay. Give me a second." I search on Spotify for exactly what I'm looking for. Depeche Mode's rendition of the old classic "Route 66" starts.

"Holy shit. Is this Depeche? I've never heard this remake before."

"Yeah. Cool, huh?"

"Not bad." After the song is over, Clay switches his phone over to the Bluetooth in the truck and hits the shuffle button on his playlist. "Carry On Wayward Son" by Kansas starts playing. "That's so perfect you would think I had planned that," Clay says.

"Ha. Fun coincidence."

We drive for a little while and I flip through a magazine. I'm bored with reading the latest celebrity gossip, so I decide I'm going to take a little nap.

I'm not sure how much time passes before Clay shakes my shoulder and wakes me up. "Lynn."

I rouse. "Are we there?"

"Not yet. We're about to cross the border into Oklahoma, if you want to get a picture of the welcome sign."

"Oh, yeah. Thanks for waking me." I get my phone ready. Since there's not much traffic, Clay slows down to pull over on the side of the highway so I can get a good photo. I roll the window down and take a few shots.

"You got it?"

I check my phone for the results. "Yep, all good to go."

He pulls back onto the highway and says, "Okay. You know I have to say it."

"Say what?"

"I don't think we're in Kansas anymore."

I snicker at him. "I know we're not. I've got photographic evidence on my phone." I hold it up as proof.

"I just thought you'd appreciate my homage to Dorothy."

"Oh, totally. Watch out for Munchkins and flying monkeys."

"Always do."

I finish off my cup of coffee to help me wake up from my nap. The brew is cold now from the time we've spent on the road, so I frown. I like iced coffees on occasion, but this isn't the same. At least there's caffeine.

As we continue along the highway, I remember something I read about the other day that I thought would be a good activity for us to do on the road. I turn the radio down in the middle of "Sex Type Thing" by Stone Temple Pilots.

"Um, helloooo… what the hell are you doing? I love that song."

"I want to do something else. Something different."

"Like what?"

"Let's play a game."

"What kind of game?"

"Sort of like *Truth or Dare*, but I'm just going to ask you a bunch of questions. So, the objective is for you to answer them. Honestly."

"So, basically, it's just *Truth*."

"Exactly."

"Ugh. I'm sure this will end well," he says sarcastically. "Are they going to be all about feelings and shit?"

"No," I laugh. "Well, some. But a lot of them are kind of mundane. I might even skip those."

"No. Don't skip those. Put them in between the feelings ones."

"Okay, that's fair."

"Do I get to ask you questions?"

"Sure. And I'll answer the same ones I ask you, if you want."

"Okay. Fire away. Start with a non-emotional one."

"Hmm. Okay." I pull up the website that I bookmarked on my phone with the list of road trip conversation starters for couples. "What is your favorite way to relax when things are hectic?"

"That should be obvious: sex with my hot wife."

"Come on, Clay. Be for real."

"I *am* being for real. Nothing relaxes me more than that."

"Please don't make this all about sex. I want to talk about these things."

"Alright. But that's my honest, truthful answer. Now you answer the same question."

"I guess my answer would be a long, hot bubble bath with candles and a glass of wine. And some instrumental spa music."

"What the fuck is 'spa' music? Is that really a genre?"

"It's this." I scroll through my *Everything Zen* playlist and hit shuffle. A song called "Timeless Wisdom" starts. The calming keyboard music plays.

"Whoa. Very haunting. Sounds like it belongs on the *Twin Peaks* soundtrack."

I chuckle as the Native American flute kicks in.

"Okay, now it's giving me Enigma vibes. It sounds like that song 'Principles of Lust.' I can see how this could be relaxing."

"Not that I need your validation," I playfully shove his shoulder, "but thanks."

"Alright, little lady. Don't get smart with me. I'm giving you understanding. Turn this off and ask the next question. Please."

"Fine." I stop the music just as the streaming birds start chirping from the speakers. "What do you wish you could spend more of your time doing?" Clay gives me a side-eye look with one of his suggestive half-smiles and doesn't answer. I shake my head. "Jeez. Sometimes I wonder if a sixteen-year-old boy hijacked your mind and body."

"Hey… I love you, and I love having sex with you. And I wish I could do it more often."

"More often than we already do? Sheesh! I wouldn't be able to walk."

"That's the goal," he chuckles.

"Goodness gracious, Clay. You're incorrigible."

"You love it."

I roll my eyes but smile inside. I do love it. "Give me another answer."

"Okay, fine. How about… I wish I could spend more time working on restoring my Charger. And now that we have the Eldorado Brougham from Aunt Mitzi and Uncle Sid, I want time to fix that too."

"That's a good answer. And when we get back home, you will be able to spend as much time in the garage as you want."

"What about your answer to the question?"

"Hmm, I think I'd like to spend more time with my art. Painting and ceramics especially."

"I can understand that. So when we get back home, you can take over Aunt Mitzi's art studio space. Paint and sculpt and glaze as much as you want. And I'll be in the garage. What's the next question?"

"What is something I do that you can't live without?"

"Well, that's easy: breathe."

"Aww, Clay." I give him a heartfelt smile. "That's incredibly sweet. I wasn't expecting that at all, considering your previous answers." I lightly scrape the back of his neck with my fingernails, a simple touch that I know he loves.

"Well, it's true though. I don't know what I'd do or where I'd be without you. I'll also say that I don't know if I could live without how much support you give me. How you give me strength. You know I've been in some dark places. But you… you make me want to wake up every day. Get out of bed every day. Live. Every. Day."

I start to get a little teary-eyed. "I took a vow when we got married, Clay. Good times and bad. Sickness and health. All that. Because I love you."

"Love you too, babe." He smiles and winks at me. "Now you answer it."

"I guess I would have to match your answer and say the same. I'd be lost without you too."

He lifts my hand to his mouth and kisses my fingers. "Okay then." He smiles. "What's next?"

"What is the nicest thing I've done for you recently?"

"Oh, that blowjob the other day was *really* nice," he chuckles.

I laugh. "Fair enough."

"And you?"

"I love when you bring me my coffee in the morning before I have a chance to make it. And when you buy me little things, because I know you thought of me. Like that travel journal you bought me a couple of weeks ago when we stopped at Barnes and Noble. That was really nice. I appreciated that."

"No problem, love."

"Okay, one more question for now. What's your favorite memory of our dating years?"

"Well, you know we didn't exactly date for years. It was just a couple of months before I left for my first deployment to the Middle East. I was gone eight months."

"Yeah. And we got married as soon as you got back. So pick a favorite memory from the two months before you left."

"It would be the night before I left. When I told you I loved you for the first time. And then we had sex… made love… for the first time."

"I think that would have to be my favorite memory too. It was one of the best and worst nights of my life all in one."

"How was it the worst?"

"Because you were leaving the next day. And I was so in love with you by then, I didn't know how I was going to survive with you across the world for an indeterminate amount of time."

"I know. I was so scared you were going to ditch me while I was gone."

"I promised you I'd wait for you."

"You did make that promise. But with how I'd been treated in the past because of my work, and how new you and I were, I was still uncertain if you'd really wait. I'm so glad you did."

"The thought never crossed my mind to leave you. I'm not that kind of person."

"I know you aren't. But still… I think that's part of why I asked you to housesit for me and take care of Shadow while I was gone. It was selfish, but I wanted to know you were sleeping in my bed every night, even if it was without me."

"I was happy to do it. And everything turned out alright in the end. It led us to where we are now."

"That it did. And speaking of that, we should be at the Route 66 Museum soon."

CHAPTER 27

Clay and I pull up to the museum and the building is a retro style of architecture, kind of Googie meets Raygun Gothic. It's boxy with pointed fins jutting from the roof near the edge, similar to those found on '57 Chevys. The whole storefront entrance of the building is fabricated with glass blocks and the name of the museum is emblazoned largely in red neon lights. The columns along the front are also made of glass blocks and have neon lights set within them. An antique convertible behind the windows makes the place look kind of like a car dealership.

"I think I need a refresher on the clue before we get out and go in search of our prize," Clay tells me.

"Yeah, me too. Okay, so the clue says, 'Head south to the Mother Road and get your kicks. There's a place in Clinton with lots of old pics. Find the booth where you can drop a dime. Inside you'll find something made with time.' Oh right, we're looking for some kind of booth where you leave money."

"I believe that's correct."

We get out of the truck and walk towards the entrance. A large, standing, marble plaque about four feet high greets us, noting that this museum was opened in 1995. It also marks the remembrance of Will Rogers.

"Apparently, Route 66 is also known as 'Will Rogers Highway.' Did you know that, Clay?"

"Yeah, I've actually seen one of the other roadside plaques placed in dedication to him. Something about Route 66 being the road he traveled that led to his career, or something like that."

"Very interesting. I had no idea."

"I believe he's from here. Oklahoma, that is. Not sure where, exactly."

I see the quote from him at the bottom of the plaque and read it out loud. "'*We are here just for a spell and then pass on… so get a few laughs and do the best you can. Live your life so that whenever you lose, you are ahead.*' Aww, I love that."

"Me too. I'd like to think we're living our life in that way." Clay leans in for a peck on the lips. "We have a great life."

"That we do."

As we get closer to the entrance, I focus on the beautiful, pale-colored, classic convertible that's showcased in the front bay window of the museum. Clay's eyes light up.

"Ooh, check out that Mustang," he says as we walk inside.

I knew he was excited about it. And of course he'd know what kind it is at first glance. The car is the first thing we take a look at in the front room of the museum. "It's so cool," I tell him. "Okay, smarty pants. What year is it?"

He cracks his knuckles. "It's a 1969 Ford Mustang. Convertible, obviously. And now I'm really going to impress you."

"By all means. Do your best."

"The paint color is Meadowlark Yellow."

"Are you sure? Because I think I remember from my Color Design class at LSU that this is most definitely Meadowlark Lemon." I smile, then whistle a few bars of "Sweet Georgia Brown."

Clay laughs. "I love when you make jokes. While there might be a car color somewhere out there named after the famous Harlem Globetrotter, this isn't it. That was cute though."

"Thanks. I'm here all week." I give a little bow. "So what else can you tell me about this 'Stang?"

"Well, I can't tell what kind of engine it has just by looking at it, but I'd like to think it has a three fifty-one Windsor."

"What does that mean?"

"More power, of course."

We move over to the exhibit placard to read more about the car. "Look, Clay. It does have a three fifty-one Windsor."

"Very nice. This is truly a kick-ass car. For a Ford."

"Don't discriminate."

"Babe, you know I'm a Dodge man. But I can appreciate this bad boy."

"I thought cars were girls."

"You know what I mean."

"So, if this were your car, what would you name it?"

"First off, this would never be my car."

"Why not?"

"Because, like I said, it's a Ford. And second, I can't just name a car on the spot, Lynn. I have to have a connection with it. I have to feel it. The car has to speak to me."

"Speak to you?"

"More like murmur."

I snicker. "It's so cute that you let your cars whisper sweet nothings into your ear."

"More like my soul."

"Wow. Where was all this depth when you were answering the truth questions in the truck on the way here?"

"Hey…" He turns me and looks me in the eyes. "I *did* get serious with you back there. And I meant everything I said. I might not be standing here today if it weren't for you, Lynn."

I take his face in my hands and give him a soft peck on the lips. "You're right. You did. I'm sorry. And even when your answers were a little shallow, I know you were telling the truth."

"That I was." He gives me a soft, sweet smile.

"Now. I have one more question that I want you to answer truthfully." He tries to hide his cringe, but I catch it. "What is it?"

"What is your Charger's name? The one you're restoring back home."

His body visibly relaxes and he smiles with pride. "That's Michelle."

"Michelle? Why Michelle? Did you name her after a girlfriend?"

"Fuck no," he laughs.

"So then, why Michelle?"

"It was 1982. I had a huge crush on Michelle Pfeiffer."

I think for a second, trying to remember when Michelle Pfeiffer's career took off. And then I laugh out loud. "That's greatness."

"What's so funny?"

"I never pegged you for a *Grease 2* fan."

Clay turns red with embarrassment. A guy with as much machismo as my husband has would never admit to being into cheesy high school musicals set in the early 1960s, or any decade for that matter. "Busted," he shakes his head and smiles. "But in my defense, it's not like I went and searched it out. Tyler was trying to woo some chick the summer after our sophomore year in high school and made me go on a double date with his crush and her friend. The girls wanted to go see *Grease 2*. The chick that was my date…" he pauses and looks up, thinking. "I don't even remember her name. Anyway, she wasn't my type in the slightest, and I didn't want to go, but… I owed Ty one."

"Why?"

"He covered for me one night when I got drunk at a party. Called my mom and told her I was going to stay at his house because I 'fell asleep watching a movie.' I'm sure she didn't believe him and probably knew what really happened, but she let it slide. So anyway, he was cashing in his favor. I wasn't looking forward to spending a couple of hours with a girl I had no interest in whatsoever. I wasn't too keen on seeing the movie either. But when Michelle Pfeiffer stepped onto the screen, I was immediately grateful for some gorgeous eye candy to keep my attention. It softened the blow of the boring girl that was my date for the night."

"That poor girl. She was probably just shy because she had a crush on you and didn't know how to act in your presence."

"Maybe," he chuckles. "But regardless of how crappy that date was, I found Michelle Pfeiffer. And when I got my Charger, I felt so fucking cool driving it. Like a cool rider. And the name Michelle popped into my head because of that song she sang in the movie."

I laugh again. "That song is about a guy riding a *motorcycle*."

"I didn't need a motorcycle. That's how fucking cool I was driving that car."

I continue laughing while singing "Cool Rider" from the movie. Clay shakes his head at me. When I finish the chorus, along with her dance moves, I tell Clay, "But seriously, babe. You don't need to be so defensive and have nothing to apologize for. We all have our guilty pleasures, and I don't blame you one bit. Michelle Pfeiffer is a knockout. And *Grease 2* is one of my favorite movies too. The character of Stephanie… I'm drawing a blank on her last—"

"Zinone."

"Right," I laugh. "Of course you would know her last name without having to think about it. Stephanie Zinone was a badass bitch." I decide to test him a little more. "Who was her love interest in the movie?"

"I don't know. I only have tunnel vision for Michelle when it comes to that movie."

"Sure you do," I say with sarcasm. "He was played by the actor Maxwell Caulfield. His character name was Michael something."

"Carrington," he blurts.

"Ha!"

"Shit!" he laughs. "Okay, that's enough *Grease 2* trivia for today."

"Fair. Now, let's get your cool-riding ass away from this beauty of a car and look for whatever booth we're here to find."

"With pleasure."

In addition to the Mustang in the display window, there are several other relics from the groundbreaking Route 66 in the front room of the museum. A piece of the concrete curb from the original highway is in a plexiglass box. Authentic road and gas station signs adorn the walls. In the corners are vintage Coca-Cola and Royal Crown Cola vending machines offering six-ounce bottles of soda. 'The Mother Road' is lit in big neon capital letters above the entrance to the gift shop, which is just beyond the front room. The soft buzz of the neon sign sounds like a hummingbird swiftly flapping its delicate wings, searching for nectar in the warm orange glow created by the light.

We walk to the front desk register inside the gift shop where a sign tells us to sign in and pay. A sweet lady welcomes us as Clay pays and I sign the guest book.

I spot a few ornaments and a t-shirt that I might want to buy. "We'll come back to the gift shop after we go through the museum," I tell Clay.

"I figured as much," he smiles.

"You won't have a choice anyway," the clerk says. "It's a forced exit through the gift shop at the end of the museum."

"What is this? Disney World?" Clay asks with a laugh.

The lady and I both laugh as she says, "It works."

"Sure does," Clay says. "C'mon, babe. Let's go get our kicks." He puts his arm around me and the two of us begin our trek through the evolution of Route 66.

The first thing we come to is a huge interactive map of the United States showing a lighted path of Route 66 encompassing all 2,448 miles and eight states that the highway goes through, from Chicago to Los Angeles. Various stops on the route are pinpointed.

We continue and walk down a hallway plastered with newspaper headlines, clippings, advertisements, and cartoons from times gone by. Some of the headlines include *Jury Convicts Capone*; *Prohibition Ends At Last!*; *The War Is Over!*; *President Kennedy Is Slain*; *Marilyn Dead*; and *Man On The Moon*. A promo for Elvis' movie *Love Me Tender* is affixed next to a public service announcement reminding people to get their polio vaccine. An advertisement for a 1936 Ford V-8 Sedan shows the cost of the car is $495. A *Tom and Jerry* cartoon depicts Tom smoking a cigar in Jerry's face.

Moving on, placards and pictures explain Route 66's birth and development. It started with a dirt road in the 1920s. The timeline moves us into the Dust Bowl era and President Roosevelt's *New Deal* of the 1930s, continuing to World War II and its aftermath of the 1940s. Each exhibit room is seasoned with music from its respective decade.

The next area we go into is a reproduction of a gas station and mechanic's garage. The gasoline pumps on display are antique ones with transparent glass cylinders and lighted globes with advertisements on top. Vintage signs with various brands of oil and gas adorn the walls. My favorite one, of course, is the one advertising Sinclair gasoline.

"Check it out, Clay," I say, pointing to the sign with our last name. "You need one like that for the garage or your man cave."

"I do need one. But I'm not going to have a man cave, remember? It's going to be called my den of seclusion."

"Oh. Right." I do my best impression of a manly voiceover for a commercial. "Den of seclusion: the swanky kind of man cave."

Clay laughs. "Exactly."

"I do think it would be pretty cool to have one of those signs though."

"Oh, I'm getting one. Soon as we get home. Unless there's one for sale in the gift shop."

"It'll look great next to your big light-up Hooters sign."

"Heck yeah it will."

When we get to the 1950s section, we're greeted by a replica of a diner with the classic black and white checkered floor; a long, polished metal counter; and vinyl-covered, floor-mounted bar stools with metal banding and chrome columns. A soda fountain at the end of the bar is fixed with ice cream bins, topping containers, and flavored syrup dispensers. Vintage signs for Sonic, 66 Café, and the local Clinton, Oklahoma Pop Hicks Restaurant hang on the wall. Several booths in a corner are set around a table to complete the look of the diner. Elvis Presley's "Hound Dog" spills from the ceiling throughout the area. Nostalgia at its finest.

"Look, Clay. There's a big booth with a table. Let's go sit down and see if we can find something to unlock."

"Lead the way, little mama," he says in his best Elvis impersonation.

The red and white V-back vinyl booths have enough room for about eight to ten people to fit around the table. As we sit down and get comfortable, I notice that the table is printed with a bunch of diner lingo that waitresses and short-order cooks used in all greasy spoons across the country. Some of my favorites include 'Burn one, take it through the garden, and pin a rose on it' which means a hamburger with lettuce, tomato, and onion; 'Adam and Eve on a raft and wreck 'em' translates to scrambled eggs on toast; 'Nervous pudding' is a fun way of saying Jell-O; and 'Bloodhound in the hay' is code for a hot dog with sauerkraut. There are many others, but those are my favorites.

"So where do you think our lock is?" I ask, looking under the table for something that might be the answer.

"Hmm… there's a jukebox right here." Clay points a thumb over his shoulder. "Maybe that's it. You could definitely drop a dime in that thing."

"Oh, good thinking. We haven't unlocked a jukebox before. And that's a piece of machinery, 'like a cash register or something,' as you put it. This weird key might unlock it."

I get up and take a closer look at the quintessential classic music machine. It's a Wurlitzer, and I think it might be original. It's in excellent shape if it is, though a few scratches and dings give it character. The vibrant, alternating colors of orange, yellow, green, and red are in plastic columns of light that arch around the lit frame of the jukebox. Trimmed in chrome and with a glittery grill, it plays 45 rpm records. There are bubble tubes set in between the colored pillars of light. I think that's my favorite part of the whole thing. The way the bubbles float up and around the jukebox makes it look alive. In my opinion, it's the most animated jukebox ever produced, and I personally believe it was ahead of its time for being invented more than half a century ago. This style of jukebox became a symbol of the sock hop era of the 1950s and was a staple in diners. It kind of reminds me of the pinball machine at the Rock and Roll Hall of Fame back in Cleveland because of all the colors and lights.

"Do you see a keyhole?" Clay asks.

"No, not on the front part. Maybe on the back or side. Where'd they exchange the records?"

Clay leans over the side of the booth. The jukebox is nearly flush against it. He winks and points at a rectangular junction and set of hinges. "Over here. About halfway down the side panel."

"Oh, cool. Um, do you wanna go see if there's anybody in the museum nearby that you might need to distract?"

"No. Let's just roll with it. Plus, we have to see if the key fits first anyway."

"Right."

"And besides, I like the risk of getting caught."

I feel a buzz of excitement and my heart beats a bit faster. I smile. "Same. It's a little thrilling, isn't it?"

"That it is. And I don't like looking for anybody in charge to let them know we're here because I don't want them to lead us to it and give it away. I want us to find it. More fun that way. And on that train of thought, I don't really like asking anybody for help until we're completely stuck."

"Totally on the same page, Sinclair."

I slide in next to Clay in the booth and get the key out of my pocket.

Since the key is small and not your standard door key, I know this is going to work. Kneeling on the seat of the booth, I see that there's just enough room between the booth and the jukebox for my hand to fit. I lean over and try to insert the key into the side panel of the jukebox, but it won't go in. The tip of the key is an entirely different style and shape from the lock on the jukebox.

"Does it fit?" Clay asks.

"No. This isn't it."

"There's probably another lock on the back panel of the jukebox. Hand me the key."

I give the key to Clay and move out of his way. He gingerly slides the jukebox away from the wall, leaving just enough room to get his hand behind it and feel for another keyhole.

"Anything?"

"Yeah. Hold on." He takes the key and fumbles around the back of the jukebox, trying to get the key to fit. "Nope. This isn't working either. We might be on the wrong track."

"Okay."

"Wow. Is that all you're going to say? I thought you'd be more upset." He puts the jukebox back into place against the wall.

"Well, normally I would be. But we've still got half of the museum to go through, so maybe we'll stumble upon something else that will work. Besides, I'm trying to listen to you and not get ahead of myself. Again."

"Look at you being all optimistic and shit," he smiles. "Good girl."

I roll my eyes. "Let's just keep going." I feign annoyance, but I kind of liked it when he called me a 'good girl.' It made me a little tingly. Maybe that's what he feels like when I call him 'sir.'

We step into a room that is full of display cases filled with tons of memorabilia from motels, diners, bars, roadside attractions, restaurants, gas stations, and any other businesses that sprung up along Route 66. There's a small bar of soap from Zeno's Motel and Steak House in Rolla, Missouri; a linen postcard from the Park-O-Tell in Oklahoma City, Oklahoma; an ashtray from MidPoint Café in Adrian, Texas; and more. I love the various old matchbooks from places such as the Silver Spur Nite Club and Café in Gallup, New Mexico; Whirlaway Stage Bar from Chicago, Illinois; Uncle

Joe's Pancake House in Tucumcari, New Mexico; and more. But my favorite of all the collectibles is the case of vintage motel keys. There's a bowl full of them, as well as some spread throughout the case. All of them have the classic diamond shape fob. Several of the keys are from Holiday Inns across the Mother Road. Also included are keys from the Fiesta Motel in Rialto, California; Lamplighter Motel in Santa Fe, New Mexico; Alura Motel in Bridgeton, Missouri; Clock Inn Motel in Oklahoma City, Oklahoma; Court Shamrock in Springfield, Illinois; and more.

"These are really cool," Clay says, admiring all the different keys.

"Yeah. Love them." I take a picture.

"You ready to keep going?"

"Yep."

As we move into the 1960s part, "California Dreamin'" by the Mamas & The Papas hits our ears. We come upon an old Volkswagen Microbus. It's painted in an array of colors and designs. The whole thing is practically a mural dedicated to the hippie movement. Yellow daisies surround the headlights. An American flag is painted on the back part of the passenger side along with a bright sun radiating glorious rays of sunlight. The side part of the roof is painted with flower boxes having colorful wildflowers springing up from them. The famous slogan 'Make Love Not War' is painted on the front passenger door. And of course, there's a large, white peace sign in the middle of the double doors on the passenger side.

"Groovy," Clay says.

"I know. I always wanted one of these hippie vans. They're so cool."

"I bet Miss Moon Sparkle drove one of these."

I laugh, remembering my persona from our afternoon on the stage at Hoyt Sherman Place in Iowa. "My dad used to have a blue one. I wish it had still been running by the time I got my license. I used to take the best naps in the back of that thing."

"It's not safe to take a nap while you drive, Lynn," he deadpans.

"Okay, smartass." I roll my eyes. "What year do you think this one is?"

"I would guess about 1968."

"You guess?"

"Yes. I'm guessing. While I pride myself on knowing a lot about a lot of different types of autos, I don't know everything about every vehicle ever manufactured."

I sigh. "I'm disappointed in you, Clay. What kind of vehicle connoisseur doesn't know the make, model, year, engine type, and options packages of every automobile ever manufactured?" I shake my head at him and *tsk, tsk, tsk* in mock dismay.

"*Now* who's being a smartass?"

"That would be me." I wink at him. "Anyway, I think 1968 is a great guess. I was thinking '69."

"Oh really? I'm down for that," Clay says with one of his sexy half-smiles as he nods.

"Jesus, Clay. Freaking gutter brain."

"You walked right into that one."

"I suppose I did."

We get closer to the van and peer into the windows. The floor and sides are covered with a flowery print material. It's all decked out in 1960s gear. An acoustic guitar rests on the back seat next to a suede vest with fringe and rivets. A pair of bell-bottom jeans spills out of a plastic, yellow, vintage suitcase. I wonder if that's what the key is for. Probably not though, since the suitcase is already opened. And has nothing to do with dimes. The key is too big for a suitcase lock anyway. A portable radio with only AM stations sits on the floor next to the suitcase. Purple, fuzzy dice hang from the rearview mirror.

"I don't guess there's anything in this minibus that you can drop a dime in that would need to be unlocked," I say to Clay.

"Probably not. Although I bet plenty of LSD was dropped in this van. Along with dime bags galore."

I chuckle. "I'm sure you're right about that."

The song in the room changes to "I Saw Her Standing There" by The Beatles. I'm still peeking into the windows of the van when Clay grabs me by the waist and spins me around. I shriek in surprise.

"What are you doing?" I laugh.

"You can't shake your ass like that and expect me to stay still." He twirls me around one more time, then finishes it off with a slap on my butt and a peck on my lips before he stops and lets me go.

"You're crazy," I snicker. "I didn't even realize I was dancing."

"I sure as hell did. C'mon. Are you ready to move on to the next room? There can't be too much of the museum left to see."

"Yeah, let's go. I hope that doesn't mean we're almost out of places to find our treasure."

"It could be anywhere, Lynn. And you know the drill: if we don't find it, then we'll ask."

"Roger that."

As we mosey into the decade of the 1970s, "Hotel California" by the Eagles is playing. We see pictures of the decline and downfall of Route 66. The diminution of the Mother Road began when the interstate network was developed in the 1950s, so as time went on, the road was traveled less and less. Photographs of abandoned and dilapidated hotels, restaurants, service stations, and other businesses along The Main Street of America hang on the walls. Accompanying those are pictures of cracked asphalt and faded 'Route 66' road striping with weeds growing through the fissures. The melancholic timeline of photos continues with images of barricades and signs reading 'ROAD CLOSED.' It's really glum. Progress paves the way for nostalgia in the heart.

"This is so sad," I say in a low voice.

"Yeah. It's literally the end of the road."

I look around, searching for something that might need a key, but nothing stands out. "Doesn't appear to be anything here to unlock."

"Nope. Looks like just one room left before we're back to the gift shop."

I sigh. "I hope we haven't overlooked it."

"Don't give up, babe. We're not done yet. Come on." He grabs my belt loop with his index finger and pulls me along to move ahead to the following room.

"Wait. I wanna snap a few pics of this, even though it's kinda heart-breaking." Clay stops and I take a couple of pictures with my phone. "Okay."

Heading into the 1980s, Bruce Springsteen's "Hungry Heart" is playing overhead.

Here we learn that by 1985, Route 66 was decommissioned and removed from maps. However, this area of the museum is uplifting. It talks about the preservation and revival of Route 66 as a tourist attraction.

Some of the landmarks that were still on the highway were restored and added to the National Register of Historic Places. Certain sections of the highway were renamed 'Historic Route 66' and reinstated to some maps.

"This makes me feel good," I smile. "Thank goodness a group of people had the foresight to save this road and revitalize it before it was too late. This stretch of road is too important to American history to have it be totally dumped and forgotten about."

"I agree. Check out the pictures of some of the restorations."

"Yeah. It's wonderful to see."

Photos of restored neon signs from many of the motels and restaurants decorate the room. The Magnolia fuel station in Shamrock, Texas has been restored and turned into a museum. Newly installed highway signs with the word 'Historic' have been added to the markers. And I think my favorite of all the restorations is the Wigwam Motel in Holbrook, Arizona. There are also photos of people enjoying their trek up and down the newly resuscitated Route 66, posing in front of various landmarks and signage all along Will Rogers Highway.

As I'm taking pictures of some of the really cool photos of neon signs, Clay taps my foot with his as he says, "Babe," to get my attention. I look up at him and he points to the corner, where a tall, black phone booth stands.

I smile. "How did we miss that?" I ask.

"It's practically camouflaged. Same color as the walls."

We amble over to the booth and I open the sliding glass door. The phone looks out of place for this to be in the 1980s section of the museum. It looks more like a pay phone from the 1950s. Maybe even the '40s.

"What do you think this is doing in this area? It should be back in the diner."

"Maybe they ran out of space and had to move it. The diner was pretty packed with props and memorabilia."

"Maybe so."

The phone is a light color, not the typical black and chrome that you used to see up until recently. With the popularity of cell phones, pay phones have been on the decline since the mid 2000s. But this phone is almost a pale pink color, with minimal chrome. It's a rotary phone, of course, with slots for a nickel, dime, and quarter at the top.

"Let's sit down on the seat," Clay suggests.

"It'll be tight."

"That's what she said." He grins.

I chuckle. "You sit, and I'll sit on your lap."

"Okay. We'll try that."

Clay sits down and I squeeze in, sitting sideways on his lap, my legs hanging out the door. "Perfect fit." I give him a kiss on the cheek, then pick up the receiver and hear nothing. "Out of service. That's good to know. At least no loose change has been putting weight down and possibly damaging what Aunt Mitzi left us. Assuming there's something in here."

"I don't think she would have risked that."

"You're right," I say, pulling the key out of my pocket. "Ready?"

"Yep."

"I just realized there are two locks though. Which one do you think it is?"

"Probably the lower one. The keyhole is a weird shape, like the key. Plus, that's where all the money goes, so there's actually room to hold something. The top lock probably opens the phone up for wiring and stuff."

"Okay. Here goes nothing." I put the key in the bottom lock, the box where coins are collected. I turn the key and hear a click. The coin vault pops and sticks out a little. I tug on the box to bring it out of the phone's housing. Clay and I look inside.

It's empty. Except for a velvet box about three inches square.

Chapter 28

Clay moves my hair out of my face as I open the box. I gasp when I see what's inside. "Whoa. It's another charm bracelet." I take it out of the satin-lined box and put it on my wrist. "I love it so much." This one is different than the last one I got in Lexington, Massachusetts. This is a Pandora charm bracelet, where the charms slide on the bracelet instead of them being fixed on the chain. Some of these charms dangle and some don't. A few that I notice at first glance are a View-Master, a typewriter, and a button. I'll have to look at them all more closely later.

"Having this bracelet is special."

"It's beautiful, babe. Looks great on you." He kisses my hand. "Are you ready to check out the gift shop?"

"Yeah. Let's lock this back up."

Clay replaces the coin box and secures it with the key.

As we exit the phone booth, "Jump" by Van Halen starts playing in the room.

"Wow. Talk about a blast from the past. This reminds me of something Tyler and I did on our senior prom night," Clay says.

I look at him and raise an eyebrow in question.

"Not like that," he laughs, when he realizes what he said and how it sounded. "What we did was reckless and stupid, but it was also exhilarating and we got a good story out of it."

"Ooh, sounds interesting. Please elaborate."

"I'll tell you when we get back in the truck. Let's go find you an ornament first. And I'm gonna buy a Sinclair sign if they have one. It's flat, so it will fit under the seat."

"Okay, babe. No problem."

When we enter the gift shop, I head straight for the ornament section and pick one out. I get the one that looks like the keychain for this stop, the Route 66 shield. Clay is looking at t-shirts and pulls one off the rack. I see him get one for me too and I smile.

This is a great gift shop. So many Route 66 items to choose from besides ornaments and t-shirts. There are magnets, tote bags, keychains, golf balls, puzzles, blankets, jewelry, and so much more. Plenty of road signs to look through as well as vintage gasoline signs and various advertisement signs from the bygone era. I even spot some metal Harley-Davidson signs, as Route 66 is well-traveled by motorcycle enthusiasts. I can't decide if I also want to get a coffee mug from here or a shot glass. I opt for a shot glass since it'll take up less room.

Clay adds a Sinclair gasoline sign to his small pile of souvenirs and we meet at the register. "I hope you like the shirt I picked out for you." He holds it up.

"It's cute, I love it." It's white with little red, silver, and blue blingy rhinestones in the shape of the Route 66 shield in the center of the shirt. "What does yours look like?"

"It looks like me."

"Let me guess. Basic black with a small Route 66 sign in the upper left corner."

"Bingo. And the back of it says, 'I got my kicks on Route 66.' You know me so well."

In addition to the sign and t-shirts, he has a potholder and a deck of playing cards.

The clerk smiles as she starts ringing everything up. "How did you like the museum?"

"Oh, it was great," I say. "Loved it."

"Very informative. Loved the fifties section," Clay tells her. "That juke-box is awesome."

"It is," she says. "One of our pride and joys here at the museum."

She picks the potholder up to scan and my curiosity gets the best of me, so I ask Clay about it. "A potholder? That's so random of you," I chuckle.

"Well, I need a new one by the barbecue pit. And I like this one, it's cool. The cards are for us to play strip poker."

"Clay!" I shake my head at him with a small chuckle and blush a bit, knowing the lady at the register heard what he said. However, I see her smile out of my periphery, so I guess she wasn't too offended. I change the subject anyway. "Wouldn't an oven mitt be better for the barbecue pit?"

"No way, man. Those things are too hot."

"Gotcha."

As the lady thanks us for coming in and hands me the bag with our stuff, my bracelet sparkles in front of her and she gasps.

"Your bracelet," she says, her eyes wide. "It's… where did… are you…" She pauses and looks between Clay and me. "Are you Lynn?"

"Yes. Lynn Sinclair." I give her a big smile. I point at my husband. "And Clay."

"I can't believe it. *Lynn*. You're actually here. And *Clay*." She lays a hand on her chest. "I'm Pearl. It's great to meet you both."

"It's nice to meet you too, Pearl," I say.

Clay nods at her. "Pleasure. You mean the Sinclair sign didn't give us away?" He smiles.

"Maybe that should have been my first clue, but it was definitely the bracelet."

"So, you knew my Aunt Mitzi?"

"I met her, but didn't know her. She stopped in a few years ago and went through the museum. When she finished, she told me about every-thing, and asked if I had a spare key to the old phone in the phone booth. After a generous donation," Pearl winked, "the historical society decided she could leave your bracelet here. A copy of the key was made for her. We were able to make some upgrades to our lighting and get our 1920s cement mixer outside refurbished with her donation."

"Wow," Clay says.

"Somehow, that doesn't surprise me," I tell her.

"She was so nice. Very sweet lady. I'm sorry to hear that she passed."

"Thanks. Was she alone when she came to visit here?"

"No. I believe she had two other ladies with her."

"Two?"

"Yes. One about my age, with graying hair, and one about your age, with dark hair."

"Oh, that must have been Flo and Julie, Flo's daughter."

"That sounds familiar." She clasps her hands together. "I'm so glad I noticed your bracelet, otherwise I would've panicked when I went to check on it. I verify that it's still there once a week. Not that anybody else could get to it."

Clay looks to my wrist. "They won't now."

Pearl laughs. "I guess not." She returns her focus to me. "All of us that work here were made aware of this special situation. I can't believe I'm the one that was actually here to witness you coming in. I feel like I've come full circle in this story, having met Mitzi and everything from the beginning. It's a beautiful bracelet."

I smile at Pearl and hold up my wrist so that we can both admire it. "That is pretty cool. Lucky too. The stars must have been aligned for us to all be here."

"This has been a really fun stop for us," Clay says. "And very interesting. I learned a lot about the Mother Road."

I nod in agreement. "Me too."

"That's wonderful. I'm glad you've both had a good time here." Pearl pulls her shoulders back and lifts her chin. "We're proud of our museum."

"As you should be." Clay turns to me. "You about ready? I'm hungry. We skipped lunch and it's almost three o'clock."

"Yeah. Now that you mention it, I'm starving." I look at Pearl. "It was so nice to meet you. Thank you for keeping my bracelet safe."

"Wonderful to meet you as well, dear. And it's been my pleasure. You two be safe out there on the highway. Where are you headed now?"

"We're not sure," Clay says. "We haven't even looked at the next clue."

"I think it's Texas," I say. "That's just my best guess."

"Well, good luck. Safe travels."

"Thanks so much," Clay says to Pearl as he grabs our bag from me to carry. He puts his arm around me as we head towards the exit. I turn back as we walk out the door and give Pearl one more wave goodbye.

"That was a really good stop," I say. "Now where to? What are you in the mood to eat?"

"At this point, I don't care. I'd even settle for the nearest McDonald's."

"So, you're okay with fast food? Or do you want a place where we can sit down and relax?"

"I'm fine with fast food, but I don't want to do a drive-thru. I want to get out and sit. How 'bout that Subway across the street?"

"Sounds perfect."

After we get our sub sandwiches and settle in at our table, I look at Clay expectantly.

"What?"

"Tell me that story about you and Ty on your prom night."

"Shit," he laughs. "You sure you don't want to figure out the next clue first?"

"Well, I am curious about that, but I'm more interested in your story right now. The clue isn't going anywhere. So stop stalling."

"Okay, fine." He takes a deep breath. "Our prom dates had a midnight curfew, and we didn't. So, we left the after-party and dropped them off back home. We sure as shit didn't feel like going home yet and didn't want to go back to the party, so we drove around for a while, looking for mischief."

"Did y'all find it?"

"I'm trying to tell you," he chuckles. "We ended up at LSU. Tyler says to me, 'Hey, man. You ever been in the underground tunnels?' And I was like—"

"Wait. LSU has underground tunnels?"

"Yeah. Well, sort of. You've never heard about them?"

"Not really. I mean I heard stories about people sneaking into the abandoned Fieldhouse pool on campus, but that wasn't until after it was shut down in the late nineties. I don't recall anything about underground tunnels."

"They exist. But it's not like, well, just listen to the rest of my story."

"Okay. Sorry. Proceed."

"So anyway, Tyler asked me if I had ever been down there and I said,

'Uh, no, dude. Have you?' He told me no, he'd never been down in the catacombs under campus, but he'd heard crazy stories about them, that they were haunted and shit. He was like, 'You wanna check 'em out?' So I thought about it for a second. That's when Van Halen's 'Jump' came on the radio. And I said, 'Why the fuck not? Might as well jump.' So we did."

"Oh my god. I'm so intrigued. This is getting good. How did you get in? And how did you know where to find the entrance?"

"Tyler knew where it was. We got the flashlight out of his glovebox and headed in the direction he'd heard about."

"Wait. Are y'all still in your tuxedos at this point?"

"No. We changed at the party."

"Thank goodness. Did you have to break in or was the entrance unlocked?"

"Lucky for us somebody had busted the lock already. The rusted chain was still on the ground. I guess the maintenance guys hadn't found out yet."

"What was it like?"

"As soon as we went in, I almost regretted it. It was so dank." Clay crinkles his nose at the memory. "You could smell mud and dirt, mildew and rot. Probably dead rats and who knows whatever else crawled down there but never got out."

"Sounds like the plot of a horror movie."

"Yeah," he chuckles. "Anyway, I wanted to see. Tyler went ahead with the light. The ceilings were really low, so we had to hunch down."

"I guess so, seeing as y'all are both over six feet tall."

"Yep. And there were bugs everywhere. Spiders. We kept having to bat away webs. I know for sure there were black widows because I saw one. Probably had brown recluses too. Water bugs, roaches—"

"Ew. I hate roaches."

"I know you do."

"That would have been it for me. No thank you."

Clay snickers. "There were pipes hanging from the ceiling, not helping with the height situation. It was hot and humid down there, because the pipes carry steam from the power plant. And they were leaking in some places; you could see the steam hissing out. Made the air even more wet. We just kept on, clawing our way through spiderwebs and sloshing through the muck."

"Why did you keep going? You could've been bitten by a poisonous spider and died."

Clay pursed his lips and nodded. "Yeah, but I wasn't going to punk out. Besides, that was the last thing on my mind."

"So you're batting away spiderwebs, and you freaking saw a black widow, but you're not thinking about spiders?" I shake my head. "Y'all are crazy."

"Yeah, well, we were a couple of teenagers that thought we were invincible. Idiots."

"I'm glad you can recognize that now. What else did you see down there?"

"There was a bunch of graffiti spray-painted all over the concrete walls."

"What did it say?"

"Stupid stuff like, 'Turn around. The end is nigh. Fuck off.' and shit like that."

"Warnings."

"Well, like I said, it looked like graffiti, not like some official warning sign. I mean, it may've been the facility staff that painted all that down there to scare students and other fools like us. It really is a dangerous place. But you don't think about that when you believe you're bulletproof. I guess we just thought it was other kids that tagged the walls."

"How long were y'all down there?"

"About ten minutes or so. We didn't get very far because of how hard it was to move along, being all hunched over and plowing through spiderwebs. After we were there for a few more minutes, we heard a low moan."

"Holy shit. Like a person?"

"It seriously sounded like it."

"Were you scared?"

"It was a little unnerving, but I wouldn't say I was scared. Tyler even hollered out to see if somebody answered that might have gotten stuck down there and was hurt, but we didn't hear it moan again. I doubt it was a person."

"Maybe the catacombs really are haunted and it was a ghost."

"Whatever it was, it started scurrying towards us. It was enough to jump start us to get the fuck out of there," he laughs. "We were high on adrenaline, trying to get to the exit as fast as we could, tripping over our feet, hitting our heads on the pipes."

"Holy shit, it was chasing y'all?"

"It sounded like it. It seriously might've just been our minds playing tricks on us, but it sure as shit seemed like a huge rat was running towards us. Like bigger than New York City rats."

"But rats don't moan. They squeak."

"Well, this rat moaned. Maybe it was a mutated black widow spider water bug roach rat."

"None of those things moan, Clay."

"How do you know what a hybrid spider bug rat mutant would sound like?"

"Touché." I laugh.

"Anyway, we finally reached the exit. Spiderwebs and dirt covered us from head to toe, mud all over our shoes. Filthy."

"I bet. And you never really saw what was chasing you?"

"No. It could've been a rabid dog for all I know. Or like I said, our minds playing tricks. Man, we were so muddy and stinky."

"I can't believe you got back in Tyler's car all dirty. He's such a clean freak."

"He had a towel in his back seat, so we cleaned up the best we could. Wasn't too bad after we brushed off and stomped the mud off our shoes."

"So then what did y'all do?"

"We went home. Got back to his house about two in the morning. We were still pumped up and too restless to sleep, so we had a couple of beers and just shot the shit for a while. Kind of an anti-climactic ending to the night. But we had fun."

"Wow. That's a wild story. I'm glad nothing happened to y'all down there though, you could've really gotten hurt. Crazy kids."

"For sure."

"You should've had matching shirts made that said 'I survived the LSU catacombs.' That would've been cute."

"Uh, not exactly our style, Lynn." He switches gears. "You ready for the next clue?"

"Yep."

I eat the last of my potato chips and Clay finishes off his meatball sub, dripping marinara on the sandwich paper spread out in front of him. He gathers our garbage to throw away while I dig the clue list out of my purse.

Clay returns from his trip to the garbage can. "Alright, what's it say?"

I take a sip of water and clear my throat. "Ahem. 'In the capital of Texas where you'll find a mass of longhorns, there's a shop with odds and ends, and maybe unicorns. Amidst all things unusual and rare, find the nacreous vanity complete with a chair.' So, we're headed to Austin."

"Looks like it. I bet Ty would be willing to meet us there. Austin's a cool place."

"Oh, that's a good idea."

"She doesn't give us much to go on as to where exactly we're supposed to go though. Some place with rare and unusual odds and ends? Unicorns? And did you say something was nefarious?"

"No. Nacreous."

"What does that mean?"

"Like, iridescent. Mother of pearl."

"Alright. And what does she use that word to describe?"

"A vanity. With a chair."

"So, like a lady's makeup dresser?"

"I guess."

"It sounds like she wants us to hit up a garage sale or something."

"That can't be right. She couldn't have predicted random garage sales. Maybe the place she's talking about is a thrift shop. Or Goodwill. Or an antique store."

"What about a curiosity shop? Stuff in those places is ordinarily odd and unusual."

"That's a good guess. 'Ordinarily unusual.' Talk about an oxymoron." Clay smiles. "I'll do a search for those types of shops in Austin." I pull up Google on my phone's web browser and look for curiosity shops in Austin. "Holy shit."

"What?" Clay asks.

"There are a ton of them."

"Well, that makes sense. The city's slogan is 'Keep Austin Weird.' I guess they're doing what they can to stay that way. Nothing says 'weird' like a city full of shops with shrunken heads, mythical creatures, and sources of all things macabre in nature."

"True that," I laugh. "Looks like we've got our work cut out for us though."

"How about instead of going from shop to shop and looking for this opalescent vanity, we go down the list and call ahead to ask if they have such a thing."

"Brilliant idea."

"How long a drive is it to Austin from here?"

I check the distance from Clinton, Oklahoma to Austin, Texas. "About seven hours."

"Okay. I don't feel like driving that far tonight. I think Dallas is about halfway. Let's stay there tonight and drive into Austin tomorrow afternoon."

"According to the map, we'll be going through Fort Worth instead of Dallas."

"Okay then. That works."

We get back into the truck and head south towards Fort Worth, Texas.

CHAPTER 29

"I'm ready for some tunes, love," Clay says.

"You got it." I pull up my *Badass Songs* playlist and hit shuffle. "Addicted" by Saving Abel starts. "How's that?"

"Perfect. Love this song."

Opening my phone's browser again, I book us a room for the night in Fort Worth and tomorrow in Austin. Then I text Annie to see how things are going with her and Stone. I text Cece to check on our house, and then text Flo to thank her for helping Aunt Mitzi finish out this quest for us after Uncle Sid died. Finally, I text Mom and Dad to tell them we're doing great and that I love them.

A few minutes later, I happen to look in the side mirror and see an older red Mustang speeding up, about to pass us. My hackles rise and my heart races. Goosebumps appear on my arms. I scoot as close to Clay as I can, even though the center console separates us. Closing my eyes and shaking my head, I curse in a whisper. "Shit."

"What's wrong?"

I open my eyes as the car passes us on the right. "That."

"Oh, shit, babe." Clay grabs my hand. "It's okay. You're okay. He's dead, Lynn. Dead."

"I know, but…"

"Just breathe, love. Breathe with me. Deep breaths. Inhale. Exhale." I mimic his technique. "That's it. You're alright."

My heart rate slows down and I begin to settle. "Thanks. I just…"

"You don't need to explain. You want me to pull over for a minute?"

"No, it's okay. I guess I just don't know what will trigger me until it happens."

"Yeah. That's kind of how it goes, which sucks. You sure you don't want me to take the next exit?" he asks as he slows down and veers right off I-40 before I can even answer. He parks on the side of the road and walks around to open my door. "C'mere."

I unbuckle my seatbelt and get out. Clay engulfs me in his arms, holding me tightly, planting a kiss on my head. My eyes immediately well. After about ten seconds or so, I pull away to wipe my tears. "Wow. I needed that more than I realized. Thanks."

"Anytime. I've got you. You okay?" He bends his knees to get eye level with me and wipes the moisture from under my eyes with his thumbs.

"Yeah. I'm okay. We can leave."

"Alright. In you go." He helps me inside and shuts the door.

I know this is just the beginning of my anxiety, but will it ever stop?

Clay pulls onto the interstate and I have to ask. "How do you do it? How do you get past it?"

"Just take it day by day, babe. You'll be okay. And I'm here for you whenever you need me. Always. When we get back to Baton Rouge, you can make an appointment with a therapist. Even Dr. Hart if you want."

"Yeah. I think I'll do that."

I switch my playlist to something a little more subdued: *Hair Band Slow Jams*. I hit the shuffle button and "When I See You Smile" by Bad English starts.

An hour passes before the phone rings through the speakers interrupting the music in the truck. Clay hits the phone button on the steering wheel. "Speak of the fucking devil. We were talking about you a while ago. What's up, Tyler?"

"I knew my ears were burning for a reason."

"Hey, Ty," I say.

"Hey, darlin'. Where are y'all?"

Clay answers him. "We're in Oklahoma right now, on our way to Fort Worth for the night. We'll be in Austin tomorrow afternoon. I was about to call you. Do you think you can meet us tomorrow for dinner in Austin?"

"Uh, yeah. I should be able to swing that. What's in Austin?"

"Not sure yet," I tell him.

"I haven't been there in a long while. I could use a little vacation after the last year. I can fly into Austin tomorrow. How long will y'all be there?"

"Um, don't know. But we can stay a couple of days so we can spend more time visiting with you. Book your flight to go back on the fourteenth."

"Okay. Sounds good. Send me the details of where you want to meet up."

"Alright, man."

"How was Lena's party?" I ask.

"It was fun. She loved the flowers y'all sent. That was nice."

"Good, I'm glad she liked them. Can't wait to see you tomorrow, Ty!"

"Same here."

"Yeah, man. We've got a lot of catching up to do."

"Truth. Alright. See y'all tomorrow. Be careful on the road."

"Will do. Have a safe flight, bro."

"I'll text you the information for our hotel in Austin so you can book a room there too," I tell Tyler.

"Okay. Great thinking, darlin'. Y'all be good."

"Later, man."

Clay clicks the phone button and music fills the cab again.

"I'm excited to see him," I tell Clay.

"Me too. It's been forever. He's been gone overseas for too long."

"Doing good work though."

"Yep."

"He's such an awesome guy. I can't believe nobody has snatched him up."

"He's been too busy for love."

"Well, when the time is right, it will find him."

"He definitely deserves it."

"That he does." I hope Ty finds a good woman to take care of him.

"So," Clay's tone indicates he's changing the subject, "how many shops are on that list?"

"At least a dozen." I pick my phone up and look at the results again. I skim each website and don't see any vanities offered for sale. "None of their web pages seem to have what we're looking for."

"Might be a good idea to start calling them then."

"Yeah. Guess I'll get to it." I call the first six on the list and don't get anywhere. One of the shops did have a vanity, and the guy was kind enough to text a picture of it to me, but it wasn't close to what I was looking for. It was black lacquer with babydoll body parts used as drawer pulls. Um, just, no.

Clay notices my reaction. "What are you scrunching your nose at?"

I show him the picture of the creepy vanity.

Clay shrugs. "Keep Austin weird and all that. Anything else?"

"No. I feel like this is a wild goose chase."

"Don't give up. How many have you called?"

"Six."

"Maybe lucky number seven will be the one."

"From your lips to God's ears."

I call the next one. The phone picks up after three rings. "Good afternoon. Thanks for calling Uncommon Objects. Chop speaking. What can I find for you today?"

"Hi, um, Chop. I hope you can help me. I'm looking for a very specific piece of furniture. It might sound like an odd request."

"There's no such thing as an odd request. At least not here. What is it?"

"A mother of pearl vanity. With a chair."

"A mother of pearl vanity," he ponders. "We do have a couple of vanities. And I think we have one like that, but I can't say for sure. Sounds familiar though. Hold on just a minute. Let me double check."

"Thanks."

He puts me on hold and the music coming through the phone is *The Munsters* TV theme show song. Fitting. It makes me chuckle.

A minute later, he comes back on the phone. "Okay. I have good news and bad news. We do, in fact, have a vanity with a mother of pearl finish. With a chair. Bad news is, it's not for sale."

"Oh, good. Okay. Thank you. That's not a problem. I just need to come by and see the vanity. I'll be there sometime tomorrow afternoon."

"Um… okay."

I refrain from telling Chop we're not interested in buying, but just rummaging through its locked drawer. "Thank you so much, Chop. Am I saying your name right?"

"Yes. It's Chop. Like a pork chop. And you're welcome. Glad I could help."

"My name is Lynn. Can I ask for you when I get there?"

"Sure thing, Lynn. I'll be here all day."

"Great. Thanks. See you tomorrow then."

I hang up and look at Clay.

"You found it," he states.

"Yes."

"Told you. Lucky number seven. So, where is it?"

"A place called Uncommon Objects. That fits with the words she gave us. 'Unusual, rare, odds, ends, and things.' All of those are words she used in the clue."

"Okay, good. Now you can stop worrying."

"Yeah. Thank goodness."

"His name is Chop?"

"Yep."

"Wonder how he got that name."

"He did say it was like a pork chop. So, maybe he loves pork chops."

"Or maybe he chops things up. Mu-wah-hah-haaaah," he laughs maniacally, stretching out the last 'hah' of his attempt at trying to freak me out.

"Don't put that in my head."

He chuckles. "Sorry. But, you know, we're headed to Texas. If he wanted to kill you, he might just massacre you with a chainsaw. Yeah, now that I think about it, that's probably why they call him Chop."

I shake my head. "I think I'm gonna take a nap. Wake me when we get to the hotel."

"Alright, babe. Sweet dreams. Watch out for Leatherface." He makes noises like a chainsaw firing up.

I ignore him and recline my seat.

In the hotel room the next morning, Clay lightly shakes my shoulder. "Babe. Time to get up and get on the road soon. I let you sleep as long as I could. It's late, after nine already. We've got a three-and-a-half-hour drive ahead of us. Your coffee is on the bedside table. I'm gonna jump in the shower." He bends down and kisses me on the cheek. "C'mon, love."

He must have just gotten back from the gym. Didn't even realize he left. I guess I was sleeping like the dead. "Okay," I rasp. "I'm up."

After we're both showered, properly caffeinated, and packed, we load back up into the truck and head to Austin.

"I got a text from Tyler earlier. His flight gets in at 6:05 this evening so he'll meet us at the hotel and then we can leave for dinner from there."

"Perfect. I'm sure we'll be done at Uncommon Objects before then."

"I freaking hope so. We've been known to spend hours looking for the target."

"Yeah, but this time, we know where we're going, and Chop will be there to lead us to the vanity. So once we unlock it, that should be it. Unless there's another clue inside, but that hasn't been the case too often."

"True." Clay scrolls down his Spotify playlist while keeping his eyes on the road. "I've got the perfect song."

"We're in Texas. That mean you're in the mood for some country music?"

"Uh, no, ma'am. It doesn't."

"You're making me nervous, doing that while you're driving. Give me your phone and tell me what song it is. I'll find it."

"I'm fine, Lynn. I got it."

"No, you shouldn't scroll and drive."

I reach for his phone, but "Jump on It" by Sir Mix-A-Lot starts.

"Told you I had it."

"Just please don't do that again. It's dangerous."

He sighs. "Fine."

"This is the perfect song though, you're right. With all the Texas cities he sings about at the beginning, including Austin. And it's such a fun song."

We sing along to the old school rap lyrics and laugh when we mess up and get them wrong.

"There are so many area codes in this song, I can't keep up with them all," Clay says.

"Yeah, and some of them have probably changed by now. You know, like Baton Rouge used to be five-oh-four, but became two-two-five in the late nineties. I bet something similar happened to most if not all the cities Sir Mix-A-Lot sings about."

"You're probably right. I believe this song came out in the mid-nineties."

My phone buzzes and I check to see who the incoming text is from. "It's Tyler. Wonder why he didn't text you."

"He probably knows I'm driving. What's he say?"

"He says he's bringing us a surprise."

"A surprise? I'm intrigued."

"Me too. Oh, do you think it's a girl?"

"Doubt it."

"I'm going to tell him I hope it's a girl."

"Please don't do that," he laughs. "Poor guy has been under pressure for that for the last twenty-five years from his mom. The last thing he needs is for you to add to it."

"Okay, fine. I'll just tell him we can't wait to see what it is."

"That's better."

"And I added a yellow heart emoji."

"What does that mean? You love him?" He chuckles.

"I do love him."

Clay gasps overdramatically. "Fine. Guess we're done. I'll have my lawyer fax your lawyer."

I laugh. "You're such a goofball. A yellow heart means love for family and friends."

"I figured as much. He's both."

When we finally get to the Hilton in Austin a couple of hours later, we check in, put our stuff down in our room, and grab a quick bite to eat before we head out to Uncommon Objects.

Upon arriving, I notice that the storefront is not as weird as I expected it to be. I guess I thought it would be more colorful, with maybe a mural or something. But it's kind of a grayish color with a light blue stripe horizontally painted across the length of the center of the building. However, there are some strange items in the three display windows that do not disappoint.

A taxidermy bobcat stands on its hind legs, dressed in a brown pea-coat, mittens, and a blue plaid scarf. It's standing next to a fox (also on its hind legs) wearing a red dress, a white fur coat and hat, red mittens, white pantyhose, and red Mary Jane shoes with white fur pom-pom shoe clips. The scene is so bizarre that it almost makes me want it, or at least be the person who would be brave enough to have this displayed in our house. The second window shows a female mannequin torso with googly eyes sporadically glued all over it. The last is a display of an old door with various tribal masks hanging on it. Some of them are kind of scary, like they could have been used in sacrifices. Maybe they were.

As we enter, a bell chimes over the door making our presence known.

"Welcome to Uncommon Objects," a woman with chartreuse hair and a lip piercing says.

"Thanks," Clay and I say in unison.

I walk over to the lady. Her nametag says 'Hello. I'm' and in the blank part where you usually write your name, she has written 'Trying My Best.' It makes me chuckle. "Hi. Is Chop here? He's expecting me. My name is Lynn."

"Oh, yes. He wanted me to tell you if you came in during lunch hours that he'll be back in about," she looks at the wall of clocks, "twenty minutes."

"That's cool," Clay says. "We'll just look around till then. Thank you, Ms. Best."

"You're welcome," she says with a laugh.

We start down an aisle of vases. All shapes, sizes, materials, and colors. Floor vases, outdoor concrete vases, ceramic vases, decorative vases, even down to tiny glass vases about three inches tall.

"Whoa, check this one out," Clay says as he points to a very unique vase. It's around a foot tall, about the same in diameter in the middle of its body. Narrow at the top, with its neck about three inches around. The bottom half is slightly tapered. The vase is completely découpaged with an array of cigar bands. Tons of different brands, some quite vintage, and even a few pink and blue 'It's a Boy' and 'It's a Girl' ones, celebrating new life.

"Holy crap. This is pretty freaking cool," I say, picking it up. "Heavy too. I would have never thought to do anything like this. Now it makes me want to start saving fruit stickers or something silly like that and découpage them onto everyday items."

"You can glue all the fruit stickers, candy wrappers, or canned vegetable labels you want on your stuff, love. Just don't mess up any of my stuff. Actually, now that I think about it, a candy wrapper *lamp* sounds kind of cool. Can you make that for my den of seclusion when we get home?"

"Sure, babe. That does sound cool. I'll put that first on the list."

"Thanks. You're the best," he says as he gives me a peck on the lips.

"I know."

I put the cigar vase back down on the shelf and we turn down another aisle that brings us into a fabricated room full of things creepy as hell. More taxidermy, including a king cobra with its hood in full flare like it is about to strike its prey, a longhorn bull head with a gaudy necklace hanging around its neck and bangle bracelets on its horns, and a white rat with a cowboy hat and lasso riding a cat like it's a horse; a plethora of disturbing clown statues, just hanging out like they are holding clown court; the wall of obligatory shrunken heads, some with bones skewered through the bottom part of their noses like a septum piercing; a bin full of loose babydoll body parts, heads with one eye open included.

"You're probably in heaven right now, aren't you?" I ask my horror-loving husband.

"A little bit. Not gonna lie."

"Please don't get any ideas in this area for your den of seclusion or I'll never go in there. Like, ever."

"That's kind of the point, Lynn."

"Um, okay, jerk. I guess that means you're taking back your invitation for me to serve you cookies and lemonade in my bikini."

"Oh shit, I forgot about that," he laughs. "Okay, I promise I won't deck out my space in creepy crap. And really, babe, you know you can visit me there any time you want. Just enter at your own risk if the guys are there."

"Deal."

The loudspeaker comes on overhead. "Lynn. Paging Lynn. Please come to the front entrance."

"Chop must be back. Let's go see." I grab Clay's hand and we walk back in the direction of the front counter.

We get to the front part of the store and I see a guy standing there who looks to be in his fifties, dressed in a Jane's Addiction t-shirt, black jeans, and Doc Martens. The length of his dark blond hair is a little past his shoulders. He extends his tattooed arm out to me as his hazel eyes meet mine when he shakes my hand. "Lynn, I presume."

"Yes. And this is my husband, Clay."

Chop and Clay shake hands.

"Clay Sinclair. Nice to meet you."

"Chop Wood. Pleasure to meet you both."

"Chop Wood? That's your name?" I chuckle.

"'Fraid so." He leans in a little closer to us and whispers, "Don't tell anybody, but my real first name is Delbert." He smiles, then resumes his normal volume. "Follow me." He leads us down a different aisle. We pass shelves of globes, random trophies, colorful glassware, and freaky marionettes.

"There's nothing wrong with Delbert," I say. "I went to school with a Delbert. Though, we did call him by his middle name, which is James."

"Exactly," Chop says. "I'm a fourth, so they couldn't call me Junior or Tré. My great-grandfather was the only Delbert. Grandad was Bert and my dad is Del. When I came along, my uncle jokingly said, 'Y'all should call him Chop.' And it stuck. So here I am. Chop Wood. For fifty-four years and counting."

"Better than calling you Major," Clay says.

I shake my head.

Chop bursts out laughing. "That's the truth." We round the corner, and when we reach the vanity, he says, "Well, here it is."

"Oh wow, it's gorgeous."

The celluloid mother of pearl vanity is way prettier than I expected, even though some of the iridescent veneer is chipped. The chair's cushion is covered with white fur that's secured to the edges of the seat of the chair with those antique upholstery tacks. The cracked round mirror is framed in tarnished silver, its mottled grays and blacks looking something like a darker version of the faux mother-of-pearl. Shaped almost like dragon wings, the drawer handles and keyhole match the same blackened metal as the mirror frame. Vintage perfume bottles rest on a mirrored tray along with a turquoise and silver hairbrush, comb, and hand mirror.

"Nice," Clay says, opening the side drawers. They're empty.

"May I ask," Chop says, "why exactly you just wanted to see it?"

"Well, I have this key," I say as I dangle the keychain, "that I assume will open this center drawer."

Clay and I give Chop the abbreviated story of our trip.

"You really knew nothing about this?" Clay asks.

"Not a damn thing. I took over this shop a few years ago and was told by the previous owner, Hilda, that this piece of furniture was not for sale. She even put a stipulation in the paperwork that this vanity is to remain here, for all time. I just assumed it was because it's a great set piece and the beauty of it makes it look like it doesn't belong here in the middle of all this craziness. I figured it was either that or some kind of curse or something." He chuckles. "Being a stop on a cross-country scavenger hunt wasn't even on my radar. Anyway, it's kind of like our diamond in the rough. I can't sell it. Literally legally. I even triple checked the paperwork yesterday. That's the real reason I had to put you on hold when you called. I knew we had it here."

"Sounds like Hilda is the one that probably spoke with Aunt Mitzi and made the deal to have this vanity stay here for us."

"Probably so," Clay says.

"And as luck would have it, we don't need to take it. Just unlock it and retrieve what my aunt left us," I tell Chop.

"Be my guest. I'm curious as hell."

"Don't give up hope," Clay reassures Chop. "It might still be cursed."

I roll my eyes, insert the key into the hole, and turn it. I feel it unlock and smile. As I pull the drawer open, it jams. With a little effort from Clay, he jiggles and shimmies it, freeing it from its wedged state. Confused, I pick up our prize when it is unveiled.

"What's this?"

CHAPTER 30

"It looks like a manuscript," Clay says.

"Holy crap. I think it is."

The stack of papers is about half an inch thick and bound with three brass paper fasteners evenly spaced on the left-hand side, their prongs splayed on the back of the sheaf.

"Oh my god, Clay." I read the title page out loud.

"'Keyholes and Casseroles
By Mitzi Santini'"

"Is it a novel?" Clay asks.

I thumb through it, noticing that the typewritten pages aren't filled with words. "I don't think so. It looks more like poetry."

"She wrote poetry?"

"I guess she did."

An envelope falls out of the manuscript. Chop picks it up off the floor.

"Looks like this is also for you. Got both your names on it." He hands the envelope to Clay since I have my hands full with the manuscript.

"Thanks," Clay says. "There may be an explanation in here about the vanity situation."

"Oh, please let me know. I'll give you two some privacy."

"No need. You're welcome to stay."

"I appreciate it, but I've got work to do. Just promise to keep me in the loop, if you will. Especially if it's cursed."

"Sure thing," I chuckle.

Chop walks away with a wave and Clay holds the envelope up to me. "Do you want to read this before checking out her poems?"

"No, I think I want to read a couple of her poems first. Here, put the envelope in my purse." I open my bag and Clay drops it in.

"Are you going to start from the beginning or just open to a random page?"

"I'm just going to open pages at random. Like I do with her diary."

"Go for it."

I open the book to a page in the middle and read aloud.

"Autumn

'Fall is the time
For brisk breezes
Falling leaves
Tumultuous seas

'Birds that fly
Dot the sky
Moving south
Fly real high

'Fire crackles
Chickens cackle
Goblins scatter
Memories gather

'Frost is coming
Last of sunning
Winter's waiting

Children skating

'The Earth is sleeping
Its beauty keeping
Spring awakens
To God's creations'"

"That's really beautiful," Clay says.

"Yeah. I love that. Let's see what else was on her mind." Flipping to another page towards the beginning, I read another one out loud.

"'Loss
'Wake with hope
The day anew
Time is fresh
Harmony in view

'Halfway done
Doing alright
Peace for now
Fear the night

'Daylight gone
Alone but not
Thoughts turn sad
My heart's distraught'

"Oh, that is so incredibly heartbreaking. She must have been writing about one of the babies she lost," I sniffle as my eyes water.

"Probably so, love." Clay rubs my back in comfort. "But it could have been anything. Could've been about your grandmother after she died."

"Maybe." I wipe a lone tear from my cheek. "I don't want to cry about this right now. It's just too sad. I can't imagine the pain they went through."

"You know, she might have even written it because ABC canceled *Matlock*."

I burst out laughing. My husband really knows how to turn things around. He's so good at that. "She did love herself some Andy Griffith."

"I know. Read one more, yeah?"

"Yeah."

I let my thumb blindly scan the edge of the pages, stop at random, and open the manuscript to read the poem. "It's called *Ode to Mayberry*."

Clay's eyes widen. "You're shittin' me."

"That I am," I laugh, then read him the real poem.

"Intangible Sentiments

'Fun: Dancing around maypoles
Hope: Reaching our set goals

'Faith: Praying for all souls
Trouble: Going through rigamaroles

'Love: Eating cinnamon rolls
Sorrow: Receiving many consoles

'Bliss: Taking leisurely strolls
Anger: Hitting too many potholes

'Peace: Watching all the fishbowls
Fear: Dreaming of ugly trolls

'Surprise: Looking through peepholes
Hate: Dealing with a-holes

'Mystery: Planning for keyholes
Comfort: Making Mama's casseroles'"

I close the manuscript as my body shakes with laughter. Clay is laughing too.

"Wow," he says, still chuckling. "Even Aunt Mitzi, who was so nice to everybody, could still pick out the assholes."

"I know," I smile. "But she was classy enough to abbreviate it, even when 'assholes' fit the meter. There's never been and never will be a shortage of a-holes on the planet. She knew how to put them in their place though, without them even knowing it. I saw it for myself a couple of times."

"Tell me."

"Well, once, we were Christmas shopping at the mall, and we stopped to have lunch in the food court. This young couple sat down next to us. You know how close the tables are to each other, so we could hear everything the guy was saying. He was trying to be quiet, but he wasn't quiet enough. He was being so mean to his wife. Cutting her down and just berating her. It was awful. His wife wasn't taking his shit though. She was giving it right back to him. When they got up to leave, Aunt Mitzi looked at the guy and said, 'I hope the rest of your day is as pleasant as you are.' And his wife almost lost it, trying to hide her laugh. He just looked at Aunt Mitzi and said, 'Thanks,' like she was giving him a compliment."

"Very cunning."

"That it was." I point to the manuscript in my hands. "I love how she ended that last poem I read with keyholes and casseroles. Guess she took those words and made it the title of her book of poetry, which makes me feel good. Like she had us in mind when she titled it."

"I'm sure she did."

"Are you ready to go?"

"Almost. We need to read the letter before we leave and see what she says, if there's anything about Hilda and the vanity."

"Oh, you're right." I fish the envelope out of my purse and open it. It's a card, not a letter, so it should be short and sweet. There's a picture of the state of Texas with Austin starred and the text says, of course, 'Keep Austin Weird.' I open it and there's a short note on the left side with a receipt taped to the right side. I begin to read.

"My dear Lynn and Clay,

I hope you enjoy this book of poetry. I've written some here and there all my life. The vanity is yours if you want it. As you can see, I've

*taped the detailed receipt, signed by myself and Hilda, as proof of my
ownership of this piece of furniture. You can choose to take it, sell it,
ship it, leave it, or whatever.*

'Love you both always, Aunt Mitzi'"

Clay laughs. "And there's our answer."

"I figured she was the rightful owner of it."

"Well, if it's okay with you, I'm all for leaving the vanity here with
Chop. He seems to like the clash between beauty and bizarre. But it's up
to you. Whatever you want to do."

I think about it for a second. I really do like this piece, but I also see how
it seems to belong in Uncommon Objects. "I'm alright with leaving it here.
Chop can keep it."

"Okay, cool deal."

I put the manuscript in my bag along with the card from Aunt Mitzi
and we mosey back over to Chop to explain things.

"That's awesome," he says. "What do you want for it?"

"Oh, nothing," I tell Chop. "It's yours."

"What? Are you sure?"

"Yeah, man," Clay says. "Merry Christmas."

"That your way of telling me it really is cursed? Some kind of Dybbuk
box?"

Clay laughs. "No, it's all yours. Curse free."

Chop smiles. "Thanks, y'all. I sincerely appreciate it. And I will keep
it. Not for sale. Besides, I could never part with it now after the great story
that goes with it."

"Sounds good. You're very welcome." I turn to my husband. "You ready
to get back to the hotel and find Tyler?"

"Yes," Clay says with a big smile. He sticks his hand out to Chop.
"Thanks so much for everything, Chop. It was great meeting you."

"Same here," he says as he shakes Clay's hand. "Lynn, pleasure meeting
you as well." He goes to shake my hand.

"Oh no, I'm a hugger," I say, and move in for a hug. "It was nice meeting you too. Take care of the vanity for us."

"Will do. Thanks again to both of you for that. Hope y'all have fun here in Austin."

"We will. Take it easy, Chop."

We wave back at him as we exit Uncommon Objects.

When we return to our room at the hotel, Clay looks at the time on his phone and says, "Tyler won't be here for another couple of hours."

"What do you want to do till then?"

"I have a few ideas," he says with a wink.

"Ooh. Do tell."

"I'd rather show you."

His lips crash onto mine and we fall into bed.

An hour and a half later, we're still lying in bed, tangled in the sheets. My head rests on Clay's chest as he flips through the channels on the TV with the remote. He stops on a rerun of *The Office*, the one where they're learning CPR. As things go awry, Dwight cuts the face off the practice dummy and puts it on his own face. He says, 'Clarice,' just like Hannibal Lecter from the movie *The Silence of the Lambs*. The two of us have seen this episode already, but we still crack up.

Clay's phone buzzes on the bedside table with an incoming text and he picks it up to check it.

"Ty just landed."

"Yay!"

"He'll be here in about a half hour, give or take. Guess we should shower and get ready for dinner."

"Okay. Where do you want to eat?"

"I was thinking we'd just stay here and eat at one of the restaurants in the hotel. There's one with a patio called Austin Taco Project. I figure we'll probably get loud so it's best for us to sit outside."

"You're probably right," I chuckle.

"They have specialty fusion tacos and a bunch of beers on tap."

"You had me at 'taco.' Plus, I'm sure Ty won't really feel like going out again after just getting here."

"Exactly."

"I'll shower first since I'll have to reapply makeup and do my hair again. You text him and tell him when and where to meet us after he settles in."

"Yes, ma'am."

Fifty-six minutes later, Clay and I are sitting at a corner table on the patio of Austin Taco Project waiting for Tyler. I'm looking at the specialty cocktail menu when I hear his voice. He rounds the corner and Clay can't get out of the booth fast enough to give him a bro hug, which turns into a full-on regular hug as they clap each other on the back. These guys have missed each other.

"So good to see you, man," Clay says as he lets Tyler go.

"You too, brother," Ty says as he turns to me.

"C'mere, you." He gives me a big smack on the cheek and a bear hug that lifts me off the ground a few inches. "You look great as ever, darlin'." He sets me down and we head to our booth.

"Thanks, Ty. As do you."

Tyler is about 6'3" and has a very solid physique. His brown windswept hair brushes his chin, setting off his blue eyes. He's wearing an army green V-neck tee and faded black jeans. His clean-shaven face, chiseled jawline, full lips, and dimples give him a look of rugged innocence.

"You hungry?" I ask.

"Starving."

We sit down and Tyler picks up the menu.

"First things first." I clear my throat. "What is this surprise you brought us?"

"Oh, it should be here in a minute."

"It? Here?" Clay asks.

As if it was planned, a smooth deep voice hails from around the corner. "What's up, Sinclairs?"

"Holy shit. Is that... No way." Clay says with a disbelieving but delighted smile.

A guy I haven't seen in a couple of years comes into view. He's tall and built like a lumberjack, with black hair in an undercut, amber eyes, and a sexy six o'clock shadow. Dressed in khaki cargo shorts and a light blue henley, tribal tattoos peeking out of his sleeves, he stands before us with arms wide open.

"Yes way," Tyler says.

"Beck fucking Jacobs." Clay stands up and gives him a bro hug. "Damn, dude. Good to see you! How long has it been?"

"Dunno, man. Too long. Good to see you too."

Beck Jacobs went through Special Forces training with Tyler and they became fast friends. When they aged out of the Green Berets, Tyler did some private security contracting and Beck went on to be a bodyguard for Hollywood celebrities. When Tyler finally decided to start his own security training company, he recruited Beck to work for him. Since Beck spends a lot of time with Tyler and Tyler spends a lot of time with Clay (apart from this last year), Beck and Clay got to know each other and they became like the Three Musketeers (or the Three Stooges, depending on how much they've been drinking). I've gotten to know him as well since the guys (along with Stone) would hang out at the house now and again.

"Lynn. Hey, beautiful," he says to me as his large arms engulf me in a long, tight hug. Holy moly he smells good.

"Hey, Beck. So good to see you."

The hug lingers.

"Jacobs. Get your hands off my woman," Clay says jokingly. But he means it. Though, it's not like he's really threatened.

Beck Jacobs is a total looker. Extreme chick magnet. Don't get me wrong, Tyler is a studmuffin too, but Ty is more like a brother to me so it's hard for me to see him like that. Not that I'm looking at Beck that way, but damn, it's kinda hard not to. And of course, we all know I only have eyes for Clay, but I'm not dead. I can appreciate a gorgeous man. Beck has a reputation for being a womanizer though, so that makes him a little less attractive. To me, anyway.

We all sit down at the table as a cute waitress comes to take our orders.

"Give us a minute, please," Tyler tells her.

"Sure."

Beck and Tyler watch her walk away in her tight shorts. I'm sure if I weren't sitting here, Clay would be watching her too. He's not dead either.

We study the menu a bit and when the waitress comes back a few minutes later, we put in orders for tacos, three beers, and a strawberry margarita.

"So," Clay says, "what the hell have you two been up to since the last time we saw y'all?"

Tyler crosses his arms across his chest. "Well, you know I just got back from my security stint in the UK. It wasn't bad, but I'm glad to be home."

Clay gives him a fist bump. "Yeah, man. Glad to have you back." He turns to Beck. "Jacobs, what about you?"

The waitress comes back with our drinks and tells us our tacos should be out shortly.

"Well, I held down the fort for this asshole," he points a thumb at Ty, "at RTS while he was gone." He's talking about Tyler's company, Rutledge Tactical Security.

"I'm sure it was in good hands," I say.

"You know it," he says with a cocky smile.

"Any women in either of your lives?" I ask both Tyler and Beck.

"Lynn, come on. Don't bother them with that."

"Why? I'm just curious."

"It's okay," Tyler says. "I dated a little bit while I was over in England. But nothing serious. Didn't want to get too involved since I knew I was only going to be there for a year. Plus, I needed to focus on the job. But I've put myself back out there. We'll see. Jacobs here on the other hand... he's got some stories," he laughs.

"I bet he does," Clay says.

"I don't think they want to hear about my escapades."

"Please, you can spare me the details." I sip my drink. "I'm just wondering if you're happy."

"Oh, he's plenty happy."

The waitress comes back and brings our tacos. I have the Backyard Brisket tacos, Clay got the Baja Shrimp tacos, Tyler ordered the Kicking Chicken tacos, and Beck has the Confit Pig tacos. Everything looks and smells so good.

"Tell 'em about the bloodhound, Jacobs," Ty says as he takes a bite.

Beck lets out a humorless laugh. "Shit." He shakes his head. "That girl was something else. But, man, she was so freaking hot and—"

"Half his age."

"So?" Beck gets a dreamy look on his face. "That tight ass, legs for days." He sighs wistfully. "Don't be jealous."

"Not jealous, dude."

Clay takes a long pull from his beer. "Doesn't exactly sound like a bloodhound to me."

"Let me finish. So, we hung out a few times and got along great, even though I could tell something was off with her."

"Like what?" I ask.

"I kept catching her in a bunch of stupid lies. It was like she was trying to impress me with wild stories."

"Example," Clay says.

"She told me she went scuba diving in the Pacific Ocean."

"What's wrong with that?"

"With piranhas."

Clay cracks up laughing. "She clearly doesn't know that piranhas are freshwater fish."

"Exactly."

"Did you call her on it?"

"Hell no," he laughs. "I'm an asshole, but not a fucking asshole. Plus, at that point, I still hadn't scored with her. Wasn't going to mess up my chances by pointing out I knew she was lying."

I shake my head at him. "What else?"

"Another time she told me that her great-great-great-whatever grandfather was friends with Jean Lafitte and helped him bury his treasure in the bayou, which I suppose is plausible, but after everything she had already told me, there was no way I believed her."

"Oh my god," I laugh.

"Arrrr you serious?" Clay asks in a pirate voice, referring to Jean Lafitte, the famous nineteenth century pirate who fought with Andrew Jackson in the Battle of New Orleans. We all laugh.

"I wish I were joking. But wait… there's more. She also told me that another one of her great-grandfathers had a map to the treasure that he found in *his* grandfather's house and hunted for the treasure, found it, and then buried it again in a different place."

"Holy shit, Jacobs," Clay says, shaking his head.

"And why were you willing to excuse her lies and tall tales? That's a little more than just a red flag, Beck."

"She was good in bed." He shrugs like it's nothing.

I roll my eyes. "Jeez. Typical playboy answer."

"Hey, don't judge me. I'm not looking for a wife."

I give his hand a sisterly pat. "I'm not judging you, Beck. You just deserve better."

"Thanks, sweetness."

"So, what happened? We know you never learned not to stick your dick in crazy, but," Clay narrows his eyes inquisitively, "what does all this have to do with Ty calling her a bloodhound?"

"Oh, her stories are just the tip of the iceberg," Tyler says.

"You mean it gets worse?" I ask.

"Unfortunately," he says with an eyeroll.

Beck continues. "She kept showing up everywhere I went. At City Café when I was having lunch with a client, at the gym while I was scoping out the latest equipment to upgrade at RTS, even at the freaking DMV when I had to change the address on my license. At first I thought it was a fun coincidence. Snuffleupagus, you know?"

"I'm sorry, what?" I ask, smiling and wondering what the loveable character from *Sesame Street* had to do with Beck's situation.

"Snuffleupagus. A happy accident."

"You mean serendipitous?"

Everybody cracks up laughing, including Beck.

"Yeah. That. Whatever." He shakes his head at himself and gets back to his story. "Anyway, she'd hang around till I was done with whatever and we'd hook up. But after the fifth time in two weeks, I knew it wasn't happening by chance. Come to find out, the crazy bitch put a tracking device on my truck."

My mouth drops. "What a *psycho*."

"Holy shit," Clay says. "What if she was a honey trap?"

"I thought about that. For a second. But there's no way this chick was that smart. Even if she had been sent to seduce me, she'd've slipped up and outed herself without even meaning to."

Tyler nods. "I don't know why anybody would try to infiltrate us anyway. It's not like our client list is that invaluable or anything. I mean, we do have some top-tier clients, but… I don't know. I think she was just batshit crazy."

"Our training methods are pretty badass though. So there's that. But still, she was never there when we were conditioning or running drills."

"That you know of," Clay chuckles.

"Oh, I know it. Triple-checked every camera inside and out." Beck points his beer at Clay.

"So what did you do after you found the tracker?" Clay takes another bite of his taco.

"Called her to come over. Banged her one more time for good measure, then threw her out along with the cheap-ass-piece-of-shit destroyed tracking device. Told her if she ever followed me again, I'd get a restraining order."

"Damn, Jacobs. Who knows how long she may have been spying on you."

"I know, right? But shit, she was smokin'. And a goddess in the sack. That was some sweet, sweet honey. Trap or not. Still haven't found a chick that can duplicate the feeling she gave me when she scratched her nails down my back." Beck sighs.

"Reminds me of that Buckcherry song," Ty chuckles.

"What song?" I take another sip of my drink.

"You know. 'Crazy Bitch.' Sounds like Jacobs could've written it."

The guys laugh and start singing the chorus.

I crack up and shake my head at them. "I forgot about that song."

"Ain't no amount of hot worth that amount of crazy," Clay says.

"Cheers to that." Ty raises his beer. He finishes it off and orders another round for the table.

A couple of hours pass as we eat, drink, talk, and laugh. We have the best time hanging out and catching up. Clay and I tell them about all the places we've been and the things we've collected, Tyler tells us more about his time in England, and Beck catches us up on happenings at RTS.

When the subject of tattoos comes up, Ty shows us a new one on his inner forearm that he got on a trip to Paris while he was in Europe. It's an ambigram tattoo, which is a word (or phrase) that when viewed upside down, reveals a new word. Or in some cases, the same word. But Tyler's reads 'courage' in one direction, and 'strength' when he flips his arm over.

"That's really cool, Ty," I marvel.

"I fucking love it, dude." Clay looks pensive for a second, but then smiles. "It suits you."

"What about you?" Ty asks Clay. "Anything new?"

"Nah. Not since I got 'CLS' on the back of my shoulder before I retired."

"Those aren't your initials." Beck looks confused. "Your middle name is Weston."

Clay looks surprised. "How do you know that?"

"Because I once heard Lynn throw your whole name at you, fussing at you for something," he laughs. "It's my mom's maiden name, so it stuck with me."

"Ah. Anyway, 'CLS' stands for 'Courtesy, Loyalty, Service.' It's the Louisiana State Police motto. But it's also for Clay and Lynn Sinclair."

I smile.

"Got it. Check this out." Beck shows us his new arrowhead tattoo on the side of his rib cage. I give him a questioning look. He explains. "It's the logo from the TV show *Arrow*."

"Isn't that a comic book?" I smile.

"Make fun all you want, but The Arrow is a fucking badass. He's the best DC character in the whole DC Universe."

"Not making fun. Just clarifying."

"No judgment here." Clay raises his beer.

"The Hood, Arrow, The Green Arrow — whatever you want to call him — is alright, but he's no Batman," Ty declares.

"Dude, I'm not about to have this argument with you again."

I switch the focus. "I want to get a tattoo."

"What?" Clay asks, surprised. "You finally wanna sully that beautiful virgin skin of yours?"

"I think so."

Tyler raises his eyebrows. "You can't just think so. You need to know so. It's permanent."

"I know. I want one. I do. Nothing too big or conspicuous though. I want us to get matching tattoos, Clay."

Beck rolls his eyes. "Of course you do."

"You hush, Beck." I look back at my husband. "Okay, not matching exactly. But complimentary. I want to get a key and you get a lock. To sort of commemorate this trip."

"Wait," Ty holds his hands up, "shouldn't Clay get the key instead?"

"Yeah, babe. You're the one with the *key hole*. Not me."

"Touché." I laugh.

"Switch it and I'm in."

"Okay, sure. I'll get the keyhole."

The waitress comes back to the table to check on us again.

"I think we're about done," Ty says, looking around at us in question to see if we all agree.

"Yeah," Clay says. "We're ready for the check."

"Okay. It's been a pleasure serving y'all," she says. She fishes the bill out of her apron and puts it on the table.

"I'll take that," Tyler says, swiping it up. He gives it back to her with his credit card before any of us can object.

"Aww, thanks, Ty," I tell him.

"You're welcome, darlin'."

"You didn't have to do that, man," Clay says.

"No sweat. I don't mind."

"He owed me one anyway," Beck says. "I bought lunch and drinks at the airport," he laughs.

"Whatever, Jacobs." Ty playfully punches him in the shoulder.

"Hey, does anybody know where I can get a toothbrush?" Beck asks. "I forgot mine."

As we're walking towards the exit of the restaurant, I stop and ask our waitress if there's a sundry shop in the hotel so Beck can get a toothbrush.

"It's closed for the night, but there's a convenience store a couple of blocks from here, right next to the souvenir shop," she says.

"Okay, cool. Thanks."

When we get back into the lobby, Beck makes a suggestion. "Y'all wanna continue this party?"

"What exactly do you mean, Jacobs?" Clay asks.

"Let's make the walk together to the store."

"You scared to go by yourself? Need me to hold your hand?" Ty asks.

"You're funny, Rutledge. I'll let Lynn hold my hand though."

"I don't think so," Clay says, as he grabs my hand and interlocks our fingers.

"I wouldn't mind the walk. Beck can get his toothbrush at the convenience store, and we can check out the souvenir shop next door. I want a 'Keep Austin Weird' t-shirt. I'm sure they have one. Plus, you can spend more time with Ty before we have to say goodnight."

"That's true. Okay, love." He turns to the guys. "We're in."

Tyler rolls his broad shoulders. "Alright."

We exit the lobby and take off down the street. Tyler and Beck are a few feet ahead of us having their own conversation.

"It's great having Ty back, huh? I know you've missed your best bud."

"I did. It's funny, I didn't realize how much until I saw him again today. Even Jacobs. I haven't hung out with him in so long. Forgot how much fun he was. I hate how he flirts with you though."

"Clay, please. You know it's nothing. He flirts with everybody."

"I know. I'm just... you're mine. He knows that."

"Exactly. Hey, I noticed you didn't bring up everything that happened, with me and the abduction, you and the shooting and all. But we can't keep that from Ty."

"I know, babe. I just didn't want to bring down the mood tonight. I'll tell him. We'll tell him. We'll tell both of them sometime before we part ways in the next couple of days. We have time."

Beck turns around. "Here we are," he says pointing at the Circle K. "Y'all need me to pick up anything?"

"No, thanks," Clay says. "We'll just be next door at the souvenir shop here."

"I think I'm gonna head in with Jacobs. I feel like I might want a Milky Way for a midnight snack. We'll meet y'all over there when we're done here. Shouldn't be long," Ty says.

"Alright, bro."

Ty and Beck head into Circle K while Clay and I walk towards the entrance of the souvenir shop. As he opens the door, his phone rings.

"Who is it?"

"Stone. I'm gonna take this. You go on in. Be there in a few."

"Okay."

He answers the call as I walk inside. The place is empty except for one employee, and it smells like chargrilled cheeseburgers in here. They must sell food in the back. The petite clerk sits behind the front counter, her eyes barely peeking up at me in greeting from under purple bangs. I smile at her. She's rubbing her fingers at her temples. I guess she has a headache.

I search the clothes racks for a t-shirt that I like and find one. It's pink and has 'Austin, Texas' on the front and 'Keep Austin Weird' on the back. It also encourages you to support local businesses. I love it.

I look back through the door and Clay is still outside talking to Stone. He catches my eye and winks at me, so I give him an air kiss.

I continue perusing the stuff in the gift shop. Lots of UT Longhorns items, various barbeque cookbooks, seasonings, and rubs. Then I notice some posters with Austin's resident bats in flight. Apparently, Austin has quite the bat population living under the Congress Avenue Bridge. They take off every night at sunset from spring to fall. I make a mental note for us to check that out while we're here.

I finally find some glittery glass Christmas ornaments. I envision adding a couple of them to the rest I've bought along our trip that will adorn our tree this year. Immersed in the details of one with the Austin skyline etched into the face of it, I barely register a loud thud coming from behind me. As I inspect each tiny star and little building on the gorgeous ornament in my hand, something niggles at me and I feel the urge to peek around the corner to make sure everything is okay. When I turn around, I see a mess of violet hair splayed across the face of the cashier on the floor. She appears lifeless, lying a foot away from her stool. I drop everything. The skyline ornament plummets from my hand and shatters to the ground as my adrenaline kicks in.

I rush to the girl and crouch down at her side, trying not to panic as I yell Clay's name. I don't know if he can hear me outside through the door though. I shake the girl, but she's unresponsive. Noticing her name tag says 'Winnie,' I begin loudly repeating it as I gently slap her cheeks. I check for a pulse and she's still breathing, thank God, but her skin is red and flushed.

As I begin to yell for Clay again, I can barely get my voice out. I'm getting dizzy. My vision is blurring. I'm becoming nauseous. I can't catch my breath. What is happening? I was fine just a few minutes ago. Wondering exactly how long I've been in the gift shop, I look at the digital clock on the wall, but I can't focus on the numbers to tell the time. I try to fish my phone out of my back pocket to call Clay, but my fingers are clumsy. I then begin to fumble for my purse, knowing my whistle is in there and I can use it to hopefully get Clay's attention. Realizing I dropped it next to the ornament section, I get on my knees and crawl back for it, but for whatever reason, my body is weakening. Before I know it, floating spots form in front of my eyes and my legs give out, just as I'm an arm's length away from my victory. I try to yell, but the sound is only a whisper. "Clay," I wheeze out, as my world fades around me.

To be continued...

About the Author

Rosie Politz is a down-home Cajun girl who loves to travel but hates to drive. She has a Bachelor of Arts degree in Anthropology from LSU and works in the tourism industry. She's a daydreamer, a trivia fanatic, and drinks more water than anybody she knows (though she does enjoy a few drinky-drinks on occasion). Some of her favorite pastimes include playing cards (especially Spades), planning themed parties, and singing karaoke. She loves perfume, flamingos, and all types of puzzles. Rosie lives in the Deep South with her husband, Tommy. *Key Holes* is her third novel.

Rosie is busy working on the conclusion to her Key series. In the meantime, please visit rosiepolitz.com for up-to-date information about the series and join her mailing list for exclusive material. She would love for you to follow her on facebook.com/rosiepolitzauthor, and Instagram @rosiepolitz.

If you enjoyed this book, please visit amazon.com and write a review.

www.ingramcontent.com/pod-product-compliance
Lightning Source LLC
Chambersburg PA
CBHW020648120726
47906CB00001B/175